FLESH and BLOOD and DNA

KING COBRA
PRESS.COM

a SCOTT JONES novel

AUTHOR PROFILE

Scott Jones has written hundreds of articles and columns for many newspapers and magazines in the USA and Thailand, authored four books (*Life in the Laugh Lane—facts, fiction, and photos in Southeast Asia, Can you spare me a smile?—a copious compendium of comedic commentary, FLESH and BLOOD and DNA—in her right mind and the wrong body,* and *Five Lives One Dream*—a metafiction novel of action, love, and adventure which spans the spectrum from severely humorous to deadly serious).

He has performed his unique style of original music, comedy, and stand-up photography in Asia, Canada, and all fifty states in America.

Scott lives in Thailand with his wife and Chance the Husky, whose name has evolved into Chancellor, the Exalted Ruler of Their General Vicinity.

COPYRIGHT AND CREDITS

DEDICATED TO

My soulmate...
without you
this novel would
never have come to me.
and without your support,
I never would have
written it.

HEARTFELT THANKS TO

My invaluable and astute
reader/editors:
Jim King
Walt Nigh
Amy D'Apice
Chuck Spencer
Michael Tangen
Pleasant DeSpain

BOOKS BY SCOTT JONES

FLESH and BLOOD and DNA
TURNABOUT: FLESH and BLOOD and DNA Finale
Five Lives One Dream
Life in the Laugh Lane
Can you spare me a smile?
Edit Yourself

CONTENTS

Day 1

Tuesday

ODORS DREDGED HER MIND FROM THE VOID.
Bacon? Coffee?

Simone had given them up a decade ago, though the smell still meant breakfast. Dishes clanked beyond the room, but she lived alone, and her two dogs certainly weren't cooking. She tried to move, and her body didn't respond. Simone felt as if she were deep underwater... or underground... or just deep under.

What's happening to me?

Her eyes opened slowly, not on her command. Something else controlled them. Dawn peering through ragged window curtains barely illuminated the room. Small hands reached up and rubbed her eyes. The ceiling sloped down to the bedside, inches above her head. A slanted Oprah Winfrey poster stared Simone in the face.

Where... where am I?

A woman's voice echoed from somewhere below. "Amanda! Up 'n' at 'em! 'T'seven a.m., girl!"

Simone's body, remote and foreign, sat up and hung its legs over the edge of the bed. The feet didn't touch the floor.

This isn't my bedroom, not my world. I must be dreaming.

The body hopped out of bed, and Simone seemed to float

within it. As the legs walked, one hand scratched scalp, the other opened the door. In the cramped hallway, feet felt rough boards of the cold wooden floor; ears heard cars passing outside on the street; eyes saw the dilapidated stairway; nostrils smelled Mr. Clean wrestling with the stench of the toilet.

This is too real to be a dream.

Simone could feel her essence melding with the energy of this body, a union and a separation at the same time—one doing, one watching. She sensed trepidation in the body, as if a cold breeze were passing through a place no breeze should be. The body jerked around and looked behind as feet stepped onto the stool in front of the sink. When the head swung toward the mirror, Simone expected to see her own angular, blue-eyed, 37-year-old face looking back. Instead she confronted a young teenaged, dark-skinned girl with chocolate brown eyes and tight black curls cascading to her shoulders.

What…? It's my patient! The girl who doesn't speak.

"Amanda! Breakfast's ready!"

Fifteen hours earlier…

"Déjà vu Monday, in between a rock and a hard place. Coco Montague's committed to ending her life, and Murray Spindler's resigned to wallowing in his. I must remember to separate their sessions with another patient who I feel I might actually be helping."

Dr. Simone Wellstone sat cross-legged on the redwood deck curving around outside her circular office/therapy room, a stand-alone structure fashioned after a Mongolian yurt with windowed walls and a white dome roof. She called it her "Sensory Sanctuary." Crisp spring air nipped her nose. Setting sunlight warmed her hair. While recovering from Coco and rejuvenating before Murray, she chatted with Mac on her lap, who recorded her professional diagnoses and personal diatribes. Depending on the moment and her mood, she called it her Diary, or her Diarrhea.

"Today Coco asked if I could arrange a secret, assisted suicide for her, Kevorkian-style. Not my style. Could I kill her with herbs and words, music and massage, crafts and other crap? Spear her with 400 acupuncture needles, then roll her down the hill? Good lord." She sighed and looked down at Mac. "What style will the world associate with Dr. Wellstone when I'm gone? Well-stoned?" Simone closed her eyes, leaned back her head, and took a deep drag on a joint from her preferred legal brand, Skywalker. "A drag a day keeps the doctor awake."

She'd never been like other people. A true empath, certified at birth by the universe, Simone wasn't merely empathetic with elusive abilities to understand and share the feelings of others. She felt her patients' pain in her own body—real, live, immediate pain—emotional, mental, and physical. Before a person had uttered a sound, Simone might say, "You've got a shooting pain in your right leg. Right here, from your hip downward. Your foot is numb and feels dead." And she'd be right on.

As a young child, she'd assumed everyone was like her and didn't understand why people treated each other badly, or why they spoke with such cruelty. Simone had been a shy introvert who preferred the company of Mother Nature. Trees, fields, and animals just lived, without all the issues that haunt humans. Public places, malls, supermarkets, even crowded rooms were overwhelming.

Inch by bitter inch during her teens, Simone realized she vividly felt other people's emotions and took them into her being as her own; separating them from her innate feelings still presented routine challenges years later. The sensitivity to her surroundings combined with compassion for the underdog became a magnet that attracted friends or strangers who burst open, spattering her soul with their worries, dreams, and nightmares.

Simone followed her destiny into counseling and psychiatry, but those fields didn't cover her extensive gifts. The internet had revealed that the moniker "Empatherapy" was taken. Since the framed parchment on her wall confirmed doctoral status, she'd chosen the title "Dr. Simone Wellstone, Empathiatrist" and hung out her shingle. Word of mouth and heart spread. Her time became her patients'.

A light rap on the sliding glass door by her assistant and gatekeeper Ming signaled the approach of her next challenge. "Mr. Murray here. I send him in?"

Since arriving six months earlier, Ming had been a welcome rock in Simone's wavering world—solid, efficient, stable. Bedrock. She took care of the business busyness which allowed Simone to fully concentrate on her patients. Ming added an Asian authenticity to the therapeutic modalities Simone practiced and to the oriental office décor. Twenty-seven, exotic, and winsome, she was genuine Chinese, descended from the Ming dynasty. Men manufactured ailments as excuses for appointments with the doctor merely to have a fantasy-filled moment with Ming. Best of all, she seemed emotionally inert. Simone might become nauseous several hours before an earthquake struck hundreds of miles away, but she could not sense what lurked behind this taciturn Great Wall of China.

Murray Spindler ambled into the room and collapsed on the couch. A lost rich kid buried in middle age, he crawled from one phobia, syndrome, or disorder to another in his search for Murray Spindler. He had no friends other than counter help or salespeople. He never wore any clothing more than once, but at least donated his daily disposal to charities or homeless folks. Simone was one of the products he purchased—a "friend" who had the patience of a stone and endured the tales of his trials and trivialities. Murray listened little, and if he ever took a shred of Simone's advice, he disposed of it later in the day like another piece of used clothing. For her, every session was a depression as she felt his failures and failed along with him.

Simone pulled up a bamboo stool and sat next to the couch as a new tactic swirled in her mind. *Today I'm gonna do the talking...*

"Rough week, eh?"

"Brutal, just brutal," Murray sighed, dragging his fingers through sparse wavy hair that seemed to be trying to escape from his head.

"I'll bet. Too much booze, jail, bail, and back on Shit Street."

The grimace on his face pleaded guilty as charged.

Simone forged ahead, trying to shake his anxiety out of her soul. "I have one question for you, and I want an honest answer."

"Okay... fine... What is it?"

"Had you heard about Alien Hand Syndrome before you grabbed the woman's breast on the bus, or did you discover that pathetic rationalization afterwards?"

Murray looked down, tapped his fingers on his knee, and bounced his leg on the ball of his foot while he pretended to think.

"Never mind. I don't care what the answer is. I'm guessing you got it from a list I found on the web, 'The 10 Weirdest Psychological Disorders.'" Simone flipped through her notes to find the printout and read aloud. "'Alien Hand Syndrome occurs when an arm seems to have a mind of its own. It moves around, grabs hold of things, and might even start to strangle the person, all without the control of the person to whom it belongs.' It's on this list with the 'Jumping Frenchmen of Maine,' whoever they are." She skipped down the printout and continued reading. "'Boanthropy, a delusional disorder when a person believes he's a cow or an ox and grazes on grass. The Alice in Wonderland Syndrome: space, time, or body image become distorted and objects may appear much smaller or larger than they really are.' I've counselled couples living in that Wonderland. He thinks it's huge, and she says it's way too small." She looked up and shook her head. "Face it, Murray. You've been going downhill for months, and last week dug yourself a deep hole in the bottom of the pit."

"But… well…"

"I'll tell you what… today… let me do the talking. Today's session is free. It's on me. One friend to another. Is that all right with you?"

"Free…?" The shock squeezed out a smile on Murray's face. "Sure!"

"It may be free, but it'll be worth ten times that amount." She grinned, pleased with her little joke. "You're not a bad person, Murray, but you did a very bad deed. I like you in spite of your attempts to drag yourself into disorders or define yourself with phobias. You've had a rough life with no help from your wealth. Your father—an angry zealot and workaholic, determined to mold you into him. Your words, not mine. Your mother—a distant alcoholic dying under your father's iron fist. Both taken from you at an early age."

Simone brushed back her non-existent brunette locks that used to hang down into her face. Last week she'd chopped them into a razor crew cut, no fuss, no muss. She could pass as a man or a woman which suited her just fine.

"I can feel you're a caring person… if you only had someone to care about. Grabbing a bust on a bus can be great if you're both mutually consenting grabbers and grabbees. Murray, you're intelligent and diligent. Your incessant research has taught me more about phobias than I ever wanted to know." She turned the page and read again. 'Allodoxaphobia: the fear of opinions…'" She looked up at him. "Probably petrified of my advice, eh? 'Dextrophobia: the fear of having objects situated to your right.' That's me again. As the object, I object. 'Sesquipedalophobia: the fear of long words.' Did I pronounce it right? Sounds to me like a cruel joke. Have you tried 'Chronophobia: the fear of time?' You could spend 24/7 on that one alone. I'm surprised you haven't mentioned the 'Munchausen Syndrome: the sufferer feigns, exaggerates, or creates symptoms of illnesses to gain attention, sympathy, and comfort from medical personnel.' Lookee here! There's a picture of Murray Spindler right next to the definition!"

His face had fallen into a frown during her verbal journey through the truth, but Murray forced out a tight grin.

"Loosen up, dude. Your lips won't rip if you widen that smirk. No doubt some of the phobias you've sampled have a modicum of validity, but how many were created by drug companies ready to sell their placebos? Or by shrinks with shrinking careers desperate to get their names in print? I can, but don't prescribe drugs. You've never shown any interest in my alternative methods. So here's my new ultimatum, again, one friend to another. We can meet for another month, no charge, but…"

Murray waited one taut moment, then searched her piercing blue eyes for the terms. "But? But what?"

"Three conditions. One, you spend your hundred dollars a week and start a Phobia Support Group. You'll meet women… and men. You might enlighten them, just don't infect them with your own phobias. You can help them and help yourself. Two, hang out with those homeless folks you give your clothes to. You'll see your life, your being, and your worthiness in a whole new light. Walk a mile in their shoes… they'll probably be wearing yours anyway." Simone closed her notebook, stood, and looked down at Murray. "Number three: don't drink and ride. Stay off the bus. Time-out for the Alien Hand. It's grounded."

"Okay," he sighed. "But I can't start a fucking support group. I'm only qualified to be in one."

"Who says you can't? I'll make you an official certificate, sign it, and frame it. But it's not a 'Fucking Support Group.' It's a *Phobia* Support Group." Speaking over her shoulder, Simone started toward the door and Murray followed. "Just do it and come back in a week. Or don't do it and have a nice life… on your own." She opened the door, gestured for him to pass, and patted him on the back. "You know the way out, Murray… and the way back in."

The Sanctuary was located behind the office/patient reception room at end of a brick walkway lined with sedum and hosta perennials blooming red and white. Murray veered left and shuffled out to his black BMW parked in Simone's three-space carport next her two-story house. After jotting notes on her final session for the day, Simone stopped at the office to bid Ming adieu.

"Now I bill Murray?" Ming asked.

Simone smiled. "No, you're not Bill Murray." Being the empath who relied on feelings and body language more than words, she loved the way Ming tore English apart and stuck it back together in the simplest sentences possible—a few conjunctions, lots of nouns and verbs, mainly present tense. "And we're not going to bill Murray. He gets complimentary sessions for a month, starting today. A new tactic since the old ones tanked."

"Okay, I not bill Murray."

"No… you Char Ming. Don't ever change."

Ming's expression turned mischievous. "Miss Simone, I have surprise. A man call on phone from Damian's Deli. They start new home delivery service and choose your name for free meal."

"My name? How?"

"You drop business card in bowl."

"Hmm… I suppose I did…"

"They bring your favorite. Thanksgiving Déjà Vu."

Simone's eyebrows arched. "Really? Monday's looking better as it slips away."

"I walk and feed dogs and go home."

"No, no, thanks. I need some time with 'em. You have a nice night now."

"You too. Sleep good. See you tomorrow." Ming slipped away to her bungalow tucked in the trees behind the house.

During the doggies' daily stroll AKA Simone's daily de-compression session, she trailed behind her best buds, an eight-legged mirror of her personality. The Irish Setter—Brandy—reserved, neurotic, and needy. The Golden Re-triever—Dammit—the world's friendliest dog, who licked everyone into wet submission, and drove Brandy nuts. Simone tolerated humans and cherished helping them but could only take the species in small doses—two hours on, then four hours off, preferably alone. She kept a low profile in the neighborhood, but did relish yelling out the door to summon in her troops for the night. "Brandy, Dammit!"

Simone roasted fresh range-fed chicken and mixed it with their premium "Chicken Soup for the Soul" dog food, finished dictating to her diary, showered, then coaxed the day out of her soul with a yoga session until the doorbell rang. She yanked herself out of semi-meditation, padded to the door, and checked out the visitor on the security screen. She'd had the system installed after two incidents with unruly former patients appearing in the middle of the night.

A burly but beautiful man stood on the steps. Tousled hair, Cimmerian eyes, black leather flight jacket, seven o'clock shadow.

She unbolted the lock, removed the metal chain, and opened the door a crack. Both dogs barked, and Brandy kept growling until he left.

"Good evening, ma'am," the man said. "Dr. Wellstone, I presume?"

"Certainly not Dr. Livingstone."

Surprised, he laughed and said, "That's funny."

"Yeah, I borrowed a funny bone from a patient. Can I help you?"

"One Thanksgiving Déjà Vu for you," he announced, "compliments of Damian's Deli on the first day of their new home delivery service," and handed her a large brown paper bag.

Simone opened the door the width of the bag and stretched out one hand. "Well, this is sweet, and I'm starved. Thank you very much." Though the man tantalized her eyes, he seemed a bit seasoned for deliveries. And too perky for deadpan Damian's. An icky sensation slithered into her stomach. "I don't remember seeing you around the Deli... *their* Deli, as you say." *This beau is faux. Not fo' real, not fo' me.*

"Well..." He hesitated and looked down, then spoke to his belt. "It's my first day on the job, Dr. Wellstone. Name's Hunter. It's a pleasure to meet you." He tipped his suede beret and started to turn away. "Enjoy your dinner. I hope to see you again at Damian's."

I don't want to see you again. With her tongue stuck in her cheek and squeezed between her teeth, she watched him lope down the street to the left toward a truck too large for a deli delivery van. Another man sat in the front seat. *Something's wrong with Mr. Right.*

As Simone struggled to sort out the situation, a growl from her stomach quashed the churning in her gut. She shut and locked the door and checked it twice. On her way to the living room, she began to empty the bag, positioned the feast on the coffee table created from a rectangular antique trunk, and slipped behind it on the overstuffed beige recliner.

Mmm. A very merry unthanksgiving to me.

Sesame-grilled turkey slices on Damian's home-baked bread made with stuffing and potatoes. One Styrofoam bowl of gravy for dipping. A side of green beans with crusty tamari almonds. A plastic glass of cranberry juice spiced with orange zest and cinnamon.

The sandwich tasted divine, and the juice hit that spot a pill can't reach, but midway through the meal she began to feel fuzzy, like a river of bubbles was flowing through every vein. Her neck fought to keep her head upright but gave up and let it fall. Chin resting on her chest, Simone saw the floor recede into a blurry square floating in the distance.

Damn... Is this... Malice in... Wonder... land?

The words in her mind stretched out like Silly Putty, then broke apart, and bounced around inside her skull. The half sandwich in her hand grew vast in her vision as a wave of nausea swept through her body. Simone's legs wouldn't cooperate when she rose and stumbled around the coffee table toward the bathroom. In slow motion the faraway floor expanded into a gigantic platform that slammed into her face as she slumped onto the shag rug. Limp and unconscious, she dreamed of alien hands on and under her skin but was too far gone to scream.

Back to the present...

As the eyes stared at their reflection in the mirror, the second hand on the clock stuck on the moment. Familiar had become alien, known now unknown, right was left in the mirror and wrong in her mind. Comprehension floundered in the flood of confusion. Most people would likely panic from the realization that they were staring out from inside a foreign body. Not Simone. Her left-brain scientist stepped up to balance her right-brain empath. Unbridled emotions gave way to one analytical thought.

What the fuck is going on here?

Simone had been in plenty of situations where her role demanded she soothe the patient to lead them out of trauma, but this time she was the patient and the doctor. She closed her eyes and took a deep slow breath to relax, a second breath to release the terror she felt, and a third to gather information. During that third breath, she noticed the chest she inhabited had expanded and contracted according to her commands. She opened her eyes to see the eyes in the mirror open in unison. These observations suggested she had some control over the body. She raised one eyebrow, then the other, quickly, like twitches. The eyebrows in the mirror moved in the same manner.

No coincidence there. Some control confirmed.

She surrendered to the commands of the host being. Science discoveries come with step-by-step processes, but empathy demands compassion. Simone could imagine this young teen's scream if she realized a foreign being was living inside her.

Thumps from a broom handle on the kitchen ceiling below vibrated the bathroom floor. "Hey, sleepyhead! You up yet?"

Amanda picked up the metal cup holding her tooth-brush and tapped four times on the pipe next to the sink.

"Well, c'mon down quick. Your food's gettin' cold!"

As Amanda continued her morning routine and splashed water on her face, a whirlpool of questions swirled in Simone's consciousness.

Is this what multiple personality disorder feels like? Schizophrenia? Or is this astral projection? Has my soul— whatever that is—separated from my physical body and attached to Amanda's? Where the hell is my body? How do I get back to it? When? Will I be trapped here forever?

Neither her knowledge of science nor psychology provided any reasonable answers. Nor did her experience with paranormal and psychic phenomena. The final events when she'd been Simone alone flashed in her mind. The weird delivery guy. The disorientation during dinner. Collapsing onto the rug in a stupor and passing out.

Someone did this to me. Who? How? Why?

Simone felt the need to try another experiment to discover more clues about this conundrum. Something simple. Normal. She thought of Murray and his Alien Hand Syndrome. When Amanda finished wiping her face with a towel, Simone raised both hands to the right cheek and gently squeezed a small pimple. She felt the twinge of pain and then focused her empathic radar on her host. Beneath her own anxiety, Simone could feel a calmness in Amanda. No alarm. No tension.

I'm connected to her nervous system. I feel physical pain. I'm connected to her medulla oblongata. Involuntary processes are intact and functioning. I'm connected to the cerebellum and have some control over her voluntary actions. I can see, hear, smell, and probably taste, but I have absolutely no connection to her thoughts. I am linked with her brain and body, yet Amanda seems to have no awareness of mine. I'm detached from my body, yet still linked with my brain. But where is my body? Mystifying yet intriguing. One more test.

Simone audibly cleared her throat. Amanda cleared her throat. She then spoke one sound, "Hmm," and Amanda spoke it with her.

As Simone had expected during the single session five months earlier with thirteen-year-old Amanda Parnum and her mother Whitney, no physical problem prevented the young child from speaking. Simone had a near pho-tographic memory for the details of her patients' cases. Valleyview Middle School had recommended they visit Dr. Wellstone as part of their counselling outreach pro-gram. Amanda hadn't spoken a word, but was alert, looked Simone right in the eye, and seemed to exude confidence and determination. Amanda's school file showed excellent grades. Whitney's comments had revealed some sketchy traumatic experiences with an uncle who had provoked them to flee their home in Florida and seek a new life twen-ty-five hundred miles west. Amanda had ceased speaking shortly before she and her mother left on their journey.

Satisfied with her revelations, Simone settled into obser-vation mode.

Amanda finished brushing her teeth, stabbed her thick curls a few times with a rake comb, skipped to the bedroom, and dressed in blue jeans, a checkered blue-and-white shirt, and tattered running shoes. The black watch had been on her wrist when she awoke. From a standing position, she dropped face-forward toward the floor, caught herself with angled arms, and pounded out thirty push-ups, not the prissy style on bended knees, thirty official full-body push-ups. Then she flipped over and whipped through thirty of-ficial sit-ups.

Very impressive! We've got a future Serena Williams here.

Simone's middle-aged, sedentary lifestyle had begun to creep into her joints and muscles. Sailing along with this fluid lass felt like smooth skimming across the waves in a new sloop.

Amanda gathered her textbooks, notebooks, folders, pens, pencils, eraser, ruler, protractor, and calculator from her study table, and meticulously placed each item into its respective pocket in her nylon backpack.

Watching from within, Simone drifted back to a time when she'd been about Amanda's age. She'd packed her bag in the same precise manner before embarking on a solo bicycle adventure in Utah's Canyonlands National Park. Her parents, Abram and Nova Albright, had rented a high-clearance, 4WD Jeep Cherokee, tackled the rocky rutted roads with their twins Simone and Simon, and set up camp at a remote site in the "Maze," fifty miles and a three-to-five-hour drive from the nearest ranger station. A vast mass of incredible geologic formations, slickrock, arches, and dead-end canyons, the Maze was regarded as one of the most dangerous places to hike in America.

Midafternoon on their second day, the temperature hit ninety-something, cool by Canyonlands standards in the summer. Simone filled her backpack with the essentials. Two water canteens, compass, power bars and trail mix, matches, rope, flashlight, extra battery, pocket knife, map, signal mirror, long-sleeved shirt, a thin emergency space blanket and—Dad was a medical research doctor and Mom a registered nurse—a first-aid kit. She jumped on her 10-speed mountain bike, called "Nomad" because that was the name on the frame and reminded her not to get mad. She rode off into the sun in search of visual and mineral treasures. Those days Simone imagined she'd become a geologist and world explorer.

She didn't check her map on the way out, because she honestly *liked* to get lost and then find her way home. After an hour or so of pedaling through twists and turns beyond her biking ability but firing her desire, she dismounted on a stunning canyon overlook at trail's end. The sun had dropped faster than she'd expected. She checked her watch.

4:45 p.m. I'll just look around for a while and have plenty of time to get back to camp.

The ground next to the trail was covered with brownish-black balls about the size of Simone's wide eyes surveying the scene.

Are these the famous moqui marbles I've only seen in books? I gotta gather some for my collection!

She selected several choice specimens, stuck some in her pockets, and reached for more marbles close to the cliff. The "solid" sandstone rock where she'd set her forward foot crumbled, and Simone started to slip over the edge. Her right hand grabbed a mesquite bush, and her left hand cupped a flat ledge of shale jutting from the edge. The bush popped out of the sand, and the moqui marbles, still clutched in her palm, rolled her off onto a steep dusty slide. Her downward tumble accelerated on the slickrock. Frantically grasping at anything within reach, Simone plunged over another precipice into thin air.

When she regained consciousness on the dry stream bed at the bottom of the canyon, the world was dark except for the faint blue light from a quarter moon. Her head throbbed, inside and out. Caked blood stung her eye. Scrapes and bruises burned on her elbows, legs, and knees. Her sprained wrist hurt when she flicked the hair off her face. Simone could barely see the canyon edge far above, outlined by the blue-black sky and pinpoints of stars. She considered screaming but decided it'd be useless.

If I attract anything, it'll probably want to eat me.

Simone removed her pack and inspected its contents with the flashlight. Everything was intact. She put on the shirt, took a Tylenol to beat back the pain, and sipped water from her plastic canteen as she looked up at the moon rising in the east, the direction she'd come. Simone took a deep breath and whispered aloud to the universe, accepting the situation, and setting her intention. "I got myself here, and I'll get back there. Yes, Mother, I hear you. 'Get a good night's sleep, honey. Tomorrow's another day.'"

She set a few rocks in a circle, gathered sticks, started a fire, and sat squat-legged while munching on a power bar, dabbing Bactine on her damaged limbs, and taping a bandage over the wound on her head. Except for her throbbing body, the scene was quite peaceful. The fire crackled as it devoured the wood. An owl hooted in the distance. The subtle smell of mesquite permeated the air, and the night sky had come alive with constellations. Simone cherished quiet time alone. She stashed her snack bag in the gnarly branches of a juniper tree. Critters will search for and destroy food supplies, and she didn't want them ripping apart her backpack. She curled up in her space blanket on the sand next to the dwindling fire and became one with the wilderness.

As dawn crept into the sky, Simone awoke and wrestled her way to her feet through the aches and pains. She gazed at the canyon's edge, at least a hundred feet up, and felt grateful to be standing at all. The slickrock, void of jagged rocks, boulders, and trees, had likely saved her life. She saw no route up the steep incline.

My bike's right above me, but beyond me. I'll hafta head east into the sun, find a way up, and backtrack to it.

She took out her Canyonlands map from the ranger station, but it focused on hiking, biking, and 4WD trails, not backcountry topography. The maze of canyons sketched on the map looked like a mass of worms spilled onto the ground, spreading in all directions. Simone thought of what her dad would probably say. "You're in a can o' worms, kid."

Hell, I'm in a whole canyon of 'em, and I hafta walk through 'em.

Simone leaned down and balanced five rocks into a cairn to mark the spot where her tombstone could have been, slung on her pack, and trudged along the south wall of the canyon. Any trepidation she felt soon succumbed to reverence of the landscape around her. She'd never before experienced, nor even imagined, a natural wonder on Earth so beautifully simple yet so wickedly complex. The worm hole canyons crawled around and through each other, twisting and turning in on themselves. Some canyons felt like dingy caves with thin slivers of sky for ceilings but offered cool respite from the sun baking her body. Along the way she stopped to stack more cairns in case she needed to backtrack through this lower labyrinth of terrain.

Her eastern trek ended in a beige, orange, and cinnamon striated rotunda rising a hundred feet on all sides. Simone felt as if she stood at the base of a massive elliptical vase sculpted by the hands of God. It opened to a circular blue heaven a hundred feet above and unreachable. A living dead-end. She wound around the rotunda which lead her back west into a canyon she'd already traversed. A few more steps brought her to the last cairn she'd built fifteen minutes earlier. Her only choice now was to find an escape route on the north wall of this maze. An hour later she discovered a narrow gulch that allowed her to scramble up and out into the high noon sun.

Simone plopped down under a short mesquite tree for a drink—the last sip of water left in her canteen. She headed east again and followed the upper labyrinth of canyon rims until they turned back west and led her back to her long-lost buddy.

Nomad, you rock and rollin' goddess! You are a sight for my sore eyes, sore body, and sunbaked skin!

Parched to the bone, shaking with exhaustion, and three precious moqui marbles in her pocket to savor for a lifetime, Simone rode into the family camp twenty-four hours after beginning her solo journey. A search party had been sent out at dawn, and her parents were in a panic when they learned of its failure from a park ranger. Her father lifted Simone from her bike into a bear hug as mama bear put her arms around both of them. Simon stood over to the side. He'd always been a bit sickly, never would have survived such an ordeal, and seldom shared the spotlight that always seemed to center on his twin sister Simone.

"If you don't get down here pronto, I'm givin' your food to the cat!"

The voice from below tore Simone from her memories. Nomad dissolved into Amanda as she bounded down the stairs. The reverie had bolstered Simone's spirits, buoyed her hopes, and set her intention. *I got myself here, and I'll get back there… wherever there is.*

The wooden stairway led down to a stark living room with a worn sofa, armchair, and coffee table typical of low-budget, pre-furnished apartments. The faded tropical print with swaying palms over the sofa would be right at home in a cut-rate motel or bargain bin at the Salvation Army store. Three steps past the furniture took Amanda to the front entrance on the right or the kitchen doorway on the left. She veered into the kitchen, its cracked linoleum floor populated with one beat-up, double-burner gas stove, one midget fridge, one aluminum table with three chairs normally found outside on a lawn, and an unknown number of invisible termites devouring the bank of dingy counters supporting a cheap metal sink and an old toaster. No frills, only the evidence of a tiny family making two distant ends meet. Amanda pecked her mother on the cheek and sat at the table.

"Hey, A!" Whitney crooned. "Congrats! You made it. Sorry, I thought you might sleep until next year, so I gave your food to Fluffy. She said you could finish hers." Whitney set the cat's bowl on the table in front of Amanda.

Amanda gave her a thumbs-up, scooped up a spoonful of Purina Cat Chow, and lifted it to her lips.

"Ma'am, lemme check again." Dressed in a red-and-white, striped TGI Fridays shirt, black suspenders, funky tie, and a short black skirt, waitress Whitney played out work at home. She raised the frying pan lid from a plate on the counter. "Oops! Guess some bacon, eggs, and hash browns are left." She replaced Fluffy's bowl with a breakfast feast. "Will this do?"

Amanda, smiled, nodded and rapped on the table twice.

Whitney sat next to her daughter. "I already ate, and we got 15 minutes to catch the bus. Today's your big treatment day! Are you okay?"

Amanda rapped twice with her fork.

"Feelin' anything weird? Anything at all?"

Amanda shook her head and rapped once, then shrugged her shoulders and rapped three times.

This must be their code. One is 'no.' Two is 'yes' or 'okay.' Three is 'I don't know.' Simone thought of Amanda's raps on the bathroom pipe. *Four times could be 'I'll be right there' or 'give me a minute.'*

"You're not sure, eh?" Whitney asked. "Well, the guy said to just be yourself and do whatever you do on a normal day. You 'member the list of dos and don'ts he gave us?"

One hand rapped once, the other delivered a forkful of eggs.

"I'm gonna read 'em while you eat." Whitney unfolded a piece of paper and laid it on the table. "Right on the top of the instructions it says, 'You might feel different, but don't worry. Just relax and go with it.' Underneath it lists three to-dos and one don't. The first to-do says, 'Wear the bracelet at all times. It monitors your vital signs and your location. If you become afraid or are in an emergency situation, spring the watch face as demonstrated to you, and press the button underneath. It will only respond to your fingerprint.' You 'member how to open it?"

Amanda rapped twice and seemed more interested in breakfast than instructions, but Simone was lit. She leaned Amanda's head toward the paper so she could scan it. *No logo, no address, no phone, no nothing on the fucking paper. Who is 'the guy'?*

"Number two says, 'Be home and ready to sleep by 8:00 p.m. You will feel very drowsy and drop to sleep soon afterwards.' No problem. My shift's done at three. I forget, sweetheart. You got a volleyball game after school today?"

Amanda rapped twice.

"Number three says, 'Stay within the city limits the entire day to assure we can carefully monitor your treatment.' You plan on leavin' the country?"

Amanda rapped once with her orange juice glass.

"Okay, number four. He made a big deal outta this one, and it's bold on the paper. '**Do not tell anybody about this treatment**, or you will not receive the rest of the payment we agreed to give you. If anything happens out of the ordinary, or if someone asks about your behavior, apologize politely and say that it might be side effects from a new medicine you are taking. WE WILL KNOW IF YOU SAY

ANYTHING TO ANYONE.'" Whitney held up the piece of paper. "Look, Amanda. That last line is in all capital letters! This is some secret, I think he said revolutionary procedure, and we signed an official contract. We don't get the rest of the money till it's over, and that's prob'ly more than I'd make in a year, so... it's pretty important to us too. Think ya can do that, A?"

Amanda pointed to her mouth and gave Whitney a withering look that said, "Get real, Mom, I don't even talk."

"I know, I know. You're not talkin', but don't even write it. Please."

Two raps from Amanda.

"Now we better get our butts in gear, but first..." Whitney lifted a box from behind the toaster and set it in front of Amanda. "I bought a little gift for ya. I spent some of the down payment on these babies you been droolin' over."

Amanda tore off the wrapping paper, opened the box, and took out a black mesh New Balance Minimus Cross-Trainer sporting a bold pink N, pink laces, and a pink-and-white traction sole. She dropped the shoe on the table and gave Whitney two thumbs-ups as she jumped to her feet and threw her arms around her mother's shoulders.

Simone listened to this new information, seething as the moments dragged on. A raft of emotions raged through her along with the words she longed to speak out loud. *"Excuse me, but I've had enough of this. I'm Dr. Simone Wellstone. We met in my office. I'm stuck here inside Amanda and have no idea what the hell is going on. Where'd you meet this guy? What else did he tell you about this treatment? How long is it?* Playing out the scene, she imagined the shock on Whitney's face, and compassion reigned in her desire to intrude. *She'd probably think her daughter's gone bonkers. Who knows what precious Amanda might do? And someone's paying them big bucks for this? Get a grip,*

Simone. Now's not the time.

Whitney gave her daughter a few tender pats on the back and whispered in her ear. "Oh, my sweet little warrior. I'm so proud of you for doing this. You are a courageous one. Maybe we'll even figure out why you ain't talkin' anymore."

During the last nine words Whitney spoke, Simone felt the bolt of fear shoot up Amanda's spine, tightening her chest and widening her eyes. She let go of her mother and seemed to shrink into herself. She put the shoe back in the box and picked up her pack.

"Aren'tcha gonna wear your new shoes, A?"

Amanda shook her head and focused her eyes on the floor.

She's got a secret buried somewhere, and she's afraid it'll be revealed. Nothing's wrong between these two here, but something's wrong out there. In school maybe? Where? Or who? The unnamed uncle somewhere? A revelation about the reality of this situation rose up from Simone's core. *How many times have I wanted to be the fly on the wall in a patient's world and experience their stories as they happen? To walk that mile in another man's shoes, instead of hearing their denials, half-truths, blatant lies, and misconceptions in my office. This is a proverbial dream come true!*

Whitney took out her beat-up iPhone, punched in a number, and the gift box started to buzz. "Okay, baby. You can wear 'em later, but right now I think you better answer your other sneaker."

Perplexed, Amanda crunched her eyebrows together. She opened the box, lifted out the buzzing shoe, dug out a small iPhone, and stared in amazement.

"It's old and used," Whitney said, "but if anything happens on your big day, I wanna know about it. You might not talk, but I bet you can text up a storm."

Amanda's anxiety vanished during another jump into

Mom's arms and a hard hug.

"Okay, okay! You're welcome again. Your security code is A-M-A-N-D-A. Think you can remember that? Want me to write it down for you?"

Amanda rolled her eyes as she slipped her pack on her back.

"Time to hit the sidewalk, A. We each got a bus to catch!"

They walked arm-in-arm to the bus stop and didn't notice the drone following them, thirty yards above and twenty yards behind. Amanda spotted the school bus approaching in the distance, kissed her mom on the cheek, and ran to meet it. As the doors folded open, Harvey the driver greeted her with a grin beaming from his dark skin, one shade lighter than his brown uniform.

"Queen Amanda! 'S'ap'nin? Y'all lookin' bea-u-ti-ful again today. You okay?"

She flipped up her thumb, hopped into the bus, turned left, but met a log jam of legs blocking her way—not accidental, obviously a premeditated misdemeanor. Halfway down the aisle, two arms waved above a wide smile.

"Take a seat, girl."

Amanda tapped Harvey on the shoulder. When he looked up, she raised both eyebrows and nodded toward the back.

Harvey sighed, set the brake, stretched his six-foot self into a standing position, and faced the sullen faces. "My pathetic little miscreants, today is the last time I will tolerate this disgusting display of racism on my bus. If y'all do not remove your legs from the aisle 'mediately or before, I will remove them from your bodies, and kick your sorry collective asses to the principal's office." He gestured over his head. "I'm sure she can identify all your lily-white faces from this here s'curity camera on the ceiling."

The miscreants grunted and retracted their legs with the speed of a pack of sloths.

"Okay, honey bun. If any legs or arms get in your way, y'all have my permission to break 'em."

Amanda shared a fist bump with Harvey, then strolled down the aisle, and took a seat next to Toby and his smile. Amanda was one of the few dark-skinned kids at the school, and Toby Park was the sole Korean. Besides Harvey and the two security guards, Toby was the only other person at Valleyview Middle School who wore a uniform. His parents (severely conservative and traditional) believed in longer school hours (7 a.m. to 7 p.m.), a strict regimental dress code (white shirt, black tie, and blue pants, exactly how Toby dressed every day) and random drug testing for everyone in their local zip code. A foot shorter than Amanda, he wore classic black nerd glasses and hearing aids in both ears. Amanda and Toby made a perfect pair—she didn't talk, and he couldn't hear. Toby compensated for his idiosyncrasies by speaking better English than many of the teachers and being the smartest kid in his class, or perhaps the entire school.

"Good morning! You made it!" Energetic and upbeat as always, Toby had a pen and notepad ready for her to write on. "If only guys are dickheads, what do you call girls who are dickheads?"

Amanda wrote 'MC' on the notepad.

"MC? What does that stand for? Let's see… malicious creatures… mischievous cretins… mephitic cocksuckers?"

Amanda wrote, "mentally challenged."

"Ah, politically correct." Toby's nodded as he fidgeted with his ear lobe. "I brought you a present. Your favorite."

Amanda pointed to herself with one finger and then raised it.

"Okay, fine. You first."

She took a Snickers Bar out of her pocket and waved it in front of his face.

"Hey, that's the same as my present for you!' Toby produced another Snickers Bar from his pocket and fenced with Amanda's.

They traded bars, unwrapped them, and bit off a chunk in unison.

"Breakfast of Champions," Toby mumbled through caramel, nuts, and chocolate. "You need any help getting ready for the science quiz on the solar system?"

Amanda wrote, "No problem. I like space. Peaceful. Quiet. No humans."

Via Toby's tongue and Amanda's handwriting on the notepad, they chatted about which planets would be the best to visit until the bus stopped in front of the main school entrance.

As they stepped onto the sidewalk, a shout rose from a group of students on the lawn. "Hey, look! It's Deaf and Dumb!" Two boys ran over, touched Amanda's and Toby's arms, and yelled, "Deaf germs! I got deaf germs! Dumb germs! I got dumb germs!" The fledgling dickheads raced back to their pod and each slapped another person on the back. "Tag, you're it! You got deaf germs! You got dumb germs!"

Amanda and Toby plodded through the bedlam as more kids tapped them and scampered around "infecting" other people.

"MC DH," Toby muttered. "Mentally challenged dick heads."

After a locker stop to pick up textbooks, they walked to geography class and sat at their alphabetically assigned desks. The name Amanda Parnum was next in line after Toby Park.

Simone soaked in these situations and Amanda's emotions while drifting through her own memories. Twenty-five years earlier, she and her twin brother Simon had attended Valleyview, one of two middle schools in town. Like Toby, Simon was a genius but plagued with physical issues. She'd often been his guardian angel, protecting or saving him from the brutal treatment of his classmates. Though Amanda seemed unfazed by the harassment, Simone had been poised to invoke the Alien Hand Syndrome. She remembered her high school history teacher who'd grab an unruly kid by the trapezius muscle on the top of the shoulder with two fingers and a thumb, then press her nails into the flesh like Spock's Vulcan Nerve Pinch on *Star Trek*. Students melted into submission under her grip.

I might give the Nerve Pinch a try if this keeps up.

Simone had also been testing her control of the body. If she did nothing, the experience reminded her of riding on the back of a tandem bicycle when she didn't steer and could pedal or not. She imagined it might be like flying an airplane. If the captain needed a break, he set the plane on autopilot, or the copilot took over. She noticed a complication when she only controlled the eyes, instead of the whole body. If Simone suddenly gazed to one side, Amanda's steps forward faltered a bit. If Simone directed the whole body, Amanda seemed to become passive and compliant.

The geography teacher doddered into the room and slumped behind his desk. As he shuffled his papers, attempted to clear away the scraggly gray hair blocking his vision, and honked into his handkerchief, Simone recognized him.

Oh my, god. Mr. Arnold is still here! We called him Mr.

Aren't You Old back then. His nose is even redder now. I can see individual veins from here!

"Today we'll be learning about four countries south of Russia: Kazakhstan, Uzbekistan, Kyrgyzstan, and Azerbaijan. Kazakhstan is the largest landlocked country in the world and its capital is Astana."

I think this is the same lecture he gave twenty years ago. None of us could spell or pronounce the names, didn't care about them then, and haven't heard about them since.

Mr. Arnold droned on for fifty minutes, oblivious of his students, the snoring in the back, or Amanda and Toby passing notes to each other in the front.

Unlike aging Arnold, the young upbeat science teacher greeted each student at the door, never sat down, and captured everyone's attention straight away. "We've talked about change being the only constant in the universe. Today I will demonstrate that concept. I don't feel like sitting through a boring test today. You can take it home and turn it in tomorrow."

A chorus of sighs and cheers echoed around the room.

"Yesterday I learned something cool that'll blow your minds." Miss Stacy's enthusiasm was contagious, and the class caught it. "Right now, you are sitting still in your seats. Are you moving?"

Toby already guessed where she was headed but raised his hand and asked, "You mean moving like breathing or raising my hand?"

"No. Good question. Let me rephrase that. Sitting still in this room, are you traveling right now?"

Toby turned around and grinned at Amanda. A month earlier, they'd watched a video on this concept while studying together. He raised his hand again.

Most kids shook their heads, but one girl blurted out, "Yes, the earth rotates, and we're traveling with it."

"Good start, Rachel, but you've got to look at the big picture. What do you think, Toby?" asked Miss Stacy.

"Yes, we are all traveling... phenomenally fast. Is it all right if Amanda helps illustrate just how fast on the whiteboard?"

"Go for it." Miss Stacy handed Amanda a marker as she walked to the board.

She drew a small earth with a tiny stick person sitting on it and an arrow curving around it as Toby began his commentary.

"The earth is 25,000 miles around at the equator and rotates on its axis once every 24 hours. That's about 1,000 miles per hour, and we're traveling with it."

Amanda wrote 1,000 mph over to one side, then drew a larger circle, labeled it "Sun", and drew another curving arrow to show the earth revolving around it.

"The earth takes us around the sun in one year at a speed of about 66,667 miles per hour."

Amanda wrote 66,667 mph under the other figure, then drew a huge oval around the earth and sun, labeled it "Milky Way", and drew another curving arrow through the galaxy.

"Our solar system revolves around our Milky Way galaxy like the earth revolves around the sun at about 550,000 miles per hour."

Amanda wrote the number under the others and drew one more immense arrow pointing away from the Milky Way.

"The entire universe has been expanding since the Big Bang that gave birth to it some fourteen billion years ago, and our galaxy moves away from that original point of creation at about 2,237,000 miles per hour."

Amanda wrote that last number at the bottom of the others, drew a line, and calculated the sum—2,855,000 mph.

"So, you see," Toby concluded, "you might think you're sitting still, alone, but we are all traveling together across the universe on Spaceship Earth at almost three million miles per hour. That's 800 miles per second!"

"Excellent!" Miss Stacy declared. "I couldn't have explained it any better. Will an A+ grade suit you two?"

Amanda wrote on the board once more. "How about an A^{10}?"

Most of the students laughed except Rachel, her face locked in a frown. Some kids even patted Toby and Amanda on the backs at the end of class, unconcerned about deaf or dumb germs.

Although Amanda remained attentive during math class, at her desk or solving equations on the white board, Simone zoned out after fifteen minutes of figures and functions. She preferred extroverts and introverts over exponents and integers. During Simone's freshman year at UCLA, she'd signed up for Calculus and become a number—one of 300 students in a cavernous lecture hall. Simone didn't understand the formulas on the board nor the professor's thick Chinese accent and dropped the course after two days. She replaced it with German, so she could read Sigmund Freud and Carl Jung's works in their original language.

Amanda ruled in gym class, the final period before lunch. A fiery Latino and competitive martial artist from Miami, Isabella was her favorite teacher and volleyball coach. She seemed more of a man than a woman, took no shit from students or staff, and valued hard work over idle talk. Isabella had recognized Amanda's gifts early on and trained her after school.

Every four weeks Isabella administered her MAP test, a Monthly Athletic Performance evaluation. Amanda ran faster, jumped higher, and did more push-ups and sit-ups than any classmate. She climbed the rope hanging from the ceiling hand over hand without using her feet until halfway to the top. A couple of girls managed to do three pull-ups. Rachel panted through one and touched her nose on the bar. Amanda whipped through seventeen full chin-ups.

After the test Isabella commanded the class, "Okay, divide into four teams, choose your badminton rackets, and beat up that birdie. I'm gonna work with Amanda on some exercises. I'll be watching you, and I wanna see real games with real effort, not just batting your pretty eyes and flailing your flimsy arms."

The workout left Amanda coated in sweat. The other girls hurried off to the lunchroom, and she took her time washing in the dressing room. When she entered the hallway, only a few students strolled past. Turning the corner, she heard a heartrending shriek and saw an altercation near her locker. A group of kids leaned against the opposite wall, laughing, pointing, or recording the scene with their phones.

"Ow! Stop it!" Amanda recognized Toby's terrified voice and froze. Rachel, Rodney, and another girl were trying to stuff him into his locker.

Riding inside Amanda while watching from afar, Simone had been feeling like a crossbreed between an adult and a teenager. This scene transported her back to the days of protecting her brother Simon in grade school, yet Amanda stood immobile.

These brats need to be taught a lesson. Alien hands won't work. It's time for alien body.

Simone sprinted toward the fray while lifting Amanda's pack to her chest. Four feet from the first girl, she launched it at the back of her legs. Heavy with textbooks, the pack buckled the girl's knees, and she fell to the floor. Simone shoved her onto her side, and then grabbed the bottom of Rodney's sweater from behind, stretched it over his head, face, and neck, and threw him down onto the first girl. Simone recognized him as the boy who'd shouted, "It's Deaf and Dumb!" and started the pathetic game of tag.

Serves you right, Rodney. Now you're blind. How's it feel?

Rachel let go of Toby and lunged at Simone's neck. Simone ducked low, pulled Rachel's short skirt down her black leggings to her ankles, and yanked her feet out from under her.

Simone picked up her pack, helped Toby stand, and led him aside.

"My glasses," Toby whimpered through tears.

She turned back and picked them off the floor, broken in half at the bridge, two framed lenses with bent bows. Rachel had struggled to her knees. Simone kicked her ample fanny and sent her sprawling into the pile of her partners.

When she and Toby were beyond the crowd, Simone whispered, "Are you okay?"

Toby straightened up with surprise in his eyes. "You talked!"

"I did?"

"You did it again!" Toby's pains seemed to evaporate into joy.

"Only to you. It's our little secret." Simone zipped her

mouth closed with her thumb and forefinger.

Toby did the same, then flashed her the Boy Scout sign. "Scout's honor!"

"So are you okay? Your forehead's bleeding."

Toby took inventory as he limped along. "I'm okay, but my leg hurts. And my head hurts." He tapped his ear. "And one of my hearing aids is dead."

"Let's go to the nurse's office and call your parents." Now that Simone had taken complete control of the body, she checked in on Amanda.

Where is she? Still frozen in time? Or sleeping? Maybe our roles have reversed, and she's riding in her brain and watching. I don't know.

Amanda, now sans Simone's control, sat in the office as the nurse gave Toby a painkiller, cleaned and bandaged his head wound, and called his parents to give her recommendation—stitches ASAP. On the front steps of the school, Amanda shared the contents of her lunch box with Toby while waiting for his mother to take him to the hospital. As Toby waved from the car window, Amanda shot him another "zip it" gesture across her lips. He returned it with one hand and a thumbs-up with the other.

This is puzzling. So I just relax into the background and Amanda rises to the foreground, or is it somewhere in between? She remembered the "zip it" move I made earlier, but what about the speaking and the whole incident? She seems calm... but what is she thinking?

Now alone on the steps, Amanda took out her iPhone, sent an "Thanks for the phone. I love you!" text message to her mother, and then checked her Snapchat and Instagram accounts. She hadn't used social media much without a smartphone but had set them up on her computer at home. Scrolling through the posts, Amanda shuddered when she came across a video from a classmate with the headline, "Girl Attacks Students at Valleyview." Her real life had transformed into a virtual broadcast in a half hour. The video only showed Amanda's dash down the hallway and what appeared to be an "assault" on three "innocent" kids. Toby appeared as an unrecognizable blur for a second at the end.

Jesus, I was only trying to help! These days life is chopped into chunks, and time is squeezed into moments that last forever. I'm still living in the Stone Age, the Wellstone age. What have I done?

Amanda switched over to Instagram and scrolled down the posts. Another longer video of the scuffle from a different perspective with the title "SHEro Saves Kid from Bullies at Valleyview" clearly revealed how Rachel, Rodney, and the other girl had tormented Toby and violently tried to stuff him into a locker. It was obvious that Amanda had rushed in to rescue him. Amanda glanced at her watch, stashed her phone, and hurried into the school.

How the hell is this going to play out?

Though this dual personality phenomenon presented endless confusion, questions, and emotional trauma, Simone had grown quite fond of Amanda. And sweet little Toby. She cherished the role of defending the underdogs and championing their cause. She'd become comfortable with her bizarre predicament and felt as if she were lounging in her office peering through a window into her patient's world. She was certain that the reason for Amanda's silence hadn't originated at school, that the harassment by some students was merely a repercussion of her decision not to speak. The root of that choice became clearer in Amanda's English class.

Mrs. Ramstad's spindly legs stuck out like sticks below her white smock. Wire-rimmed glasses roosted at the end her substantial pointed nose stretching down from her slanted forehead. Peering over the lenses at the class, she resembled a near-sighted stork.

"We've talked about fiction, and read fiction, and today you're going to write fiction. Let your mind and heart wander where they will. No holds barred, no boundaries. At the end of class, I want you to hand in a beginning, a middle, and an ending. On your marks, get set, imagine!"

A jumble of fear and resolve churning in her gut, Amanda sat for a minute chewing on the wood of her pencil. She took a breath into the bottom of her lungs, let out a sigh of surrender, and began to write.

"Andy was born on the Rainbow Planet. People of all sizes and colors lived there. Blue people, purple people, red people, orange people, yellow people, green people, and every color in between. All the people got along, and there were no wars.

"One day he fell into a deep sleep and woke up on another planet. The land and buildings and plants and animals were every color of a rainbow, but all the people were shades of brown. White beige, light beige, light brown, chocolate brown, blue brown, and black brown. And only some of them got along with each other.

"Most people thought the Boogeyman was fiction and didn't believe in him. But Andy met one in person, and believed. The Boogeyman was dirty white on the outside and black as midnight inside. He was lazy, wicked, mean, bad, nasty, and smelled like sweat and stale beer. Wherever the Boogeyman touched Andy, dark scars stained his skin. Andy tried to wash them off and scrub them away, but they stayed. They itched and hurt inside his body.

"Andy lived with his two best friends, and one day he saw the Boogeyman make one of his friends disappear. The Boogeyman said, 'If y'all ever tell anyone, I'm gonna do the same to you and your friend.'

"Andy was really scared. He and his friend left on a spaceship that took them to another planet. It had more brown-skinned people, and most of them were pretty nice except for some kids who had already started to become Boogeymen.

"Andy and his friend felt happy and safe, but he knew that someday the Boogeyman would find them. Andy had to protect his friend because she was weak. He made himself strong and hid magic weapons in his bedroom. When the Boogeyman came to their door, Andy would drop from the roof onto his shoulders and send him away forever. And even if Andy fell into another deep sleep, maybe, just maybe, he'd wake up on the Rainbow Planet again."

Amanda set down her pencil and stared at Toby's empty desk in front of her. The emotional rollercoaster inside her raced faster and higher. She put her hand on the paper and started to crumple it. She paused and bit into her pencil, then reread the story and changed a few words. She glanced up at the clock. Two minutes to the finish line. As the seconds ticked down, she titled her story "The Boogeyman" but didn't include her name, slipped it on Mrs. Ramstad's desk, and walked out as the bell tolled.

Simone had followed every word as Amanda wrote them. Each one was a clue to the insight she'd sought to explain Amanda's mute behavior.

Thank you, Andy Amanda. You get an F for Fiction and an A for Authentic. So, who is the boogeyman, and what did he do to you?

Amanda checked Snapchat and Instagram after settling into her desk in her last class of the day. The amount of people who'd viewed the videos had doubled.

The teacher distributed soft pastels for the students to experiment with a new medium. The aisles between the desks were wider to accommodate Miss Garfield's width. She embodied art in a body broad enough to contain every artistic style. Her rotund face smiled like a teddy bear head on a 300-pound panda dressed in flowing robes, neck draped with scarves, and appendages adorned with eccentric necklaces, bracelets, and rings.

"Let's get abstract today. Pretend you're a cubist Picasso, modernist Mondrian, or surreal Salvador Dali. Create something you see in this room, anything, and make it into something else. Be as weird as you want. If you need any help, I'll be doing the same thing at my desk."

Amanda thought for a few minutes, separated the pastels into dark and light shades, and set them on both sides of her sketch book. She outlined a large distorted oval in black in the middle, added two eyes, one lower in blue, one higher in yellow, one like a teardrop, one like the sun, and drew an oversize purple mouth drooping on the left and curving up on the right. Using thick black lines, she divided the background behind the strange face into random geometric shapes, and then carefully colored them with dark shades on the left melding into light shades on the right.

From the back of the second row, Amanda looked up at Toby's empty desk at the head of the third row and sighed. Attracted by movement in her peripheral vision, she glanced over at Rachel who was wagging a piece of paper at her from the first row. Under the headline "Deaf and Dumb" stood two naked figures. Toby had breasts, and Amanda had a penis. With a wicked smirk, Rachel passed the drawing to Rodney who sat in front of her.

Amanda didn't react visibly, but Simone shared the anger she could feel coursing through her host's young body. *This has got to fucking stop! And right now, sweet girl, whether you're ready for this or not, we're going to give the class a reality check and a lesson in behavioral psychology.* Simone took control of Amanda, marched up the aisle, snatched the paper from Rodney, and approached the teacher's desk.

"Excuse me, Miss Garfield," she whispered. "I'd like to make an announcement to the class… please."

The pink pastel in her hand and her jaw dropped. "Amanda, dear!" she gasped. "You're talking now?"

"Now, yes. For a few moments, please."

"Why not?" Miss Garfield gestured to the front of the room. "Be my guest."

Students nearby who'd heard her whisper exchanged shocked expressions. Simone slowly walked in front of Toby's desk as all the faces in the room turned toward her. She let the silence sit while sorting her thoughts and settling her emotions.

"We all make choices, every minute of every day. And one choice can change your life forever. Months ago, I made a choice to stop talking, but today, I choose to speak calmly…" Simone's voice rose into a shriek during her next words. "Even though inside I am screaming I'VE HAD ENOUGH!" She slammed her fist on Toby's empty desk. The vibration from her blow reverberated through the desk, into the floor, and up everyone's legs.

She paused, scanned the spellbound faces, and resumed her former tone of voice. "This desk is vacant because today three students made a choice to violently attack him and try to stuff short-and-sweet Toby into his locker. I'd guess you heard about it or watched the videos on the internet. His glasses were smashed, one hearing aid is dead, and right now he's at the hospital getting stitches for the gash on his

head…"—Simone paused again to let the facts sink in— "…
while we are presented with this." She held up the artwork.
"I don't know who's work it is, but I suspect it might be one
of the attackers. Our despicable nicknames have expanded
beyond 'Deaf and Dumb' to include slogans. 'Toby or not
Toby?', a play on words that would probably piss off Wil-
liam Shakespeare. Mine is 'A man? Duh!' Despicable, but so
clever, yes? I have some suggestions on how to evaluate this
whole situation." As she spoke, Simone wrote the grades
and categories on the whiteboard.

"The artist gets an A for Abstract. Assignment directions were followed. Get weird and create something out of
something else. But just so you know for sure, I do not have
a penis, and I seriously doubt that Toby has breasts and a
vagina."

A few kids snickered. They'd never heard those words in
public outside of Biology or Sex Education Class.

"A+ for Anti-social Behavior that is racist, sexist, abu-
sive, and full of hate." Simone stared directly at Rachel and
Rodney, but they were both looking down at their desks.

"B+ for Bullying. No question there.

"C+ for Consequences. Your friends, your family, Toby's
family, your friends' families, and your teachers will see the
videos or find out another way. You'll be judged harshly
or perhaps punished. The reputation of Valleyview Middle
School is already being tarnished throughout our local
community, across the county, even around the globe…
as if we matter to the world. If you were older and out of
school, you could be arrested for Assault and Battery, sentenced in court, and carted off to jail.

"D+ for Damages. Emergency stitches at the hospital?
At least five hundred dollars. The cost of new glasses? Maybe two hundred. High-tech hearing aids like Toby's? About
two thousand dollars for one." She'd written the numbers

while talking and then added them together. "That's a total of two-thousand, seven-hundred dollars. Who's going to pay for this? You? Your parents? The school?"

"E+ for Enemy. For some reason, you've made Toby and me into your enemies. But what have we ever done to you? Why do you hate us so much? Because my skin is darker than yours? Because Toby's from another country? Because you think we're flawed with disabilities? Because he's smarter and studies harder than any of us? Because I'm stronger and workout more that you? Because you are beaten and abused at home? Because you blindly follow some misguided gang leader at school? Sit in your soul and think about it.

"F+?" Simone signed and gazed at the ceiling for a moment. "Here's where choice come in… one simple choice." She looked over at Rachel. "We could simply be friends. We could put this behind us and move on. We could stick our differences into the past and create an F+ for the Future."

Simone plodded back to her desk. "Once again, I've had enough. We've all had enough." She picked up her pack from her desk, walked to the door, and turned back toward the pensive room as she grabbed the knob. "Thank you, Miss Garfield. I apologize for interrupting your class so I'm sending myself to the principal's office. She and I have to talk."

As she shut the door, a smattering of applause sounded from behind it. Simone hoped Amanda had heard it too.

Simone led Amanda into the main office, leaned on the principal's door frame, and peered into her room. Principal Bernhardt stood next to her desk while gathering papers into a file. They'd met before when the school contacted her about Amanda, and Simone had been impressed by her concern and compassion. Simone grunted, "Ahem."

"Amanda! I was just coming to find you. The Superintendent of Schools just gave me an earful on the phone."

"I'm sure he did."

"What?" The principal's eyebrows shot up in surprise. "I'm stunned."

"Yes, today I'm talking, but I'm not sure about tomorrow. I even talked in art class today. I'm taking some new medicine."

"It certainly seems to be helping."

"We'll see. I don't have much time because I've got a volleyball game after school. Can we chat for a minute?"

"Sit! Sit!" Mrs. Bernhardt pulled a chair close to her desk. "It's been quite a day, but I'm happy to see you... to hear you!"

Amanda sat, put her elbows on the desk, and rested her head in her hands.

I didn't do that! I would never get so comfy in a meeting like this. Amanda moved on her own!

"I hope you know I didn't attack—"

"Stop. I never even considered that possibility. Thank you for rescuing Toby. Those were some fancy moves, Amanda. Did you learn them from Isabella?"

"I didn't wanna hurt anyone, just break it up and get him out. I wish I coulda been there before it started. Do you know how he's doing?"

I didn't say those words! That's Amanda speaking!

"I returned from a conference a half hour ago, so I'm still getting up to speed on the events. I've watched the videos. I've talked with some teachers and students. The Superintendant of Schools talked to me, and then talked some more, but I think the verdict is clear from the video. The nurse will be keeping tabs on Toby. I've got three voice mails from his parents. At least we'll have something to talk about besides uniforms, longer hours, and drug testing."

"Mrs. Bernhardt, you know it's so much easier to have a conversation when I'm talking instead of writing."

"I agree, and I hope you keep talking!"

"I think you should see this." Simone laid the drawing of Toby and Amanda on the principal's desk. "This was being passed around art class. I didn't actually see Rachel draw it, but she's the one who had to make sure I saw it. All three of the kids in the video were in the art room."

"Oh, my." Mrs. Bernhardt's smile dropped into a frown.

"Remember the shooter at Hawthorne High School a few months ago? A boy who'd been bullied by classmates?"

"How could anyone forget?"

"There's a lot of great kids here, but you've got some bad ones in the bunch. We're not the only ones being bullied. You don't have to worry about me, and Toby wouldn't hurt a fly. He avoids stepping on ants."

Hmm. Amanda's words just slipped in again. I haven't seen other kids bullied, and I didn't know that about Toby.

"You're very perceptive, Amanda."

"It'd hate to think it would happen here, or what kids might learn here and carry into high school."

"One session of the conference today addressed these issues, and I have a new plan of attack." Mrs. Bernhardt covered her mouth with one hand. "Bad choice of words."

"I'm not trying to tell you how run a school, but you don't see everything that goes on here during the day."

"Unfortunately, that statement is too true. Thanks for sharing this drawing with me. I always appreciate our little chats, and this one especially." Mrs. Bernhardt winked above her warm smile.

"Maybe we'll talk again soon, but now I gotta change and get to the game. Thanks for your time."

"No, thank you for coming in. My door and my heart

are always open for you."

When I thought I was in control, Amanda moved on her own during the conversation. And those last words were hers, not mine. She seems to feel safe and relaxed and must've had other chats with the principal. Are we merging into one being? A dual personality named Simanda?

Amanda hurried to the dressing room, donned her uniform and sweats, and strode across the open courtyard next to a pond outside the gymnasium building on grass slick from the afternoon rain. A school van carrying the entire volleyball team except for Amanda sat on the main driveway. Parents waited in cars. Students milled about in cliques.

Some kids seemed to be watching her too closely for comfort. Simone's internal radar picked up the tension in the air as if an earthquake were imminent.

Rachel lurked in the bushes on the lawn thirty yards behind and to the left. She jumped out and sprinted toward Amanda.

Simone's senses seemed to stretch out from the physical being of Amanda. She could hear the soft flap of Rachel's feet on the wet grass. When she felt the vibration on the earth right behind her, Simone dropped Amanda to her knees.

Rachel's outstretched arms shoved air instead of sending Amanda flying. She tripped over Amanda's back, fell forward onto her chest, and slid on the slippery grass through the mud and into the pond.

Simone let go as Amanda turned her head toward the pond, stood up, walked over to the edge, and extended her hand to help Rachel out of the water. She lifted one muddy arm and flipped Amanda the bird.

Simone sighed inside. *Hopeless. Rachel gets two more F's*

for Finger and Fuck you.

Amanda boarded the van to cheers and high-fives from the team.

The Valleyview Hornets shutout the other volleyball team, 3–0. Amanda's power serves screamed over the net and ricocheted out of bounds off her opponents' hands. She slammed the ball down their throats, and routinely set up spikes for her teammates. She seemed to be everywhere on the court and made diving saves that amazed the other team. Simone felt as if she were lashed onto a wild carnival ride that she never dared tackle in her teens.

As the school van dropped off each team member at their homes, Amanda took out her new iPhone to message her mother, but the battery was depleted. She signaled the driver to stop at the bus stop on the main road, so he wouldn't have to back out of the dead-end street where she lived.

At six p.m., the sun had slipped behind the hills and wouldn't set for another hour. The day had been long and charged with emotion, but Amanda breezed along the sidewalk, smiling and humming, still dressed in her long-sleeved, purple-and-white jersey, and purple sweatpants.

Suddenly she stopped mid-step as if her skeleton had turned into petrified wood. She scrunched her head down and stared at a beat-up, shit-brown pickup truck parked in front of her duplex apartment building. Fear flattened Amanda against the hedge on the right of the sidewalk. She slunk low and inched closer to the truck.

What's going on? When Amanda paused again, Simone could see the truck had a Florida license plate.

Amanda backed up thirty yards, still crouching, then stood and sprinted to the bus stop, turned left around the corner, and left again into the alley behind the buildings. Like a wary spy, she crept around trees, cars, rotting garages, and piles of garbage until she reached the house just beyond her duplex. In this rundown slice of town, most structures needed repair, remodeling, or demolition. Hiding behind her neighbor's hedge, Amanda scoped out her tiny backyard. Her two-story apartment on the right mirrored the one the left—two bedrooms and bath upstairs, living room and kitchen downstairs, a porch with a sloping roof attached to the back. No one in the yard. No people or movement visible through the windows in the kitchen or Amanda's second-story bedroom.

On the neighbor's side of the hedge, she slipped toward the front yard of their duplex. The hedge stopped five yards before the sidewalk. Amanda crawled around the end through the uncut grass and weeds until she lay under the picture window. The curtains had been pulled shut except for a two-inch gap between them. Amanda slowly rose to her knees and peered into the living room.

A bulbous, stubbled man overflowed from the wingback armchair in the corner across the room. His greasy hair glistened in the light from the floor lamp on his left. A semi-automatic pistol lay on the side table to his right. On the coffee table, a fifth of Jack Daniel's sat next to a pocket mirror holding a razor blade, an empty packet, and a small pile of white powder. Underneath his unbuttoned, flannel shirt, a stained wife-beater tank top stretched across his porcine belly. A rope tied to his arm stretched beyond Amanda's vision to the right. Shifting to the left, she could see that the rope ended in a noose tightened around her mother's neck. Whitney huddled on the tattered sofa two feet away from the armchair. Her hands had been bound with another rope and her TGI Friday's shirt ripped. Bruises darkened her cheeks. A thin stream of blood trickled down her temple.

This white trash must be Uncle Boogeyman. Simone emotions raced along with Amanda's as she tried to comprehend their dilemma. *He's a big fucking brute. The bottle's half-empty and he's probably hammered. And sky-high on cocaine. In Amanda's story, she dropped on the boogeyman from the roof. That's not gonna happen. What do we do? Her iPhone's dead. Run to a neighbor's house?*

Simone only knew sketchy information about this man, but Amanda had lived through the horror and heard the history from her mother. The boogeyman's name was Darryl Foster, and he had plagued their lives for years.

Amanda never met her father. "You were conceived in love," Whitney had said, "but your real father, his love, and his promise of marriage vanished after three months of my pregnancy."

For eight years Whitney raised Amanda alone while scraping together money by suffering through shit jobs around a picayune town in the Florida panhandle. Then she met Charlie Foster, a sweet man who became Amanda's loving stepfather. He worked as a traveling life insurance salesman, prospered, and moved his new family into a modest apartment.

Charlie had been adopted at age six by Eloise Foster, a kind woman who took him in after his parents abandoned him at the local Primitive Baptist Church. Dark-brown skin was merely another shade of humanity to Eloise, but her nine-year-old son Darryl had already assimilated the rampant racism of the community. He'd hated Charlie from the beginning. Charlie was smart and industrious; Darryl, an inanimate human parasite. As Whitney had described him, "He fell out of the stupid tree and hit every branch on the way down." Charlie had a paper route by age eleven, worked odd jobs, and contributed money to help out his mother. Charlie gave, and Darryl did nothing but take. After Charlie married Whitney, he'd still give Eloise monthly cash which often disappeared from her purse. Once his mother passed, Darryl focused his greed on his little brother, and Charlie continued to support him.

When Charlie died, Darryl targeted Whitney. His miniature brain imagined he'd move in with her and Amanda. "Ah'll take care o' y'all." His sentence should have ended after "Ah'll take."

Darryl's violent streak surged with physical abuse of Whitney and threats to Amanda. One morning Whitney pleaded with him to leave the apartment. He communicated his answer via drunken roars, vile epithets, and punches while Amanda cowered in the corner. Whitney grabbed her steam iron and slammed it into his face. He collapsed on the floor with blood and alcoholic saliva drooling from his mouth. Whitney and Amanda stuffed clothes and necessities in two suitcases, withdrew their meager savings from the bank, bought bus tickets, and rode out of town to a new life.

The vision of her mother's battered head through the picture window matched that pivotal moment in Amanda's past. A soldier snapped to attention inside of her. She crept around the corner to peek through the small window behind the armchair where Darryl sat under an open staircase leading to the second floor. She saw no one else in the room. Amanda dashed around the corner to the back yard and scaled up the side of the house on the drainpipe extending down from the roof gutter like she'd done on the rope in the gym.

Simone thought for sure the nails holding the rickety drainpipe would rip out of the wall. *This kid is a mad monkey on a mission. She must've done this before. But what's the mission?*

Amanda eased onto the porch roof, tiptoed across to her bedroom window, pried it open, and stepped silently onto the floor. She paused to listen, then padded to the hallway to hear the voices from below.

Darryl's thick drawl slithered up the stairs and her spine like a centipede. "When's that brat o' yoursh comin' home, anyway? It'sh damn near shix o'clock."

Whitney's reply sounded submissive and meek. "I told you. When she has a volleyball game, she gets home late."

"Well, let'sh get to it then. Y'all got any sexy tunes on that there phone o' yers? I wanna shee you shtrip and shake 'em fer me, baby!"

He is shit-faced danger fueled by Jack and Columbian marching powder. Scary combo. Simone struggled to think of a feasible plan. *Shit-faced could be good or bad news.*

Amanda pulled open the top drawer of her dresser and took out a polished wooden box with her name hand-carved in the lid, a birthday present from Charlie where she kept her treasures. Amanda lifted the cards, trinkets, and papers from the box to reveal a switchblade and an ice pick honed to a fine point.

Ah, these are the 'magic weapons' from her story. Does she really dare use them?

As Amanda held them in her hands and pricked her finger on the point of the pick, another minute passed before faint music floated up the stairs—"Rock the Boat" by Aaliyah, one of Whitney's favorite songs.

Amanda slunk into the hallway, bent low, pulled back her curly hair, and nudged one eye around the corner. Darryl's sat six feet below her and a foot ahead. His slimy skull was bobbing to the beat. The smell of his rancid sweat and fermented breath bit her nose. Whitney swayed halfheartedly two feet in front of the armchair.

Amanda stuck out her head, caught her mother's hollow gaze, and raised one finger perpendicular to her lips. Whitney's eyes widened as she nodded to Amanda with the beat of the song.

"C'mon, bitch. Get it on! I wanna shee movin' an' shakin'!" Darryl grabbed the pistol and waved it at Whitney. "If y'all don't rock mah boat, ah'm gonna fuckin' sink yers."

A decade earlier, Whitney had taken a job as a stripper at a local redneck dive but only lasted three days. She now had a reason to dance in spite of the noose around her neck. Her moves became fluid and seductive. "If I'm gonna rock you, sugar, you'd better get rock hard between your legs."

Back in the bathroom, Amanda took her metal cup off its hook, and rapped four times on the pipe to the beat of the music. Rap, rap, rap, rap—no raps for four beats—rap, rap, rap, rap.

"I'll be right there." Amanda's got a plan. She's going to drop on him from the top of the staircase. I'll bet she's been building up her body for this exact moment.

"What'zat sound?" Darryl mumbled as he rocked in the armchair.

"That's the beat, sugar bear," Whitney purred, slipping off her torn shirt. "That's the countdown to your climax."

"Lemme shee more shkin, baby doll." Spittle dribbled from his grin to his chin.

"I'm gonna take a picture o' you, sugar, so y'all can show

your buddies what they're missin'." Whitney danced her hands down to the coffee table, picked up the iPhone, and licked it. She pressed record and lowered it to her crotch, pausing to video the pistol in his hand. "Hey, you stud, show me how rough and tough you are."

Darryl screwed his face into a grotesque farce of a gangster.

Whitney eased the iPhone around into a selfie. "Oh, Darryl Foster, y'all're one han'some dude!"

Simone pictured the pistol. *Where is it right now? First we've got to deal with the gun. Amanda and I seemed to have a quantum leap of connection at school. Is she really listening every time I speak? Are we truly Simanda now? A tiny team of two?* She whispered out loud. "Amanda, the gun first. Use the magic weapons next. First get rid of the gun."

Amanda's head jerked backwards in thought. She looked around the bathroom until her gaze centered on the toilet. She cleared off the cover of the tank, removed it, returned to the bedroom, and set it on the bed. She bound her hair with a black stretch headband and stuck the switchblade into her left sock. With the ice pick in her right hand, she picked up the tank cover on each of its long sides and hefted it in front of her. Amanda squinted and spoke softly with steel resolve. "I watched this monster murder my stepdad. Let's do this."

She crept to the stairway and peeked into the living room. Darryl's left hand lay on his leg, holding the rope tethered to Whitney's neck. The pistol under his right hand lay on the side table. His bloodshot eyes were fixed on Whitney.

Simone didn't dare speak aloud this close to their foe, but her thoughts seemed to physically vibrate in her head.

Drop it on his wrist and then jump with the pick. I'll focus on the gun.

Working together, Simanda positioned the tank cover above Darryl's wrist and twenty inches in front of her body. Whitney exaggerated her erotic moves, flipped open her shirt, and teased him with her cleavage. Simanda let the cover drop and jumped a half-second later, targeting his knee with the ice pick.

"Ee-yahh!" Darryl screamed as the bones in his hand crackled. The pistol discharged and flew off the table into the corner by the picture window.

He screamed again when Simanda landed feet first in his lap and plunged the ice pick through the flesh behind his kneecap. "Son of a bitch!"

She slammed the pick in further with her left hand and vaulted off him to grab the pistol.

His brain raging with pain from two wounds, Darryl tried to yank out the ice pick with his right hand, but the crushed fingers wouldn't curl. As he moved his other arm toward it, Whitney leaped onto the sofa, leaned back on the rope around her neck, and wrenched away his hand. Her face was turning red as the noose tightened when Darryl struggled to pull his arm back toward his body.

Simanda scrambled on the floor, retrieved the pistol from the corner, and sprung up in front of Darryl. She leveled the pistol at his chest and yelled, "It's over. Don't move!"

Bolstered by Jack Daniel's liquid anesthesia, Darryl smirked through the burning pain in his hand and knee. "Oo, Amanda'sh a tough cookie now with a gun. Big gun for a little shquirt. Ya think ya know how to use it?"

The advanced option of Simone's self-defense course had included learning to handle a Beretta M9 semi-automatic at a shooting range. She didn't care for the noise but thought the kick of the gun was kind of fun.

"I took some lessons." Simone racked the slide, ejected a bullet, gripped the pistol with both hands, and fired a round into the wall to the left of Darryl.

Darryl flinched but recovered with a taunt. "Betcha never shot a person, bitch."

"You're right." Simone smiled and shot him in the left shoulder. "Now I have."

"Goddamn fucking hell!" Darryl's arm went limp, but Whitney kept up the pressure on the rope.

The scene became a face-off between Team Simanda and Team Jack Darryl Daniel's Cocaine. From some inebriated backwater in his brain, he summoned the strength to lurch out of the armchair, propelling his body forward with his uninjured left leg.

Adrenaline pumping, Simone backed up and shot him in the groin. "Men like you shouldn't be allowed to reproduce."

With a final howl, Darryl fell flat on his ugly mug with both hands clutching his balls.

Simone pounced on his back, pressed the gun barrel into his neck, and growled, "If you even think of moving, it'll be your last thought."

Amanda pulled out the switchblade from her sock, sprung it open, cut the rope attached to Darryl's arm, and held it out toward Whitney so she could slice the rope around her wrists.

Thirty seconds later, Darryl grunted, arched his meaty carcass, and rolled over. Simanda tipped off to the side onto the floor.

Whitney snatched the Jack Daniel's bottle from the table, yelled, "Deja-fucking-vu, you prick!" and slammed it into his face.

After a minute of unison panting and staring down at

the immobile lump, Amanda asked, "Is he dead?"

"I hope so," Whitney sighed, then gave her daughter the look of love that only a mother can. "Hey, A… you're talking now."

"Yeah."

"That's gonna make me sap happy after we wrap this creep up like a mummy. I'll call 911. You get the packing tape in the kitchen drawer." As they secured the boogeyman with rope, tape, and the lamp cord through his mouth, Whitney had a few more questions. "I see you're pretty handy with an ice pick now?"

Amanda nodded. "I guess so."

"And guns too?"

"Just today."

"I love hearin' you talk, but I gotta sit down. My body's shakin', and my heart's about to bruise my ribs." Whitney slumped down on the floor next to the couch. "How are you doin'?"

Amanda kneeled beside her mother. "Shakin' like you but somehow kinda calm inside."

"Wha'd'ya mean, sweetheart?"

"I just knew he'd come sometime, and I've been preparing. He's fat and weak, and I had to make myself strong. We beat him… and now it's over."

"God almighty, I hope it's over. For months I've been prayin' it wouldn't start." Whitney wiped the sweat off her forehead with her shredded shirt. "Let's go sit in the kitchen, away from this pile of shit."

"No, Mom, stay here! We gotta watch him. Everytime they leave the criminal alone in the movies, he unties himself and gets away."

"Okay, baby. You got the gun, and I got Jack Daniel's club. He ain't goin' nowhere. How 'bout I order a pizza, and we chat more when the police split?"

"Sounds great, Mom. I'm starved."

"Pepperoni?"

"Pepperoni, thin crust, please."

"You got it."

As Whitney phoned the Pizza Hut, a squad car pulled in front of the apartment. The policemen questioned, photographed, gathered evidence, and watched Whitney's damning video of Darryl on her iPhone. Paramedics arrived and carted away the taped mummy in an ambulance. The boogeyman wasn't dead, but he wouldn't be walking or reproducing for a while.

Amanda had one fact from the past for the police. "I saw him murder my stepfather Charlie in Florida, but I never told anyone."

When Whitney and Amanda walked outside to meet the pizza man, no one took any notice of the EDNA truck parked down the block. A new delivery company, EDNA had sprung up in town during the previous year. On each of their canary yellow, panel vans, a cartoon drawing of the bust of a stern, older woman with her hair in a bun captivated the public with a cheery smile. This logo rode beside the maroon acronym EDNA—"Express Delivery. Now. Anywhere." They seemed to be everywhere, all the time.

Simone hadn't noticed the truck that followed the school bus to Valleyview, parked in the school lot for the rest of the day, and then shadowed the school van to the game and on to Amanda's apartment. Nor that the deli delivery van parked in front of her house the previous evening had been the exact size and model as the yellow EDNA trucks but painted blue with "Damian's Deli" stenciled on the side panel in white.

It was after eight when they sat at the kitchen table and Whitney served up the pizza. "Talk to me, sweetheart."

Amanda took a bite and spoke with her mouth full. "I was outside prowling around one night in Florida when I saw Darryl murder Charlie right down the street from our apartment. I think he saw me too. I hated him so much. He'd put his grubby hands on me, but I always ran away. He said if I ever told anyone anything, the same thing that happened to Charlie would happen to you and me."

"I'm so sorry all this happened, A. I learned via my Florida grapevine that a warrant had been issued for his arrest. Someone in a bar heard him bragging about killing Charlie. He's been on the run for months. I don't know how he found us."

"I was so afraid, Mom. I only stopped talking to make sure I'd never accidentally say anything."

"Well, A, you are a brave, smart girl, and I am proud of you." Whitney picked up a slice of pizza and tapped Amanda's slice in a toast. "Now what about you handlin' that gun like a professional?"

"That wasn't me. Someone else was inside of me all day. In the morning I was scared at first. Suddenly my body'd move but I wasn't moving it. When that happened, it kinda felt like I was dreaming. But I remembered the instructions and just relaxed and went with it."

"Wha'd'ya mean by 'someone inside' of you? Like it was the treatment?"

"It felt like the someone was a woman. A nice lady, but really strong. She was always trying to help me. Somehow, she spoke through me. I didn't feel so alone or like a cripple. She made me a super hero at school."

Amanda gave her mother a rundown of the day's

events—Deaf and Dumb tag, saving Toby, writing her story, talking in class, meeting with the principal, Rachel sliding through the mud, and kicking ass at the volleyball game. Their roles switched—Amanda spoke while Whitney rapped on the table. One for no. Two for okay. Three for I don't know.

When they finished the pizza, Amanda sighed and rested her head in her hands. "I'm soooo tired, Mom. And smelly."

"It's after eight, and that's what the guy said would happen at the end of the treatment. Let's get you to bed after a hot shower."

Burned out but squeaky clean, Amanda put on her favorite velour pajamas and slid under the covers. Whitney sat next to her on the bed.

"Mom, what's that puppet on strings called?"

"A marionette?"

"Oh, yeah. That's what I felt like today. I was the marionette, and the lady and I were two puppet masters moving the strings."

"Spooky, eh?"

"Spooky but kinda cool." Amanda's voice started to ramble and trail off. "I gotta call Toby, but... my iPhone's dead. An' I gotta do my science homework for tomorrow... The lady inspired me today, Mom. She was my guardian angel... kinda like you."

"You are my super shero and always will be." Whitney stroked Amanda's hair and kissed her on the forehead. "Close your eyes, sweetheart, and try to get some sleep."

Amanda mumbled, "I wonder where my angel is now?"

As Simone listened to these words, she shed a few tears inside that pooled in the corners of Amanda's eyes.

I'm right here, Amanda.

They joined each other in the void.

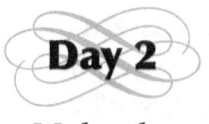

Day 2

Wednesday

S IMONE'S PSYCHE ROSE UP FROM THE ABYSS OF NOTHING
into an unconscious, pitch-black dream.

She could hear no sound nor see any variation in the Stygian gloom, though it seemed to be vibrating and smelled vaguely medical. She tried to sit up and felt the pressure of straps on her chest, arms, hips, and legs. As if bathed in the flash from a camera, the space around her lit up for a split second. The ceiling and walls were close like an intensive care cubicle in an emergency room.

Something touched her forehead and paused there, then her neck, then touched a wrist and paused again. She heard faint breathing like a nurse bending over a bed, then sniffing like a predator examining its incapacitated prey. The touches spread to other areas below her waist, as if the first intruder had been joined by two others. The pace and volume of the breathing increased as she felt moisture in her groin. The three intruders morphed into a tongue licking her genitals and two hands stroking her legs.

In direct contrast to the numbing terror she felt, Simone's body was aroused and involuntarily arched up to meet the mouth. The rush of emotions coursing through Simone dragged her mind into semi-consciousness. She started to struggle to free herself from the straps, but they were no longer there. She bent her knees and clamped her thighs around the head between her legs.

Now fully conscious and eyes wide open, Simone rolled over to one side then the other, slamming the head back and forth and dislodging its mouth. Confused grunts and cries of pain emanated from the white sheet that lifted above her lower body like a ghost. "GET"—she coiled both legs into her chest—"OFF"—and kicked the apparition with a force that seemed beyond her strength—"ME!"

The shrouded form flew off the end of the bed, smashed into the wall, crumpled to the floor, and shouted, "Jeez, Diego! Wake up! It's me! Jimmy!

Questions inundated Simone's head as it twisted around to assay the situation. *Who's Jimmy? Who's Diego? Where am I?*

A circular stained-glass window above the wailing voice. Forest green walls below a sky-blue ceiling stretching into a lofty peak. A desk, laptop, and full-length mirror across the room. A wooden coat and hat stand hung with an array of clothing. An ornate oriental rug on the floor. In the bed and attached to her head, a ripped, tattooed, naked body. Six-pack abs. Strong, sinewy, hairy legs. And standing tall between the thighs, an impressive erect penis.

Oh, god, here we go again. Déjà-fucking-vu in some dude! Diego? Diego... I remember... Diego Fierra. Another one of my patients. Simone focused her consciousness inside instead of on the external scene. She could feel her host waking to his world. *Back off. Stop protecting someone who probably doesn't need protecting.*

Diego Fierra sat up and rubbed his eyes. "What's going on?"

Jimmy crawled out from under the sheet and toward the bed. "You were asleep. I was just giving you a surprise gift on your birthday."

Diego scanned the rumpled bed and the floor. "What gift?"

"A little head."

"I think… I was having a nightmare."

"You kicked me off the bed into the wall."

"Sorry… I'm taking some new medicine. Might have some side effects."

"I'm sorry too, Diego. Didn't mean to freak you out."

"Don't ever do that again."

"I did it once before. You remember that?"

"Jimmy… just don't do it again."

"Yes, sir. You're the boss."

"What time is it?"

"Eight a.m. or so."

"You're s'posed to be helpin' set up for the party."

"Yeah, boss. We've been workin' on it since seven."

"Well, finish it. I've got stuff to do."

"I'm on it, boss. Sorry again." Jimmy scurried out of the room.

"Hey, Jimmy!"

Three seconds later, a head poked into the room.

"You rang?"

"You could bring me a little birthday present from downstairs."

"You name it."

"One cuppa Java, please. My morning fix."

"Black?"

"You got it."

Jimmy snapped off a military salute. "Not yet, but I'll get it."

Diego stood tentatively, stretched, padded to his bathroom, and assumed his standard urination stance.

I've always admired the ability of men to stand and pee outside wherever they want, but inside? Why don't they sit down and relax?

Unlike the two toilets in Simone's living space and office frequented mainly by two women, Diego's lid and seat were up. The sign above her office toilet clearly displayed the etiquette required. "If you lift it, put it down. If you miss it, clean it up. Gentlemen, please stand close. It might be shorter than you think."

With Diego's flaccid yet still formidable penis resting between his/her fingers, Simone got to experience one of her pet peeves first hand. Diego stood six foot two, so the waterfall began about three feet above the pool. She could see the mist of urine splay off the main stream onto the rim of the bowl. She could feel the fine droplets of urine splash up from the bowl onto his/her feet.

After the final squirts of the session, he squeezed his penis like a toothpaste tube and then started shaking it.

Simone took control and halted his hand mid-shake. *God, why don't men see or feel the pee, or care about the consequences of their lofty position? Are they marking their territory like dogs?* As she stared down at the situation, Simone noticed the black watch on his arm. *That's exactly like the watch Amanda wore yesterday.*

Diego moved over to the wash stand, brushed his teeth, and washed his face. He combed back his short black hair, tapered down to skin above his ears, then messed up the top with his fingers.

As he slapped cologne on his cheeks and leaned closer to the mirror, Simone looked him in the eyes. *Diego Fierra in the flesh, all of his gorgeous flesh. How could I forget him? How could anyone forget him? A single, handsome hunk attractive to males, females, and all shades in between. Gentle, introspective, and intelligent. I wished then that we'd met as woman and man instead of doctor and patient.*

An inviolable rule from the almighty APA, the American Psychiatric Association and its Principles of Ethics in Practice plodded through her brain "Any occasion in which the physician interacts with a current or former patient in a way that may be a prelude to a more intimate relationship should be avoided."

Diego took a jock strap from his dresser, pulled it up his legs, and arranged his penis and scrotum before slipping it on.

I can't imagine having my private parts hanging outside my body, flapping on my thighs, or erect and ready at the wrong time.

Diego threw on a black singlet, red nylon shorts, and Under Armor "Charged Escape" black running shoes. Four raps on his bedroom door set the beat for "Happy birthday to you" sung in an array of random keys by tone-deaf athletes. He opened the door and took in the scene with a smile. Surrounded by The Fit Nest staff, his mama held out a glass of orange juice and a plate of huevos rancheros, his favorite breakfast—a corn tortilla topped with black beans, jalapeno peppers, salsa, avocados slices, feta cheese bits on the side, and two sunny-side-up eggs in the middle. Next to each egg stood a lit white candle in the shape of a four and a zero.

"Thanks, Mama, you're the best."

"Feliz cumpleaños, mi hijo," she said as the song ended in a flurry of discordant notes. "Life starts at forty, you know."

Diego took a piece of the white feta and put it between the candles. "This year I'm gonna move the decimal point to the left. 4.0 sounds more like an upgrade." Laughter and cheers arose as he blew out the flames and took the plate from Mama, almost two feet shorter than Diego, though her stiff, four-inch-tall hairdo decreased the difference. "Do I have to cut this into slices for everyone?"

"All for you," Mama said, "Breakfast in bedroom."

Jimmy held his cuppa java over Mama's shoulder. "And your morning fix, your majesty."

"Thank you, every one of you. I'll see you in a few. Gotta check my email."

And I gotta check mine. I had clients yesterday, and I have clients today, right now. And I have two dogs and a million questions that need some answers. Simone had wanted to connect to her personal and office email while inside Amanda, but the day had careened from one adventure to the next, and cell phones were off-limits in class.

Diego sat down and logged into his email. As he scrolled down the page, Simone spotted a recent message from "the office of Dr. Wellstone," took control, and clicked it open. It had been sent mid-morning on Tuesday while she'd been in Amanda and in school.

Dear Valued Clients and Friends,

Please accept my deepest apologies. I'm sorry to inform you of my absence with such short notice, especially those of you who have appointments today, Tuesday. Last night, I had to leave town on an urgent mission and will be out of the office for five days. If you'd like to reschedule any appointments that you'll miss this week, or schedule a new one, I'll in the office and available starting next Monday. Please contact my assistant Ming via the email address or phone listed below.

Once again, I am truly sorry for any inconvenience I may have caused you. Please forgive me.

Sincerely,

Dr. Simone Wellstone

Odd. It came from the office email account, and sounds like what I'd say, but who wrote it? Ming? Simone switched to her personal account, logged in, and scrolled through the spam to a recent email from Ming.

> Dear Dr. Simone,
>
> I email message you send me. I hope you are okay. No worry about office or Brandy and Dammit. I feed and walk them. Let me know anything else to do. See you next Monday.
>
> Regards, Ming

Simone checked her sent folder and found the email she'd written to Ming, late on Monday night, hours after she'd had entered the void, which included the exact words of the message delivered to her clients and another apology to Ming.

So she came into work, saw the email, and did as I asked, but I couldn't have written this. What the fuck is going on? Someone must've hacked into my email account, and Ming doesn't know my password. It says I'll be gone for five days, and today is day number two, trapped in another patient. Who's next? Three more patients? Did they pry into my patient files to get the names and info? I've been kidnapped, but there's no mention of blackmail, and they're paying Amanda and Whitney for this "treatment." Why, why, why? Who has technology to do this that I've never heard of or imagined possible? Some competitor of mine? But who benefits? Amanda seemed to. Will Diego? Maybe I should write an email to Ming. Yeah, right. "I was kidnapped, lived inside a kid, and now I'm trapped in another patient. Call the police. Save me!" She'd think I'm completely out of my mind. I'm still in my mind, but where the hell is my body? Ming would've seen it slumped on the floor. Scenes from Simone's morning dream flowed in. *I was strapped down on a bed or something. In a tiny room that was vibrating or bouncing. Are they schlepping my body around town in some mobile hospital? God, give me some answers!*

Simone logged out, switched back to Diego's email account, released him from her control, and faded back into observer mode.

Like Amanda in the beginning, Diego seemed to have no recognition of her presence, though he blinked his eyes as if awakening from a daydream. He read a few emails and logged out, then opened the desk drawer, removed an exact copy of the instructions Whitney had read to Amanda, and scanned its contents.

The sound of a thud and shattering glass broke the silence. Diego leaped up and raced down two flights of stairs into the main reception area of The Fit Nest, his new martial arts and workout studio, prepped and decorated for its official grand opening on his birthday.

He'd repurchased and remodeled his family home and the house next door into one building with new floors and a roof spanning the two houses. The reception desk, juice bar, and weight-training area were first-floor center. In the family house to the right, Diego had restored the bedroom, bath, kitchen, and living room for Mama. In the house on the left, he'd knocked out all the walls for Nautilus fitness equipment and exercise bikes. Second-floor center held canvas workout mats, Wing Chun wooden dummies, punching bags, and other martial arts paraphernalia between locker rooms, saunas, and massage chambers. Diego's living space in the attic overlooked the river.

"Where is it this time?" Diego demanded.

Jade Lafitte, his bronzed and burly Fit Nest manager from Montreal pointed to the right, her daunting bicep slightly deflating as her tricep bulged on her uncurled arm. "Front window in Mama's living room."

"It's daylight. Did we get it on camera?"

"Haven't checked yet."

"Do it."

Jade kneeled behind the reception desk and scrolled through the security video files on the computer. A five-foot-eleven, body-building instructor with a business brain, she was the first employee Diego had hired. Her hard feminist exterior belied her soft unisex core. When he'd presented Jade with her "Manager" name tag, she snapped it in half with two fingers and replaced it with a new one that said "Womanager." Diego didn't dare complain.

This was the fourth incident in two weeks. Diego had gotten a low-interest loan from the city to "gentrify" the neighborhood, but xenophobes, racists, and homophobes still raged on the fringes. He picked up the rock that had smashed through the window and muttered to anyone listening, "We'll catch this fuck-stick and string him up as a new punching bag."

Only Mama was near enough to hear him. "¡Oye! You're in my house so watch your mouth."

"Sorry, Mama. How about 'We'll have to teach him a lesson?'"

"That's better. You probably used to do the same thing when you were out gallivanting in the hood. What's a fuck-stick?"

"An idiot. A piece of shit."

"Language!"

"Hey, Mama. You just said fuck-stick!"

She rolled her dark brown eyes. "That was an educational question."

"Diego!" Jade yelled. "Check this out!" She'd paused it mid-pitch of the jagged rock that lay on Mama's floor.

He kneeled next to her in front of the screen. "Hmm. A teenage fuckstick. Stupid too. Dressed in bright white, turquoise hoodie, and camo pants. Clear shot of his face. Great. He'll be history soon. How are you doin' with party prep?"

"Should be done by noon," Jade said, muscles rippling as she dead-lifted a 170-pound full keg of beer.

"You want some help with that?"

"Nah, I got it."

"Well, make sure everything's done by noon. Official party time is two p.m. but some members'll come early. Anyone givin' Mama a hand with the food? I'd guess we'll have fifty guests."

"They got the grills ready in the backyard and are slicing and dicing as we speak." Jade still held the keg.

"Okay, sounds good. I'm off for a run."

"A mile for each year again?"

"Gave it up after last year's torture. Too many hours to do it and too many days to recover. Five miles to pick up my new birthday bicycle and five or ten to return. I'll be back in a couple hours. Call if you need me." Diego opened the door to leave, then turned back. "One more thing. I think you should workout less."

"Why?" Jade scrunched her eyebrows together in disbelief.

"Your arms are gettin' bigger than mine."

"Afraid I'll beat you in the arm-wrestling match, eh?"

Diego grinned and headed out. "I'm afraid you'll just beat me."

The Fit Nest sat on a boulevard that curved alongside the Antelope River. The sun had burned off the morning mist to reveal a cloudless sky though the temperature stayed cool, ideal for a blood-pumping, deep-breathing jaunt. Diego ran across the road, down the steep riverbank, and wound around the bends on a bike path Simone had often cruised. She'd tried jogging but didn't care for the pounding or wear-and-tear on her knees and spine. Smooth cycling suited her better.

This is a sweet city tour but I'm going to demand a detour on the way back. And maybe take a peek at the office.

After about a mile, a voice interrupted the reverie of the run. "Diego! Hey, Diego Fierra!"

Diego scanned side to side, then stopped and spotted the source above him on the grass by the road. "Benji! 'S'up, man."

Benji Dorfman was a lending officer who'd helped him with the bank loan to fix up The Nest and fit the stereotype—average height, mid-thirties, prematurely balding, pasty complexion, a couch-potato paunch, thin arms and long fingers. Instead of his standard blue tie and pin-striped suit, today he wore a yellow sweat suit that didn't quite match his cubicle personality. He looked like a banana with a bulge in the middle. Benji struggled down the slope to the path. "Mind if I join you?"

"Sure, if you can keep up. Not slaving over facts and figures today?"

"Nope. Day off. I'm a runner now."

In the periphery of Diego's vision, Simone noticed a black disk hovering in the air about thirty yards above and to the rear of Benji. She slipped up Diego's sunglasses to the top of his head and squinted as the disk veered behind trees. *No strings on that disk, and a kite doesn't do that. A tiny UFO? Kids playing with some high-tech flying toy?*

Diego set his sunglasses back over his eyes, turned, and continued down the path. "I didn't know you were an exercise guy. How long you been runnin'?"

"This is my second day," he said proudly.

"Cool." Diego nodded to the beat of his feet. "Two in a row. Good luck. You mind if we don't talk? I run for the silence as much as the workout."

"Sure. I can't talk and pant anyway." After a half-mile, Benji benched himself on a log.

Diego kept the pace and shouted over his shoulder. "Grand opening at The Fit Nest at two! Stop by if you're able!"

"Okay!" Benji called a taxi to take his spent body home.

A few months earlier, Diego had phoned Dr. Simone Wellstone to schedule an appointment because he wanted "to explore my sexuality." When Ming opened the office door to announce the new patient's arrival, she seemed unnaturally giddy. "He look like Robocop. On the cover of GQ magazine. Nice on the eyes."

Simone stood up from the couch while raising one eyebrow and tilting her head to the side to raise it further. "You're wearing a sly smile today. What do you mean?"

"You will see."

Diego stepped into the room cautiously. Black leather boots below faded blue jeans. Thin hips and waist leading up to a widening physique accentuated by a leather motorcycle jacket—not the classic black jacket with zippers—a sleek spacesuit-style, padded on the shoulders, chest, and elbows. He cradled a skull helmet in one arm like a decapitated head. A rugged face with thick black eyebrows, matching stache, and a soul patch on his chin that couldn't disguise the angelic countenance glowing from his eyes— one dark brown and one dark green. Contrary to his commanding presence, he looked nervous. "Hello, ma'am, I mean Dr. Wellstone. My name's Diego Fierra. We talked on the phone."

"I remember. It's great to meet you in person." She extended her hand as Ming's words echoed in her mind. *Nice on the eyes.* "How about calling me Dr. Simone. Personal yet professional." Simone gestured to the couch. "Have a seat or lie down. Your choice."

He set down his helmet, sat, and surveyed the room. "Nice space, ma'am, I mean Dr. Simone. Peaceful."

"Thanks, I call it my Sensory Sanctuary."

"Nice name too." He sat on the couch and assumed The Thinker statue pose. "I've never been to a shrink before. Sorry, maybe that's a bad word. A psychiatrist."

He doesn't speak like I'd imagined. Softer. More vulnerable. Notebook in hand, Simone perched on the bamboo stool next to the couch. "I don't mind shrink. It's a fun word. My website says empathiatrist."

"Right, I read that. I didn't know what it meant."

"Most people don't. Or really understand empathy. I simply feel more than other folks. Hyper-sensitive, some call it. Intuition on steroids. Sometimes I can actually feel other people's emotions or pain in my body. For instance, if your shoulder hurt, so would mine."

"Huh. That'd come in handy in a martial arts match. If I knew where they hurt, I'd hit 'em there again."

Simone laughed harder than she wanted to. "Now there's a use I hadn't considered! I try to add a little compassion to the mix. Now if I recall correctly, you said you wanted to explore your sexuality."

"Yeah, I guess, but I'm not exactly sure what that means either. Overall, life seems A-OK. I'll be forty in a few months, opening a new business with some buds, money's not a problem, but… I've been straight and I've been gay and I'm not sure which I am anymore… and I got a hole in my heart."

"That doesn't sound good. Considering surgery?"

"Not that kind of hole."

"I didn't think so." Simone nodded with a warm smile. "Tell me more. Just talk. I like listening."

"Maybe I'll lie down like they do in the movies."

"Relax in any position you choose."

Diego tried, but his boots were on the couch and his head hanging off the other end, so he scooted back and forth on his back like a confused caterpillar until his ends justified the means. "Okay, where do I start?"

"Your call."

"At the beginning?"

"I like beginnings but start wherever you want." *He's trying to get comfortable but he's not. More like a stiff soldier on a break, still poised to leap into action.*

"Well… the beginning, eh?" Diego took a moment to rewind his mind. "My father and Mama immigrated from Mexico, met in America, and pumped out my sister, two brothers, and me in four years. Our happy-go-lucky life was dandy till luck took a dive along with the neighborhood in the 1980s. Crack cocaine invaded big-time, and our block went from old-fashioned to new-fucked." Diego bowed his head a bit, raised his eyebrows, and glanced over at Simone. "Pardon my French."

"My mom used to say that every time she swore, which never got any raunchier than 'Damn, pardon my French.' For years, I assumed damn was a French word, and thought they must be cool people."

"So you don't mind if I say fuck during our talk?"

"Of course not!" Simone scoffed. "It's a great word—an interjection, noun, verb, adverb, or adjective that can mean a million things. Fuck was totally out of bounds with my mom. She didn't like me using any words that even started with the letter F."

"That's funny," he chuckled. "Okay then. Fuckin' drug lords ruled. Gangs roamed the streets. No one was safe. My father was a solid, strict Catholic who didn't take any shit unless it was scripture from the Good Book. He worked two jobs to buy our house and keep it goin'. Mama had a little restaurant that served bangin' Tex-Mex fare. She and I were always tight, but I don't remember ever being close to my father. He was the 'almighty father' in his own private heaven, and I was one of his minions below... or heathens below. I used to leave the house for Sunday School and then hide in the garage. I just didn't buy all the tall tales. If someone really believed God created the earth in seven days, made Eve out of Adam's rib, and a snake convinced Eve to eat an apple, I didn't trust anything else they said."

"So you didn't trust your father, either," Dr. Simone probed.

"I trusted him to get biblical when he learned I'd skipped out on the words of the Lord. He wouldn't say, 'Spare the rod, and spoil the child.' He'd shout, 'He that spareth his rod hateth his son! But he who loveth him chasteneth him betimes!'" Diego relaxed and clasped his hands behind his head as his story flowed out. "The worst part was when he'd make me deliver a new switch. If I brought back some wimpy stick, he'd double the punishment and send me to find a stiff one. I'd be cryin' before the whippin' even started."

"Did you ever resolve any of these conflicts with him later on in life?" Simone could feel the tension building in his body as Diego took a deep breath and let it out slowly.

"Fate resolved 'em. When I was fourteen, I came home from school to find his and my older brother's bodies in a bloody heap on the porch. Snuffed out by the local lords. For what reason? My family was Mexican and in their way. That was a brutal fuckin' day."

"Whew. It's brutal to even hear about it."

"We couldn't afford to keep the house, and shit, didn't even want to live there anymore, so we moved into an apartment a few blocks away. Us kids found odd jobs to help out

Mama with expenses, but soon I joined one of the neighborhood gangs and found lots of wicked odd jobs that paid better and quicker. We were 'The Lats' for Latinos. The main gang of monsters called themselves 'The Coup'—short for Ku Klux Klan. We called them the 'Cuckoo Crackheads,' red necks from the top of their skinheads to the bottom of their rotten souls. I don't even want to remember all the shit we did back then. I'm surprised I'm alive to not remember." Diego jerked up and sat on the edge of the couch. "But I do remember our gang cheer. Wha'd'ya think it was?"

Simone pumped her hand two inches into the air and chanted, "You, rah, rah, rah. Go Lats."

"Cute. You looked like a two-foot-tall cheerleader."

"I missed the tryouts in school. I was probably locked in the science lab."

"One of my gang brothers would yell, "What's evil spelled backwards? The rest of us would shout, "Live! Live! Live!"

"That's grim."

"Yeah, well, the old neighborhood became a grim slum known as Darwin's Kitchen, where only the fittest survive. After my father was murdered, I got my own religion. Wild Diego, they called me. One word. Wildiego. The Able Cain-raiser. I let my hair grow into a righteous Afro, wore any leather duds I could get my mitts on, and commissioned this cobra tattoo windin' up my arm grabbin' the apple of my eye." Diego took off his jacket to reveal the black cobra with its fangs buried in a red apple on his shoulder with "Mama" inscribed in the middle.

"Sweet," Simone said, examining it closely. "A hell-raiser with a heart. Seems like you've changed a bit. And you haven't mentioned the word sexuality yet."

"Oh, back then there was some sex, but no sexuality. Boys had to be rough and tough. The girls were even rougher and tougher. Rough guys treated their tough girls like things, playthings, nasty things. You don't loveth your squeezes, you scorneth or berateth them. That didn't turn my crank." Diego slumped back down on the couch. "The heat started to descend on the Kitchen. Cops breathin' hard down everyone's necks. Gang members behind bars. When I graduated from high school, I got out o' the grind and enlisted in the army. I wanted to be proud to hand Mama some legal tender instead of illegal dinero I'd stolen, scammed, or snaffled in the hood. The army scrubbed me up and beat some common sense back into me. I was born more physical than mental, so I fit in like a cog and greased their wheel. They could see the rage in my eyes and soon learned that my weapon of choice was whatever they put in my hands. They weaseled me into the Army Rangers, and I rose up the ranks. Sergeant Wildiego was shipped off to raise hell in the desert for three tours in four years until they let me go."

Simone had been scribbling as he spoke but needed a break. "Why am I working so hard here? You should be the one writing a novel. You write it, and we'll trade for treatments."

"Nah, this is just more shit I don't want to remember."

"You must've been in your mid-twenties by then. Bushy Afro to buzzcut. Crook to commando. What next?"

"I came home. Twenty-six years old. I felt good but the hood still sucked. I'd disappeared off the face of earth, and no one knew me anymore. I worked as an undercover pseudo-cop for two years and helped the force pick up the trash. I knew who killed my father and brother... they're not around anymore. More shit I don't want to remember."

"Huh. Normally I try to help people remember. You want me to help you forget? Have you tried drinking yourself into oblivion?"

"Nah. Gave it up."

"How about Drugs?"

"Gone."

"Now what?"

"Lemme tell you about the part I want to remember. The part I can't forget no matter how hard I try."

"I'm all ears and notepad."

"I gotta stand up. Can't lie around too long. Is that okay?"

"Of course. You're paying, sir. I'm just the hired help."

"How much time left?"

Simone thought *all the time in the world*, but said, "Almost half-time."

"This next chapter is seven years long." Diego strolled over to the picture window.

The doctor followed him, soaking in his athletic frame. "Go for it. If you don't finish, you can come back anytime."

"Your backyard looks like a temple of God in Japan."

"You're close. Gotta switch two letters. It's my temple of Dog."

Simone's entire rectangular yard was fenced in behind the house and office to the four-room bungalow where Ming stayed. The circular deck around the sanctuary kissed a larger yin-yang circle—one green teardrop colored by fine fescue grass, the other brown from smooth river stones. A round teak gazebo sat in the wide section of the stones; a small, round, polished-concrete pool sunken in the grass section. The circle of the sanctuary and the yin-yang design formed a figure eight, the symbol for infinity. Blooming flowers, bushes, and fir trees flowed beyond to the fence to create a secluded hideaway.

"How about a quick half-time show?" Simone asked, "You can meet my whole family. No parents, no kids, just two of woman's best friends."

"Sure. I like dogs. Never had one, but met a bunch along

the way."

Simone pressed the intercom button to ring Ming.

"Yes, Dr. Wellstone?"

"Send in the clowns, please."

"Okay, I do." A minute later, the door cracked open, and two noses flung it aside. Ming watched the introduction through the doorway, her gaze intently focused on Diego.

"Meet Brandy and Dammit," Simone said, as they zeroed in on the new human. Lady Brandy sniffed Diego suspiciously. Dammit wagged himself into a frenzy with a tennis ball in his mouth as if greeting a long-lost buddy. "Careful, he's very dangerous. Might lick ya to death."

"Interesting names," Diego said, stroking Dammit's head now jammed into his crotch. "What inspired you?"

"What color is Brandy?"

Diego scanned her as she hovered on the other side of the room. "Brandy?"

"Correct. What color is Dammit?"

"Gold?"

"Think of bees."

"Honey?"

"That's the first name I gave him. And what would you say if your puppy couldn't get the hang of paper training, and you routinely stepped into a pile of poop with your bare feet?"

"Dammit."

"Correct again. Honey became his last name. Had to change my vocabulary cuz whenever I said dammit, he thought I was mad at him, so I switched to fuck it. Put a whole new light on getting angry. Instead of cursing something, now I say, 'Fuck it' as in 'let it go' or 'just do it.'"

"A year ago I took in a scrawny stray cat. It's a fat cat now and keeps to herself. She seems to think if I picked her up, I'd throw her back on the street. I call her Princess Aloofa."

"Fits any feline I've ever met. I'm not a cat girl. They need too much therapy." Simone opened the door and the dogs raced outside. She sat on the steps of the deck and motioned for Diego to join her.

The second he sat, Dammit demanded he play with a tennis ball. Obliging both his canine and human hosts, he threw the ball and started the seven-year chapter of his life story. "I met the love of my life by accident."

"I don't believe in accidents," Simone countered.

"Okay… everything happens for a reason. Is that it?"

"Yeah."

"Then how about…?" Diego smirked. "I met him during a traffic synchronicity."

"Good word. I believe in synchronicity. Another tall tale to you?"

"No, but it is strange how life plays out." Diego again pitched the ball for Dammit. "One day I happen upon a fender bender. Big pickup rear-ends a sporty little MG. A big-dick dude who matches his big-dick truck is shovin' a little guy who matches the MG. I'm the innocent bystander with an attitude and make the dude back off. I call the cops, and my buddies arrive pronto. Tow truck hauls off the MG, and I haul the little guy into a bar. Nathan. Beautiful Nathan Fontaine. One look into his eyes, and I see my soul." Diego sighed, resting his elbows on his knees and chin in his hands. "Cliché maybe, but I swear my heart skipped like a kid with a jump rope. We hit it off right away. Even though I could tell he was gay, it didn't matter. He was just a human. A humane human."

"I'll bet they didn't care for gays back then in the hood."

"That's an understatement. When I was a know-it-all but naive teen, homosexuals were persona non grata. Fuckin' faggots. Backdoor bandits. Daffodils." Diego got to his feet again. He had to walk and talk with his hands and his body, in between routine flings of the tennis ball. "I served with some gay guys in the army. Great guys, devoted, tough as titanium, and had my back, not my backdoor. My prejudice faded away. When the news exposed the networks of pedophiles—the pathetic priests my father had praised—any lingering connection to organized religion I had dove into the deep end and drowned. I'd seen the Catholic casualties in the hood and in the army, scarred by the 'words of the Lord'"—Diego made quote marks in the air as he spoke—"they'd learned from some fork-tongued devil in robes."

"My parents were scientists," Simone mused, "and I only went to church a few times with friends. I took a theology course in college because I thought it'd be prudent to read the Bible to help me understand my future patients. The Good Book took a tumble in Chapter One. A verse on the first page has stuck with me ever since. Genesis 1:27. 'So God made man in his own image.' I think Mr. Genesis mixed up the words. He should've written, 'Man made God in his own image.' Each man shrinks infinity down his own level and goes to war to defend his personal image. Too many of his gods are demons."

"I agree. Despicable demons."

"Let's go back to the beginning for a sec. When you were little Diego, did you feel like you were, or would be, straight, gay, or both?"

Diego pondered the question for a while. "Straight, I guess. I had a couple girlfriends and had my first sex experience at fourteen. Didn't last long, but felt good. Seemed natural, but taboo. No love, just sex."

"Fast forward a few years. It sounds like you evolved into someone else."

"You know... I'd hear the words heterosexual, homosexual, bisexual, and I guess I just thought... 'Fuck the categories. I'm sexual, pure and simple. That didn't change when I met Nathan, but it sure got more focused. I'd never really experienced the combination of sex and love before."

"Thanks for the detour. Tell me more about life with him. I interrupted Diego and Nathan's Big Adventure."

"Well, you and I were talking about religion, and along the way Nathan introduces me to the words of the Dalai Lama. 'My religion is simple. My religion is kindness.' Nathan doesn't just say those words; he lives them. And for seven years, we live them together, all over the world. Besides bein' a down-to-earth, natural guy, he's a computer whiz and investment genius." Diego paced around the circular pool in the grass with Dammit at his heels. "Nathan makes more money in an hour on the beach with his laptop than I make in a month as a grunt. He seems to be able to see into the future. He'll research a company, buy, sell, trade, or whatever he does, and score every time. And then he gives away his profits, helping people in need along the way, and money flows from Wall Street into the streets of the world. As Freddy Mercury says, 'Money cannot buy happiness, but it can damn well give it!' We travel through Europe, across Asia, to Australia and New Zealand, to the pyramids in Egypt and the Sahara in Morocco. I study massage in Thailand, Japan, and Sweden, and then combine the techniques into my own style. I get jobs on cruise ships, and he rides first class in his mobile office. My hands become weapons of healing instead of hell. Traveling with him teaches me more about life than the distorted facts rammed into my brain at school. I learn how to live and truly love another human being." Diego paused by the pool and gazed into the water as he stroked his soul patch and chin between his forefinger and thumb.

Grey rain clouds had slipped in and started to drizzle onto the scene. Simone walked over to Diego and rested her hand on his shoulder. "Let's get under the gazebo."

"Okay." He shuffled behind her, and with a heavy exhale, plopped down onto one of the curved benches surrounding the circular table in the center of the gazebo. Dammit gave up and lay between his new buddy's feet. Brandy waited back on the deck under the eaves. Diego's elbows rested on his knees, his chin almost on the table.

"Your mood seems to be sliding downhill. I have a feeling your relationship came to a rough conclusion."

He sat motionless, searching for the words, his earlier energy draining out of him. Sorrow shaded his voice as he continued his tale. "Another traffic synchronicity. Full circle from the day we met, but this time I can't save him. He wants to tackle 'The Road of Death,' and it lives up to its name. One moment he's next to me, full of life and joy. Fifteen macabre moments later, he's dead and gone. Another bloody heap on the floor, this time on a bus at the bottom of a jungle ravine in Bolivia. Somehow, I survive, but Nathan's crushed by humanity and its baggage. I wish I'd been taken instead. The world needs more like him and less like me."

"I'm so sorry for you. And sorry I never met him."

"Yeah, he was this devil's angel."

"Sounds like you grew some wings along the way."

"Maybe," Diego sighed.

"I don't know if you noticed, but when you tell me about your time with Nathan, you speak in the present tense, but when you talked about the rest of your life, you spoke in the past tense, like your memories of him aren't memories, and Nathan is alive, right now, in your mind and in your heart, even though your heart has a hole in it."

"It's seems like only yesterday that he died, but when I close my eyes, he's here."

"How long have you been without Nathan?"

"Three years…"

"Have you—"

"Eleven months…"

"Have you—"

"Twenty-four days…"

Simone smiled. "Hours?"

"Don't remember. Forgot which time zone."

"Aren't you a veritable rollercoaster of emotions? Happy, sad, happy, sad."

"Mountains, valleys, mountains, valleys."

"Have you been with anyone else since then?"

"A few moments at a time."

"Men or women?"

"Men. I'm terrified of women."

"The Able Cainraiser is terrified?" Simone chuckled. "In case you haven't noticed, I'm a woman. You seem okay with me."

Diego picked at an imaginary pimple on his chin. "Female friends are fine, but when I'm the least bit attracted to one, daring Diego becomes a bumbling idiot."

"Why? What do you feel inside of you when that happens?"

"I dunno." Diego scratched a few non-existent itches on his scalp. "They're like a different species. They're vegetables, and I'm a fruit."

"That's Doctor Vegetable to you," Simone joked. "Why'd you choose to see a female shrink?"

"A friend talked about you. I checked out your website. You seemed… more human than the rest."

"Like Nathan."

"Damn straight. I want him back."

"Sure you do. I'll bet he's the hole in your heart. You may be extraordinary, but you're normal. And even though you probably know somewhere in your brain that he won't be coming back, your heart aches for him. And aches for the special kind of human love you shared with him."

The Diego coaster was about ready to roll into a puddle of tears. "Yeah, I've got a lot of close friends, but it's not the same."

"Have you talked with anyone else about these feelings?"

"Nah," he said to the table. "No one'd understand."

"Loneliness is a formidable foe. Your weapon against it was Nathan. A humane human, as you say. Given seven billion people on this planet, there's gotta be a few humane humans out there somewhere, waiting for you to appear. I doubt if it matters whether they're male or female. I've heard that Thailand and Buddhism in general have historically recognized three or four genders, and that more than two percent of the population are gay. And because of the cultural acceptance, many boys decide they're gay as early as puberty and gravitate to a support group of those who'd already assumed the gender."

Diego's elbows rested on his knees, his chin almost on the table. "Yeah, sounds true," he mumbled. "Nathan and I were at ease and accepted there. The Land of Smiles."

"You've had a lot more experience interacting with men, but hey, both men and women are Homo sapiens, and you loved being with a human. Some folks might say it's in your DNA, and you're born gay. Others believe you're influenced by your environment, and you make a choice to be gay. Medical textbooks might ramble on about dysfunctional family relationships and a disoriented psyche seeking a surrogate father. The Bible preaches that homosexuality is an abomination but says the same thing about eating shellfish. Multiply two negatives to get a positive. Maybe two gay men are good to go if they're having sex while eating shrimp."

"You're starting to sound like a conversation over dinner on *Sex in the City*.

"Sorry. We psycho-docs always feel the need to sum up

stuff and shrink it down."

"No, no." Diego raised both palms like bookends beside his head. "I only said that because you were funny, like the TV show."

"Ah. Never saw it. Well, here's the bottom line from this headshrinker. I'd say you should do what feels right for you. Start with the heart, and your body will follow."

"Good call, but a hard one. How do I find him… or her?"

"Good question, but a hard one. The answer?" Simone shook her head. "I don't know. Ask and ye shall receive? Be open to every possibility? Match.com?"

"How about your receptionist? Is she single?"

"Ming? You're attracted to her?"

"Well, she was nice to me. And she's pretty cute."

"I've never seen her bat an eye at anyone. And I'm not going to tell you what she said about you. It'll go to your head. Professional confidentiality, you know. I'm not in the match-making biz. You'll figure it out. You've already conquered a fistful of foes. Give synchronicity some time. And unfortunately, our time has run out today. It's been a pleasure to meet you and hear the saga of Diego Fierra. Keep in touch. You're always welcome here."

As Simone, Brandy, and Dammit walked him across the yard and through the sanctuary, Diego said, "By the way, I bought back the old family house and the house next door. I'm renovating them into a martial arts and workout studio called The Fit Nest. The grand opening won't be for a few months, but we're up and running in place. Drop by sometime."

"How fit do I have to be? What are the requirements?"

He stopped, put two fingers on each side of his chin, and looked her up and down. "Well, let's see. You have a mind… and a body. You qualify. I'll be your personal trainer, and you can help me write the novel."

"Thanks for the offer. We'll see." Simone herded the dogs into the reception area with Ming, who she saw wink at Diego, and walked him down the sidewalk.

"You know, I have a temple too. The Fit Nest. TFN. Temple for Nathan. I couldn't have created it without him, the funds he left behind, and the new life he awakened in me."

"Then I'll definitely drop by."

He donned his helmet and mounted his Ducati Monster bike. "Thanks for listening, Dr. Simone. And talking. I'm still sad, but happier."

"Mountains and valleys."

"Yin and yang." Diego turned the key, revved the engine, and screeched away from the curb. He never came back.

Diego's running route to the bike shop diverged from the river path, behind Copper Butte into historic Halliday Park past rusty iron statues of local heroes during the days of the old wild west and replicas of covered wagons, then zigzagged through tidy neighborhoods creeping up the piedmont to the outskirts of the city and the mountains on the horizon. Simone guessed he was heading to her bicycle shop of choice, the Cycle of Life, managed by cycle-maniacs who lived to ride and repair. They offered a wide variety of styles or built customized bikes from the exact components requested by their clients. Diego sprinted the final 100-yards into their parking lot, reining in his legs right before opening the door. He greeted counter help with outstretched arms and a booming "Where's mah baby?"

"Hey, dude. I'm pretty sure she's out of the delivery room and in the nursery. Lemme summon the doctor."

"He'd better spank her to life cuz today's my birthday, and she's my present to me."

The owner of the shop, Augustine "Gus" Blaszkiewicz—a long-haired, long-bearded leftover from the sixties who'd never owned a vehicle with more than two wheels—rolled in the newborn princess. "Miss Santa Cruz Stigmata Cyclocross with Feather-light Titanium Frame, Shimano Hydraulic Disc Brakes, and Hutchinson Bulldog Tires, meet your father."

"Oh, baby," Diego purred, "come to Papa." He stroked her as if she were the love of his life. Her red frame, silver components, and black wheels perfectly matched his running outfit and the thin streak of gray in his hair.

"Diego buddy, are you rollin' in dough these days? The frame alone on this cost almost three grand."

"Some greenbacks came my way, and I didn't want 'em to get moldy. Would you prefer I'd put it in an IRA for the future?"

"Oh, no! The future is now or never. I gave her a test-ride, and she is beyond words. You will 'be here now' forever on this beauty." From behind his back, he handed Diego a black Bell bike helmet with an adjustable rearview mirror already installed. "Helmet's on the house. Happy birthday, buddy."

"Gus, you are the official hero of my day." Diego engulfed the little guy in a big hug. "Thanks, man."

"On the road or off, you're good to go."

"Time to ride." Diego donned the helmet, hopped on, counter help opened the door, and he rode out of the shop.

This mama is going to ride this baby too. Tandem in the back for now but handling the bars soon. Whichever route Diego picks, my office will be a stop along the way.

He followed the road up the incline of the piedmont until the city limit sign and, obeying his treatment rules for the day to stay within the city, made a quick U-turn.

Once again, Simone saw the black disc in the sky, further away, but clearly the same shape.

I'll bet it's a fucking drone. They hear and track us with the wrist watch and see us with a camera in the drone. And I'll bet the cash that "came Diego's way" was the down payment he got for the treatment. The mastermind behind this scheme must have money to burn. Why? What's the big picture? Why me?

Diego cruised along the streets, sidewalks, paths, and gravel upgrades testing the all-terrain capabilities of his new baby. Simone let him ride with his eyes on the road ahead, while she followed the drone behind when he glanced into the rearview mirror on his helmet.

When the bike approached her neighborhood, Simone commandeered the handle bars and wove through back streets to approach the office from the rear. *Mmm, this baby is responsive, geared by the gods, and tight yet smooooooth. Wish I had his calves and thighs for an engine every day.* One block from the office, she slowed to a crawl, peering through the foliage to see if the dogs were in the backyard. *No sign of any activity, canine or human. So why am I here besides to hug my babies?* She dismounted and walked the bike around to the front walkway. *I want information, but how will I get it from Ming? I'm in Diego. Will she even let me into the office? She was around when I installed the deadlocks, alarms, and cameras, and knows how important security is to me. Do I dare tell her the truth about being trapped inside another body? Get real, girl. She'd never believe it and might call the police to report a crazed patient.* Simone leaned the bike against the railing, put a foot on the step, and pressed the red intercom button. *What should I say as Diego? He hasn't been here in months. He doesn't have an appointment to reschedule. So why is he here today? "Dr. Simone asked me to come over and play with Brandy and Dammit?" Pfff. Ming wouldn't buy it.*

With these questions and options preoccupying in her mind, Simone had let her control of Diego slip away after she'd pressed the button. Suddenly the door flew open.

"Mr. Diego Fierra! What a surprise?" Ming wrapped her fingers around his arm and tried to lead him through the doorway. At five-foot-four, she was nearly a foot shorter than Diego. "Come in, come in!"

Reacting as he'd done earlier when Simone had released Diego, he seemed to be drifting out of a dream. He glanced from side to side to get his bearings. "Um… sure… but I can't leave my bike outside."

"Bring it in! Plenty of room. I can help you carry it."

"No, no… that's okay. I got it."

I'm in! Shit. He's in, not me. Now what?

"Here. Sit!" Ming gestured to the sectional sofa spanning one wall and wrapping around a corner of the reception area. She plopped down first and patted the cushion next to her.

Simone's dogs started to whine behind the door into the living area as Diego propped up his bike next to the desk and sat on the sofa slowly, still in a daze. "Your name is Miss Ming, right?"

She rested her hand on his knee. "Just Ming for you. Why did you come here today?"

"I'm not sure." Diego's words trudged off his tongue. "I started taking new medicine today… and sometimes I zone in and out of La La Land."

"Sounds like fun."

"No, not fun. Strange. I came because… I think I was daydreaming about Dr. Simone's dogs. Dammit and…"

"Brandy."

"Right. Brandy. Can't forget a name like Dammit. Is Dr. Simone in?"

"She won't be in the office until next Monday. Maybe

she'll come back Sunday."

"Oh, yeah, I got an email. I dreamed she wanted me to hug the dogs. Weird, uh?"

"I remember Dammit liked you a lot. I'll get them."

"Okay, if it's not too much of a bother. I can't stay very long."

This is not the Ming that I know. The emotional stone. She seems playful, even frisky. Odd. Her English has improved. In two days? Past tense, articles, contractions. Very odd.

When Ming opened the living room door, Dammit and Brandy raced across the room, leaped onto the sofa, and smothered Diego with affection—licking, wagging, barking, spinning in circles—not only everybody's-my-best-friend Dammit. Thick-skinned Brandy frolicked as well. They weren't reacting to Diego; they were responding to Simone.

Oh, my babies! I missed you so much! Her separation with Diego melded into an uncontrollable love festival of hugging, kissing, and petting.

Wearing a scarlet-trimmed, black-silk Cheongsam dress that caressed her curves, Ming stood and watched with a half-hearted, half-smile that suggested she wasn't really watching—she was planning her next move. "We can take them outside. Dammit, Brandy. Let's go!"

They followed the happy dogs through the Sensory Sanctuary and into the backyard. Dammit brought his tennis ball, and Brandy carried a squeaking plastic chicken. All four of them leaped around the backyard like little kids who'd eaten too much sugar for breakfast. Ten minutes later, Diego and Ming paused to rest under the gazebo. Not for long.

"You didn't see where I live when you came before. Come with me now." She took his hand and led him into her bungalow just beyond the gazebo.

The bliss Simone had felt during the romp with the dogs sunk into suspicion. *What's she up to? Has she done this with other patients?*

Ming gestured around her abode proudly with a shade of seduction in her tone. "I have a living room, little kitchen, toilet, and back there, a cozy bedroom."

"It's charming," Diego said. "How long have you lived here?"

"I come from China six months ago and start to work for Dr. Simone soon." Still holding his hand, she escorted him to the burnt-orange futon sofa. "Over here, you sit. It's very comfy and can make into a bed." She sat next to him, thigh to thigh, and put her arm over his shoulder.

Comfy? Cozy? Make into a bed? When the cat's away, the mice will play? This mini-mouse has morphed into a vixen pussy high on catnip and toying with her mark. Simone could feel Diego was wide awake and alert—all ears, eyes, nose, and skin.

Ming's wet lips slipped into a calculated meek smile. "You know what I said to Dr. Simone when I saw you first?"

"No, what? She wouldn't tell me. Professional confidentiality or something."

"I can tell you." Ming's smile turned angelic. "He looks like Robocop. Nice on the eyes."

"Well, thanks. I felt the same way about you. Not the Robocop part. Nice on the eyes."

Ming kissed him on the cheek. "Mmm, that is so sweet for you to say."

Professional confidentiality? This is stretching professional ethical behavior beyond its borders! Diego seems so relaxed and confident. What happened to the "bumbling idiot" when he's with a woman? Maybe our one-and-only session inspired him, and he's been practicing.

"We're both wearing the same colors," Diego said, stroking the sleeve covering her arm.

"You noticed! In China, black is the color of heaven, and red means good luck. Black and red like my dress, black like my hair and red like my lips." Ming puckered her lips into an irresistible invitation as a Queen tune rang in his back pocket.

Diego kissed them, quickly, checked the number on his cell phone, and silenced it. "You are truly enchanting today, and I'm sorry, but I can't stay very long. It's my birthday, and we're gettin' ready for a grand opening in the studio at two p.m."

"Oh, good luck! Happy birthday!" Her face seemed to glow from within. "Maybe I have a present for you."

"A present?"

"Yes! How do you say in English?" She paused with one finger on her lips. "A quickie! How about a quickie?" She didn't let him answer. "You wait here, and I slip into something more comfortable." She flashed him a fetching grin and scampered into the bedroom.

OMG! I didn't think anyone actually said that! I should stop this fiasco now. The American Psychological Association would bar me in a nanosecond and then crucify me on their code-of-conduct cross. This is not merely an example of a "slippery slope" leading to doctor-patient boundary violations. This is a greased playground slide straight to hell. But wait a minute. I'm not doing. I'm only watching, like examining patients in a room behind a two-way mirror, or observing their interaction at a family wedding, or joining a patient at a twelve-step meeting. I'm in the holistic, humanistic, living world, not locked in the anal, analytical prison camp that demands sterile client communication, no touching, no outside-the-office contact, no dual relationships whatsoever, cross your heart and hope to die, just remain elevated in your illustrious ivory tower while dispensing omniscient wisdom, prescribing exorbitantly expensive drugs, and addicting innocent bystanders to your weekly monologues. Then again, Ming is my assistant. How does that spice this pickle? Who would ever find out? If the APA did, they wouldn't believe it, shit, I can hardly believe it. I'd have to plead permanent insanity, foam at the mouth, and maybe lunge over the table at the president during the disciplinary hearing. Okay, get a grip. My bottom line is the welfare of my patients. Hovering right above that line is the concept of using sound clinical judgement—flexible and tailored to each of their needs—to provide them with successful healing and therapy instead of pandering to impersonal, authoritative dogmas and despair. APA? For today… go fuck yourself and the rules you rode in on. I'm gonna sit back and try my hardest to enjoy the show. God help me!

If the whole truth and nothing but the truth were to be told by Simone, she'd have to admit to having a bit of confusion over her own sexuality. She'd never married, yet counseled heterosexual and gay couples. She wasn't a lesbian, nor been intimate with a woman, yet counseled LGBT patients. She'd had few relationships with men and limited sexual experience. She was attracted to Ming, and to Diego, as a woman and a man, and as human beings. And she was curious, personally and professionally. What's it like to make love to a woman? What's it like when two men have sex? What does a man feel during intercourse with a hard phallus on the outside of his body with the proverbial mind of its own while engulfed by a woman's soft vagina which often seems attached directly to her heart? She'd remained single and somewhat distant to both sexes because "I'm married to my work." But on late lonely nights, she wondered exactly where she fit in the multifarious mix of options and when she might find out.

Ming emerged from the bedroom dressed in a see-through, scarlet camisole that revealed her lithe frame and hung down to the bottom the V of her ebony pubic hair. She slunk up to Diego and purred, "You like my lucky red nightie?"

"You are definitely tempting now. But I'm kinda sweaty."

"I like it. You smell like a strong man who works hard. And maybe plays hard too?" She sat beside him and brushed her fingers across his ripped triceps and biceps. "Mmm, hard muscles. But not as hard as this muscle standing under your lucky red shorts." She bent over, pulled down the elastic band, and licked it once.

Diego stretched his right arm around her back and found her firm breast with his hand. As he stood, his left arm slipped under her legs, lifted Ming off the sofa as if she were light as a pleasant thought, and carried her toward the back. "You haven't shown me the bedroom yet."

"You show me the bedroom," Ming whispered, "and I'll show you what happens in the bedroom."

With time flying past noon, Diego pumped the pedals faster than Simone thought possible. She wanted to be still in her own space, invisible, neither controlling, nor considering controlling anything or anyone. The last scene at the bungalow had been intense beyond her expectations, a short course in sexuality never offered at any medical school, nor had she ever experienced such unbridled passion. During Simone's mental soliloquy about ethics, she'd neglected to factor in her empathic powers. Whatever Simone had imagined in the living room became a completely new balling game in the bedroom. Her original image of "watching" was less like observing patients through a window than viewing a wrestling match from inside the ring with the sweat of the athletes soaking her body. The encounter became a ménage à trois with no avenue for escape. Without controlling one cell in Diego, she'd merged with him into a single being, and the emotions of the threesome had commingled into one orgasmic ecstasy. As the bike leaned into tight curves and swerved around potholes, Simone swung between guilt and awe, then between guilt and dismay, then between guilt and satisfaction, and finally settled solely on guilt.

Diego pulled onto the front sidewalk at The Fit Nest by half-past twelve. In one fluid motion, he jumped off his bike and rolled it through the open double doors. As he'd predicted, members had come early to hit the machines and mats. A chorus of happy birthdays drowned out the music booming from the speakers.

Jade was on him first. "Where you been, boss? Thought you'd be back by eleven."

"Ran into an old friend by accident. Couldn't get away."

"How old was she? You stink like sweat and perfume."

"Just take my bike, please, and put it in the back."

"Oo-ee! This baby's rad. Maybe I'll store it in my room."

"How's Mama doin'?"

"She's got the cookin' thing down, man. That one little lady's way ahead of all of us."

"Sixty-five years of practice makes perfect. Just check in on her, will ya? I gotta take a shower and get some shit ready upstairs." Diego tore up two stairways, two steps at a time. He showered, shaved, trimmed his stache, and gelled his black hair to resemble an incarnation of Freddy Mercury. He'd grown up getting down with the multifaceted rock group Queen, four misfits playing for other misfits, and that resonated with Diego. Their lyrics and music had inspired him for decades. He selected the appropriate athletic attire—black nylon Nike sweat pants and t-shirt with their original slogan in white. "Just do it." Sitting at his desk, he laid out a clean sheet of paper, and scribbled ideas about what he might say as an official welcome for his guests.

After three raps on Diego's closed door, Snake delivered a warning through the crack. "Hey, boss. We got a storm on the horizon. Hostiles approaching."

Diego jumped up from his chair, unlocked the door, and motioned Snake in. "Wha'd'ya mean? Who? Where?"

"Check it out from your porch. Joey from down the block called to warn us. Here's a pair o' binocs."

A hundred yards down the street a crowd of twenty or thirty guys straggled around an older man carrying a hand-lettered placard that read, "NO FAGS!" Peering through the high-powered binoculars, Diego could see they carried a baseball bat, hockey stick, golf club, a garden hoe, one tire iron, and several open beer bottles. "Most of 'em look smashed and staggering in their slaughterhouse uniforms."

"It's the nightshift zombies from Wild Bill's Bar and Grill who crack eggs in their beer for breakfast," Snake said. "I made the mistake of goin' in there one morning. They get off work at the packing plant at eight a.m., and noon's the midnight prowling hour for the half-dead."

"Hmm. This could be a riot, as in fun, as in a battle with a barrel of drunken monkeys. And guess who's helpin' roll out the barrel?"

"A messenger from God himself?"

"They probably all think they are. That young rock heaver we ID'ed on camera is front-row center." Diego flipped the binocs to Snake as they headed into his bedroom. "Keep an eagle-eye on the silent ones in the back. A few are packin' something in their pants, but I can't tell if it's their gut, hardware, or a hard-on. You lock 'n' load 'n' lie on the porch. I'll summon the troops." He snatched his black duster and Jason hockey mask from hat rack, and strapped his samurai sword over his back.

Synchronicity kicked in as Diego descended the stairs to the main room of The Nest, and he shouted along with Queen singing through the speakers. "The Show Must Go On!" When he reached the reception desk, he turned down the music and yelled, "All you Fit Nest misfits, report for duty now! Get your butts in gear! Time for a huddle!" When the staff had assembled, Diego laid out the plans. "We got a barrel of drunken monkeys rolling down the street lookin' for trouble. Jimmy, get out the Bluetooth earbugs and mics so we can all talk to each other. Now."

"I'm on it," Jimmy said.

"Who's on DJ duty today?"

"Me. Disc Jade."

"Good. Open the front windows, turn the speakers to the outside, and set up the mic and stand on the sidewalk, halfway to the street, right in line with those huge elm trees on both sides. Test the mic and make sure it's live. Then crank up 'Another One Bites the Dust' and come back to the huddle. Do it now."

"Will do."

"Snake's on sniper duty up on the porch in case any are packin' heat. Watch the quiet dudes in the back of the pack real close and keep on your tippy-toes. This is the fuckin' US of Angst, and who knows what could happen. Conan, Masaru, Chick, Norman, and I will position ourselves in two rows behind the mic stand. I'll be up front with Conan on my right and Masaru on my left, both one step behind me. Jimmy, link up all six of us via Bluetooth. Hurry!"

Jimmy handed out the earbugs and looped the microphones around their necks, then raced up to the porch to outfit Snake.

"Norman and Chick, you stand behind us. Figure out a quick demonstration of your skills for the monkeys." Diego grinned at Conan. "'This guy's a demonstration when you just look at him."

Freddy Mercury sailed through the neighborhood as Jade returned to the huddle for her next command. "Okay. Five of us are gonna walk out and meet the monkeys. Jade, get 'We Are the Champions' on deck for our grand entrance. I'll signal you to start it from in here. Cut it when I slice my finger across my throat outside."

"Got it."

"Then cue up 'We Will Rock You.' Your signal will be 'Music please, Maestro.' Fade it in slowly through the intro beat and Freddy's first verse till I yell 'Crank it up!' when the chorus starts."

"Can't wait."

"The rest of you, keep calm and do your thing. It's gonna get theatrical so these members'll wanna watch. Keep 'em inside. I want to stop this fiasco before it starts."

The staff dispersed and went about their duties. Diego tested the Bluetooth microphone and heard seven 10-4s in his earpiece. His brain kept churning as he peered out the door and watched the monkeys advance from the right on the grass across the boulevard.

Pleased to be in the background as the spectacle unfolded, Simone watched as well. When Diego looked to the left, she had a déjà vu from two nights earlier. A large truck parked down the street reminded her of the delivery from Damian's Deli. *That's like the vehicle the guy came in except this one's a yellow EDNA truck. And come to think of it, an EDNA truck was parked at Valleyview Middle School the next day.* She scanned as Diego continued to scan the area. *No drone in sight. Is this truck on a tag team with the drone? EDNA's a player in this scheme?*

When the monkeys paused across the street, Diego shouted to Jade, "Get ready to cut the music for a few seconds. The monkeys meandered over to The Fit Nest and bunched together in a clumsy pack. Diego yelled, "Cut it." He counted down five seconds while waving his four-member troop toward the door. "Hit it!" In five more seconds, Diego donned his Jason mask and strutted through the doors with his warriors. "We Are the Champions!"

The monkeys had settled into a single chant—"No fags in the neighborhood! No fags in the neighborhood!"—but it could barely be heard above the music. Folks living on both sides of The Fit Nest had already gathered on their porches and lawns.

When Diego reached the mic stand, he threw his right hand above his head with a flourish and then slashed his finger across this neck. The pack went silent. For a few mesmerizing seconds, the chirping of birds was the only sound. He stood motionless to let his visage sink in—Halloween mask of horror above a black leather, full-length duster flared at the bottom and an engraved ivory sword handle looming above his shoulder—the Dark Vader of the Neighborhood.

He flipped off his mask and hung it on the mic stand. "Good day, gentlemen! I'm Diego Fierra, owner of The Fit Nest." His amplified voice attacked the pack from the speakers and their soused heads reared back. "How can I help you today?"

A volley of "No fags! Yeah, no fags!" rose from the middle of the pack.

Diego switched tone from commanding to casual. "Sorry, but we don't sell fags here. You'll have to get your cigs somewhere else. I see you boys got a baseball bat, a golf club, a hockey stick, a garden hoe, and a tire iron. Didja get a flat tire on the way to some multi-sports event?"

The older man in front holding the sign frowned. "Don't get smart with us, boy."

Diego took the wireless mic out of its clip and walked

up to him. "Ah… right. Don't get smart. Good advice. So what's your mission here today, Mister… Sorry, but I didn't catch your name." He held the mic up to the man.

"Didn't give it."

"Right again." Diego nodded with a sigh. "Mission, sir?"

"Simple. We don't want no queers in our neighborhood."

A chorus of angry epithets arose behind the man. "Yeah, no queers here! No fudge packers allowed! Homos are an abomination to the Lord! Go home to Sodom!"

"Okay, thanks. That's pretty clear. Well, we gotta mess o' members and don't care what they do at home, only what they do here." Diego paced in front of the pack as he spoke into the mic. "Let's get a few facts straight before you boys continue with your mission. Number one. Security cameras are recording this little event of yours, sound included, and the police should be able to easily identify everyone here." Diego pointed to the teenage kid next to the older man. "We already know this vandal threw the rock this morning and broke my Mama's front window. Shoulda changed clothes, kid. Wearin' a white hoodie, jeans, and turquoise tennies ain't camo. It's a spotlight."

The kid inched backwards. Most of the pack lowered their heads or pulled down their ball caps except the squinty-eyed, silent statues in the back.

"Number two. Lemme read this sign above our door to you. 'The Fit Nest. Martial Arts Studio. Weight training. Massage. Sauna. Juice Bar.' It doesn't say *Marital Arts.* No counseling for you and your wives. We teach a bunch of techniques from self-defense to how to kick the shit out of people like you, no matter what their race, religion, or sexual orientation. Now if you boys wanna dance today, first let me introduce you to my five partners. You can't see Snake. He's invisible, but you might feel his bite. He earned the name cuz o' the way he'd slithered up a mountain to set up his sniper nest. He's lurking somewhere behind me. "Hey, Snake, how many confirmed kills did you have in Afghanistan?"

A voice came from somewhere above. "77."

"And how many on the next day?" Diego chuckled and turned back to the pack. "That was a little joke, the next day part. Not the 77 kills."

No one laughed as fifty eyes scoured the building for a rifle barrel.

"This mound of muscles on my right is your local, mild-mannered Conan the Barber, our shit-kicking instructor. That's short for Sergeant Conan the Barbarian, the name he earned while training American Marines and leading them into battle in the Middle East."

Silver rings pierced both eyebrows above Conan's handlebar mustache. Two skull earrings hung next to his bald head. He either had no neck, or it was hidden under trapezius muscles bulging above his shoulders to his jawline. Tattoos of tigers rippled down arms the size of the men's thighs in the pack.

"Hey buddy, are you gay?" Diego asked, extending the mic to Conan.

A sinister smirk slipped onto Conan's mug as his gravel voice vibrated through the speakers. "Not gay. Happy. Happy to dance."

"He's workin' as a barber now and gettin' to be an expert with a razor blade. On my left, meet the honorable Masaru, our martial arts instructor. He's got a black belt in black belts—karate, Judo, jujitsu—and his name means 'the law.' Might be gay, might not. I've never asked him."

Elegant in his white canvas *karate gi* robe, belt, and pants, Masaru bowed slightly to the pack.

"He's sportin' his nunchucks and a chain whip today. I've only watched him beat up dummies, but I'll be tickled to see the damage he can do to a few live ones. In the second row we got Chick Filet. She teaches defense against knives and offense with 'em."

Hatched and hardened in Kingston, Jamaica's inner city, Chick was a short, cylindrical, steel girder with Rasta dreads snaking down to her shoulders. Christened sweet Mary Campbell at birth, she'd been forced to evolve quickly into a little hellion. Chick glared at the pack without blinking while rotating both thumbs on her fingers as if winding them up for war. To her right, Smilin' Norman leaned on a black carbon-fiber cane, the image of that nice next-door neighbor who'd secretly buried sixteen bodies in his backyard. Norman tossed an apple to Chick. She snatched a combat knife from its sheath on her belt and slashed twice. Four apple slices hit the ground.

Diego put the mic back on the stand. "I'll let you find out about Smilin' Norman's talents on your own. As for me, I teach tactics I used as an Army Ranger and stuff picked up on the streets that's downright ugly. I don't know karate, but I know crazy, and I'm not afraid to use it. I also do massage therapy, I repeat, *ther–a–py*, not the hand-job you boys might imagine in your dirty little minds." Diego held up both hands beside his head. "These hands can heal, or they can hurt." He yanked the samurai sword from its sheath on his back and stabbed the sky. Diego turned his head and hurled the sword into the elm tree to right. It stuck with a "thunk" that reverberated up the spine of the pack. Two more thunks pierced the silence as Chick nailed the left elm tree with two Cold Steel tactical knives. Diego grinned at her as they retrieved their blades in unison. "Wicked! Stereo mayhem!" In one smooth move, he slipped his sword back into its scabbard and gestured to his left. "Masaru taught me that."

Masaru honored him with another bow.

During Diego's keynote address, most of his audience—who might have previously considered themselves a loose pack of rowdy wolves—had transformed into a tight herd of sheep in search of a barn to hide from the cameras and their personal visions of a shearing by Conan the Barber in their immediate future.

"As you can see, the odds aren't in your favor today. Six professional maniacs on my team and only twenty-some amateurs on yours." Diego grabbed the mic, strolled up to the sign guy, and locked onto his eyes—five inches ahead and five inches down. "There's one more issue I'd like to make clear. You, Mr. Nameless, used the words 'our neighborhood.'" Diego stepped back and stretched one arm toward the pack. "How many of you boys here were born in this city?"

Four hands shot up and waved as the pack looked itself over, plus one stiff middle finger raised from a silent statue in the back.

"Only four." Diego pointed to the ground. "And how many of you were born in this neighborhood, this slum we used to call 'Darwin's Kitchen' where only the fittest survive?"

No hand waving. No sound. One more middle finger.

Diego's voice lowered and his eyes narrowed as he pointed over his shoulder at The Fit Nest. "I was conceived in this house. And forty years ago—today—I was born in the hospital, two blocks away in this neighborhood. My daddy lost the house along the way, but I bought it back, and with the help of this city of ours, I restored it and the house next to it. If you think you can drive me out of my own fuckin' neighborhood, you'd better picture one hell of a battle you will lose."

Snake hissed a warning to the troops. "Three silent statures in the back are definitely packin' and plannin' somethin', mumblin' away and eye-ballin' each other. Middle one's got his hand on a lump under his jacket. I got him in my scope. Deal with the other two."

Diego bowed his head to his chest and barked his orders. "Masaru, take out the one on his left. Norman, the right." He paused as he tore into individual eyes in the pack with his scowl. In his peripheral vision, he caught sight of two police cars converging from both directions and assumed a cheerier tone.

"Music please, maestro!" The pulsating beat of "We Will Rock You" began to build in the air. "Now then... you boys have two options. One, take some lessons here at The Fit Nest to prepare yourselves before we dance. Or two, if you wanna dance now, I guarantee every one of you a ticket to the emergency room that's right around the corner." He waited for three seconds until Freddy finished the first verse. "No answers? Then let's get it over with! Crank it up!"

"We Will, We Will Rock You!" Diego sung along and taunted the pack. Masaru flowed through a sequence of moves into his karate combat stance—both legs bent, one stretched to the rear, left hand on his hip cradling the nun-chucks, his right extended to the front with fingers wrapped around the metal chain whip. Chick brought her left fist up to her chin, a tactical knife chest-level with her right, and cocked her knees. Conan remained stern-faced, standing at attention. Smilin' Norman stopped smiling.

The pack had been transported into another reality, but the flashing red lights and squeal of the sirens brought them back to earth. Monkeys on the sides panicked and bolted toward the river. Suddenly the hockey player had a safer game to attend, and the farmer choose an easier garden to hoe. The baseball player threw down his bat and ran home. As rocks pelted The Fit Nest, the auto mechanic lunged at Conan and swung his tire iron. Conan ducked, grabbed the man's ankles, wheeled him around through the air, and flattened him on the tree trunk. No one dared tango with Chick, Diego, and their blades.

The three silent statues in back had come alive. The tall man in the middle yanked a Servu Super Shorty shotgun from under his jacket and lifted it over the crowd to fire. The loud "crack" between the beats of the song came from Snake's rifle, a nanosecond before the resounding "tzing" when his bullet hit the gun barrel and blew it from the man's hands. Most of the monkeys cowered or fell to the ground.

Masaru and Norman were already in motion. Norman sprinted around the right side of the pack, Taser cane raised in front of him, and delivered a million volts into the right statue's stomach before he could remove the pistol tucked in his waistband. Masaru's right arm swept up and his left swept down as he darted ahead two steps, summersaulted sideways, whirled around on his feet and unleashed the chain whip from his hand, swinging it over his head and around the wrist of the left statue brandishing a revolver. With the hook of his cane, Norman caught the first man-sans-shotgun by the neck and hurled him onto the ground next to the twitching man stunned by the Taser. Norman smiled again, standing over his first victim with the tip of his cane buried into his windpipe. "If you ever want to speak again, don't move a muscle now."

Jade turned Queen down a notch as two squad cars vaulted over the curb and screeched to a halt on both sides of the pack. Seven policemen leaped out with guns drawn. With Masaru and Norman's assistance, two cops cuffed the grounded men by the street while the other four took their positions at the front and rear bumper of each squad car. Chick, Conan, and Diego tightened the human noose around the pack on the sidewalk between the elm trees. The officer in charge stalked around the chaos toward Diego.

Police Captain Eddie Bardow had worked with Diego and Conan cleaning up the neighborhood a few years earlier—Eddie leading the force, Citizen Diego and Conan the Barber behind the scenes. Uncommonly broad-minded, he'd also called upon Dr. Simone Wellstone for assistance as an unofficial, human lie-detector with certain suspects and trusted her extra-sensory perception in vexing cases.

Welcome, Captain Eddie, the only uniform in this area who accepts the notion that there's more to a situation than the eye can fathom or the ear can analyze.

"Eddie, my man!" Diego greeted him with their below-the-belt, all-fingers-entwined secret handshake. "You came all this way to bring me a birthday present?"

"Forgot, sorry. Happy birthday. That's is all you get. Joey called. Said you might need some help."

"Me? Maybe them." Diego nodded at the remainder of the corralled pack who now seemed to be wishing they were anywhere else but there, most likely back at Wild Bill's Bar and Grill. "Three were packin' heat, some carryin' weapons of minimal destruction, but the odds are a little lopsided. Six of us and only fifteen of them left. Maybe they'll let you guys be on their team."

"Six?" Eddie raised one eyebrow and counted again. "I only see five."

"Jimmy's hiding in the crow's nest."

"Ah. These days, you never know, do you?"

"Nope, and I didn't want to guess too late. The tall one with the shorty drew first, and Jimmy destroyed his toy."

Officer Eddie snapped off commands to his men as they loaded the four armed assailants into the squad cars, then turned to Diego and gazed over his shoulder at The Fit Nest. "I see you got another broken window."

"Yeah, a bird flew into it."

"Big fuckin' bird."

"A blue-footed booby, I think." Diego winked at the kid in the pack. "I can show you a picture."

Dressed in a flowing, multicolored, Mexican party dress and carrying a plate of steaming tacos, refried beans, and red rice, Mama glided through the doorway and shouted, "Ay, caramba! Enough talk, let's eat!" The Fit Nest troops moved aside as she strolled by and paused next to the talkers. "Good afternoon, Eddie."

"Hey, Mama, how are you doing?"

"Just fine, but impatient. Nice show, Diego, but…"

"Thanks, Mama, but what?"

She raised one finger and pointed at his mouth. "Language!"

"Sorry, Mama."

"You too, Eddie."

"Sorry, Mama."

She continued beyond them to the man holding the sign, patted his ample belly, and held the plate under his double chin. "You look like a boy who knows how to eat. Some of the skinny sticks who come in here only nibble on seaweed and wheat thins. C'mon in. It's my son's birthday, for God's sake!" The man's brain seemed to be stuck in the deep end, treading reality. She took his arm and led him toward the door while addressing the pack. "C'mon! All of you! I made enough for everyone. You too, Eddie. Bring in your boys if they're not busy picking up the litter."

Diego looked over at Eddie and shrugged his shoulders. "The peacemaker defuses a Mexican standoff."

"She's brilliant! An international diplomat. We could use her on the force."

"Please excuse me, bud. I need to tell Jade to put a lid on the beer for a while. Most of these monkeys are already lubricated on a cellular level."

The party proved to be a rousing success, a grand opening of The Fit Nest and the minds of its unexpected guests. The monkeys became men, and The Fit Nest members became more human in the eyes of the men. Walls of belief weakened, and people chatted through the cracks.

Diego cornered the blue-footed booby chowing down a taco. He learned the kid had a biblical name, Adam, and his "old man" was the sign guy. It seemed to be a clear case of parental prejudice rammed down the throat of the offspring, and Adam had been doing as he was told. Diego made him an offer that lit him up.

"Tell you what, Adam. I could teach you how to be a real criminal who won't get caught, but that's not a career I choose to revisit. It's a one-way road to hell. So I got a deal for ya. If you work here part-time to pay for the windows, I won't show Officer Eddie our movie of you heavin' the rock through Mama's window. You can help clean up or blend smoothies at the Juice Bar. If you do the job well, you could become one of our staff. You might even have some fun."

Adam accepted the offer with relish plus three more tacos with salsa.

When Diego identified who'd shouted "Homos are an abomination to the Lord," he discussed the Good Book with the man. "I got a question for you about all these rules in the *Bible*." He'd borrowed Mama's copy from her bedroom and bookmarked two sections. Diego flipped it to the first one and showed it to him. "It says here in Leviticus 25:44 that people are allowed to possess slaves... male or female... if they're purchased from neighboring nations. Mama's from Mexico, I was born here, and we're both American citizens. Can I bring some relatives in from Mexico as my slaves, or do I have to head north and capture some Canadians?"

The man murmured, "Well..."

Diego flipped to another verse he'd marked. "And it seems to me you're violating Leviticus 19:19 by wearing garments made of two different kinds of thread." Diego rubbed the fabric of the man's shirt between his fingers. "I'm pretty sure this is a blend of cotton and polyester. Don't worry. I won't tell anyone."

The man said, "Well..." and stumbled through a random explanation that didn't even make sense to him. He finished in confusion with a confession and a resolution. "I read the Bible every day, but I haven't read the whole thing. Maybe I'll look at some of those other chapters."

One pack member faced Conan the Barbarian in the arm-wrestling contest and discovered it was like trying and failing to move a fire hydrant.

Conan smirked and grunted, "Use both your arms."

Even with two arms and his feet braced on the table leg, the man couldn't budge his right arm while Conan munched on nachos with his left. Diego lost to Jade, and Jade lost to Conan, who also won the leg-wrestling contest by default because no one dared oppose him. After Masaru gave a nunchucks demonstration, an inebriated member of the pack asked if he could try them and nearly knocked himself out.

The pack partied hearty but didn't last long, and soon straggled away. The festivities continued with Fit Nest regulars, guests, and the staff tapping the beer keg, eating cake, and presenting an array of gifts to Diego. Most offerings were shades of black except for the red, blue, yellow, and green circles on the white plastic mat of a Twister game, which was immediately placed on the floor and played for a riotous hour. Smilin' Norman complained that he'd sprained his gut while laughing his ass off. Diego's birthday present from the universe came soon afterwards.

Simone had relaxed in her balcony seat watching the play of the day, and feeling Diego's fervor behind the scenes. Her mind drifted back to the previous day, and as she focused on Amanda, her internal vision once again peered through the young girl's eyes. She sat at the kitchen table while having dinner with her mother, chatting about what had happened at Valleyview this afternoon.

My connection isn't as clear and united as yesterday, but I'm still able to be with her. Amazing. She seems happy and content. How much control do I still have? In between Amanda's spoonfuls of macaroni and cheese, Simone picked up the glass of soda, took a sip, and smiled. *Huh. I still have some control. Remarkable. I wonder how long this phenomenon will last?*

The consternation Simone felt after the encounter with Diego and Ming at her office had dissolved into exhilaration as the activities at The Fit Nest bloomed, exploded, and resolved while she observed the proceedings from her private balcony inside her host. The uncomfortable claustrophobia she'd experienced during two intense days in two different worlds in two foreign bodies had subsided, though she was exhausted from the barrage of emotions and its vast cast of characters. In her daily routine, Simone sought silence between each patient to restore her energy and external focus. Even after ten hours straight of being on-call or center stage, Diego seemed to have an endless supply of energy coursing through his body.

As the party was winding down, Simone selfishly took control. *Just a short stroll outside. I need a tidbit of peace and quiet.* She pulled up Diego from his chair and announced, "I'm gonna get a little fresh air. Won't be gone long. Party on!"

At seven p.m. the sun hadn't set but was slipping behind the trees along the river. Simone walked down the sidewalk, missing her canine companions, processing the day, and attempting to calm her mind. An EDNA delivery truck drove toward her, and she tried to see the driver through the window as it passed. *I thought their trucks were identical, but this one has dark tinted windows. I wonder if it's the same one that was parked here earlier?*

Simone turned away from the river and spotted a 7-Eleven. She, or Diego, felt thirsty and entered the store to pick up a beverage. With a bottle of cranberry-apple juice in hand, Simone stepped behind the last woman in the checkout line and felt a sudden surge of sensation inside Diego. Whether it was from sound, smell, or sight, she couldn't tell, but one thing was certain. *He knows this woman.* Simone released him into the moment.

Diego blinked his eyes and took a deep breath. He looked around, breathed again, and inched closer to the person ahead of him. If a meter had been tracking his emotions, the needle would've been buried in the red zone. His heart beat harder and faster while scrutinizing the woman in front of him—sandy brown hair cut short and tapered down the neck, smooth skin, shapely figure, casual maroon jacket and matching slacks, leather slip-on loafers. He moved sideways to peek at her face, but she looked down, dug into her handbag and paid for her goods, then left the counter and walked out the door. Diego followed as if drawn to this woman by a magnetic spell. On the outside patio, he called to her, "Ma'am, excuse me, ma'am?"

She turned, and he froze. Her jaw dropped, and Diego's heart pummeled his lungs.

"Laurel?" he murmured.

"Diego!" she shrieked, leaped forward, and flung her arms around his neck.

He wrapped his arms around her waist, buried his head in the crook of her neck, and sucked in an involuntary breath that ended with a whimper or a sob or a heave of his chest or all three at once. The familiar spicy smell was overwhelming, intoxicating, divine. His body disappeared into the present as his memory materialized in the past. It was the smell of his lover Nathan, his sweat, his cologne, his family, his little sister Laurel.

They separated slowly, silently, locked onto each other's eyes.

A uniformed, pimply teenager stood by the doorway with his elbows bent and hands on his hips. "Hey, mister!"

Diego jerked his head toward the sound.

"You didn't pay for the juice."

"Sorry, dude." With his right hand holding the juice, Diego's left fought with his pocket to free his wallet. "She's an old friend I haven't seen in years. How much is it?"

"A dollar and forty-nine cents."

Diego fumbled through the bills in his wallet. "I wasn't tryin' to steal it."

"Yeah, whatever."

"Here's two bucks. Keep the change. Sorry." He turned back to Laurel and his previous state of shock.

"So I'm an old friend now?" Laurel said, feigning irritation.

"Well, you are definitely older. I still think of you as sweet sixteen when we met. Man oh man, how long has it been since I saw you?"

"You and Nathan split for seven years. I moved out of town. Four years ago at the funeral, I guess, for a second."

"I was a basket case then." Diego shook his head. "I could barely be with myself, let alone with other people. And life just hasn't been the same without him. I'm still a recovering basket case."

"I know what you mean," Laurel sighed. "Mom was never the same either and kept getting worse. The big C finally took her down, but I think she just gave up."

"I'm so sorry to hear that. She was a special lady."

"Thanks. I miss her to death. Wait. That sounds bad, like double death. I can't even find the right words for it. I just miss her. Dad had a stroke, and he's hangin' in there, but his memory's not so good. The doctor says it could be Alzheimer's, but I think he just doesn't want to remember. I quit work and moved back a week ago to take care of him. I heard you were in town and was gonna to look you up."

"Well, I looked up in this lucky 7-Eleven, and there you were. And I tell you what... that made my day, and you are still makin' it right now. I am so happy to see you! You were cute as hell at sixteen and still look fabulous at what, twenty-sixteen?"

"Is hell cute? Was that a compliment? Are you saying I look like hell?"

Diego's hands sprung up in front of his chest. "No, no, no. You are beautiful, Laurel. Beautiful as ever."

Laurel's face transformed from a fake snarl into a precious smirk. "Damn, you are as gullible and lovable as you used to be! I'll tell *you* what... when you two split town, I don't know which one o' you pissed me off more. You takin' Nathan away from me, or Nathan takin' you away from me." Every time Laurel said 'you,' she stabbed one finger at Diego as if the finger were shouting along with her. "You guys left me behind in this shithole, and I had one serious crush on you back then. I didn't mind if you or Nathan were gay or not, but I was kinda pissed at every gay guy. Seemed like all the nice, decent men around here were gay, and they were already taken by other gays. That left slim pickin's for us young chickens."

"You're killin' me here. I'm not sure whether to laugh or cry."

"Yeah? Well, do both."

"I must admit I had a crush on you too… no, not a crush. That wasn't legal. I just liked you a lot. You were a young, fun, ball of fire, and I already felt old. Look at you now. Gorgeous and in great shape."

"I try. Workout, jog a little, eat right. Yoga helps. Tried Pilates for a while but the people were too weird. I need to find a club or gym in town. You know of a good one?"

They hadn't moved an inch from the moment they'd hugged. People walked around them as they entered and left the store, but Diego and Laurel were oblivious to the world around them.

"Are you doing anything now?" Diego asked.

"Yeah, talking to you."

"No, I mean, is there anything you have to do right now?"

"Yeah, talk to you. Why?"

"Not on your way somewhere? To meet someone?"

She shrugged her shoulders. "No place to go, no one to meet, no job, and no shit to take from anyone."

"How'd you get here?"

"Dad's car. What're you getting at?"

"I live right around corner. You gotta see it, Laurel. Wanna drive or walk?"

"Around the corner? Oy! Are you one of those potatoes who rides an exercise bike bolted into the basement floor and then drives three blocks to work?"

"Actually…" Diego counted in his head. "I have six of those bikes at home."

"Now what're you talking about? You're weird. I hope you're not into Pilates."

"You'll see. Let's walk."

As they approached The Fit Nest, Laurel slowed the pace. "Wait a minute. Isn't this the block you used to live on? Nathan brought me here one time and showed me some dilapidated druggie hangout."

"This was and is that place. I helped the police cleanup the neighborhood. It's pretty safe these days." He pointed to The Fit Nest. "Here's the hangout now."

"The Fit Nest." Laurel read the entire sign menu aloud and slapped him on the arm with the back of her hand. "You sly fox, you! Why didn't you tell me?"

"I wanted to show you. Surprise!"

"Cool. Is it open?"

"Prob'ly. I live here."

"What? Get real."

"C'mon in. We'll give Mama a heart attack."

"Don't say that!"

"Sorry." Diego took her hand and led her through the double doors. "C'mon. I'll show you around."

All the guests had left, and the lights had been dimmed. Jade swept the floor, and Jimmy dealt with the sound equipment. An immobile snoring mass, Conan lay stretched over two beanbag chairs. Snake leaned against the wall with his eyes fastened to his smartphone.

"I'm back." Every head turned toward Diego and Laurel except Conan's. One quick look at her face and avant-garde pixie hairdo didn't suggest any gender, but one glance below the shoulders verified female. The best plastic surgeon in the world couldn't transform a man into a woman that well. "I ran into an old friend of mine."

Laurel smacked Diego on the arm again.

As Mama walked in from her living room, Diego put his arm around Laurel's shoulder and nudged her ahead. "Guess who's here?"

Mama stepped forward to take a closer look.

"Hi, Mama," Laurel said. "Good to see you again. It's been a while."

"Well, well, well. Little Laurel Fontaine, all grown up."

"I hope not. That's gonna take a few more years."

Every feature on Diego's face seemed to be smiling. "She's my birthday present from the universe."

"It's your birthday!" Laurel shouted. "Why didn't you tell me, you shithead?"

"Language!"

"Sorry, Mama. I meant that in a nice way."

The entire staff was now grinning and exchanging glances in the background.

"And I'm so sorry about Nathan," Mama sighed.

"Yeah, me too," Laurel agreed. "But we move on, don't we?"

"We try. Do you still live here?"

"Just got back."

"Good. Stay. And don't be a stranger."

"No stranger than your boy here." Laurel heard her own words and regrouped. "I meant that in a nice way too."

"I know, honey. Strange but amazing."

Diego's fingers had been fidgeting with each other, signaling his itch to exit stage left. "We're goin' upstairs an' talk for a while."

"I stowed the rifle," Snake said, "but left the case on the porch. Just set it aside, and I'll fetch it in a bit."

As Diego and his present strolled up the stairway, the audience overheard Laurel's voice. "A rifle? Are you shooting wild game from the porch? Or people? I hope you're using a silencer." And from the top of the stairs, "Jeez Louise, are we pathetic or what? You still live with your mom, and I live with my dad."

Simone weighed in from the virtual balcony. *I'm not a matchmaker, but this feels like one made in heaven.*

While Laurel snooped around his space, Diego removed the rifle case from the porch and brought in two state-of-the-style beanbag chairs – memory foam instead of beans with black micro-fiber covers, more like round mini-beds.

"Boss digs you got here." Laurel sunk into one of the circles. "Are you really the boss?"

"I built it. Someone's gotta keep it going."

"How long have you had it?"

"Today was the grand opening, hence the rifle. Had a pack of gay bashers out front and wanted to prevent anything before it happened."

"Did you?"

"Not quite. We had to defuse the disorder. Police arrested four foiled bashers, but Mama invited the leftovers in for the party. Turned a few around. Three guys waited till their buddies left and signed up for family memberships."

"You're kidding."

"Nope. It's been a long fuckin' day. I'm gonna give Mama the Neighborhood 'Noble' Peace Award." Diego flopped down on his back on the vacant lounge chair next to Laurel's. "What job did you quit?"

"Number crunching at a big nonprofit trying save the world. I majored in Busyness in college. Accounting seemed to be in my DNA, and Nathan massaged my genes early on."

"You could help us out here. Numbers aren't my thing."

Laurel rolled over on her side and eyed Diego. "Speaking of your thing, are you still gay?"

"You don't beat around the bush, do you?"

"Why bother? Beating takes up too much time. After a thousand 'nonversations,' I got addicted to terse truth and its consequences."

I like this girl. Could be good for the boy. C'mon, Diego. You've definitely changed since you were in my office. Tell us both what's in your heart these days.

Diego's tongue seemed to be tied while he tried to untangle his feelings into a straight answer.

"Well…" Laurel prodded. "Are you gay or not?"

"I think it's fading away."

"So… you have been with women too, or are you celibate?"

"Both. A couple women for a couple moments and celibate in between."

When Laurel heard his answer, she started moving closer to Diego, perhaps at first in her heart, then with her tone of voice. "How was it?"

"Without love, sex with a woman or man seems about the same. Empty. Have you heard this saying? 'Love can get you through times of no sex better than sex can get you through times of no love.'"

"No, but I should have. Woulda nixed some regrettable nights." She rolled onto her stomach and lightly ran one finger from the tail to the head of Diego's cobra tattoo on his bare arm.

"Like you said, back then the decent guys were gay, and one took me away. The girls were rough, and I'd had enough."

She raised up to her knees and crawled into Diego's soft circle. "Nathan told me one of his elusive business and investment guidelines. 'Two plus two is somewhere between three and five.'" Laurel's voice had gotten quieter as she'd counted out the numbers by tapping on his chest with her fingers. "He said it applied to genders too. 'One plus one is somewhere between one and three.'" She gently slide one finger across her lips.

"Sounds like him. Genderless, a human in between."

Laurel stretched on her side next to Diego, rested her head on his shoulder, and whispered in his ear. "I'm not in between. I'm a woman."

Diego lay like a lump, though his heart beat like a football fan stomping in the bleachers to rev up his team.

Wake up, Diego, and smell this wholesome, human rose that's right in front of you. Simone was aching to take over, wishing he'd take some direction like Amanda had done. *What happened to that suave stud at my office? Even the bumbling idiot you talked about would be better than a manikin. Kiss her already! She's asking for it but doesn't want to start it! Will I have to do it for you?*

Laurel sat up and stared down at him. "Psst? Diego?" She addressed him as if he were four years old.

He answered as if he were the 4.0 age he'd talked about that morning, without the upgrade. "Yeah?"

"What does your t-shirt say?"

"Um…" He tilted up his head and read his chest. "Just do it."

"Thank you! You finally asked!" She bent down, kissed him full on the lips, and slithered her tongue between his teeth, gently but powered by a reservoir of pent-up passion. She sat up slowly, sucked in a deep breath through lips puckered into a circle, and then relaxed them into a calm smile as she exhaled through her nose. "See how long it takes to beat around the bush? I should've done that ten years ago."

Diego morphed from manikin to man and sprung up to his knees. "You want the terse truth? I was afraid that meeting you tonight was just too damn good to be the truth. I swear I felt your presence and smelled you in the store before I truly dared accept it was really you. Not just the Old Spice cologne you and Nathan wore a decade ago, the essence of family. I smelled the familiar odor of its skin. A bolt of… of… How can I describe it? Love shot through my senses into my cells. I thought my heart might stop or beat a hole in my rib cage. You were taboo until today. You were your daddy's little girl. You were my lover's precious sister. You weren't in the cards." Diego slipped his palms under her hands, intertwined their fingers, and lifted them to his lips as if they were delicate, crystal treasures. "But now you are here, and the universe has dealt me the Queen of Hearts." He upped the ante of her first passionate kiss with another full of compassion that flowed into an extended hug. Diego tried to rise from his knees with Laurel in his arms but swayed to one side and nearly lost his balance. "Whoa. Dizzy."

"Are you okay? What's happening?"

"Gotta lie down. On the bed."

Laurel helped him through the door into the bedroom.

"I think I'm fine. Just gettin' very tired."

"I thought men usually fall asleep right after making love, not right before."

"No, no, it has nothing to do with you, Laurel, mi amor." As he caressed her cheek with his hand, Diego noticed the time on the black watch on his wrist. "It's eight-fifteen. My new medicine is kicking in… or out."

"What's it for? Something bad?"

"No, no." Diego waved away her words in slow motion as if he were half-cocked. "I think it's something good. A new treatment. I'll tell you later. They said I should be in bed by eight, and I'd soon be gone."

"Can I lie down here with you?"

"Of course, por favor mi amor."

His bed was a single, and except for Diego's shoulders, they were both pretty thin.

"I thought you were having a premature bedgasm." Laurel massaged his temples and ran her fingers through his hair. "You know, you look a little like Freddy Mercury."

"One of my all-time heroes. Ever listen to Queen?"

"Listen to 'em? I heard 'em before I was born! Mom saw 'em live and fell in love. She told me I'd be dancin' in the womb when she played their albums. Even made the nurse play 'Love of My Live' over and over in the delivery room."

"Sweet." Diego's speech started to coast like a car with an empty gas tank. "The ringtone on my phone is Queen's... 'Somebody to Love.'"

"You're kidding, right?"

"Why would I kid about that?"

Lauren kissed him on the cheek and whispered, "So is mine. Did anybody find you somebody to love?"

"My shrink said... someone was waiting for me to appear." Diego's voice softened, and his sentences broke into pieces. "Maybe... we both found each other... the somebody...for each of us... who..."

"Go to sleep, Diego baby."

"Do what Mama said... stay."

"Don't worry. I lost my Mom. Dad's on his way out. I lost Nathan. I lost you. I'm tired of losing. Finding sounds good. I'm not going anywhere."

"This is like... a dream come true... that I never imagined... I could ever dream..."

During one final thought, Simone drifted into the void with Diego. *Maybe he did evolve a bit since his session... and maybe I helped a bit today. I took him for a walk to lucky 7-Eleven.*

Day 3

Thursday

SIMONE'S JOURNEYS INTO THE VOID at the end of the previous two days were nothing like her normal nighttime routine. She seemed to travel deeper than the four levels of non-REM and REM sleep into another realm—a melding of anesthesia and coma yet with an element of intense internal activity. Simone might capture some fleeting memories along the way, but the vague sensations of primordial movements, genetic alterations, electro-chemical reactions, disconnections and reconnections were almost unremitting and all incomprehensible. The only feeble analogy she could formulate was "my entire being seems to be fizzing like an Alka-Selzer tablet dropped into a glass of water."

Rising above these subterranean suspicions of liveliness into a dream state, Simone had the pervading apprehension of a massive object levitating above her that could drop at any moment and crush her. Though this foreboding menace was invisible, she imagined a five-ton boulder or a giant hand threatening to flatten her as if she were an insect.

Earlier this morning her psyche had settled into a recurring dream depicting a recurring experience during her childhood. Nine-year-old Simone lay asleep on her bed. She felt rhythmic jabs into her side by a small finger from the past. Twin-brother Simon stood next to the bed poking her and issuing commands with each poke.

"Wake up." Poke.

Young Simone lay motionless.

"Let's go." Poke, poke.

She stirred and waved him away with a grunt.

"Wake." Poke. "Up!" Poke. "Let's." Poke. "Go!" Poke.

"Leave me alone!" Simone whined. "I told you I don't wanna. Go away!"

Six pokes, one delivered precisely with each word. "Wake up! Let's go! Simon says!"

When Simon had learned the game "Simon Says" at the impressionable age of four, he believed it had been created solely for him, and thereafter, with disgusting gusto, used his presumed power to coerce his family and friends into serving his every wish.

Simon's jabbing grew aggressive and the tone of his voice increased in fervor. "Wake up! Let's go! Simon says!"

As the dream progressed and Simone crept closer to consciousness, the pokes softened. The words of the commands mutated and seemed to emanate from a younger child with a higher-pitched, playful voice. "Wake up! Let's go! Simon says!" morphed into "Make us friend's toes with cimmonum!" Poke, poke, poke, poke. "Make us friend's toes with cimmonum!"

Simone opened her eyes to view a cracked ceiling and a circular light fixture with a dingy glass cover darkened from the battery of bugs that had died inside. She lifted her head to determine the origin of another "Make us friend's toes with cimmonum!" and gazed into the sky-blue eyes of a pint-sized cherub with curly, strawberry-blond locks.

Here we go again. And where are we going? This little angel is not one of my patients. So where is my host today? Still sleeping, or am I me again? Simone raised one arm from under the covers and drew in a quick breath as she winced from the pain in her shoulder. *Ow! Jesus, that hurts!*

Before she could speak or think further, the cherub boy threw his arms around her neck in a warm hug. "G'morning, Grammy!"

Grammy? Simone followed her arm wound around the boy's waist to see its thin skin, bulging veins, age spots, and an opulent diamond wedding ring stranded between arthritic finger joints. *Oh, no. God, no. That's Coco Montague's rock. This is a patient I'd rather not inhabit! And this sweet boy must be the joy of her life she told me about.* "Well, good morning to you too! And what's your name?" *And where's Coco and why isn't she awake?*

"Silly Grammy. You know."

"Of course I do!" Simone picked up a few of the pill bottles littering the nightstand next to a pack of Marlboro Menthol cigarettes. "Your name is Gollum, right?"

"Nope."

"Is it Poopsie?" Simone squinted at the tiny type on the bottle labels but they were a complete blur. She could make out Coco's eyeglasses next to the bottles, put them on, and the words became legible.

"No!"

"Now I remember! It's Barthomew Humphrey Bogart Armageddon!" *Valium, sleeping pills, nitroglycerin, Caffeine Energy pills, Extra-Strength Tylenol. All the ingredients for a damn roller coaster ride to chaos.*

"No! My name is Connor!"

"I knew that." Simone gave him a little fist bump on the shoulder. "I was just testing you. I thought maybe you forgot." *And here's her bottle of the dieter's buddy Contrave which can cause nausea, headaches, dizziness, insomnia, and suicidal thoughts. Bingo!*

"Will you make us friend's toes and cimmonum?"

"Sure, but I need to wash up first." *And try to wake up the real Grammy.* "Okay?"

"I'll wait in the kitchen with my Game Boy."

Dressed in a pink, frilly, grandma gown that she'd never be caught dead or alive wearing, Simone swung her legs onto the floor and pushed herself upright with her hands. Joints crackled, one knee buckled, and her head started spinning. She toppled to her left and barely caught the short bedpost to stop her body from slamming into the floor. She slumped back down and sat on the mattress. *Great. I declined to help Coco with an assisted suicide, and now I'm going to kill her before she wakes up. I doubt I'd care to live in this body either.*

While Simone waited for the wooziness to subside, she perused the framed photos on the wall—a gallery in memory of the ascent, zenith, and collapse of the life that Coco Montague relished and missed. Quite poised and lovely, she graced snapshots and formal portraits with Hollywood moguls, celebrities, and politicians in exotic locales around the USA and abroad, with and without her three trophy husbands. During her four therapy sessions, Coco had droned on about these days gone by while denying today's reality now revealed to Simone by the drugs on the night stand and the wretched state of her physical mind and body.

After high school, Coco had fled to the left coast, attended the Fashion Institute of Design and Merchandising in Los Angeles, and soon after graduation found work in the film industry. At age twenty-five, she married a fresh, dashing, young director who, after two years, Hollywood declared had become rancid, dashless and old hat, and spat him out. Unwilling to accept his lack of income or any blemish that could possibly spoil her blossoming career, Coco spat him out as well.

Less dashing, though lucky and loaded, her next film-producer husband wrapped the impressive Coco around his wrist like a gold Rolex while attending star-studded events, but afforded her the freedom to do as she exorbitant-ly pleased. Since money had become no object other than the objective of her initial affection, Coco quit the work-ing grind in the movie costume biz and became a critic of the entire entertainment scene. Although she had no writ-ing experience, she'd been a self-appointed connoisseur of complaining about most any topic for decades. Her fiery style succeeded as she exalted the influential and erased the insignificant. After ten years of cohabitation with her inattentive beau, Coco discovered his habit of copulation on the casting couch, packed up her jewelry, and squealed away in her BMW in search of another benefactor.

Even at the over-ripe, La-La Land age of forty-two, Coco had a horde of ardent admirers. She tantalized the line-up for a few months before settling on Herbert Ginsberg, a fi-nancial manager of a major production studio. He looked like the mole in the background that he was. Although Herbert's face had an oddly handsome aspect, or at least a secondhand attraction—or third-hand, in Coco's case—its first and lasting impression was that of a formidable schnoz supporting two miniscule magnifying glasses extending too far ahead of his beady eyes. To Coco, Herbert's three main attributes were his absolute adoration of her, his fi-nancial devotion to her desires, and the unlikelihood that any other woman would want to have an affair with him. Over the years his fourth and fifth attributes did capture her heart: he was fiercely intelligent and had a irreverent sense of humor that buoyed her spirits. She fondly referred to Herbert as "Bert"—her Bert.

As Coco's career shifted from entertainment critic to cranky social gossip columnist, her maternal instincts demanded proof of procreation. Her Bert obliged, her son was born, and Cobert Ginsberg became their prized possession.

Herbert and Coco remained together for twenty years until fate wrote the finale of their fairy tale. With the same strict secrecy of his financial matters, Herbert had kept his medical condition buried in his mole tunnel. One day Herbert was there, and the next day he was gone. He'd burrowed into his idling black Mercedes parked in their garage until the carbon monoxide transported him to his next destination. During a therapy session with Dr. Simone, Coco had shared the note he'd left on the seat, an inspiration for her own suicidal desires.

DEAREST COCO,

I'M SO SORRY TO LEAVE YOU BUT
MY HEART IS FAILING RAPIDLY. I'D
RATHER YOU REMEMBER ME CONTENT
IN LIFE AND PEACEFUL IN DEATH. THE
"CREATIVE FINANCING" I SET UP TO
SUPPORT YOUR LIFE-STYLE HAS GONE
SOUTH, BEYOND ANTARCTICA. MY JOB
HAS BEEN TERMINATED, AND I WILL
LIKELY SERVE TIME IN PRISON RATHER
THAN SERVING YOU, MY ONE AND ONLY
TREASURE. I WILL HAVE TO PLEAD
GUILTY TO FALLING IN LOVE AND DOING
EVERYTHING IN MY POWER TO MAKING IT
LAST. ALTHOUGH IT'LL BE DIFFICULT, YOU
WILL LIVE LONGER AND MORE SECURELY
WITHOUT SPENDING ANY OF THE
REMAINING FUNDS FOR MY NEEDS. MY
HEART ONLY BEATS FOR YOU IN THESE
FINAL MOMENTS AS I CHERISH THE
MEMORIES WE SHARED.

LOVE FOREVER, YER BERT

Amplifying the devastation of losing him, Coco's life in California disintegrated. Herbert had also remortgaged their home and "borrowed" from his life insurance policy which depleted the death benefit payment. Once her material world vanished, the "friends" she'd made suddenly had "so many other things to do." The acquaintances she'd squashed while climbing her career ladder slithered out of the ground into the streets like night crawlers after a thunderstorm. Tinsel Town transformed from her dreamland into the script for a B-grade horror flick.

Coco soon fled Hollywood in her aging Jaguar crammed with jewelry and a suitcase stuffed with clothing. Defeated and demoralized, she returned to her hometown to live with a high-school friend while she regrouped and pawned her jewelry to survive. Similar to Coco's exit from her first husband, her son's wife left him when the financial support of his father vanished. Cobert and one-year-old Connor came to live with his mother in her less-than-luxurious flophouse.

Simone didn't dislike Coco, but was perplexed about her professional role in this unusual case. Gratification came when Simone helped people, not when they paid her, and she seemed incapable of helping Coco. Untrained as a hospice therapist, Simone considered herself more of a life counsellor. She could teach a person to drive, but Coco wanted a mechanic to tow her rusty body to the junk yard.

Coco had gone through a harsh period of self-realization, changed her ways, and committed herself to assuring the well-being of her son and grandson by leaving a legacy of giving instead of taking. During each of their therapy sessions, Dr. Simone had absorbed Coco's sorrow, disappointment, and suicidal desires, became cranky and demanding right along with her, and felt like a failure when her patient dragged herself out the door.

Simone eased Coco's legs off the bed, shuffled over to the door she assumed led to the bathroom, and opened it to reveal the clothes closet. "Connor! Where's the bathroom?"

"Silly Grammy!" His voice came from somewhere beyond the bedroom doorway. "You know! It's next to the kitchen!"

"Keep talking so I can find you and the bathroom!"

"You're funny today, Grammy!"

The house was small and austere. Padding through the living room reminded her of Amanda and Whitney's apartment—dingy walls surrounding low-budget furniture and a threadbare rug. Through the picture window, Coco's ruby-red Jaguar parked out front appeared to be in the wrong neighborhood. *God, is that my breath I'm smelling. Maybe I can find a Brillo pad to clean my tongue.*

Simone began to realize that this frail body was only one cause of her mobility issues. The combination of drugs her host had taken increased her subtle stupor and also the difficulty of rousing Coco. Standing at the sink, Simone washed her face, neck, and chest with cold water, scrubbed harder than usual, brushed her teeth, gums, and tongue till they were raw, pinched her skin, and slapped her cheeks a few times. *No response. I don't like this at all.* She considered pressing the emergency button on the familiar black watch on her wrist, the same instrument Amanda and Diego had worn. *Not yet. I'm sure Coco signed up for this treatment program to make some money. Or... god forbid... in hopes it would go awry and kill her. What can I do here and now to wake the dead? Hmm. Connor could be the key.*

Simone found him in the kitchen engrossed in his vintage Game Boy Advance. "Is your father home?"

"Nope." He kept thumbing the buttons and didn't look

up. "Daddy comes home at nine. He's working at the graveyard shit."

"I think you mean graveyard 'shift'?"

"No, Daddy says, 'I hate this graveyard shit.'"

"I see. Okay, Mr. Connor. If you'll put down your Game
Boy, we're gonna play a little game."

"What kinda game?" he asked, then stood up, intrigued.

"A fun one. What's the biggest, scariest monster you can
think of?"

"Um... T'ranasawus Rexstuff!"

"Tyrannosaurus Rextuff?"

"Yeah, they wreck stuff and eat people."

"Oh. They certainly do! Would you scream if one were
chasing you?"

"Yeah?" Connor's tone of voice said that Grammy had
asked a really stupid question.

"Okay, now pretend a Tyrannosaurus Rexstuff is right
behind you and then scream as loud and long as you can
so everyone in the neighborhood will come and save you."

"As loud as I can?" Connor's brows arched high over his
delighted eyes. "That's *really* loud."

"Even louder than that. Okay now, scream when I say
go. Are you ready?"

"Ready." Connor took a couple of breaths to warm up.

She counted down, "three... two... one... go!"

"AIEEEEEEEEEEEEEEEEEE!"

Simone felt a sudden surge inside, and like a patient re-
ceiving an electric shock on the chest after cardiac arrest,
Coco came to life. She blinked, shook her head, and tried to
get her bearings before shouting, "Connor! Connor!"

"Grammy! Grammy!"

She slunk down to her knees and grabbed him by shoulders. "What's wrong? Are you okay?"

"I'm fine, Grammy. That was fun!"

"What was fun?"

"You told me to scream cuz a T'ranasawus Rexstuff was gonna get me."

"I did?"

"Yeah. You're funny today."

"What do you mean, honey?" Coco frowned in confusion. "I just woke up."

"Noooo. I woke you up a bunch o' time ago. You forgot my name and called me Gollum. And Poopsie."

"I did?"

"Yeah, and you even forgot where the bathroom is. Will you make us friend's toes now? With cimmonum?"

"Of course I will. Just let me wash up first."

"You did that five minutes ago."

"Okay, fine. Friend's toes it is then. Good heavens! I've been walking, talking, *and* washing in my sleep."

Simone took a deep breath and sighed along with Coco. *Thank god she's alive. I need a break. And I haven't made French toast in years.* Simone liked to hang out with young kids when clients or friends brought them during their visits, but liked it even better when they went home. People often tried to convince her to have children, but she gave them a standard answer to cease their crusades. "I've considering adopting one but not until it's finished college, gotten married, and has a house of its own."

She guessed Connor was about four, her favorite age of innocence. While he and Coco prepared breakfast, Simone wandered back to her wee ages with brother Simon. She hadn't thought of him much in the past two years since he'd lapsed into a coma during the terminal stages of ALS, amyotrophic lateral sclerosis, but the interaction with Connor and her morning dream triggered the memories. Simone wasn't even sure if Simon was still alive.

⚈⚈⚈

The ultrasound of Nova Albright's womb had revealed two babies in one placenta, a sure sign of identical twins of the same sex formed after one egg fertilized by one sperm cell split and created two embryos. However, two months later in the next ultrasound, it became apparent to the doctor that the twins were male *and* female.

"If I hadn't observed this pregnancy with my own eyes, I would have said it had a snowball's chance in hell of happening," he told his skeptical colleagues. "Perhaps this statistically inconceivable event occurred on a cold day in heaven."

The twins, neither fraternal nor identical, fell into a third rare category called semi-identical twins. In this case, a single egg had been simultaneously fertilized by two sperm cells before it divided. In identical twins, the embryos share 100 percent of the same DNA. These semi-identical twins shared 100 percent of maternal genetic material and only about 75 percent of paternal genetic material—*differing* genetic material from their father—because sperm may look the same but each carries a unique and random sampling of DNA.

Honoring the matrilineal tribal tradition of her Hopi grandparents, Nova named the offspring. Simone was first out and frisky. Simon lagged an hour behind, emerged fragile, and spent a week inside an infant incubator at the hospital, a harbinger of the remainder of his life.

Some twins develop cryptophasia, their own secret language understandable only to each other, but these twins could communicate mentally. Simone remembered experiences while playing and guessing each others thoughts that flowed into silent conversations. The phenomenon faded over time, but during their elementary years, Simone didn't have to hear a terrified scream like Toby's to alert her. She *felt* Simon's distress wherever he was in the school.

When Simone disclosed this uncommon ability, her mother smiled, nodded, and gave her that familiar knowing look. "You can thank your great-grandfather. He was a Hopi healer, medicine man, and shaman rolled up into a single human. He didn't like fancy titles and would say, 'I'm just one of The Old Ones who learned The Old Ways.' He could speak without talking, and you'd hear him with your soul. Once in a while I've had a similar experience with my patients."

Though the twins seemed to be the classic "two peas in a pod" during their toddler years, divergent streaks appeared around age four, accentuated by Simon's recently discovered power game. A series of incidents were still etched in Simone's mind.

Little Simone had become fascinated by ants and their ability to toil together whether they were female workers or winged males, to move a huge leaf alone or with help from their buddies, to communicate with their antennae and have little chats as they met each other on long trails between the anthill and some project undertaken on the other end of the yard. She could watch them for hours, helping the workers with their tasks by scooting a dead fly toward the anthill with her finger or by laying down itty-bitty sticks for a bug bridge across a mud patch.

In complete contrast, Simon was hell-bent on torturing them. He'd stomp on the ground near an anthill and then stomp on the ants when they swarmed out. Or steal matches from the kitchen and fling them into the fray. Or set up sick situations so he could yell his new pet command. He'd grab one black ant, drop it at the entrance of a red anthill, and scream, "Simon says kill!" None of Simone's scolding or begging stopped him and that drove her crazy with anger and grief.

One morning in their back yard, he started picking up

individual ants, whispering "Simon says die," crushing them between his fingers, and flicking their mutilated bodies across the lawn.

Simone sat seething until she couldn't take it anymore. She'd formulated a heartfelt question that seemed certain to convince him to cease and leaped up to deliver it. "Simon! Stop it! How will those poor little ants' mommy feel when her babies don't come home for dinner tonight?"

He gave her a blank look and said, "Nothing."

"Nothing?" She was shocked. "Why not?"

"I got her too!"

Simone's jaw dropped as she sucked in a gasp of air and covered her mouth with both hands. For a few eternal seconds, she was speechless, paralyzed with horror. She ran up to her bedroom, locked the door, and collapsed on the bed in tears. Simone couldn't talk to or even look at her brother for three days.

Unlike the demeanor she chose to exhibit during her sessions with Dr. Simone, Coco treated her sous-chef Connor patiently even when he dropped a raw egg onto the kitchen floor. Red-eyed Cobert returned from the graveyard shift, and the family of three polished off the French toast, scrambled eggs, and orange juice. Simone gagged during the first sip of the secret screwdriver—into which Coco had poured her glass half-full from the bottle of vodka hidden behind the vegetable oil—while Connor cleaned up the egg scrambled on the floor.

I guess happy hour starts early on Thursday, or is it everyday several times a day? Alcohol doesn't mix well with that stash of pills on her nightstand.

"You made perfect French toast, Chef Connor. Next time you can bring it to me in bed." As Coco gathered the dishes, she clattered them around Cobert's head buried in his arms on the table. "I found some extra money laying around, so Connor and I are going shopping in the mall before I drop him at Bright Eyes. He's outgrown most of his clothes. You'll pick him up at five, yes?" She paused, glaring down at her immobile son. "Cobert? Cobert!"

"Yeah, Mom. What?"

"Pick Connor up at five. Go to sleep. You're welcome for breakfast."

"Yeah, Mom. Thanks." Cobert stood and strolled toward his bedroom.

"Thank Connor," Coco demanded.

"Thanks... Connor." He threw the words behind him in the hallway.

"Think you can manage to take out the garbage?"

"Yeah, Mom." Cobert opened his bedroom door.

Each of Coco's next words sounded more vehement than the one before it. "Will you do it today? You promised you'd to it today yesterday!"

"Yeah. Good night, Mom." He slammed the door shut.

Coco shouted at the vacant hallway while Connor grabbed his Game Boy and ducked into the living room. "And you could try sweeping the driveway for the first time in your pathetic life!"

Now there's the Coco I know, but who's speaking? Coco, the drugs, or the vodka?

Coco stomped into the bathroom and spent a half-hour reconstructing her face and reducing her perceived age with Pure Radiant-tinted foundation, Camouflage Cream concealer, Touché Olé brightener, an array of powders and bronzers, petal-pink blush, bone-color shadow, salmon lipstick, and a final coating of coral lip gloss.

Never having witnessed this process in real time on her own face, Simone was captivated by the length of time and the artistry required to cloak reality. *This reminds me of renovating the facade of a decaying building.* Simone owned no lipstick, but occasionally used Chapstick. She'd make up her own skin care products in the kitchen—avocado-yogurt mudpacks, cucumber-slice eye pads, olive oil and honey lotion.

On the way through the living room toward phase two of her preparation for the world at large, Coco issued her marching orders to Connor. "We're leaving in fifteen minutes. Get dressed and ready for preschool."

"Yes, Grammy."

Coco struggled into her body-shaper waist belt in the bedroom, but discarded three pairs of slacks onto the closet floor before finding a beige pair that fit. The long, scoop-neck, salmon tunic she chose didn't quite match the slacks but concealed her expanding mid-section and complemented the color of her lipstick. Coco's next garment selection bewildered Simone—a wide-brimmed, floppy sun hat that effectively concealed one eye, half the brighteners, bronzers, blushes and shadows she'd added, and matted down the blonde hair she'd just fluffed up.

It must be hell trying to live up to the former beauty-pageant standards haunting her in the photos on the wall. Oh, no. Not high heels too. I haven't worn them in a decade!

In the driveway, Coco opened the car door for Connor and strapped him into his booster seat. While Coco strolled around to the driver's side, Simone noticed the dented bumpers, smashed taillight, and scratches along the length of the aging, luxurious Jaguar S-Type. Like Coco, its sleek elegance existed only in the past.

Straining her stiff neck to glance behind while backing out, Coco didn't notice the compact car cruising down the street, partially hidden by Cobert's beat-up truck parked at the curb. Simone saw it, shouted "Watch out!" and slammed on the brake. The driver shook his fist at Coco as he passed.

"What the hell?" Coco asked. "Who said that?"

"Grammy swore!" Connor wagged his finger at her. "Bad Grammy. Bad Grammy."

"Be quiet! That car was speeding." Coco backed out and prematurely shifted the Jaguar into forward, grinding the gears, and then shot off down the street.

Too fast. Too crazy. Simone pressed on the brakes with Coco's left foot to slacken the pace. *She's out of control, and why isn't she under my control? She heard me yell! This isn't like Amanda or Diego! So what is this? A battle of wills?*

"Dammit," Coco grunted. "Who's driving this car anyway?"

"Who are you talking to, Grammy?"

"Never mind."

"I'm scared, Grammy."

"Just be quiet!" Coco's agitation heightened during the next two blocks.

When the car came to a halt at the red light, Simone pinpointed their location. *This is close to Amanda's house, and the mall is straight ahead on the right.*

Coco started to inch the Jaguar forward. In their peripheral vision, Simone caught the blur of a car on their left, tearing toward the intersection, bent on running its yellow light. Coco's stoplight turned from red to green, and she punched the pedal.

Focusing her inner energy and willpower, Simone thrust her right arm over to protect Connor, gripped the steering wheel hard, jammed both feet on the brakes, and screamed, "Stop! Car coming!"

Connor echoed Coco's scream as the oncoming car swerved at the last moment to avoid the Jaguar by the width of one coat of paint. The three of them nearly sucked out all the air inside the car before letting out a unison sigh as

Simone continued through the intersection and pulled over next to the curb.

Simone had taken full control but could still feel Coco squirming inside like an animal caught in a net. *I'll bet she can still hear me talk. Now what?* Her candid question directed to the universe in general brought to mind the words of Gandhi and a simple plan. *Be the change you wish to see in the world.*

She leaned close to Connor, speaking slowly and tenderly while stroking his hair. "We're okay, honey. I'm really sorry to scare you. I scared me too. But I won't do that anymore. I'm going to drive very carefully now. I'm taking some new medicine today that made me kinda weird, but I'm okay now. Are you okay now?"

Connor nodded and wiped his wet eyes with both hands. "I'm okay, Grammy."

"Bad Grammy, right?"

"Yeah, Bad Grammy."

"You'll probably have to spank me later, right?"

A smile crept onto Connor's lips. "Maybe a little spank."

"Now we're gonna drive real slow to the mall and park in the lot and then walk inside and get you some cool new clothes and maybe you'd like to go to that fun place where you bounce around inside those colorful, plastic balloon buildings."

"Yeah. I like to bounce."

"I could use a good bounce too."

Connor pointed at her feet. "Your sharp shoes will pop the buildings."

"You're right. I'll just watch."

As she'd promised, Simone drove slowly while trying to sort out this new development with Coco. *Amanda and I connected, even worked together and said a few words to each other later in the day. Diego just zoned out when I took control, unaware I was there. Maybe female genes have some special bond? Maybe it's the drugs Coco's taking? Maybe, maybe, maybe. God, I hope this ends soon.*

Coco spoke quietly, calmer than before. "Who are you?"

"I'm your treatment," Simone answered.

"My tree man?" Connor asked.

"No, treat... ment," Simone said. "Like a treat that you like. Don't worry. The treatment is something you decided to try that would help you. Remember what the guy said. You might feel different, but just relax and go with it."

"Okay," Coco said.

"You're not talking to me, are you?" Connor asked.

"No, I'm just talking to myself," Simone replied. "Do you ever do that?"

Coco and Connor responded together. "Yeah."

Once she'd secured Connor in the Bouncy Housey at the mall, Simone sat on a bench in a quiet corner within sight of the kids' attraction. Coco seemed to calm down as the exasperation of the drive and the confusion of her identity subsided, and Simone had been able to slacken her control. She took the Galaxy phone from Coco's handbag and held it next to their ear. "Coco, are you with me?"

"I guess so."

"I got out your phone so people won't think we, or you, aren't a mentally challenged person chatting away with herself. And you are definitely not suffering from some multipersonality syndrome. You're just Coco, and you're okay. This whole situation is unbelievable, but it's happening, so please bear with me while I tell you the little that I understand. First of all, you know me. I'm Dr. Simone Wellstone, and today I am trapped inside your body."

"That's impossible."

"I agree, but I'm me, you're you, and I'm inside you. Last Monday night I was drugged in my home and woke up the next day inside another patient, a thirteen-year-old girl. Yesterday I woke up inside a different patient, a forty-year-old man. I don't know why, how, or who is doing this, but I've learned it might be over by Sunday. Like you, the other patients signed up for this treatment, and they're getting paid to participate. You're wearing the same black watch on your wrist as the others, and I'm sure the treatment gurus gave you the same instructions, but it's *not* a treatment; it's a vile experiment and we're their guinea pigs."

"I can't talk about it to anyone," Coco said. "I'm just taking some new medicine."

"Right, and I'm the goddamn medicine. We don't have to talk about it; you just need to accept it. And if they decide not to pay you, *I will pay you*, whatever the cost. We're kind of like Siamese or conjoined twins with two brains and one body. I cannot read your mind, but I can feel via your senses and am aware of your emotions. Later during the first day, the young patient and I worked out some serious circumstances together and communicated verbally. I didn't want to frighten the sweet girl in the beginning, but I tell you what—I was scared at first. Each day's experience has been different. Whenever I took control of the man, he seemed to drift into a dreamlike state. No communication. You are more connected to me than either of them."

"Were you the one walking, talking, and washing in my sleep?" Coco asked.

"Yes. I woke up before you and had no idea where I was, or who Connor was, until I saw your wedding ring. It took a while to wake you up! I didn't want to barge into your life like I did in the car, but you're driving scared the shit out of me."

"Sorry. So what do you want me to do?"

"Like the treatment instructions said, just do whatever you'd normally do. Get Connor's new clothes. When you take him to preschool, please let me drive. Relax and pretend you have a Tesla with auto-pilot. No sleeping in the car though. I still need your eyes, hands, and feet. I don't really want to take over at any other time because I might sprawl us on the ground while I learn how to walk in high heels again. But if I need to do something, please chill out and go with the flow. If you resist, it won't help either of us. I'm your friend as well as your doctor. We don't know who the hell these treatment devils are. Right now I need to make two phone calls, and then I'll fade into the background. One call to my assistant and one to a doctor friend who might be able to shed some light on what's going on. Does that sound all right with you?"

"Do I have any choice?"

"Sure, cooperation or conflict, unity or disunity. Coco, you trusted me enough to schedule four therapy sessions. Think of us as two girlfriends on a new adventure—no doctor, no patient, just two explorers."

"Okay then. Option one. Make your calls, and let's get on with it." Wringing her entwined fingers, Coco frowned and scanned the lobby for an exit. "I need a smoke."

"One more thing before I forget. I didn't realize you were taking so many pills. You might want to be careful with your alcohol consumption. It doesn't mix well with Contrave, nitroglycerine, Valium, or Tylenol. It's a recipe for disaster."

"Isn't that why I came to you in the first place?"

Simone sighed along with Coco. "Well... life or death is certainly your choice, as is suicide. But today, please don't take me with you. How do I make a call on your phone?"

Coco put her thumb on the sensor and selected the correct app. "Now enter your number. It's a smartphone but every time I use it, I feel stupider."

Simone rang the office as her anxiety level rose, and Ming answered immediately.

"Dr. Wellstone's Office. How can I help you?"

"Hi, Ming. It's Simone. Are Dammit and Brandy okay?"

"Dr. Simone! They are okay but I think they miss you. Are you okay? Do you have a cold? You not sound the same."

"I'm fine. Are my patients rescheduling appointments?"

"Yes. Many call."

Simone couldn't resist asking, "Has Diego Fierro rescheduled any visits?"

"No."

"Someone hacked into our email accounts and patient database. Who do you think could've done that?"

"I don't know." Ming paused. "Maybe those men who fix internet. No one else come here."

Except Diego. Ming just told me a little white lie. "Did you hear or see anything strange last Monday night before I disappeared?"

"No. You tell me you need no help, and I stay in my bungalow."

Hmm. Her English has definitely degenerated since yesterday with Diego. "Please make sure the security system is always activated and the doggies are fed, walked, and loved."

"Yes, Dr. Simone. You come back on Sunday like you say in email?"

"I hope so. See you then or before." Simone disconnected and drummed her fingers on her knee. *The dogs might be okay but something's not. What is it?*

She located the browsing app on the Galaxy phone, found the number for Dr. Theodore Frank, a jolly and progressive soul who had been her favorite psychology professor while attending medical school at Johns Hopkins University. Upon discovering they shared the same birthplace, the friendship bloomed, and they'd kept in touch over the years. Dr. Frank had recently retired and returned home, but Simone hadn't seen him for months.

"Good day. Dr. Theodore Frank speaking."

"I need to see you. Are you free today?"

"That depends on who's asking."

"It's your forever student, even though she's become your competition."

"Simone Wellstone? Your voice sounds different."

"Good ears. How are your eyes these days?"

"Failing but bifocaled. How are you? You've been a stranger lately."

"Well, I'm even stranger now. I look strange too. In fact, I woke up inside another body today. And in a different body yesterday and the day before."

"Simone, what are you talking about? Is today April Fool's Day?"

"I may be a fool, but I am *not* joking. Can I come over in an hour or so?"

"Of course. My curiosity is already killing me. Hurry."

"Until then, I need you to chant your own words over and over. You always used to say, 'When you're confronted with a new concept which may appear implausible or even impossible, suspend your beliefs. And then challenge your disbeliefs. View the situation again with the open mind of a child.'"

"Are you certain I said that? Sounds way too profound."

"Are you feeling like a child today?" Simone asked.

"Sure, if you don't mind one addicted to Ibuprofen."

"I'll be there soon. Start chanting."

For the next hour, everything went smoothly. Connor and Coco had a grand time spending money, and Simone didn't have to concentrate on remaining upright on high heels. When they finished, Coco strapped the boy in his seat, sat on the driver's side, and let Simone take the wheel while she and Connor chatted.

It's much easier taking full control of a body. This sharing the load is like having several brains that aren't in synch. The next time I have a patient with multiple personalities I can say, "I know how you feel. Been there, done that."

After they'd dropped off Connor at Bright Eyes Day School, Simone announced, "Coco, if you don't mind, we're going to visit my good friend and mentor Dr. Frank. Feel free to say what you like, but please let me start the conversation. This is a real-life *Ripley's Believe It or Not*, and I have no idea what his reaction will be. Okay?"

"Okay, but I think I like you better as a chauffeur than a therapist. Do you have a day rate?"

Simone smirked and let the question ride. *Good, she's relaxing into her standard abrasive self.*

Dr. Frank's office was in the original servant's quarters behind a four-story, hundred-year-old mansion overlooking the river. Simone parked, walked to the porch door with her head down, and tugged the cord of the antique bell.

The doctor opened the door, and with a cheery greeting, gestured for her to enter.

"Hi, Dr. Frank. Don't look at me." She ducked under his arm and into the office.

"Simone, I presume?" he asked, following behind her.

"No... Simone, *for sure*. Before you look at me, I want to make certain that you believe I'm me." She kept her head lowered, half-hidden under Coco's floppy hat, and slumped into the leather wingback chair in front of his desk.

"Well, you're definitely not dressed like Simone, and I've

never seen Simone in high-heels. And your voice doesn't sound like her."

"Stop looking! Please face the other direction."

"Yes, dear." Dr. Frank turned toward the book shelves lining the wall. His unruly beard and six-foot height distracted the eyes from his width. Constrained by a tight tweed vest and khaki pants, he had a Freudian appearance but without the cigar or the frown. "Now what?"

"Do I talk to you like Simone does?"

"The only person who talks to me like Simone is Simone, and yes, your words are like hers."

"For irrefutable proof, we're going to recall an experience we had together, one we vowed would remain a secret."

"Which one?" he asked. "There are so many."

"When I was your teaching assistant in Baltimore and helped you correct all your students' final exams we went out on the town under the guise of—"

"Observing humanity in its native environment."

"Very good."

"Thank you. I was sober when we started that trek."

"We drank ourselves stupid in a strip club called..."

"Wait." He paused and closed his eyes. "It was right down the block from the Performing Arts Center. It was... of course! Art's Performing Center."

"Survey says? Correct again. The final question has two answers. That night, you tried a new cocktail for the first time ever and dared order three more. What was its name, and why was it called that?"

"Oh, my. The Flaming Blue Jesus. An oppressive shot glass layered with four liquors the bartender set on fire and made me chug in one gulp. I've haven't had one since, nor wanted to."

"Good, but... *Why* did they call it that? You didn't ask anyone until after your third glass."

"By then, my memory was disabled." Dr. Frank shook his head and sighed. "I surrender. Why?"

"Because after you chug one, you turn blue and wheeze, 'Jeeezus!'"

Dr. Frank chuckled. "I can't forget that night no matter how hard I try. Okay, trust me. I believe you're you, but you woke up in different bodies? Three times? How is that possible?"

"That is *exactly* the question I came to ask you. You can turn around now."

"Please tell me more." Dr. Frank ambled over to his desk and sat facing Simone.

With her head still lowered, Simone gave an abbreviated account of the events she'd shared with Coco. "Back to the big question at hand. How is that possible? Right now, recently conjoined twins with two brains and one body are sitting in your office, but one of the them—yours truly—is somewhere else." Simone raised her head and removed the hat. "Dr. Frank, meet my patient, my friend, and shared body, Miss Coco Montague."

Nothing Simone could've imagined happening at that moment happened. For three silent seconds, three brains attempted to process the information revealed before the next chain of reactions could commence.

Dr. Frank's frozen face thawed into a glimmer of recognition. "Coconut?"

Two more seconds passed as a surge of emotion infused Coco's upper body. "Teddy Bear?"

"Yes, yes. Your Teddy Bear." His whole being seemed to glow with joy as he stood, hurried over to Coco, bent down on one knee, and took her hand. "Theodore Franklin Remington the Third at your service! My, god. How long has it been?"

"A lifetime. Or two. Three. I don't know." Coco wiped a

tear from her cheek. "It seems like forever."

"It's been fifty years. Our high school reunion is scheduled in July. Are you going?"

"I don't even know what I'll be doing in ten minutes or where I'll be doing it."

"So you're one of Simone's patients? You must live here. For how long? Are you still married? Designing clothing? Writing?"

"Teddy Bear, take it easy. Too many questions. You haven't changed a bit."

"Well, there's more of me now," he said, patting his stomach. "They sent out old photos with the reunion invitation, and I looked like a kitchen mop. I think my hippie hair weighed more than the skin and bones."

"So it's Dr. Frank, now?" Coco asked. "What happened to that well-heeled name Remington?"

If Simone had been sitting in the room controlling her own arms, her head would've been buried in her hands. *So much for my big question, and I am incapable of interrupting their precious pinch-me-I-think-I'm-dreaming moments. I asked him on the phone if he felt like a child today. Look at them! They both just got fifty years younger! Time out, Simone. Back to the balcony. Maybe they'll remember me later.*

Later continued to be postponed as Coconut and Teddy Bear exchanged stories while wandering hand-in-hand through the Remington family mansion. They'd been committed boyfriend-girlfriend in high school and had planned to reunite after college. He went east to Yale in Connecticut, and she headed west. Their relationship slipped away as their redefined lives carried them farther apart.

Invigorated by a renewed hope of companionship and visions of living the good life in Teddy's lap of luxury, Coco's demeanor turned demure yet blatantly amorous. She hung on his every word, gushed over each room, and fluttered her fake eyelashes at his constant stream of compliments. She never mentioned Simone or the treatment to assure Dr. Frank's attention remained riveted on his Coconut.

It felt a bit creepy holding the hand of her mentor for an hour, but Simone learned one thing they had in common that Dr. Frank hadn't divulged. Teddy Remington had changed his surname to avoid being associated with his family. Although his father was not in the rifle clan, the name Remington still meant guns and wealth to most people, two words that didn't quite gel with the image of a humble, kindly professor. "Frank" fit the psychology scene so he lost the "lin" in spite of Theodore Franklin Remington the First and Second who'd spawned the Third. This decision sealed his reputation as Black Sheep of the Family, but he was also the only lamb, and once his parents had passed, Dr. Frank returned to his childhood home to tend and spend the family fortune.

Back in the office after the tour of the Remington mansion and the past, Dr. Frank finally addressed Simone. "I sincerely apologize for ignoring you, my dear Simone, and I haven't forgotten about your big question. I have been engrossed in my own big question in a different category. How is it possible that two high-school sweethearts suddenly are reunited after fifty years of estrangement? While you're pondering the unfathomable answer to your question, please let me pose one more for both of you. I helped start a little non-profit called the C.A.F.E. That stands for Creative Arts For Everyone, and today we're having a rather festive benefit event. Would you two lovely ladies like to accompany me at five this afternoon? I'd be glad to pick you up wherever you live. No place is very far away in this town! Simone, that would give me a bit of time to research my uneducated guesses about your big question."

"I'm game if Coco is," Simone said. "I'd planned to go,

even marked it on my calendar."

"I'd love to," Coco purred. "That sounds marvelous!"

"Splendid!"

"What is the evening's dress code?" Coco asked.

"Please wear whatever makes you feel comfortable. I'm sure you'll see a kaleidoscope of outfits from artistically torn Levis to Armani silks. I'll be wearing this." Gesturing to his outfit, he looked down, paused at his feet, and raised both bushy eyebrows. "I might have to ditch the slippers."

Back in the Jag, Simone resumed her role as chauffeur while her passenger transformed from cranky Coco to chipper Coconut. With a self-satisfied simper fused to her face, she chatted about Teddy, the weather, and even expressed her gratitude to Simone. "I guess I owe you at least three thank yous. Two for those close calls in the car and one for taking me to see Teddy. What a coincidence!"

No, synchronicity, Simone thought, but didn't want to delve into the difference. "You're welcome," she said, and relinquished control of the vocal cords for the remainder of the afternoon.

At home Coco hummed as she prepared a tuna-salad sandwich and sipped another screwdriver, whistled through her wardrobe while laying out options on the bed, and spent the next hour in the bathroom showering, setting her hair, powdering every square inch of her skin, and relandscaping her face. Simone reveled in the chance to lapse into her own world.

I wonder if I'm still connected to Diego like I was with Amanda yesterday? Simone concentrated until she could see Diego's laptop screen on his desk. She turned his head to scope out the room and lifted his arm to rub his ear with one finger.

Amazing. Still connected. Crimeny... what someone could do with a power like this.

Through Diego's eyes, Simone watched Laurel emerge from the bathroom wearing a black-and-white checkered skirt with black-and-white striped arm sleeves, black leotards, a pair of clunky, ugly, dad-shoe sneakers in white, and a black t-shirt printed in olive-green letters—**We can do whatever the fuck we want.** She stretched out her arms, palms up, and asked, "Wha'd'ya think?"

"Well, you can do whatever the fuck you want," Diego answered, "but it's a pretty harsh statement for our slice of humanity. The kids'll love it, but the adults'll raise hell."

But am I really still connected or only visualizing this scene and his actions? A self-induced daydream, perhaps?

At 4:45 p.m. Cobert dragged his sleep-deprived body out of the bedroom and knocked on the bathroom door. "Mom, I'm going to pick up Connor. You need anything?"

Coco stopped preening and with a meek smile, cracked open her door. "Thank you so much, honey. I'm so sorry for yelling at you this morning. I know you work hard, and are tired when you get home. I'm just on edge from some new medicine I'm taking, but I think everything will be better soon."

"It's okay, Mom. I'm used to it. You've been on edge for the past three years."

Dr. Frank arrived at five and pressed the buzzer. Dressed in a long flowing black dress that covered her legs and trailed behind her high heels, Coco flung open the screen door with a flourish. Teddy Bear's face lit up like a child who'd just received a present better than any he could have dreamed. "You look ravishing, Coconut! What an elegant dress!"

"This old thing? I wore it once before at the Oscar awards ceremony. I hope it's not too much."

"Oh, no, just enough, but you'll definitely be the chic Queen of CAFE. Come and revisit another old thing." He took her hand and escorted her down the walkway to a bright orange, 1967 MGB roadster convertible with the top down.

"You've still got the Great Pumpkin! You drove me to the airport in this car when I left for California!"

"This baby still forces people to grin when they see him. I could not part with my Great Pumpkin, so I mothballed him for a few decades. Remember how we used to park on Park Drive and try to get close enough to neck in those hard bucket seats?"

Coco gently cupped his chin and pecked him on the cheek as he bent down to open the car door. "Kissy-face, rubby bod. I remember everything about you."

After a block or two of chit-chat, Dr. Frank asked, "Simone, are you still here?"

"Unfortunately I am," Simone sighed, "not that I don't enjoy your company, but I'd rather be at home with my doggies, my own bed, and myself."

"My heart goes out to you, and I wish I could settle your troubled mind. I'd like to say I found the answer to your big question during my afternoon research but I'm afraid it's out of my intellectual reach."

"That's okay. I just needed to talk to someone about it and be the patient on the couch for a change."

"I do have thoughts on the matter, but my Great Pumpkin lecture today won't be like those in class when I vaguely knew what I was talking about. Today's lecture will be mere musings of an elderly novice. Let's see if this old brain can recall and regurgitate all the new facts."

"I'm all ears... well, I'm all Coco's ears."

"I zipped around the web gathering eclectic information from the fields of biology, medicine, genetic engineering, quantum mechanics, computer science, and even space exploration." He glanced from the road ahead to his bonded passengers. "Class ready?"

"Ready and waiting," Simone said.

"Don't try to take notes. Some of the numbers are longer than this car. From some secret location, probably not far away, you are able to control Coco's speech and movements. That is quite extraordinary, but consider this. NASA landed a roving vehicle on Mars, maneuvered it on the ground, and retrieved data from *140 million miles away*. Scientists have split an atom and separated the particles by 350 miles. When they altered the rotation direction of the particles on one half, the other half immediately changed to match its long-distance twin."

Simone smirked and slammed her fists on her knees like Connor might have done. "But how is that possible? How is this possible?"

"Beats me, but I believe the explanation of your predicament lies in the manipulation of very, very tiny things. Your body contains 40 trillion cells, give or take three or four, or a billion. Strands of DNA, each one an electron-microcopic blueprint of your body, are found in almost every cell in your body. That's a lot of DNA, and it just loves to replicate itself. How much DNA is contained in the nucleus of one cell? Are you sitting down?" Dr. Frank looked over at her again.

"Still sitting. Eyes on the road, please. I happen to know the answer to that question. Six feet, about as tall as you."

"Smart girl. Now multiply six feet times forty trillion cells, calculate how many miles that makes, and how many times your own personal DNA molecules could stretch from the earth to the sun and back, take an aspirin, get some rest, and call me in the morning."

"Okay, Doctor, if you stop staring at Coco and watch the

road. I can hear you just fine." *Jesus, I'm the invisible back-seat driver in a car with no backseat.*

"Sorry, dear. Besides being distracted by Coco perched right next to me, the facts of this next discovery nearly stretched my mind out of my head. Scientists have created synthetic DNA and learned how to digitally store data on it. How much data? Still sitting down?'

"I'm still sitting!" Simone pointed out the windshield. "And you're still driving."

"215 petabytes of data—about 215 million billion bytes—in a *single* gram of DNA."

"Are you sure you got that figure right?"

"I read it over several times, but then, my brain's entire memory storage capacity is a measly 2.5 petabytes."

Simone shook her head. "I've never even heard of a pet-abyte."

"Neither had I."

"I do have two pets, but they don't bite."

"I can see I'm losing you, or are you losing it on your own?"

"Brain fluid is leaking out of my ears, but please go on."

"Bear with me. The CAFE is close, and the lecture's winding down. Only three more mind-boggling concepts to go. There's talk of organic computers made from DNA that can process data while *inside* a human body. Research-ers have developed DNA-based, miniscule, nano-mechani-cal devices able to control motion. DNA robot walkers can supposedly carry molecular cargo and deliver drugs inside the body." Dr. Frank let out a sigh. "So... back to the big question. How is it possible this phenomenon is happening with you?"

Simone took a stab at the answer. "I'd guess that some-one with unlimited resources and personnel has taken a precise selection of these tiny puzzle pieces and glued them together into a new picture on the box cover of my jigsaw puzzle. A quantum leap has occurred, and science fiction has evolved into science fact."

"I concur with that conclusion and couldn't have stated it better. I can envision the wonderful benefits for the psychiatric community. I remember you and I tossing around the concept of being a fly on the wall and clandestinely spying on our patients. However, an even bigger question looms. What will they do with this technology that allows them to really control another person? You can imagine all sorts of humorous situations on one end of the possibility spectrum, but on the perverse end? Impenetrable espionage, global masquerades, political manipulation leading up to an 'innocent' finger pressing the red button."

"Scary," Simone said. "Okay, the final question of the moment is... and I don't expect you to answer, but I need to know soon... Why choose *me* for this experiment? And why didn't they contact me? And why all the covert bullshit? Sorry, that was three questions. Seriously though, if they'd asked me first, I might've even agreed to do it."

Dr. Frank sighed as he turned the corner and slowed the car. "These people are indeed an unsavory lot, and to be bluntly nonacademic, I think the whole thing stinks. I'm worried about your well-being and your safety. Sorry to ignore you, Coconut. We're almost there. The CAFE is just down this block."

"Don't worry, Teddy," Coco answered. "It's all quite fascinating. I'm designing costumes in my head for the Hollywood movie. They should cast Richard Gere as you and Julia Roberts as Simone. Sharon Stone would make a perfect me."

"Dr. Frank and Coco," Simone said, "I have one request at this gathering. Forget about me. I'm off and you two are on. I don't exist. Please relax and enjoy yourselves. Okay?"

"We'll certainly have no trouble with that request!" Dr. Frank parked across the street from the CAFE as people stared, smiled, or pointed fingers at the Great Pumpkin. Walking through the guests mingling outside, the doctor pressed the flesh with the mayor and his wife, the police chief, the high school principal and his family, and several local business owners. He flashed a thumbs-up over the heads in the crowd to Diego, the official greeter for the event who motioned madly for him to hurry up.

As they walked up the sidewalk, Simone saw Laurel next to Diego welcoming folks at the double doors. *My vision today wasn't a dream. I am still connected to him.* Laurel was dressed the same as when Simone had seen her emerge from the bathroom, except for the new black t-shirt with white letters that still expressed her views but were more appropriate for a creative arts benefit: **I'll stop wearing black when they make a darker color.**

"Hey, Doctor Frank 'n'... Stein?" Diego gestured at Coco. "Theodore, buddy, she doesn't look like a Stein to me. Please introduce your enchanting companion."

Dr. Frank gripped Diego's arm while addressing Coco. "Diego Fierro, who has been instrumental in bringing this CAFE to life, I'd like you to meet Coco Montague, a very good friend from high school."

"I am delighted," Diego said with a slight bow as he kissed her hand.

"Nice to meet you," Coco said, blushing but reveling in the attention. "Are you an artist?"

"Yes, ma'am, the martial kind. All arts are welcome here. And Miss Coco, you'd best steer this man inside because he needs to be welcoming everyone in about ten minutes. And everyone who is anyone in this town is here."

Coconut took Teddy's hand and led him into the room. "So you're the man of the moment tonight, eh?"

"Oh, no. Just one of the men, and besides Diego, the *only* one who isn't afraid of a microphone. During a thousand lectures, my students may not have absorbed much, but at least I learned one useful thing. It's hard to believe that public speaking often ranks as people's number one fear, even ahead of death."

"Well, I'm not a big fan of getting up in front of people, but as the years wear on, death does sound comforting. Teddy Bear, I see guests with wine. I'd love a glass or two."

"Follow me, Coconut, and your wish will come true."

A renovated, red-brick historic building, the CAFE's premises had once been home to Foster's Pharmacy, General Store, and Soda Fountain. The first floor of the CAFE was a fusion of the present and the past. The original fountain counter sat on the left with its shiny stools and padded vinyl seats. Vintage Coca-Cola displays, framed automobile ads from the 1950s, and magazine covers featuring Norman Rockwell paintings lined the stucco wall behind it. The wall opposite the counter had been finished gallery-style with track lighting illuminating artwork created by participants in programs offered by the CAFE. Antique ceiling fans rotated above the high-school woodwind quintet performing a mix of classical and contemporary music. As predicted, guests were dressed in a motley assortment of attire. A frisky group of kids hawking raffle tickets circulated amongst the crowd. Some folks perused the silent auction items on tables across the room.

Dr. Frank and Coco joined the throng huddled near the fountain for the appetizers and wine-tasting carafes laid out on the counter. While he chatted with every person in his general vicinity, she sampled three wine varieties before settling on the fourth, a rich burgundy, and convinced the volunteer bartender to fill her glass to the brim.

Simone savored lounging in the background, though it

was odd to be surrounded by people she knew, including several of her patients, and friends she'd normally have engaged in conversation. *This feels like a masquerade but I'm the only one wearing a costume... a live costume.*

"Coconut," Teddy said, raising his glass. "A toast to us. I want you to know I didn't spend the entire afternoon researching the universe and Simone's big question. I thought a lot about the wonderful world where you and I once lived. Do you remember the big cosmic message which convinced us that we were made for each other?"

"Of course I do!" Coco clinked his glass and grinned. "Our garage door openers were on the same frequency! You'd drive by my house, press your remote, and suddenly my door would go up. Drove my dad nuts."

Teddy chuckled. "You performed our devious prank considerably more than I. My mother was convinced ghosts lived in the garage and wouldn't even get in the car until my father had backed it out. That suited him just fine because he could have as much man-time in his workshop whenever he wanted."

Diego patted Dr. Frank on the shoulder. "Okay, Dr. MC. It's time. You want me to gather the minds of our guests?"

"Why not? I'd rather not be the only face of the CAFE."

In the center of the far wall, the stairway leading to the second floor served as a raised stage. Diego waited until the quintet finished their piece, grabbed the mic and yelled as he mounted the steps, "Yo! Listen up! Everybody in this zip code! Our dear friend and founder has a few warm words for you, and will clue you in on what's hap'nin' here tonight. So please put your paws together for—try not to spill your wine now—Dr. Theodore Frank!"

A smattering of applause filled the air. Accepting the mic from Diego, Dr. Frank whispered, "Ah, the inimitable Fierro style." He faced his audience as he'd done so often at the university and paused until they quieted down.

"Thank you so much for coming and supporting our new charitable venture, Creative Arts For Everyone. As we neglected to print a schedule, I'd like to give you a quick rundown of the events. In forty-five minutes the silent auction will close so make your final bids by then, and please don't erase any bids that are higher than yours." He paused again until the snickers from his audience verified they'd gotten his quip. "At 6:30 we'll adjourn to the second floor where the raffle and auction winners will be announced, and you'll be treated to a showcase of talents in our new performance space—a real stage with real seats for a real audience. And after the screening of the final three short films in our CAFE Canned Film Festival, you folks will be our esteemed judges and choose the winner. First place takes home a new MacBook computer donated by Albright Pharmaceuticals which will be presented by their vice president, Paul Roberts."

Hearing the name Albright Pharmaceuticals sent a shiver through Simone. *Bah. Fake philanthropy, for sure. Bogus compassion from merciless merchants. But Tall Paul is here? How'd I miss him?* Paul Roberts had been a close friend of her father, and she'd known him for thirty years. Simone searched the room and saw him leaning against the picture windows. At six-foot-six, he was easy to spot in a crowd.

Despite holding up two posters, Dr. Frank still managed to speak into the microphone. "We're introducing two new programs I doubt you'll find anywhere else in the world. In our Art of Life series, Conan Carlson will be leading a hands-on, self-defense course on Saturdays called 'Try to Bully Me and I'll Rearrange Your Face.'" Dr. Frank motioned to Conan who stood to the right of the stairs. "Do you have any comments about your new course?"

Conan clenched both fists above his head, flexed his biceps, and growled at the crowd. Two thin adolescent nerds in the front high-fived each other and shouted, "Yes!"

"In the Fine Arts series, our resident avant-garde sculptor and graffiti artist, Sonya Dynamite, is offering an inspirational course for all ages on Tuesdays entitled 'Art as a Kick-ass Career.'" Dr. Frank gestured to Sonya on the floor in front of the stairway. "Any words for your prospective participants, Sonya?"

"I apologize if the title offends anyone," Sonya said from the middle of the crowd, "but catchy names beef up the attendance. Any wannabe artists in any genre are welcome. C'mon down and do your thing. We'll figure out how you can do what you love and still pay the rent."

"I might join that course myself," Dr. Frank said. "Since I have a bit more time on my hands, I should resurrect my easel from the storage closet. Once again, thank you all for coming and remember... every penny from every donation or purchase goes directly to the kids, our facilities, and our programs. Our volunteers' only compensation is the joy of giving and sharing."

Dr. Frank wound his way through a flurry of pats on the back, sidled up to Coconut, and took a healthy sip of wine. "Okay, I'm out of the spotlight. For the rest of the evening, my spotlight will be on you."

Coco entwined her arm around her Teddy Bear's. "You're just as charming here as you were up there."

Paul Roberts came up behind Frank and tapped him on the shoulder.

The doctor turned to find himself looking at the caps of three perfectly aligned fountain pens clipped into the breast pocket of an ink-stained, pin-stripe shirt. "Ah, Paul, there you are!" he said, craning his neck to look up into a face lined with anxiety. "Hey, are you OK?"

"Y-yes," Paul dissembled, handing Frank a buff envelope. "I want to give you our quarterly donation check because I must rush off before the award presentation."

"If you insist, but first let me introduce you to my companion here. Coconut, meet Tall Paul Roberts, one of our most consistent donors."

"Pleased to make your acquaintance, Miss Coconut."

Coco raised her wine glass and spoke in a manner that betrayed her semi-woozy state. "Same here. My name is Coco, and that's the way the world knows me. Coconut is a nickname reserved only for my Teddy Bear here."

"All right then," Paul said, his pursed lips concealing a smirk. "Dr. Theodore Bear, you need to revise one statement you made. I haven't been VP at Albright for months. They brought in a new management team and demoted me to Financial Controller. I never cared for being the president of vice anyway. At least I can still deal a few donation cards into your hands."

"Well, they, and you, are much appreciated." Dr. Frank reached up to Paul's shoulder and drew him down to his level. "How's the CEO doing these days? I heard some time ago that his days were numbered."

"The company is trying everything to keep him alive. ALS has no cure at this point, but he's still hanging in there."

"I forget the man's name..."

"Simon Albright."

"Oh, yes." Dr. Frank turned his head and squinted at nothing. "Hmm... Why does that suddenly sound familiar." He glanced over at Coco and asked, "Simone, what was your surname in college before you decided to—"

Simone via Coco's foot silenced Dr. Frank with a kick in the ankle.

"Simone?" Paul asked, his chin down and eyebrows up. "Pardon me, but I thought your name was Coconut... or

Coco... which rings a bell."

"Simone's my middle name," Coco said. "Last name's Montague."

"I see. Ding, ding," Paul chimed.

"You ever live in Hollywood? I used to write for the newspaper. Maybe those are the bells you're hearing."

"Different belfry I believe, but thanks for the information. After a brief hesitation he drew a MacBook from under his arm, stooping to add in a lowered voice, "Dr. Frank, here's the MacBook. Please extend my absence apologies to the winner who won't care a whit about me anyway. Excuse me now, but I'd better mingle a bit before I disappear."

"Thanks so much," Dr. Frank said to the back of Paul's striped shirt as it melded in with the other guests. "Sorry, Simone. I'd like to blame the wine for the slip of the tongue, but I'm afraid—"

"Forget about it. Sorry to kick you like that. Coconut, thanks for trying to cover for your Teddy Bear. Paul's a good man. Sharp as a tack but dulled by Albright Pharmaceuticals. He knows something about this. He knows I am in Coco. I can feel it in my bones... wherever they happen to be right now."

Dr. Frank leaned in close. "Now that no one's around, what was your original surname?"

"Albright. Simon is my twin brother." She paused to let that sink into his stunned ears. "We drifted apart into two different worlds... terminally. Like you, I didn't want to be associated with the family name anymore."

With every word that Simone spoke, Dr. Frank's face seemed to melt further into dismay and shock. "Oh, my God," he whispered to himself. "What have I done?"

Simone's father Abram founded Albright Laboratories, an

innovative and respected medical research facility devoted to curing disease and helping humanity. Paul Roberts had been with Albright Laboratories from the start. His financial and organizational wizardry freed Abram to focus on the science and healing. As a toddler, Simone might accompany her father to work, and when he'd vanish into his lab for hours at a time, Paul was there for her, like her personal Jungle Jim she could climb on. He'd never married, but "Uncle" Paul became an integral part of the Albright family.

In their late forties while "vacationing" as participants in a Doctors Without Borders project in South America, Abram and Nova Albright died when their single-prop plane crashed in the jungles of Paraguay, and Simon took over the company.

Contrary to Paul's advice, Simon redirected the company's benevolent mission to developing pills and placebos for the populace. He assimilated marketing tactics from Madison Avenue—create a problem, fuel the fear, sell the solution—and fabricated new disorders and syndromes that the company's products could mitigate or mask. Whenever Simone read the latest list of bizarre phobias, she'd wonder which names Simon had coined. His best income-generators were the drugs prescribed with a lifetime of daily payments, till death do they part. This supported the key concept to which he subscribed: "A patient cured is a customer lost."

Simon incorporated the company and changed the name to Albright Pharmaceuticals, peddled inadequately tested drugs to lenient, loophole-laden countries around the globe, and raked in millions of dollars. Neither the drugs nor the pseudo disorders nor the connection to the reckless, stinking-rich corporation with the debased Albright reputation resonated with Simone, so she chose the surname Wellstone when she began her practice as an Empathiatrist. The fact that brother Simon had obliterated the legacy of their father still tore her up inside.

Coconut and her Teddy Bear strolled over to the silent auction and browsed through the offerings. He bid on anything that caught her eye.

Dr. Sugar Daddy and his sweetheart in a candy store. Here I am again, a merry matchmaker, the master of synchronicity. I'll have to add the title to my business card. I do hope he can afford her and give her a reason to live.

Simone had been Dr. Frank's assistant when his wife passed in her fifties. Shaken to the core, he tried to fill the hole in his heart with work. Though surrounded by good friends and adoring students, the centerpiece of his contentment always seemed to be missing.

While Teddy and Coconut hunched over and bid on an abstract painting of a unicorn, a hand attached to a long arm set a folded sheet of paper on the table in front of them. After reading the single word on it—Simone—she looked up as the messenger disappeared into the crowd, his head bent down above the guests.

Simone picked up the sheet, opened it, and recognized Tall Paul's handwriting. Unlike his normal precise style, this note appeared to be scribbled in haste with erratic spaces between the words and the lines.

Dearest Simone,
I am so sorry. Only two days left.
I tried to stop this project before it started. Beware of
your brother. Like you control Coco, he can control me and
other people as well. Please do not look at me or talk to me.
His eyes and ears are everywhere.

Simone stood motionless as an ice sculpture, her brain burning with outrage. If Coco had tried to move even one of her muscles, it wouldn't have responded. *How fucking dense am I? How deep into denial have I dropped? My nightmares, my pathetic empathetic intuition, the subtle hints and blazing arrows pointing to the perpetrator. All useless. And his goddamn eyes and ears are everywhere?*

Snapping back to her surroundings, she faced Dr. Frank and mimed the see-no-evil, hear-no-evil, speak-no-evil monkeys, and threw in a zip-your-lips sign as an exclamation mark. Mimicking Coco's sing-song, happy voice, Simone issued her imperative. "C'mon, Teddy Bear. Let's look at the rest of these delightful silent auction items together. It's so wonderful to be alone with you even though we're in a crowd."

What does Simon the Shit want with me? If he wants to continue living in my body after he dies, then why isn't he practicing his control over me now? Maybe I'm the subject of a macabre experiment because he too inherited some of mother's paranormal skills and wants to witness the control abilities in action but without the risk. Why didn't he ask me first? Because he's a egotistic dickhead and knew I'd refuse. I can already hear his feeble, two-faced snivelings. "Gee whiz, I thought you'd love experiencing a few lives and helping them more effectively and then using this amazing technique with all of your patients." Okay, Miss Compassion. Suspend your beliefs, even though your disbeliefs are overwhelming. He's still the frail little boy afraid of dying and he needs my help. This is a breakthrough to cracking the genetic code and finding a cure. Sorry, disbelief crushes that belief. He's going to monetize this for all its worth. Money is no object because he can taste the billions this technology will demand. And that explains the secrecy. First one to market makes the killing, and we're merely disposable pawns in his vile venture. And who else is he controlling? His egghead minions? Ming? His buddy the senator? Key players in his international network of plutocrats? God help us all.

Diego's voice blaring through the speakers snatched Simone from her grim diatribe. "You have three minutes to place your final bids in the silent auction. Any bidders caught wrestling over the pen will be disqualified. Please make your way up this stairway to the next station on our long and winding CAFE road. No beverage service upstairs, but you can bring your drinks to our performance area. Feel free to slip ten or twenty appetizers in your pocket."

Before Paul's note appeared, Coco had been the sole conveyor of wine from glass to tongue. Simone had doubled its distribution during her internal rant. As Coco started up the steps, her legs wavered, and she braced herself on Dr. Frank's arm for the rest of the uphill trek.

I could feel the effects of Coco's drinking earlier, but not to this degree. Gotta watch what we're doing more closely.

As they reached the top of the stairs, Simone felt something being pressed into her left palm, ending with a light squeeze of her fingers as if a father were wishing his daughter good luck before a marathon. She forced herself not to look, but as Dr. Frank selected their seats, Simone caught a glimpse of Tall Paul in the shadows leaning on a wooden support column. The stage, lights, and screen were set on the short end of the space with a hundred-some folding chairs stretching toward the back of the room and divided by one middle aisle where Dr. Frank and Coco sat. After giving her hosts another zip-it sign, Simone unfolded the second note.

> They spy on you via their drones, EDNA delivery trucks, and the black GPS tracker on your wrist which also contains a microphone to pick up your voice and sounds around you. They want to be sure you're alive and well, for now at least. When you're hidden inside a building, take off the watch and turn up the tunes. If you venture outside, be invisible. Your next patient is a young man named Raphael on the same list as Coco. Saturday's name was crossed off. I'm scheduled to pick you up at eleven on Sunday morning and take you to see Simon. FYI: the EDNA company is a facade, another of Simon's schemes to secretly move things around. It stands for Enhanced DNA.

Her head still reeling from the first note's revelations and effects of the wine, Simone didn't notice that Coco had reached into her purse and taken two more pills.

What's he getting at? Does he expect me to go out and do something? Dr. Frank was right on track with his very, very tiny things lecture. Enhanced DNA? It sounds guilty until proven innocent by the FDA.

The lights dimmed, Diego introduced the first act, music blared from the speakers, and six teenage girls rocked the house with a ballet-meets-hip-hop-dance routine. Their rousing performance distracted Simone from her dilemma for a spell, then the second act nearly put her to sleep—a trombone solo by a small lad a tad larger than his instrument. After dedicating the song to Jesus, he played three plodding, wordless verses of "Amazing Grace," each one identical with no accompaniment, no dance steps, and no charisma. His parents applauded wildly for an encore; the rest of the guests clapped lightly with relief that the honking had ceased.

Simone knew the words to the song, and one phrase echoed in her mind. *"I once was lost, but now I'm found, was blind but now I see." Paul found me, or vice versa, and now I see bit of the puzzle. But I'm more like one of the five blind men who touched different parts of the elephant and none of them had a clue about the big picture.*

During the third act—a mime artist trapped in a box that kept getting smaller and smaller which made Simone silently scream "Stop already!"—Paul crept down the middle aisle on his knees as if recording the performer with his smartphone. He held the phone with his left hand, slipped another note into Simone's lap with his right, and then retraced his crawl backwards into the shadows.

This is the last note tonight. I'll try to find out more info and put it in an envelope. By noon tomorrow I'll tape it to the underside of the Discount Trader newspaper dispenser in front of the 7/11 store on Hickok Road and third avenue. Good luck and be careful. People at Albright have been disappearing. You are a survivor. Now please destroy this note.

The sentences on this note had been scribbled as sloppily and irregularly spaced as the last two. *He's paranoid as hell and writing these in the dark or while looking somewhere else or talking to someone to distract his eyes from the page because Paul said Simon can control him... and other people. But not everyone at once, all the time, I hope... God forbid. And now he's talking about survival? People disappearing? God help me. Someone help me.* Simone could feel her thoughts getting as erratic as Paul's notes, like her brain had detached and was slogging behind through a bog.

Exposing her inebriated state, Coconut leaned into her Teddy Bear, collided with his head, and announced, "I'm going to find the ladiesh room." She stood too quickly and grabbed the back of the chair for support. Clutching the handrail on her way down the stairs, Coco said, "Shimone, I don' need a bathroom. I need a shmoke. Let's go outshide."

Jesus, we're both the walking wounded here. Pull yourself together, Simone. You need to save both of us.

Breathing the fresh crisp air outside the CAFE building cleared Simone's head a bit, and while smoking the cigarette, she was reminded of Tina, her best friend in high school. They bought a pack of Camel Lights halfway through their senior year and pledged to finish it by the end of the semester. Once in a while they'd take two or three puffs to get dizzy. At a graduation party they shared the final cigarette and too many margaritas. That was the last she'd smoked besides the one she'd suffered through that morning outside the mall with Coco.

Simon had been with Simone at that party to celebrate their latest achievement together. Despite their brother-sister trials and spats, they'd been close in their teens. He seemed to have inherited more of their father's analytical, calculating left-brain traits whereas Simone took after her mother: emotional, intuitive, compassionate, driven by the heart. He was academically ahead of his class and kept his distance from those he'd decided possessed inferior mental capacity—those being everyone else in the school. Simone became heavily involved in social activities and made many friends, but Simon was a lone wolf, and often a lame one plagued by physical problems.

We were good friends back then. He never hurt me intentionally, and I always helped him. There must still be goodness left in him. Simone's foggy mind floated through their years together, but came to a standstill at a bonfire of enmity ignited by their final contact, a snapshot in her soul she desired never to revive.

Two years earlier, she'd visited Simon at Albright Pharmaceuticals. Bed-ridden and broken, he lapsed in and out of consciousness as the ALS ravaged his nervous system, slurred his speech, and disabled the muscles throughout his body. While Simone swabbed his forehead with a wet cloth and gazed into his sad, helpless eyes, Simon had slipped away into yet another comatose state. She left the intensive care unit, wandered through the halls of Albright, and noticed a row of metal cages housing dogs, monkeys, and small rodents. She peered through the glass door of the lab next to them and witnessed the hidden horrors of Simon and the corporation he controlled.

Strapped to an operating table, an Irish setter lay on its back, a dead specimen with its chest sliced open, its head and neck lashed down, its legs splayed out on both sides. It might as well have been her precious Brandy being tortured on the table. Like the day decades before when Simon had been killing and flicking the ants, Simone burst into tears, covering her face with her hands as she rushed down the hallway and out of the building. It was the last time she'd had any contact with Simon, and on that day, Simone vowed to never see her brother again.

Coco threw the cigarette butt onto the sidewalk and tried to crush it with her shoe. She missed, tried again, and lost her balance, but hung onto the railing and remained upright.

A shudder vibrated Simone's body as she forced the brutal memory from her mind. Squinting to focus her blurred vision, she spotted an EDNA truck parked on the next block. As she stared, the branches of the trees transformed into writhing snakes like those on Medusa's head. Anxiety-laced nausea crept up from her stomach. Fatigue and restlessness battled each other in her limbs.

We're not just feeling the wine. We're feeling the contraindications of drugs combined with alcohol, plus I have no idea what pills loco Coco has popped. I need to take control now, even though everything seems out of control. I am in need, and where is my friend indeed? And who? Simone considered people on her close friend list, but imagined the immediate bewilderment and potential danger to them in the near future. *Who can I trust? Office Eddie? Diego? Diego... Yes, Diego. Wildiego, the Able Cainraiser. He will believe, and he will help.*

Coco had become inert, back to the same state Simone had experienced upon her awakening that morning. Stabilizing her vertigo with a hand on the doorway, Simone stepped carefully inside the building. The high heels didn't help, so she kicked them off and continued barefoot. She hobbled to the fountain counter and hoisted her numb buttocks onto the stool. Fumbling through Coco's purse for a pen, she found Paul's final note. Simone read it again, memorized the location of the envelope drop, and crumpled it. As she pried open Coco's multi-slot, plastic organizer, some pills spilled onto the floor. No labels in the slots, just an assortment of blue, pink, yellow and white tablets. She located a pen in a side pocket along with Paul's second note and slapped them both on the counter. Like a baby who can't quite control its head, Simone scanned for any prying eyes to her left and right, then flipped over the paper and scrawled a plea of her own. Her lethargic hand could barely hold the pen.

Diego, my former patient, the Able Cainraiser,

Please suspend your beliefs and challenge your disbeliefs. This is beyond anything you can imagine. I am Dr. Simone Wellstone and I need help. Right now I am trapped inside my patient Coco's body against my will. Yesterday I was inside YOU, against my will. The day before that I was inside controlling another young patient of mine. I was your treatment. I was there when you woke up and kicked Jimmy into the wall. I was there when you picked up your birthday bike. I pedaled you to my office when you saw Ming. I watched through your eyes when you wrangled the drunken monkeys. I heard through your ears when you and Laurel were on the porch, and she whispered, "I'm not in between. I'm a woman." I need a friend and have no one else to turn to. Tomorrow I expect to find myself inside another patient and then will try to find you. The other side of this note was given to me by sympathetic friend who works at the corporation that's responsible for this wretched treatment program. If I can contact you tomorrow while I'm in another person, please listen with an open mind and heart. I don't know how you can help, but please, please believe me. And please, please, please do not tell ANYONE ELSE about this!

Sincerely and scared shitless, Dr. Simone

She folded the paper to conceal its contents and wrote six words in bold capitals in the blank space. PLEASE READ THIS LATER... BUT SOON! Simone eased her torpid legs off the stool, shuffled to the bathroom, tore Paul's third note into scraps, and flushed it down the toilet. Fighting an overpowering urge to lie on the floor, she leaned on the wash basin, splashed water on her twitching face, and inhaled deeply several times to gather her remaining energy. The black watch on Coco's wrist caught her eye.

I doubt I can overcome this onslaught of complications. I'm too fucking weak and my loss of muscle control is spreading. And I doubt Coconut wants to part with her Teddy Bear right now, once and for all. The emergency room at a hospital? No. I don't want to be another miscellaneous slab of meat forced to fill out forms for an hour. I'll deliver my message to Diego and press the black button. As Paul wrote, "They want to be sure you're alive and well, for now at least." If I don't finish my mission now, there might not be any later.

She drew in another deep breath, turned to grasp the door knob, maneuvered Coco's failing body into the main room, and slowly side-stepped toward the stairway, hugging the wall as if sliding along a narrow ledge on the outside of a skyscraper.

The volunteer behind the counter rushed over to her. "Are you okay? Can I help?"

"No, I'm not okay, and yes, you can help. Please get me up these stairs to Diego."

With both hands on the railing and the volunteer's arm around her waist, Simone coaxed her anesthetized legs to haul her body up to the second floor. The room was now dimly lit by a blue haze from the screening of the first short film and reverberating with Carl Orff's "Fortuna Imperatrix" from *Carmina Burana*.

"Diego's in the back behind the sound board. Shall I get him?"

"No, I don't want to disrupt the show. Thank you. I can make it from here." *Like a zombie complete with a Halloween sound track.* Holding the note in one outstretched arm and Coco's pill box in the other, she shuffled up to Diego.

He looked up from the mixing console, and his expression sagged in concern the closer she came. "You don't look good. Lemme get you a chair."

"Stop. I don't know how many moments I have left." Simone pointed to the black watch on her wrist. "The treatment program. The same watch you wore yesterday... I'm gonna press the emergency button, and they will come. They're just down the block. But first..." She held up the note in front of Diego's face and waited until he read the six words, nodded in agreement, and put the note in his shirt pocket. Summoning her final modicum of strength, Simone grabbed his hand and wrapped his fingers around the pill organizer. "Here's Coco's medicine... Give it to whoever comes..." She sucked in a short breath. "Tell 'em she drank a screwdriver for breakfast, another for lunch, and I dunno how many glasses of wine tonight. See you tomorrow, I hope." Simone pressed the button on the watch as her legs gave out, her knees buckled, and her brain surrendered to debility.

Diego caught her and carried the limp body to a mat on the floor behind the sound board. Two paramedics arrived three minutes later. As a gurney carted Simone across the ground floor and outside, her consciousness blinked on and off like a slow strobe light. Through moist slits between her eyelids, she caught a glimpse of Dr. Frank's distraught face, of a rotating ceiling fan, of Diego conferring with a stranger, of the waving snake trees, of the yellow rear door of an EDNA truck, of a mini-ICU the size of a cubicle like the one in her recent dreams. And for five seconds before total shutdown, Simone glared at the tousled hair and Cimmerian eyes of Hunter, the paramedic inserting the IV into her vein—the Hunter who'd delivered her complimentary meal from Damian's Deli and initiated her downfall.

Day 4

Friday

A FAINT MALODOR OF MEDICINAL RUBBING ALCOHOL and gasoline tainted the customary hint of incense seasoning the living room. Gusts of wind in the darkness outside seemed to shake the walls and whisper to Simone, deep in sleep. "Simon says. Simon says."

Simone lay on the recliner where she'd eaten her last deli supper, shaking her head in bewilderment while wading through the book *Human Genetic Engineering: A Guide for Activists, Skeptics, and the Very Perplexed*. Alert at her feet with ears perked, Dammit and Brandy exchanged grunts and growls. As Simone let out a long sigh and glanced up from the book, she detected motion on the opposite end of the room. Brow taut, she rose from the recliner and walked toward the windows while the dogs crept beside her. Suddenly Dammit barked, sprinted ahead to the right, and put his paws up on the sill. Brandy raced to the left window, bared her teeth, and pounded her snout on the pane, snarling viciously, her saliva dripping down the glass. A black and yellow drone hovered in the shadows outside each rear window. A quick scan around the room revealed another drone at the side window and two more floating outside the picture window behind the recliner.

She yanked the cord to close the front curtains, lowered the window blinds, grabbed the steel poker from the fireplace, and stormed to the front door. With Dammit and Brandy flanking both ankles, Simone jerked open the door and stepped onto the cement landing. A fleet of five EDNA trucks were parked at the curb. The two drones at the picture window turned toward her, joined moments later by the others. Each had two beady camera eyes attached to a crab-like body with four outstretched legs beneath four circular rotors. As the dogs howled, she lifted the poker above her head to strike the swarm but her arm froze in position, like a medieval queen with an upraised sword leading troops into battle... or a novice conductor preparing to direct an unruly quintet of robotic bumble bees. Try as she might, Simone couldn't control her arm muscles, though she could hear the EDNA truck drivers laughing.

Moments later, her arm went limp and dropped to her side. With a determined grimace, she herded the dogs inside, slammed the door, set down the poker, and picked up her iPhone. She punched in a 9, then a 1, but her hand froze mid-motion, her forefinger suspended a centimeter above the final 1. Once again she'd lost control to another force manipulating her body.

The manipulator set down the iPhone onto the coffee table and picked up the poker. He tested its heft and feigned a few lunges at Dammit who recoiled in confusion. After tapping the poker on the table as if testing its strength, he placed its sharp tip in the soft spot underneath Simone's chin, stroking the skin and stoking her fear. "Simon says watch your step, sister dear," he hissed.

Simone's eyes widened in terror and disbelief as she struggled in vain to regain control.

The manipulator slowly lowered the poker and regripped it with both hands as if it were a yard-long ice pick. "Simon did *not* say..."—he raised the handle vertically above his head—"call 911!"—then plunged the poker through the phone, burying it into the recesses of the coffee table. He snapped Simone's body upright and released control. She toppled onto the recliner as the fragments of the phone began to ring an unfamiliar tune.

In synch with her new host, Simone awoke Friday morning at dawn to a sublime and haunting Azan, the Islamic Call to Worship sung by a priest on a hilltop and echoing through the valley below. The peaceful scene defused the scream she'd been ready to unleash in her dream, though the last conscious moments at the benefit streamed in. *Where am I? Not at home. In that EDNA truck? In Coco? No. It must be tomorrow morning. SOS DD.*

Lying on his back with eyes still closed, her host stretched an arm from the two-inch-thick mat on the floor and silenced the smartphone alarm tone with one fingertip. He took a full breath of the brisk morning air, rolled off the mat onto his knees, and bowed his head to the floor three times while chanting, "Allah is the greatest. God is the greatest. Yahweh is the greatest." He kept his knees close together, heels beside the buttocks, then sat on his legs and the soles of his feet. Assuming the yogic Diamond Pose, he placed his hands on his waist, thumbs pointing backward, fingers forward, and began to meditate.

Although Simone's mind had calmed, the memories of her session with this patient intruded upon the stillness. *I must be in Rafi who Paul called Raphael in his second note— a sweet young man with a horrific past. I hope his recent life has been less grisly than the chapters he shared with me.*

Two months earlier, Hawthorne High and the entire community had entered a list that didn't exist when Simone attended her alma mater, a list every town dreaded to occupy—School Shootings in America. Around one p.m. on a Monday afternoon, sixteen-year-old Dennis Scruggs had complained in class about stomach pains and left the premises. Preparing at home for his mission, Dennis shredded his stepfather, emptying an entire 30-round magazine of an AR-15 into his body before returning to school. He knew the security guard routine and entered undetected just before classes ended. Calmly walking the hallways while strafing walls and windows with bullets, Dennis seemed to be in no hurry yet hell-bent on destroying the building as much as its inhabitants. He killed two students in the cafeteria and severely injured eleven more before taking his own life in the theater.

Dr. Simone had phoned the principal and offered to help with anything she could, pro bono. One week after the carnage, she spent the day meeting with a steady stream of students and teachers who'd signed up for counselling sessions. In an attempt to put her distressed teenage clients at ease, she wore penny loafers, torn Levi's, a purple t-shirt sporting the Hawthorne Hawks mascot she'd extracted from her memorabilia box, balanced by a navy-blue blazer to suggest a modicum of psychological expertise. In between sessions at the school while jotting notes about the previous student, Simone sat on a low metal stool near the front of an unused classroom populated only by rows of desk chair combos. She didn't hear the door open.

"Ahem... Ma'am?"

Simone's head sprung up followed by her whole body. With pen and notebook in hand, she walked toward the swarthy, wiry young man standing straight as his thin necktie, the vertical pinstripes on his long-sleeved shirt, and the precise crease on his trousers. One hand jingled keys in his pocket while the fingers of the other drummed on his thigh. "Good morning!" Simone said, extending her arm. "Please come in!"

"I am already in."

"Yes, yes, you certainly are. Sorry, I didn't hear you."

"I walk softly and speak softly but do not carry a big stick like President Teddy Roosevelt."

"Well, speaking softly is splendid but I never cared for the big stick part. I'm Dr. Simone Wellstone and..." She checked the schedule taped to her notebook. "And you must be the science teacher, Mr. Raphael Mansur, age 24." She smiled and met his eyes. "And that's all I know about you." *Looks older, seems older.*

"I am he, but Rafi will do."

"And Simone will do for me." *I doubt he's from the US but his English is perfect with no accent.* She gestured to the front of the room and strolled forward. "Please have a seat." She turned and pointed to a desk chair next to her stool.

Glancing to the left and right, Rafi hadn't quite made it to the front. "Would you mind if I take that chair in the corner?"

"Of course. Whatever is best for you." *Wary like a cat exploring a foreign room.*

Rafi sat with his back to the wall, pulled his chair a few inches closer to Simone's stool, and tried to figure out what to do with his hands. "What type of doctor are you, if I might ask?"

"In general, psychology. Specifically, an empathiatrist."

"I have not heard that word. What is an empathiatrist?"

"Do you know what an empath is?"

Staring out the window, he thought for a moment. "I think it must be... someone who can actually feel what another person is feeling. Am I correct?"

"Yes, and I think only one percent of the population on earth knows what it means. Empath is the 'speak softly' part of the title and 'iatrist' is the big-stick psychiatric certificate on the wall."

"What am I feeling now?" he entreated, looking directly into Simone's eyes. His black-brown irises seemed to enlarge the black pupils into wide pools of emptiness waiting to be filled.

"Okay..." *He asked for it. Give it to him.* "I just felt a sigh of relief inside your body when you folded your hands together, set them on your lap, and relaxed your shoulders." As she spoke, Simone noticed the disfigured skin on his neck peeking above his collar and the scars on his scalp he'd trained his hair to cover. "I can feel a tight knot here, just above your navel." She touched her own body while describing his. "It doesn't really hurt, but it's uncomfortable. The muscles on your back next to the spine ache and transmit the pain to the base of your skull."

"You are right," he said, somewhat stunned. "You can actually feel my pain in your body?"

"Yes, strange but true. And sometimes these feelings come as mental images." She closed her eyes, hesitating a few seconds while her internal vision materialized. "I'm imagining a new house you recently painted but are still renovating inside. It's surrounded by a tidy yard and a strong wire fence at the perimeter that you can see through. Many rooms are stocked with textbooks and reference books and files..." She paused. "And a small room with scrapbooks and souvenirs from your travels..." She paused again, tightening her closed lids. "In the basement, storage boxes have been buried and covered with cement, but something... or someone from a box has escaped and is taunting you."

"Hmm." Since arriving, Rafi's expression had been lifeless, a composed portrait of his face, but now his lips slipped into a thin grin. "How perceptive you are. And I think that someone must be me."

"Maybe now you trust me enough to talk about *you* instead of asking questions about *me*."

"PTSD."

"PTSD?" His response lit up Simone as if she'd been presented a surprise gift. "You're experiencing Post-traumatic Stress Disorder? Don't worry. At Hawthorne High right now, it's quite common."

"In my case we must alter the P-word to Perpetual."

"*Perpetual* Traumatic Stress Disorder? Well, I doubt it'll last that long, Rafi. I believe it's possible to cure or at least relieve it."

"I was created in chaos and disorder."

"Okay, talk to me." She surrendered with a sigh. *Shut up, Simone. You sound like a hopeful but hopeless cheerleader. Remember? Rearrange the letters of the word listen, and they spell silent.*

"My early life story is quite different than those experienced in the USA. I was born in Iraq during the reign of Saddam Hussein, near the city of Samarra about sixty miles north of Baghdad. The catastrophe last week was terrible and traumatic, but compared to over half of my years on this planet, it was just business as usual... and it did not even last very long."

"I'd like to hear about that, but let's start with last week. Did you know this Dennis Scruggs? Some people have described him as 'a quiet kid who just snapped.'"

"He was a student of mine, a lost soul I thought, straggling behind the rest. I tried to help him after classes. He did not know basic facts and skills most students absorbed long before high school, like addition and multiplication tables, how many items in a dozen, the names of a few planets, how to write cursive. I know he attempted to study, but whatever knowledge he acquired seemed to slip away, as if his brain cells were coated with Teflon. Tests tortured him, and he failed them with one flying color... red check marks. No one called him Dennis, just 'Dense.' The two students killed were probably the worst bullies in the school. Dennis did not snap. I believe the kids snapped him with their constant harassment, in person and online."

"I tend to think social media does more alienating than mediating."

"I agree. The computer seemed to be his only friend, and he was an absolute whiz at video games. Dennis could not focus in class, but he seemed to meld with a screen. I tried to interest him in mathematics or English educational games instead of slaughtering enemies and monsters."

"I wish I could have met him, months ago. Let's get back to you and PTSD. What happened on that day through your eyes?"

"Okay." Rafi gathered his thoughts, rested his elbows on his knees, set his chin on his folded hands, and stared at the floor. "I was in the theater helping construct sets for the school play, *The Mouse That Roared*. We heard rapid gunfire, screaming, doors slamming, windows breaking, the clatter of footsteps. Everyone either ran out the back or sought safe hiding places like we had been instructed to do during active shooter drills. I chose a pathetic position crouched into a ball and encircled by the bunched up curtains, stage left." As he recounted the experience, Rafi's whole body had bunched up. He appeared smaller, younger.

"Dennis stalked down the aisle, aiming the AK-15 at the spotlights and anything that appeared to move even though the room was deathly still. He climbed the side stair onto the stage and then stopped to shout at the top of his lungs, at no one. I saw his tormented face through a slit in the curtains. I heard him panting. He was only a foot away from me. I could have grabbed him, and then what?" Rafi extended both hands, palms up, as if pleading innocence. "I am not a fighter; I am a teacher. I do not have a violent cell in my body! I was petrified with fear, eleven years old again with the last words my father ever said to me looping through my mind." Rafi's voice trembled as he spoke them. "'Do not move. Do not make a sound. Be invisible and you will survive.' Seconds later the police stormed through both front doors and spread out into the rows of seats. A few shots were fired. The final shot came from Dennis... with a pistol in his mouth... and... and then his blood, bone, and brains spattered on the red curtain where I cowered... I burst into tears."

Neither he nor Simone spoke for a full minute. It felt like ten.

In his apartment, Rafi inhaled deeply, blinked his eyes, and began to rise from the Diamond Pose. To determine the extent of control over her new host, Simone stood, raised his arms, balanced his right sole on his thigh, and held the Tree Pose for thirty seconds. She released control, and Rafi stepped into the bathroom, seemingly unaware of any interruption in his actions or thoughts.

Simone then turned her host to the left and circled around his one-room, one-window, efficiency apartment. *Well, he certainly lives a Spartan existence. Is everything he owns in this room? A book shelf, Scrabble game, framed desert photo on the wall, clothes rack, double-drawer dresser, a folding table with one wooden folding chair, a laptop, a sleeping mat, acoustic guitar, bicycle... excellent, we're gonna use that later... tiny microwave, blender, toaster oven, a mini fridge... and what's this?* She bent down to scrutinize a white handwritten poster taped to the fridge door. A mechanical pencil on a string attached to a magnet hung next to the poster. Beneath the headline, "The 100 Things Challenge," a hundred individual things were numbered in a list. Some item names had been carefully erased and replaced with new ones. Everything she'd viewed in the apartment was on the list. The titles of each book on the shelf—*Qur'an, Bible, Supersymmetry and String Theory,* Krishnamurti's *Think on These Things* plus six others. A fork, a spoon, a table knife, and a utility knife. Numbered items of clothing with each pair counting as one. Toiletries constituted one thing as did 'bike and bike supplies.' *Rafi must be trying to balance his perpetual disorder with absolute order. And judging by my sense of his whole being, he's succeeding.*

"Rafi, I need your help today. May I borrow your bicycle?" Simone paused for a response. None. "And I'd like to communicate somehow with another patient of mine." *Huh. The same as Diego. No resistance, no reaction. On or off like a light switch with no dimmer.* Once again she released him, and he padded into the bathroom.

A framed, multicolored chart of The Periodic Table of Elements hung next to the mirror over the sink. The sheet of instructions for today's treatment leaned against the mirror. Rafi read it and set it aside.

While he washed and groomed, Simone noticed the changes in Rafi since she'd last seen him. *The fear and confusion in his eyes have subsided. His hair's longer, free to grow as he wants, not as the administration demands—still orderly, but a smidgen disheveled. The stubble I saw before has become bona fide sideburns, beard, and a trimmed soul patch. You're lookin' good, kid.*

He donned beige suede work boots, socks, underwear, blue jeans, a white t-shirt, plaid flannel shirt, red bandana, and a green cap embroidered with a Celtic symbol given to him by his employer, then hung sunglasses on the second button of his open collar and slipped his phone into his back pocket.

Ten items. Ten percent of his hundred things. I wonder whether he's dressed for work or play. I don't want to disturb his day, but sometime after noon I need him to retrieve the next note from Tall Paul.

While Rafi meticulously prepared and mindfully ate a breakfast of whole wheat toast and fresh fruit with yogurt, Simone drifted back to the rest of his life story revealed during his session at Hawthorne High.

Simone laid her hand on Rafi's shoulder and broke the stillness in the vacant classroom. "By the time Dennis entered the theater on that godawful afternoon, I doubt there was much else you could do. He played out the suicide scenario he'd planned. You honored your father's words, hid in silence behind the curtain, and survived. You may have cowered, but you certainly were *not* a coward."

"Yeah," Rafi sighed. "I have said the same things to myself, but the moments are still eating me up."

"I'm beginning to understand that this PTSD event relates to another one in the past. Can you share it with me?"

"One?" he repeated with a wry smile. "Sometimes it seemed like one or ten per day. It is one long story."

"Maybe you could give me an overview. Today our session's only a half-hour, but we could meet again next week."

"I will try, but I barely understand it myself." Rafi's chest swelled with a full breath of air. He let it out slowly before he began, gazing at the ceiling like a man summoning help from heaven before walking barefoot across burning coals. "I was born in 1995. Twenty-one years later in 2016, the USA marked a rather shameful milestone: twenty-five years of bombing Iraq. After the 1991 Gulf War had obliterated our infrastructure, economic sanctions created a scarcity of basic food, water, and medical care that devastated its citizens. Human rights violations under Saddam Hussein had become endemic—secret police, state terrorism, torture, mass murder, rape, deportations, assassinations, chemical warfare and genocide campaigns against the Kurds." Rafi stopped speaking and seemed to look inside himself before resuming his story. "Those are big words and concepts I did not know then, but I could feel the anxiety in my parent's voices during hushed conversations... and experience the chaos in the streets. Kids had moms but no dads. One day neighbors would be there; the next day they would be gone. My family was like a little green island floating through a sea of lava inside an active volcano that could erupt at any time. We were gentle Shi'a Muslims in a nation run by Sunni Muslims. My father was a simple medical doctor who cared about people—their race, religion, or ethnicity meant nothing to him. If they were sick, they needed treatment."

"It must've been abominable," Simone said, "but your father sounds like a good man. Reminds me of mine."

"It was and he was, but it got much worse. The American Operation Desert Fox in 1998 to disarm Iraq's supposed weapons of mass destruction caused its own brand of mass destruction. In 2003 at the age of eight I survived the US-led invasion of Iraq. Though toppling Saddam's regime, it plunged Iraq into an era of bloody sectarian strife. Car bombings, suicide bombings, rampant shootings, Shi'a against Sunni, neighborhood against neighborhood, US forces against militias against hardened criminals capitalizing on the chaos. Everyone was wrong or right depending on when or where they were speaking and who they were with. America fought a civil war between the North and the South, but Iraq's internal battles were waged amongst a kaleidoscope of factions from all directions with ever-changing sides—no center and no end in sight. Instead of one terrifying tyrant, you had hundreds. Keeping your mouth shut used to keep you safe. Not anymore. Innocent people were murdered for having the wrong beliefs, birthplace, or even the wrong name!"

Rafi had become more animated as he spoke though Simone spirits had sunk. She now mirrored his previous position with her elbows on her knees and chin resting in her hands. "You know... I've followed this war from afar, but hearing your personal account makes my chest ache."

"Bear with me. I am getting to the *one* PTSD event you have asked for."

"Please go on. A touch of discomfort is nothing compared to what you've been through."

"February twenty-second, 2006. Sunni members of al-Qaeda planted a bomb in my hometown at the al-Askari Mosque, one of the holiest sites in Shi'a Islam. People were not injured, but the blast severely damaged the mosque, and widespread violence exploded immediately. More than a hundred bullet-ridden bodies were found the next day. I was eleven years old. Mid-afternoon, three days later, we heard screams and gunfire in the neighborhood. My father stepped outside our home to see what was happening. As the sounds of ricocheting bullets and agonized cries swelled, he rushed back in, led me into an open closet, shoved me against the back wall behind the clothing, and said, 'Stay there.' A minute later he returned with a board that barely covered my body. '*Uhibuka abni,*' he whispered, *Allah ysal-mak.*' I love you, my son. May God protect you. He hugged me close, then wedged the board under the clothes rod to hide me, and raised a finger to his lips. 'Do not move. Do not make a sound. Be invisible and you will survive.' I was awash in a cold sweat."

Rafi dragged the fingernails of both hands along his

scalp, disheveling his carefully coiffured hair. "Moments later a death squad entered. From which faction or what their motives were exactly, no one will ever know. I heard screaming and pleading in the room. Through a thin crack in the board, I could see my parents kneeling on the floor, praying. I watched a sword rise up before slashing down and beheading my father. Then up and down again. I heard them drag my parents out of the house." Rafi paused, fingers entwined and contorting his hands under his chin. Beads of perspiration dripped down his neck. "After an eternity, when the screaming faded into the distance, I crept outside. I thought my heart would hammer a hole through my chest. Bloody torsos lined the street. Men, women, and children wailed. I found my parents in a pile of bodies... and their severed heads. I picked them up and crumpled onto the ground..." His fingers trembled as he bent his elbows and held his palms in front of his stomach. "Cradling my mother's head in my left arm and my father's in my right... I joined everyone's sorrow... the tears seemed to squirt out of my eyes into my lap..." Attempting to continue, Rafi choked on the words and settled into silence.

Simone had bowed her head nearly to her knees. Tear drops flowed down her cheeks and dripped onto the floor. Haltingly she raised her eyes, peered through murky pupils, and murmured, "Rafi, you don't have to go on."

His eyes were moist, but no tears fell. "To go on..." After a few seconds, Rafi unbuttoned his collar, loosened his necktie, and drew in a deep breath. "That is what I did. I went on. And that is what I'd like to do now. Those moments were the bottom of that basement pit cemented over in your vision. I have not spoken of this in a decade. I did not wish to see the pity or sympathy in people's eyes, but I feel something else from yours. Please let me finish with an uplifting chapter. The next person's session can wait a few minutes. It took me twenty-four years to get here for mine."

"I'm with you. Take me on the rest of your journey."

"I became one—one of the hundreds of thousands of orphans, one of the millions of Iraqi refugees living in or trying to leave our own country. Somehow I made ends meet on the streets, scavenging and sharing scraps of food with the dogs. Revenge ruled as more Shi'a and Sunni mosques were destroyed. Christian churches, too. Rampant violence spread like a plague and seemed to bring out the worst in everyone. Instead of creating peace, the 2003 invasion heightened the hate against foreign intervention and strengthened terrorist organizations. A month after my parents were murdered, I was captured by another al-Qaeda squad and chained by the neck in a room with other boys destined for enrollment in a jihad training camp." Rafi pulled down his shirt collar to reveal the scars. "I noticed you looking at my neck. Now you know why. The last word my father spoke became my mantra. Survive." Rafi closed his eyes and chanted aloud. "*Baqi hayana. Baqi hayana. Baqi hayana.* I escaped a week later. It should have been sooner but my fingers were raw and blistered from scratching the adobe wall around the stake that secured the chains."

"Is this really the uplifting chapter?" Simone asked, eye brows arched in doubt. "It seems like we're still going downhill."

"It is all relative, is it not? When you sink into quicksand, but grab a solid branch and pull yourself out, you feel better even though you still have to crawl across a desert."

"I suppose that happened to you too."

"No. I saw it in a movie." A meager smile slipped onto Rafi's face. "I started helping other orphan boys survive on the street and felt a little like my father. We went into the hills and found a cave to live in. It seemed more secure because we could see anyone approaching for miles. Kids came and went and quarreled and fought amongst them-selves, and eventually I set out on my own."

"You were indeed a courageous child. I am amazed."

"Let me ask you a question."

"Ask away, but I might be out of answers."

"If you were surrounded by lions, jackals, wolves, wild hogs, rats, snakes, and scorpions, with whom would you make friends?"

"The lions I suppose." Simone had straightened up and sat with one leg draped over the other like Rafi. The ache in her chest had subsided, and the session began to evolve into calmer conversation.

"And the lions were..." Rafi asked.

"The foreign troops?"

"Correct, and to be specific, the United States Lions. I became Rafi the Runner at Camp Ashraf. I would bring the soldiers goods from the city, run errands, shine their boots, whatever they wanted. They taught me some English, and I translated things for them. Captain Johnny even found a shed for me to live in. Late in 2007 the IRC, the International Rescue Committee, helped get me out of Iraq."

"Thank god," Simone interrupted. "If I had a bottle of champagne, I'd pop it open right now."

Rafi raised one finger and wagged it. "That is against school policy."

"Maybe next time we'll meet in my office. It's less strict and safer."

"I accept your offer. For a year I lived with Captain Johnny's brother and his family in Portugal. Sherman and his wife Sandy taught science and English at an international school in Lisbon. They unofficially adopted me and home-schooled me in their spare time. I spent every day learning English on my own and exploring the wonderful books they had collected. Their two children became my best friends. I was living in love instead of hiding from hate. One evening we all watched the movie *Lawrence of Arabia*, and after seeing the bitter disputes among the Arab tribes during the First World War, I remember thinking, 'Have we not learned anything?'"

"Reminds me of my trip to Vietnam in 2003," Simone said, shaking her head. "At a small village market, all eyes were fixed on a TV mounted on the tin wall. Footage of the attack on Baghdad streamed in live. I thought as you did, 'Haven't we learned a damn thing?'"

"Perhaps we watched the same broadcast together in different countries. Here is another *one* for you—*one* experience that definitely uplifted my life."

Simone's eyebrows leapt up. "I can't wait. I feel like we've almost survived the desert with lions at our side."

"One day Sherman showed me a periodic table of elements. The orderly colors in the rows and columns with numbers and two-letter symbols immediately fascinated me. The more he taught me about it, the more intrigued I became. All the elements of life were organized exquisitely by facts and precise calculations instead of opinions, beliefs, and superstitions. I imagined a chart for people based on their similarities and differences and how they could connect to become something better. Sodium alone can burn your skin; chlorine is a chemical warfare agent that will kill you. Put them together and you have...?"

"Sodium chloride, the first half of salt and pepper. Put salt and pepper together, and your eggs taste better. Maybe we should change the P-word in your PTSD to periodic. Periodic Traumatic Stress Disorder."

Rafi nodded with a smile. "I like that. Periodic sounds better than perpetual."

"I suffer from periodic stress, too... whenever I drop a leash handle and one of my dogs runs into the street."

"I was good at math in school, but the periodic table seemed to give my skills a distinct purpose and inspired me to learn more about science. I became addicted to education and discovery. Sherman taught me to play the guitar and understand music notation. Very exciting! And more math! Whole notes, half notes, quarter notes, eighth notes, whole rests, half rests—"

A knock on the door halted Rafi's enthusiastic narrative, and Simone raised her forefinger. "You rest now and give me one minute." She hustled to the door, bartered with a meek girl staring at her feet, and returned to Rafi's saga. "We have three minutes. Ready? Go."

"No problem. The IRC located my father's brother Mahmood in Brooklyn, and Sherman paid my airfare to America." Rafi talked with his hands as much as with his mouth. "Uncle Mahmood was overjoyed to see me after thirteen years. He built custom cabinets and taught me his trade. With the help of a private tutor, I continued my studies, entered ninth grade, and completed high school. I was offered a scholarship to Swarthmore College in Pennsylvania, became a US citizen two years later, finally graduated with honors in chemistry and education, and started my first teaching job right here, down the hall, seven months ago. Finished."

"Whew." Simone feigned wiping off sweat on her forehead. "This has been a marathon and a half in a half-hour."

"I feel like I weigh less than when I came."

"That's good! I feel somewhat balanced again. My heart gained and then lost ten pounds during your blow-by-blow, epic tale. Thanks for sharing it with me." She handed him a business card. "Sign up if you'd like to talk here at school next week or call me anytime. Best of luck to you, Rafi. Your father would be proud of how you've survived and thrived."

"Thank you so much for listening and caring... and

empathizing." He stood and rested his right hand over his heart. "I am deeply honored and happy to have met you. I hope to see you again. I leave you with wisdom from Rumi, the beloved Persian poet, scholar, and Sufi mystic. You have demonstrated to me what this quote of his truly means." Rafi gathered the words in his mind and delivered them eye-to-eye, heart-to-heart. "'Be a lamp, or a lifeboat, or a ladder. Help someone's soul heal.' You, Dr. Simone Well-stone... have helped me heal."

Rafi bowed his head slightly, strolled to the back of the classroom, and with a smile, opened the door for the next soul in line.

The next Monday, Rafi was not on Simone's counselling list, but the following week he phoned. "Dr. Simone?"

"That's me."

"It is Rafi the Iraqi."

"Rafi! I'm glad to hear from you. I missed you last week."

"I do not feel comfortable at Hawthorne High anymore. I resigned and will leave in three weeks."

"Whoa. I'm a bit shocked. And curious."

"I hope I am not bothering you, but you said I could call anytime. Right now I am on a bike ride and wondering if you have some minutes to spare. Not for an official session, just an update."

"No bother and good timing. I'm done for the day."

"I have your card with your address. I will be there in five minutes."

When he arrived, Ming led Rafi behind the office to meet Simone who smiled and invited him in with both arms outstretched. "Welcome to my Sensory Sanctuary. Please sit where you like. No corners and one round wall."

Rafi turned around slowly as he took in the entire room. "Your sanctuary is beautiful and serene. I choose the center of the floor." He sat cross-legged on the thick wool rug. "Nice carpet. Persian I think, like Rumi."

"You seem quite cheerful today, even optimistic." Simone joined him on the floor, face-to-face, knee-to-knee. "But you quit?"

"I am, and I did. Have you heard the wild rumors about me at the school?"

"Probably, though I think the word rumors is inadequate to describe them. I'd call them xenophobic, senseless, disgusting, fabricated fake news which makes me embarrassed to be an American or even live in this town. The terrorist recruited hapless Dennis, bewitched him with his heathen Muslim spells, and planned the whole thing. God, I just say it, and I wanna vomit."

"The latest twist is that while I was behind the curtain, I told Dennis to shoot himself so no one could question him and find out that I was the mastermind behind the shooting. You should see the way people look at me now, or step around me as if I had some highly contagious, fatal disease. I should change my name to Raf-ebola."

"That's sick, but funny. If I had the authority, I'd be on my knees apologizing for the entire community. They don't know you," Simone sighed. "They're slaves to their own fears."

"Completely unfounded fears. The irony of it is almost comical. If anyone cared, or even considered the years I experienced and dreaded this kind of hostile behavior, or knew the peaceful Muslim way my parent's taught me to live, they might feel differently. As a senior in high school, I thought I would pursue a career in biology because it was a *life* science. After one day of barely surviving a frog dissection, I dropped the course and switched to inorganic chemistry. The concept of killing to learn about living was beyond my comprehension."

"So what will you do next? Leave town?"

"The only Iraqi in this town is the one I see in the mirror each morning. I do not mind being a misunderstood minority, but maybe not the only one in a tightly knit society of 1,200—pardon me, I have learned a lot of English words that I normally choose not to use—tight-assed academics and naive children."

"I understand, Rafi. In my senior year, I couldn't wait to get outta there. Hawthorne's never been a haven for open-minded instructors or worldly students. With its Victorian turrets, tiny windows, and phallic clock tower, the main building looks like a medieval prison that mated with an insane asylum. Pardon me now, but we used to call it the cock tower."

Rafi smirked. "The kids still call it that."

"Thirty years ago its hands stopped at 1:38 when the cogs rusted together, and time has stood still since then, just like the incognizant minds trying to preserve the past. That dingy, red-brick eyesore must be over a hundred years old by now."

"And some of the teachers seem even older than that."

"Still? A few were already geriatric when I was there. My history teacher passed away in class so he actually *became* ancient history."

"Are you serious?" Rafi asked, eyebrows pinched.

"Nah, that was just one of our sick jokes back then. But he did sleep a lot in class."

"After being stuck inside square rooms for a decade of institutional education, I am ready to think and live outside the box. There are many good folks around here, and I am good with my hands. I will find work in a smaller organization. Once again, it is time to go on."

"I'll give you the names and numbers of a couple friends of mine." A cocky grin twisted Simone's lips. "One owns a coffee slash ice cream shop and discriminates against locals in favor of foreign nationals."

"That would be very kind of you. But now let me leave you to your evening. I feel a close bond with you and am certain we will see each other again, at a better time in a better situation." Rafi grinned and gently shook her hand. "Salt and pepper on eggs, you know."

Simone walked him out of her office to the street. While he slung his leg over the bicycle seat and fastened his helmet, she straddled the front tire, wrapped her fingers around the handlebars, and faced him. "Rafi, I want you to know that you've helped make my life a little better. One winter I drove through Chicago during a blizzard and saw this elderly blind man trying to walk over four-foot, icy piles of snow on the side of a busy street. The entire landscape of his world had changed overnight. One wrong step and he'd slip into the traffic. So when I'd have a so-called problem, I'd think, 'Compared to that guy, I've *never* had a problem.' Now if I'm having a bad day I say, 'If Rafi can survive for two decades, I can make it through the week.' Thank you for sharing your inspiring story with me."

His eyes moist, Rafi once again placed his hand over his heart, nodded, and pedaled away.

After breakfast while Rafi washed his only plate, bowl, spoon, and kitchen knife, Simone got a glimpse of the neighborhood through the sole window in his apartment and started to plan her day. *Now I see where we are. There's the public beach on the river, the sporting goods shop, and Rafi's room must be on the second floor of Flanagan's Saloon and Eatery. A bit of a trek to the drop-off location of Paul's*

note, but just down the road from The Fit Nest and Diego.

The two-story building stretched from the sidewalk to the steep wall of Copper Butte that dominated the skyline. In this historic section of town, only two roads fit in the narrow strip of land between the butte and the river. Park Drive, the paved street in front of Flanagan's, was four feet above the river bank, and the unimproved dirt road was twenty feet higher, level with the building's roof in the back. The apartment entrance adjacent to the main saloon led upstairs to the second floor and continued up to a rear door in an enclosed vestibule on the roof. A wooden walk-way spanned the ten-foot gap from the roof to the dirt road, so tenants could exit onto the high road in the rear or the low road in front.

Rafi filled his plaid thermos with apple juice, stuck a raw frozen bone into his jacket pocket, left the apartment, and walked up the rear stairway. Once on the roof, Rafi hunched onto his knees and crawled toward the front of the building, his body hidden by the parapet rising above the roof.

What is he doing now?

Halfway to the front, he peeked down into the dusty backyard of the adjacent one-story building, only half as long as the saloon. The butte wall curved around the other side of the neighbor's property to create a natural enclosure.

That's the old jail house. I didn't know the Rudd's had a Doberman Pinscher.

Lying beside a makeshift doghouse, the sleek black dog lifted her head and let out a low growl. Her tan ears were taut, tuned in to Rafi's dark face looming over the roof. Reflecting the clear morning sky, her eyes glowed like blue neon orbs of light below the tan circles on her brow.

"Zara," Rafi crooned quietly, caressing her name with a melodic, three-tone chant. "Zara Zarina."

The tip of her thin tail twitched tentatively as she rose on her front legs to reveal tan feet and bikini-shaped markings on her chest.

Rafi sang louder as he stood. "Zara Zarina, Rafi is coming."

Zara's tail began wagging her whole body, and she answered his song with a welcoming yelp.

Still singing, Rafi strolled back to the rear of the building as Zara followed below until reaching the end of her metal choke chain staked into the ground. He crossed the walkway, ran along the steep dirt road, and climbed down the sloping rock wall into the neighboring yard. Zara became joy incarnate, racing circles around him, licking, sniffing, and searching for her snack. Besides trying to calm her, Rafi's biggest challenge was preventing the chain from wrapping around his legs and sending him sprawling on the ground.

Rafi had moved into the apartment a month earlier and first saw the dog when he ventured onto the roof. Every day he'd spoken quietly to her and dropped a biscuit or special treat over the edge. For a week, she'd only stare or growl and flash her sharp fangs, but he'd persisted and soon started calling her Zara Zarina. He occasionally saw a grey-haired woman refill the water and food bowls, but that was it—no interaction, no physical contact, no desire by either party to engage. Rafi knew too well how it felt to be chained by the neck, to be alone, to mistrust everyone.

One morning he climbed halfway down the slope and bounced a optic-yellow tennis ball into Zara's yard. She'd growled and ignored the gift, but that afternoon Rafi spotted it inside her doghouse. During the next two days she'd tucked two more balls inside her dilapidated den. Each visit he crept closer to the flat dirt ground until Zara finally accepted a gentle pat, an ear scratch, and a biscuit from his hand. That day the play began, frantic and ecstatic.

Two weeks later during his daily visit and frolic session, the woman had come outside to fill the bowls. Her jaw dropped in shock. "I can't believe you dare come down here! She hates everyone!"

"She has learned to like me." Rafi smiled, resting his hand on Zara's head as she leaned on his leg. "Zara and I are kindred spirits."

"Zara, eh? I call her Dobette. My husband calls her The Monster. He doesn't like dogs, and she doesn't like him."

"Zara Zarina. It means beautiful, bright as the dawn." He extended his hand. "I am Rafi. I live in an apartment next door and am helping the Flanagan brothers build a new bed and breakfast."

"Well, it's very nice to meet you, Rafi. I'm Clara Rudd."

"If I may ask, why do you have her?"

"Our son came for the holidays and found Dobette living under a ledge in a canyon. Skinny, mangy, and starving. He coaxed her into his van, brought her to us, and left town. I've tried to find her a home, but she scares everyone away."

"I must go to work now, but if you do not mind, I would like to continue my visits with her."

"Oh, please do! She needs a little TLC. From now on, I'll call her Zara. It fits."

"Thank you very much, Mrs. Rudd." He kneeled in front of Zara, kissed her on the snout, and whispered, "Sweet Zara Zarina, I must leave you now, but I will soon return."

This morning during their rambunctious meeting, Simone could sense the warmth in Rafi's chest, perhaps due to his heart racing during their play, perhaps from the joy he was feeling, or perhaps it was in her own heart. *Zara is a beauty, and this boy is blessed to find his sweetheart.*

Zara could smell the bone in Rafi's pocket and kept poking his pants with her nose.

"Can you sit, Zara?"

She sat and wagged.

"Good girl. Smart Zarina. This is a cold but juicy bone!"

She took it gently, raced to her doghouse, hid the bone, returned with a tennis ball, and dropped it at his feet.

"Are you a good catcher today?" He flipped the ball in the air. She leaped up, caught it, and shoved it back into his hand. After ten minutes of intense catch and fetch, Rafi bent down to bid her adieu. "Until tomorrow, Zara Zarina. I must go to work now."

Zara licked his chin, whined, and tugged at his heart strings with her sad brown eyes.

Rafi scaled the back wall, turned to his right on the dirt road, and ran to a wood staircase leading down to the B&B under construction next to his apartment building.

On the bottom step below, one thumb wrapped around his overall strap and the other holding open the cover of his pocket watch, Kyle Flanagan stood counting down the seconds. "Seven, six, five, four—"

"Good morning, Mr. Kyle. Eight o'clock sharp."

"Shite in a bucket, Oi was hopin' ya'd be late fer once in yer life."

"Sorry, sir. My father was very strict and precise. He taught me that time waits for no man. I remember him always saying, like clockwork, 'If I'm not early, I'm late.'"

"Aye, ya should give Ronan a lesson er two. The only t'ing my kid brother's ever been on time fer is happy hour."

Oh, this should be good. The Rafi Iraqi and the Irish boys. And what a pair o' characters—two brothers from the same Irish mother but with two different fathers, one Irish and one

American.

They didn't look alike, and their age span magnified the incongruity. Kyle was pushing sixty while his brother pushed the civil limits of forty. Ronan stood a foot taller, not including his two-inch, spiked, bleached-blond locks. If Kyle had a strand of hair left, only his missus knew, because he never removed his tweed Irish flat cap in public. He sipped milk in the morning and a single pint of stout at home in the evening. Ronan slugged a shot of Jameson for breakfast and Milk of Magnesia before bed—in his bachelor pad, one of his maidens' homes, or on the couch behind the bar. Kyle constantly chewed on a crooked pipe but hardly ever lit it. A cigarette butt hung off his brother's lip 24/7. Kyle had majored in business, and Ronan had become a master of monkey biz. It made for a perfect love-hate relationship.

"What will you have me doing today, sir?" Rafi asked.

"Ya been workin' 'ere for a month now sure, so Oi'm givin' ya a little test with a special reward if ya pass. C'mon."

"You should have told me. I would have studied harder."

Kyle rested his calloused hand up on Rafi's neck as he walked him toward the B&B. "No studyin' needed, jus' doin'. Oi know yer a scientist, an' today... yer gonna move space."

"Move space? Hmm. Maybe I should get my book on string theory."

"No strings attached. Jus' wood, nails, an' elbow grease. And yer reward... if ya finish pronto and precise... ya can head on." Kyle's gold front tooth highlighted his smile as he patted Rafi on the back. "Done fer the day with full pay."

"That is very kind of you. And now I had better crack on, as you might say."

"Yer learnin', lad."

A young woman shouting from the street turned both

of their heads. "Hey, Kyle! Ronan told me to tell you he'll be down later."

"Does 'at mean later today or later nex' week?"

"You never know, do you?" She waved and jogged away.

Kyle shook his head and sighed. "Useless dosser. Spends most of his life horizontal." Kyle pointed to the second floor of Flanagan's. "His flat's right up dere. Can't even drag himself to de window to wag his tongue. Let's take a gander at de job upstairs. Ya should be able to knock it out by lunchtime sure."

The B&B's internal framework, the skeleton invisible after final construction, was nearly complete—the floors, exterior walls, window frames, rigid plywood sheathing, interior support walls and stairs, door frames, rafters, trusses, and roof deck.

Kyle gestured to the open space in the wall ready for an all-weather window. "Oi was daft to let my eedjit halfbrother lay out de measurements up 'ere. This six-foot frame should be four feet to de left. Ronan must've been standin' on his 'ead when he read de blueprints... if he read 'em at all. My client's advertisin' de river view, not a close-up of a rock wall."

Rafi stepped up and peered out the opening. "So we need to move space and change our point of view. That sounds very philosophical."

"More physical than philosophical, Oi'd say. You'll be after rippin' out an' movin' de header, de sill plate, de side supports an' all. Dat'd been hard 'nough two weeks ago before de plywood panels tied everyt'ing tight." Kyle ran his fingers over the wood, scrutinizing the construction, and spoke as if he we're miffed. "An' if ya had'na built it sound as a pound in de first place, yer job'd be a tad easier."

Rafi's face drooped. "I am so sorry. I thought that a sturdy frame is what you—"

"Oi'm only coddin' ya, mate!"

"Coddin'?" Rafe asked quickly. "Is that good or bad?"

"Jus' pullin' yer leg..." Kyle chuckled. "Yankin' yer chain."

"You mean you were joking, right?"

"Aye, yer work's bang on."

"Bang on? Good or bad?"

"Better'n good like everyt'ing ya done 'ere. Yer suckin' diesel, lad!"

"That does not sound appealing at all."

"Yer slayin' me 'ere." Kyle snorted out a giggle and practically gagged on it. "Yer English is deadly, but yer Irish is brutal!"

The highly contagious waggery infected Rafi as well. "I have no idea what you just said to me." He threw up his hands and stammered through his snickering. "Should I apologize again? Can you give me an Irish-English dictionary so I could study?"

This is way better than watching a movie. I'm an extra on stage in a Broadway farce. Wherever my body happens to be, I wonder if it's shaking like Rafi and me?

"Stall de ball fer a minute, will ya?" Kyle leaned over with his hands on his knees and tried to stop laughing. "Whew! De ol' ticker's goin' ninety to de dozen." He sucked in a breath and straightened up. "Right then. Crack on. De client's comin' this afternoon, and Oi don't want 'im to see this window here. Holler if ya need help at all."

Rafi studied the space modification project for several minutes, checked on their lumber supply, and located Kyle inspecting floor joists in the basement. "Excuse me, sir, but I need a little advice before beginning my test. That's a load-bearing wall up there, and I must have used 500 nails to secure all the boards in the window bracing. It could take the rest of the day to rip out everything while trying to save the pieces, if that is even possible. Please trust me. I am not trying to avoid working."

"Oi'm listenin'," Kyle said. "De scientist is speakin'."

"May I suggest we keep the existing construction and support the current opening, then cut the required new space and fashion the frame with virgin lumber? I checked our stock, and we have plenty on hand. That would strengthen the wall instead of weakening it along the way. I doubt you want cracks forming later when the room is finished and painted."

Kyle paused, his chin pinched between his thumb and fingers, then erupted in delight. "Brilliant idea! Ya passed yer test 'fore ya even started. Jus' don't tell no one Oi didn't t'ink o' that. Only noticed de error this mornin' now."

"Thank you, sir. I am deadly on it, with diesel."

As Kyle strolled away, Rafi dove into his task, calculating, measuring, marking, sawing, fitting, assembling, and stitching the puzzle pieces together with steel fasteners driven in by a pneumatic nail gun.

Although fascinated by the complex process involved to house a simple window pane, Simone was concerned about the time and anxious to learn more about her plight. *Somehow I've got to find a way to communicate with Rafi. Retrieving Paul's next note and having a clandestine discussion with Diego are daunting tasks. Amanda and I were a team. I only led Diego to my office or took him for a short walk. Coco and I talked in real-time. Rafi's totally in or out. But he's so damn smart that he'll probably grasp the reality of the situation and be willing to help. He's been captured and trapped like I am now. But how can I reach him? Write notes like Paul gave me?*

At the ten o'clock breaktime, completion of the window frame project by noon seemed feasible. Rafi surveyed his progress, snatched a drink from his backpack, and skipped down the stairs to find Kyle sitting on the porch, staring squint-eyed at his brother trudging across the lot in front of the B&B. The weather had taken a turn, and Ronan seemed to be towing a dark rain cloud behind him.

"Top o' the mornin' to ya, Mr. Ronan," Rafi said with a tentative wave.

"Well, at least you're tryin', but that's an English phrase that somehow landed in America and is now blamed on the Irish."

"It ain't de top," Kyle grunted. "It's de end o' de mornin'."

"Ooo, the gaffer's a snarly one today," Ronan retorted. "Yer face is that sour ye could make yer own yoghurt. Ya get out o' the wrong side o' the casket today?"

"Rafi's fixin' the frame after yer measurin' upstairs went arseways."

"Sorry, bossman. I told ya I'd take care of it."

"Hmph. Client's comin' today, an' Oi don't want 'im to see it."

"Did ya bother tellin' me that then?" Ronan asked. "Oh, my bad. And oh, I forgot... you never make a mistake and know everything and I'm s'posed to read yer feckin' mind."

Rafi exchanged a quick glance with Kyle, backed off, and starting sorting through a pile of lumber.

"It's after ten feckin' a.m., Ronan. Too ossified last night to rise today?"

"Perhaps it slipped outta yer cracked skull, but Thursday nights while yer loafin' at home holy home, I am bartendin' and closin' Flanagan's at one a.m. An' this mornin' I been takin' care o' your bizness and talkin' with the cops."

"Now what'd ya do? Actin' the maggot again?"

"Eff you, ya old fart." Ronan flicked away his butt and lit another cig. "Last night some o' yer precious customers almost got shot."

"What?"

"Shot. S-H-O-effin' T... Shot."

"Jesus, Mary, an' Joseph!" Kyle's pipe dropped from his lips to his lap. "What 'appened?"

"If ya start actin' like my brother Kyle 'stead o' just another Dick, I might tell ya. Or call the shades yourself."

"Sorry. Oi'm feelin' a bit narky with de client comin' round an' all."

Rafi had been eavesdropping and wandered closer to porch. Ronan pulled up a step sawhorse, sat two feet in front of Kyle, and covered his eyes with his hands. "I can't get this shit scene outta my head. It just keeps playin' over an' over. About midnight this scruffy dude strolls in... big guy... taller 'n me, maybe thirty-somethin'. He looks round the room as he struts between the tables, then stands at the bar. Doesn't sit on the stool, just stands. Never seen 'im before."

"What'd he look like?" Kyle asked.

"Like a..." Ronan closed his eyes. "Skinny guy with a skin head. Shiny... like a rattlesnake. Weird eyes too far apart. Sliver-thin mouth. Flat nose like someone smashed it. If you'd seen 'im before, you'd remember." Ronan stood up behind the sawhorse as if it were the bar at Flanagan's. "So I greet 'im and ask how he's doin'. He jus' says, 'I wanna Coke.' I say, 'We got Pepsi. Zat okay?' He says again, 'Coke.' He looks pissed... not plastered, pissed as in effin' angry... like he's gonna eat the head off me. I smile and say real nice, 'Sorry, buddy, but we only got Pepsi.' He jus' stares at me an' finally says, 'Water.' The dude seems stone cold sober, but mainly jus' cold. Cold stones fer eyes. I bring his water, but he doesn't drink it. Jus' stands there mumblin' over the glass. I keep watchin' him close while servin' the other customers. He starts mumblin' louder, sayin' shit like 'goddamn wogs, wops, spicks, niggers.' When his list hits 'fucking immigrants,' I can't take it no more and say, 'Hey, buddy, zip it. This here's a respectable establishment owned by a fine Irish immigrant, now an American citizen. If you don't like it, you can leave anytime.'" Ronan stopped talking and lit up another cig.

Kyle, Rafi, and Simone had been hanging on every syllable of every word.

I don't even want to hear the rest of this. And I'm sick of reading about it every day.

"I would have been terror-stricken," Rafi whispered.

"Yeah," Ronan paused and looked up at the threatening clouds. "I didn't think about bein' scared. By this time I was riled somethin' fierce. The dude is dissin' my friends! He scrunches his face real hard an' turns kinda orange like he's trumpin' himself up for a battle. Suddenly he whirls around and yells, 'America is full! America is for white people only!'"

Realizing he'd shouted the man's epithet, Ronan snapped his head around to see if anyone else had heard, then rested his hands on the sawhorse and leaned in close to his rapt audience of two.

"Musta been at least twenty-five people there, all flippin' out. I get a grip on my Louisville Slugger metal bat behind the bar. The dude's screaming now." Ronan tried to scream in a whisper. "'Mexican rapist scum! Jew bastards! Arab terrorists! Yellow chinks!' Then faster than you can think, he whips out a handgun, points it at an Asian family in the front, and roars like a wacko maniac. 'I don't want you in my country!' The whole fam'ly is wimperin' and bowin' and cryin' and I'm jus' waitin' for the right moment. He mumbles some shit I can't even understand, then tips back his head, raises both hands, says 'God help me,' and fires a bullet into the ceiling."

Ronan picked up a short two-by-four stud from the ground to act out the scene. "The moment arrives... my moment. I swing the bat an' slam a home run upside his head.

He slumps sideways, I bash his wrist an' the gun goes fly-in'." Ronan smashed the sawhorse with the stud. "He falls to the floor, so I leap over the bar an' land on his chest. Now he is cold... out cold... an' the customers can't get out the doors quick enough. I tie 'im up tight, call 911, turn a table upside-down on his comatose carcass, an' wait'll I hear the sirens."

Rafi and Kyle hadn't moved, as if they we're holding their breath.

Ronan stared at the ground, breathing hard. "I sat on the table, half-wishin' I'd killed the scum. Last night I could hardly sleep. I kept on seein' his mug with a forked, devil-tongue flickin' in my face."

"What'll we be doin'?" Kyle asked, his voice weak like a lost child. "It'll be on de news, in de papers..."

"I dunno," Ronan sighed. "Install a feckin' metal detec-tor? Hire a security gorilla? Escape from this sicko country where ya ain't even safe in yer own backyard? A shade told me that a hundred Americans are killed with guns... *every feckin' day*... and hundreds more shot and injured."

Kyle only shook his head in shock.

Ronan kneeled behind his brother on the porch and massaged his shoulders. "You never really hung out with yer father cuz he left, an' then you had to *be* the father and take care o' Mam. You 'member my dad takin' me to Dublin when I was ten? You lived there till ya were twenty, ya lucky stiff. That was the first and only time we ever got to see the legendary Éire you missed so much. Dad an' I toured round the island... it was sooo grand an' green an' everyone was sooo kind an' friendly. Right now, bein' an American immigrant in Ireland sounds like a slice o' heaven 'stead o' dealin' with the gobshites over here."

"Maybe... maybe..." Kyle chanted faintly.

"You relax, ya ol' gaffer. We'll finish the window sure."

Ronan linked his fingers and stretched his arms over his head. "Rafi, the clouds are startin' to weep. Let's crack on that frame and stick it in the past. Me brain may be a wee gammy, but me mitt's are itchin' to bash some boards and pound some nails."

The underbelly of the US of A is gettin' uglier every day. What happened to our cherished melting pot? The feckin' pot itself is melting. Maybe I should follow Ronan to Ireland. I love to hear these guys talk. So why didn't I hear a gunshot right below Rafi's apartment? Do the masterminds put Rafi and me that far under? Anesthetized with an IV drip? Maybe I wasn't even inside him yet. When and where does this bizarre transfer of cognizance take place? Is there some DNA transfusion in an EDNA mobile lab? Are they cartin' my carcass around town? I gotta look inside one of those trucks. God, so many questions.

Rafi and Ronan traipsed upstairs and worked together, quietly, each one in their own space. After a half hour, Ronan broke the silence. "I know ya went through this violent shit at the school and that got me thinkin'. Yer the only Muslim I ever met an' yer a great guy. But I don't even know what a Muslim is. Mind if I ask ya a couple of questions?"

"Go ahead. Most people have already made up their own answers."

"Let's sit a spell. I need a pint o' the black stuff." Rafi retrieved his apple juice from his backpack, Ronan brought out a bottle tucked behind a scrap pile, and they both squatted on the floor. "So I've heard Muslim's worship some other god named Allah? Is'at right?"

Rafi smiled. He'd been asked this before. "Allah is simply the Arabic word for God."

"Oh." A tiny light bulb flicked on inside Ronan's head.

"There is only one God, but man has many names for God. Deus in Latin. Dios in Spanish. Yahweh in Hebrew.

Bog in Russian. Chen in Chinese. There must be a name in Irish?"

"Dia, I guess. Lots of Irish folks got another G-word for God." He held up his black bottle. "Guinness. How come you know all that?"

"I took a college course in Comparative Religions—quite an eye and mind opener. It should have been called *Competitive* Religions."

"I heard Muslims got a different bible. 'Zat right?"

"Yes, the Qu'ran, different and the same. Both contain passages of peace and love mixed with passages of war, hate... and stoning your neighbors. The Christian Bible, the Islam Qu'ran, and the Hebrew Tanakh all have similar roots, like the prophet Abraham, and similar concepts, like one God, but they disagree on Jesus of Nazareth. Muslims believe he was a prophet before the time of Muhammad, but not the Son of God. Christians believe he's one of the Holy Trinity. Judaism teaches that Jesus was an ordinary person, like you and me. Just another Jew."

"Aye, a carpenter like us."

"Mankind's belief about one man influences their belief in one god. If I wrote my own holy book, it would be very short. Ten words. 'God is. God is you. God is everything. Stop fighting.'"

"Savage! The Brief Book of Rafi. Ya can memorize it in a minute."

"My professor required we read one book that was not on the course syllabus—*Think on These Things* by J. Krishnamurti."

"Never heard of 'im."

"Jiddu Krishnamurti, a teacher and author from India, who claimed no loyalty to any nationality, religion, or philosophy, and spent most of his life traveling the world, speaking to people about experiencing truth by understanding their own minds. I savored every one of his words, but three of them explained human behavior so simply." Rafi sighed and drifted away for a moment.

"Come back, lad." Ronan tapped him on the knee. "You got me goin' here. And the three words are..."

"Belief divides people."

"I thought belief unites people."

"So did I. But when you consider history or today's reality? Beliefs might unite a few against a few or a multitude against a multitude but then the united continue to divide. Muslims split into Sunnis and Shiites fighting over who would be Mohammad's successor. It is nearly impossible to keep track of how many factions exist today. Judaism separated into Hasidic, Conservative, and Reform plus more ethnic divisions. Christianity fractured into Orthodox, Catholic, and Protestant."

"I'm gettin' yer drift, lad. We studied the Great Schism when the Catholic Church split into east and west. A few hundred years later, King Henry Number Eight got cheesed off cuz the Pope wouldn't let 'im divorce his first wife, so he proclaims himself the Supreme Head of the Church of England, sticks the divine right of kings clause into the Constitution, and makes himself a god. Then the cheeky bastard takes five more wives and declares his arse King o' Ireland too."

"Centuries later the Episcopal Church in America split from the Church of England, and landed somewhere between Catholics and Protestants, who have splintered into hundreds, or some say, *thousands* of denominations! Belief unites? No."

"An' yer not even talkin' 'bout religions fightin' against each other."

"Or fighting between nations or within neighborhoods. Or racial, sexual, and cultural discrimination. Or global terrorism."

"Rafi, don'cha find it a wee twisted that America declared a global war on terrorism? A country 'sponsible fer millions o' deaths 'round the world with their feckin' drones, conflicts, coups, secret ops, weapon sales, and economic sanction that tear apart innocent lives? Maybe America should declared war on itself."

"You confronted an American terrorist last night who seemed quite similar to an Islamist terrorist. The terms are confusing. The word Muslim means to 'surrender to God.' Islamists are a separate sect of Muslims, fundamentally anti-everything that isn't Islam, anti-anything that isn't exactly what they believe, and are on a mission to make the world slaves to their ideas. Does that sound a bit like the Christian Crusades?"

"You know, I don't really give a shite what the next bloke thinks. I just don't like 'im pushin' his beliefs on me."

"I totally agree." Rafi raised his apple juice in a toast and clunked Ronan's bottle. "I have seen Muslims, Christians, and Jews living peacefully next each other in America and in Iraq. And I have seen them destroy each other."

"Did this Krishnawhoti have any sorta solution?"

"His writings reminded me of wise words from Buddha. I cannot remember them exactly, but the gist is... 'Do not believe in anything simply because you heard it or because it is rumored by many or written in your religious books. Do not believe in anything simply on the authority of your teachers and elders or in traditions handed down for generations. But after observation and analysis, when you find something that agrees with reason, for the good and benefit of one and all, then accept it and live up to it.'"

"Fierce words, 'specially the 'for the good of all' part. I might have a chat with me brother Kyle 'bout that. He's got a collection of opinions set in Stonehenge."

Rafi stood and leaned on wall next to the supports for the relocated frame. "I prefer the facts of science and math over the judgments of belief. Two feet plus two feet equals four feet, the exact size of this window. I might say water freezes at zero, and you say thirty-two degrees. I speak centigrade, and you speak Fahrenheit, but we're both stating the truth."

"I think there's a song about that." Ronan waved his hands and hips as he belted out the lyrics. "'You say tomato and I say tomahto.'"

"I believe you." Rafi grinned, patting the wall to the beat of Ronan's tune. "And now I believe we are ready to cut this new opening, but how?"

Ronan polished off his Guinness. "It's time to haul out the trusty Sawzall."

"*You* are the master of that formidable tool, although I like the name—a reciprocating saw. Interchange, give and take, equivalent." Rafi took a step backwards. "Please show me how it is done. I will watch closely... from over here."

"I'll rip it from inside, then we'll pound out the plywood, cut off the studs, patch the other hole, and Bob's yer uncle."

"Bob's my uncle?" Rafi asked, puzzled. "Mahmood is my uncle."

Ronan laughed. "That means it's sorted. Game over. Some Brit named Robert appointed his nephew Arthur to be Chief Secretary of Ireland. Guess it pissed people off. Artie mighta had qualifications for the job, but his main one was... well, Bob's yer uncle."

Rafi watched him wield the blade from a safe distance by another window frame facing the river.

Simone turned Rafi toward the street and rested his elbows on the sill. *So where's the EDNA truck? Haven't seen any drones today. Probably because we're so close to his home. I wonder how Coco's doing?* As she'd done with her previous hosts, Simone focused for a few moments and tried to connect. *Nothing. I hope she's okay. Maybe far gone like yesterday morning. She had a rough end to her evening.*

"Hey, Rafi, gimme a hand over here."

Simone immediately released control.

"Hey!" Ronan repeated, now standing with the Sawzall in his hand. "Earth to Rafi! I thought ya wanted to watch the master in action."

Rafi blinked and waggled his head as if shaking off a daydream. "Sorry, I went away for a minute."

"Took a little trip to Rafi Land, did ya?"

"I started taking some new medicine today, and it seems to send me into another world."

"Sounds fun. If ya got any extra, lemme pop a tab."

They finished the job at noon-fifteen and found Kyle tidying up the first floor in anticipation of his client's imminent but unknown arrival time. "Ya finished upstairs, boys?"

"Bob is our uncle," Rafi replied proudly.

"Ya mean, Bob's yer uncle."

"That is what I said."

"No," Kyle chuckled, "ya said 'Bob is our uncle,' but Iraqi Irish is fair play on my team."

"Perhaps I would speak Irish correctly if I started drinking Guinness, yes?"

"Damn straight," Ronan answered. "But if ya start, you'll never stop."

"Don't listen to 'im, lad," Kyle said. "He is not de full shilling. An' now yer free to go. What're yer plans for an afternoon off?"

"My plans were to work, but now I have no plans. I will most likely go for a bike ride and read."

"Not at the same time, I hope," Ronan quipped.

Rafi raised his right fist. "Bang on. See you Tuesday."

Perfect! Those plans fit right into mine.

After polishing off a cheddar cheese sandwich, spicy nachos, and a ginger ale, Rafi stuck his arm through his bike frame, slung it over his shoulder, and headed down the stairs. The clouds had cleared, the sun burned bright, and tourists strolled the wooden walkways in this historic section of Buffalo City.

Unlike Diego's high-tech, light-weight speed machine, Rafi's vintage Trek mountain bike had been a garage-sale bargain. About the same age as Rafi, it came equipped with canvas panniers hanging over the rear tire for groceries or a small selection of his 100 things. A silver bell mounted on the handlebars tinkled with a flick of the thumb. Though the bike weighed half as much as its rider, Rafi had scientifically tuned and lubed it for optimum performance. He put on his helmet and rode along Park Drive, the most expedient route out of the city.

On the outskirts of town, Simone took control. *Sorry, Rafi, but we've gotta take a detour.* She turned left onto the bridge over the river, paused next to the guard rail, removed the water bottle strapped to the frame, and took a sip while casually scanning the area. No drones, but an EDNA truck slowed to a stop fifty-some yards behind on Park Drive. *We have to make this as innocent as a Friday afternoon bike ride should be. The EDNA goons might've heard Rafi voice his plans to Kyle.*

At the speed of a sight-seeing vacationer, Simone headed in the direction the drop location on Hickok Road. After a twenty-minute circuitous route, she parked on the sidewalk in front of 7/11, stretched a bit, and entered the store to purchase a snack. Five minutes later, she emerged with cranberry designer water and a banana, set the bottle on top of the metal *Discount Trader* magazine vending box, and peeled the banana. As she ate, her gaze drifted from seeing the sights to the box next to her. She crouched down, peered through the hinged door's plastic window, and lowered it with her left hand while feeling underneath the box with her right. She extracted one *Discount Trader* and feigned reading until her fingers located the envelope taped to the bottom. Standing quickly, Simone tucked it inside the magazine, grabbed her drink, and leaned on the bike, perusing a few pages and sneaking a peek at the EDNA truck parked down the block.

She tucked the water bottle into the pannier, rode toward the river, turned right on Riverview Road, and cruised for ten minutes before stopping at the city park next to Cozy Cottage Resort. She flipped open the pannier and grabbed the *Trader* and the book Rafi had brought—Bill Bryson's *A Short History of Practically Everything.*

Figures. A phenomenal book. Should be the textbook for every science class in the world. Resting under a shady oak tree by the river bank, Simone opened the envelope and unfolded Paul's note.

Simon was originally inspired to create this technology because of the way you and he could communicate without speaking when you were kids. He was convinced that unique properties of the DNA you shared caused the phenomenon. He wants you to be a part of the process and thinks its a great opportunity for you to introduce it's developments to the psychiatric industry. He hoped if you experienced the amazing possibilities that you might change your mind about him. Simon even said he would like you to take over the company since his days are numbered. He just wants you to come and talk about it on Sunday. Like the other treatment participants, a large sum of money earmarked to be transferred into your account.

Expecting more pertinent info about the dangers of her plight, Simone turned over the note to reveal a blank page. Her eyebrows slammed together in dismay.

That's it? What the fuck? Paul's other notes were dire warnings. This reads like a dubious invitation, a rotten carrot on the end of a sharp stick trying to prod me into hell. What happened to his I am so sorry and beware of your brother? I don't even know what to think about this.

After a few moments of not thinking, her heart remembered her host. She stuffed the note back into the magazine and replaced it with Rafi's book.

I have to give the day back to the boy. I hope he doesn't freak out. One minute he's on his bike, then he's... he's... I have no idea where... then suddenly he's under a tree across the river an hour later. If that happened to me I'd probably head for the hospital psychiatric ward. I hope he remembers that the treatment instructions said he might feel different.

The moment Simone relinquished control, Rafi seemed confused and jerked his head to the right, then to the left, trying to get his bearings. Simone could feel the tension in his chest and imagined him experiencing a flashback of his precarious life in Iraq, alone on the streets.

I hate this! What right do I have to take this sweet boy for a ride without his consent? And Simon wants me to be a part of this shady process? Due process of the law needs to put a stop to it. Simple wiretapping is illegal. This is a whole new realm of lawless disrespect for life and liberty.

Nothing was threatening about the peaceful setting by the river. Songbirds crooned in the trees. A lawn mower purred next door and flavored the breeze with the smell of freshly cut grass. Kids climbed on boulders bordering the bank in front of the resort. An occasional fishing boat with an outboard motor or canoe rented from an outfitter upstream passed by. Rafi's heartbeat slowed as he began reading his book, and Simone drifted into her simmering world of unanswered questions.

The river narrowed to fifty yards and deepened to ten feet along this stretch causing the current to accelerate and the surface to ripple. A few hundred yards downstream, the river became raging rapids as the sloping channel wound its way into a steep canyon. Fed by snow-capped mountains in the distance, its water remained frigid until midsummer.

After fifteen minutes, Rafi set down his book and gazed at the serene scenery. A canoe carrying a small woman in front, a young girl sitting on the yoke in the middle, and a sizable man at the stern with a body built on beer floated into the picture. The man's heavy bulk in the back lifted the bow six inches out of the water.

A veteran of wilderness canoe trips, Simone recognized

these folks as novice paddlers, not the local, gnarly, weekend warriors. *If they've ever been in a canoe before, they don't remember anything they learned. Both parents are paddling on the same side so the canoe's leaning left. Dad has no clue how to hold a paddle. Mom looks as if she's dipping a stirring spoon into an antique teacup.*

As the canoe reached the center of Rafi's vision, Mom's paddle slipped from her grip and into the river. Shouting an angry epithet, she whirled around, leaned over to catch it, and missed. Hulking Dad bent over the side to grab it, failed, lunged once more, and tipped the canoe, catapulting the young girl into the current. Mom and Dad disappeared underneath the canoe. Three eternal seconds later, Mom gurgled to the surface, screaming and coughing. Dad emerged like a breeching whale and attempted to dog-paddle. His too tiny, too tight life jacket ensured his body remained vertical while his arms flailed in the air as if he were trying to swim straight up.

Rafi leaped to his feet but then stood motionless, save the throbbing of his heart. Shivering and shrieking "Mommy! Daddy!" the girl had already floated five yards to the left, downstream from the capsized canoe.

She needs help, Rafi! The parents can hang onto the canoe, but the girl will soon be gone.

Rafi scanned right and left as if expecting park rangers or medics to come to the rescue, but made no move to help.

Rafi can't swim either! Of course not! He's from the desert.

Praying that a skill or two from her high-school lifesaving course would bob to the surface of her brain, Simone flung off Rafi's flannel shirt and bent down to remove his boots. *Goddamn laces! Precisely wrapped and tied twice.* She glanced up at the river to see the girl drift beyond the trees and out of her sight line. She emptied Rafi's pockets, threw the magazine and book into the panniers, and bolted toward the shore. Mom and Dad's rescue efforts had degenerated into screaming "Help!"

"I'll get the girl!" Simone shouted. "Save yourselves!" *Can't swim to her from here. Or get closer on the bank. The boulders would kill me. Gotta catch her at the boat launch.* Simone sprinted down a path through the woods, tripped on an arched tree root, and nose-dived into the dirt, scraping her palms raw as she slid across the packed earth. When she reached the clearing, the little girl appeared in front of the sloping concrete launch. Simone calculated the diagonal to intercept her and plunged into the river next to a family wrangling their boat onto its trailer. *Fucking freezing! Pump it up, Simone. Gotta warm those muscles.*

In between each four-stroke cycle of the front crawl, Simone lifted her head, refined her route, and yelled encouraging words to the girl. "I'm comin to get ya! Stay with me, girl!" *Cold, very cold, but we're gonna make it.*

During the last few yards the girl had stopped squealing and, with arms outstretched in front of her, was trying valiantly to swim to her savior. Propelled by a final butterfly kick, Simone thrust her head through those frail ghost-white goalposts raised above a stringy-blonde, waterlogged hairdo. "Grab onto my neck and hold on tight! Pretend you're riding on the back of a friendly seal!"

With a vice grip disproportionate to their size, tiny hands locked onto Simone's throat.

"Good girl!" Simone rolled over and began breaststroking toward the river bank. "Okay, that's a little too tight. Don't strangle the seal. What's your name, sweetheart?"

"Marla. Thank you for saving me. I was scared."

"Me, too. How d'ya feel now?"

"Cold."

"Me, too. We'll find your parents and get ya warm real soon."

"What's your name?"

"Simo... *Oops.* Simply Rafi."

"Your beard is scratchy."

"Sorry Marla, I can't shave right now. Just don't let go."

By the time Simone had crawled onto the grass and dislodged Marla's arms from her neck, an EMS ambulance pulled into the boat launch. Several bystanders were still recording the event on their smartphones as two elated parents raced over and embraced their soggy daughter.

Okay... to keep control or let it go. I don't know. God, I'm sick of this. What the hell. You're on your own again, Rafi.

Moments later, Marla's dad was practically shaking Rafi's arm out of its socket. "Thank you, thank you, thank you for rescuing out little girl!"

"I did?"

"Oh, such a humble man," her mother purred, stroking his other arm. "You are our guardian angel."

"I am?" Rafi looked down at his soaked clothing and bootless feet. "I am very wet. I remember watching you fall out of the canoe, but then..." He gazed up at the sky, flexing the wrinkled, blue-white fingers extending from his red scratched palms. "But then my mind is blank. It must be the new medicine I am taking."

Dad switched from shaking hands to patting Rafi's back with his big beefy paw. "I can't believe you tore through the woods, then dove into this ice-cold river, and swam fast enough to reach Marla!"

"I swam?"

"Like a friggin' fish. Somehow the ol' lady and I got the canoe to the bank, but we heard your call and trusted you'd save our little girl. What's yer name, kid, so I can remember it forever?"

"Rafi. And yours, sir?"

"I'm Bart, and this is my wife, Patty."

"We three are so blessed to meet you," she said, making the sign of the cross.

"Amen," Bart added with a warm smile.

"It is very nice to meet you both, but I think I had better find my bicycle and the rest of my clothes... and warm up a bit."

The older, grey-haired paramedic had been off to one side eavesdropping on the conversation. "Scuse me, sir, Mr. Bart. I'd like my partner to tend to yer little girl. And yer wife's got a nasty bump bulgin' on her forehead." He turned to Rafi. "And you, son... yer lips are blue, yer shiverin' somethin' awful, and yer hands need disinfectin'. How 'bout we find your bike, patch ya up in the truck, and give you and yer wheels a lift home?"

"Well, if it would not trouble you. I live above Flanagan's Saloon, and I hope my bike is still in the park next to Cozy Cottage Resort."

"No trouble at all," the paramedic said. "Cozy Cottage is where these folks are stayin'."

Within the hour, Rafi's was swaying with his eyes closed under a hot shower in his apartment. After toweling off and putting on warm clothes, he set his phone alarm and lay down on his mat for a nap. When the chirping alarm tweeted thirty minutes later, he picked up the phone and saw one of his light blue post-it notes stuck on the screen. "Rafi, it's four p.m. Check email on your laptop now."

The words 'Who wrote this?' were written in the puzzled expression on Rafi's face. He circled the room with his eyes, then got up and checked the apartment door. Locked. He cautiously cracked open the bathroom door and peeked inside. Empty. The lone window in the one-room apartment was ajar. He tiptoed over and peered out. No fire escape, only a flat, twenty-foot, red-brick wall. Rafi paused and scanned the room once more before sitting at the table to power up his laptop.

The second after he entered his email password and the Inbox loaded, Simone took control. She clicked on the Compose button, entered Rafi's email into the To field, added a title in all caps in the Subject field, and wrote her message. She sent the email, waited ten seconds until it showed up in the Inbox, and then released control of Rafi.

Alert and focused in a moment, he opened the email at the top of the list.

IT'S DR. SIMONE. READ THIS EMAIL NOW!

Friday, April 29, 4:09 PM

Hello, Rafi...

We haven't spoken for a while, but right now, it's very important we communicate with each other. Before you read the rest of this email, please note the exact time I sent it which you can verify above the email message field.

Remember that the instructions you were given for your treatment today said, "You might feel different, but just relax and go with it." So now please just relax and go with ME, because I AM YOUR TREATMENT.

The instructions should've also warned you and said something like, "Very strange things might occur. You might feel like you drop in and out of a dream state or be unaware of what you were doing during certain times of the day." I know these two strange things have already happened to you today. And I'm sure you're wondering who wrote the post-it note stuck to your phone and how it got there.

I've been with you all day. This is not a joke, Rafi, nor is it science fiction. It is deadly serious. A quantum leap has occurred in science, and we're both part of a bizarre experiment that seems incomprehensible.

Please respond right away and notice the blank pad of paper sitting next to your laptop.

Your friend always, Dr. Simone

Rafi read the email and then read it again. He fidgeted with his fingers while trying to figure out what to write. He glanced down at the blank pad, then composed a short email reply, and fired it off. "Dear Dr. Simone, it is nice to hear from you but I do not understand. How can this be possible? My screen says that I sent this message to me, today, two minutes ago. And how do you know about the note on my phone? Sincerely, Rafi"

Simone resumed control and sent him one final email.

Thanks for the quick reply. I have just now handwritten a message to you on the pad of paper in front of you. Please read it.

She then used his pen to write the message on the pad.

Rafi, now please close your email account, disconnect the laptop from the internet, and load Microsoft Word. We'll communicate that way, and you'll soon understand what is happening.

When her latest email appeared on the screen, she released control. Rafi read the email message, followed the directions on the pad, opened Microsoft Word, and waited. Simone took control again and settled in to tell it like it is.

Thank you for trusting me, Rafi. I heard what you said to Ronan earlier today. "I prefer the facts of science and math over the judgments of belief." I don't know all the hows and whys, but here are the facts. The masterminds behind your treatment have discovered a way to transfer my consciousness into your body. You're a science guy and might understand more than I, but their method is probably a combination of genetic engineering, DNA manipulation, and nanotechnology. My brain is somehow connected to yours for one day. I can't read your thoughts, though I can feel your emotions like I'm normally capable of doing. I can control your physical body, though when I do that, you drop into some sort of dream state. I can hear you when you speak, but when I talk, you can't hear me because your senses seem to become inert. That's enough facts for a start. Maybe they'll help you understand what happened to you today. What do you think about all this? Control is back in your court. Take your time. Write whatever you want in bold italics so we can keep track of who's talking!

Rafi read her words and leaned back on his chair to process them. After a couple of minutes, he added a blank line to the Word document and replied in bold italics.

Dr. Simone, thank you for telling me what is going on. I was very confused today when I could not remember what happened, like a drunk person who had blacked out. I don't consume alcohol but people have told me about it. This is all quite fascinating and frightening at the same time. I think of

the havoc a despot like Saddam Hussain could cre-
ate if he had this technology, or some fanatic who
could send someone like Dennis into a school on a
shooting rampage. If you can hear me, why not let
me talk and you write to save time?

They can hear what we say, Rafi. They spy on us with
the black watch on your wrist that contains GPS and
a microphone. They follow us everywhere with drones
or in EDNA trucks. EDNA doesn't only stand for
"Express Delivery. Now. Anywhere." It stands for En-
hanced DNA. Here's the sinister side of this situation.
You volunteered for this treatment and are being
compensated for it. Not me. They drugged me in my
home and kidnapped my body!

Simon'es anger escalated as she furiously pounded out
the facts.

Four days ago, I woke up inside another patient
without warning, without my consent, without a clue
as to what was happening, then each day another pa-
tient, and today inside you. You and I are like white
rats in a laboratory cage at the mercy of unsavory
scientists conducting their experiment. I choose this
clandestine method to communicate because I don't
want these people to realize how much I've learned
about them and their motives. And honestly, I'm
afraid for my safety. I still don't even know where my
real body is!

Although Rafi had sunk into a subconscious state while
Simone wrote, he surfaced straight away when she stopped.

Wow. Scary. I think I understand and am very
sorry for your predicament. The only man I met

*was very secretive and warned me not to tell any-
one about it. I did not like him, but the treatment
sounded intriguing, and I was drawn in by the fast
cash, not a prudent reason for doing anything.*

*Rafi, please know this. If they don't pay you, I will!
And I'll be glad to pay! I think tomorrow will be my
last day inside another patient, and then I'll meet
the mastermind on Sunday. I enlisted your help
today without asking your permission, but I might
need more help. I don't like taking control, taking
you away from your life like they've done with mine.
I hated seeing and feeling your confusion when you
suddenly woke up in another location, in the park
or at the river. I realized you couldn't swim so I took
over and saved the girl. But really, you and I did it
together. Your legs, body, and bike got us to the park.
You just took a little nap while I raced through the
woods and went for a swim. Sorry, but I fell on the
path and scraped your hands. When this is all said
and done, we can find a new therapist to counsel us
both on PTSD!*

**Thank you for the offer Dr. Simone, but I am not
concerned about the money. The universe always
presents me with new opportunities. You said you
might need more help. I am very willing, but how?
What can I do?**

*Rafi, I don't really need your help, just your permis-
sion to take control. Around six p.m. I must meet the
patient I inhabited last Wednesday. He might be able
to help protect me from the mastermind. He only*

lives a few blocks down the river, but I need to get to him secretly. I want to remove the black watch so they can't track my (our) movements, and then sneak out through the crowds. I'd like to turn on music so it seems like you (we) are spending the evening in the apartment. It should only take an hour, and then you'll (we'll) be back by eight like the instructions require. These people treat us like helpless pawns, and I'd rather we were hopeful teammates together.

Well, you certainly have my permission! I have speakers for my laptop and can find some extended music tracks on YouTube. I like Beethoven, Bach, or The Beatles. What would you prefer?

You decide on the music. Thank you so much, Rafi. Until then, please forget I'm here. If you decide to delve into your Bryson book, I might look over your shoulder. Amazing stuff in that book about DNA and how science marches on to new discoveries. I've read it three times, and every time I finish I think, "Damn, it's over again!"

I'll leave Word loaded on the laptop if you want to chat. My password is RafiTheIraqi. Don't do anything to me that I wouldn't do to me. :^)

By five-forty-five p.m. Rafi had eaten dinner, dressed in dark clothing and a wide-brimmed cowboy hat, removed the black watch, and cued the tunes.

Simone took over, wrote two words on the pad—"It's

showtime!"—and released control so he could read them.

Rafi started the music program with Beethoven's dramatic *Fifth Symphony*, adjusted the volume to a notch or two below party level, smiled, and gave his team a thumbs up in front of the mirror.

On a busy Friday evening, tourists streamed in and out of Flanagan's, and Rafi-Simone had no trouble blending in with the crowd. She crossed to the river side of Park Drive and veered left to The Fit Nest on the bike/foot path Diego had jogged on two days earlier. *No drones in sight. I'm good to go.* Simone had been hatching this plan during the afternoon, and without the GPS on her wrist, felt confident she could evade the EDNA goons. Hoping the conversation would be heard or recorded, she'd chatted with the paramedics in the EMS ambulance and complained about being frozen to the bone marrow level. "I can't wait to get home, take a hot shower, and read in bed for the rest of the night."

Lowering her head, she picked up the pace while passing an EDNA truck on the other side of the street. The eight-block trek only took ten minutes. With a silent prayer for Diego's presence, Rafi-Simone entered The Fit Nest and greeted Jade behind the reception desk. "Hi. Is Diego around?"

"I think he's upstairs. Is he expecting you?"

"I hope so. Could you please tell him Rafi is here?"

Jade punched in Diego's quarters on the intercom. "Hey, Bossman, a guy named Rafi on floor one wants to see you."

"Finally," he said. "Would you mind bringin' him up?"

"Yes, master. Your minion will escort him in a flash."

Thank god. A man with a heart and an open mind.

Dressed in green camo sweatpants and t-shirt with the gold CAFE logo on the chest, Diego was standing in the doorway when they arrived. "Rafi, my man! Or my human... whoever you are. Nice Stetson. You almost look local. Step inside. I was beginning to think you weren't comin'." He turned to Jade. "Thank you, Miss Minion. We don't want to be disturbed for a while, but first would you please bring us a couple glasses of fresh-squeezed whatever you have at the juice bar?"

Jade bowed. "Yes, massa. Your every wish is everyone's command."

Diego closed the door, pulled up the chair from the desk, and with an engaging but tentative smile, motioned toward the bed. "Make yourself comfortable, Dr. Rafi. This time you get the patient's couch, and I get the counselor's seat."

"You are my personal hero today. Thank you so much for believing."

"Truly believin' this is a stiff task, but I've been challenging my disbelief as requested." Diego tapped her on the wrist. "Where's your black watch? I wore one. Coco wore one."

"I didn't want the GPS tracking, the drones following, or remote ears listening. I left it at the apartment enjoying an extended program of classical music. I'd rather talk than pass notes."

"That note last night from Coco, or Simone, or someone in between, stretched my brain to the snappin' point. Part of me didn't want you to show up. Tell me this, how do I really know this cowpoke Rafi sittin' in front of me is Dr. Simone in disguise?"

"A fair question. Right now Rafi-Simone knows the entire story of my life, including what Coco-Simone wrote in that note, and what you heard Laurel whisper in your ear two days ago. 'I'm not in between. I'm a woman.' How do you explain that?"

"Coco and cowpoke here are in cahoots," Diego grunted. "And two days ago someone coulda planted a bug on me... or in the room."

"That could pick up a whisper in your ear?" Simone lowered her chin and raised her eyebrows in doubt.

"It's possible."

"Well, you'd know that better than I, but if we're all in cahoots, let's go back three months when you visited me at my office. When you left that day, the last three words I said were, 'Mountains and valleys.' You replied, 'Yin and yang,' and then rode away on your Ducati. Remember that moment?"

"Yeah." Diego sat with his elbow on his knee and fist scrunching his cheek.

"You think I bug all my clients everywhere and have been planning this for months? And for what possible reason could we have for concocting this outlandish stunt?"

"No, and I have no idea." Diego threw up his hands in surrender. "Okay, okay. Just tell me what the hell is goin' on! I remember what the head of the US patent office a hundred years ago said. 'Everything that can be invented has been invented.' He'd roll over in his grave at the thought of heart transplants, or smartphones that let you talk to and see people around the world, or this insane technology. So you were in me, Coco yesterday, and now him... Rafi? Mind boggling. If someone did this to me, I'd... I'd... I don't even wanna think about what I'd do."

Simone gave him a complete rundown of her last four days up to the present moment—the first humbling experience with Amanda, the amazement during her union with Diego, and her recent fears as the magnitude of her plight escalated.

As she finished with a deep exhale, Diego took a deep breath and asked, "So... we don't have to mention my encounter at your office to anyone, right?"

"Your fling with Ming? Don't worry. Patient-counselor

confidentiality. It's written in titanium in the industry. The incident did enlighten yet puzzle me about my coy employee who transformed into a seductive vixen. I'm not sure who to trust anymore."

"Certainly seems like you can't trust connivin' Simon. Some nasty rumors about him are still hangin' on the grapevine. Like you requested, I haven't told anyone about this, but I did call up Officer Eddie to ask if he had any dirt on Albright Pharmaceuticals or EDNA. He said unexplained disappearances and suicides have been reported about people workin' there, but no concrete evidence to suggest foul play. And I've been wonderin' who gave you the note, that 'sympathetic friend' you mentioned within the company?"

"Paul Roberts. He was there at the CAFE benefit last night. He worked with my father. I've known him for thirty years." Simone pulled an envelope from her pocket and offered it to Diego. "I picked up another note from him today, but it's weird."

"Another note from Paul?" Diego asked as he opened the envelope, his tone and expression suddenly perplexed. "Today? When?"

"About one p.m." Simone could feel the tension that had invaded his chest. "Why do you ask?"

Diego paused to gather his words. "You must not have heard." He paused again, head down, scratching the back of his hand with his fingernails even though it didn't itch. "Paul committed suicide this afternoon. It's been on the news. He threw himself off the Rooftop Restaurant at Baxter's Hotel."

"What?"

"A waitress in the restaurant recorded it on her phone. Paul was leanin' on the retaining wall and lookin' out over the city. Then he climbed onto the wall, turned to face the tables, smiled, spread his arms, and dropped backwards out of sight."

"No... no, no, no!" Simone shot up from the bed and paced in a tight circle, fingers clenched into fists. "Paul would never do that! When spirits were low at Albright, Paul always stood tall. Calm. That's one reason my father loved and respected him." She fell back onto the bed with tears soaking her cheeks. "Oh, Paul. Tall Paul. Sweet Paul."

"I was shocked when I heard. He seemed okay last night, maybe a little nervous about being in the spotlight, but okay." Diego bowed his head as he waved it side to side. "He was a good man, and truly cared about the CAFE kids."

Neither of them spoke for a long minute.

Simone sat upright and stared at Diego, her wet sky-blue eyes narrowed. "My brother did it. In his first note, Paul wrote that Simon could control him and other people as well... like I controlled Coco. When I was inside of you, I could've walked you off a bridge or into an oncoming train." Simone stood and continued her pacing. "The first note! What happened to the first fucking note? I gave you Paul's second note. I tore up the third one and flushed it down the toilet. The first note... the first note." Simone stopped, whirled around, and faced Diego. "I must've put it in Coco's pocket or purse! When the EDNA goons carted us away, they found it and alerted Simon! Paul wrote that he was so sorry this was happening to me, that he tried to stop the project, that Simon's eyes and ears were everywhere. He said, 'Beware of your brother.'"

"If all this is true, murder now tops the list of Simon's other felonies—kidnapping, fraud, and burglary, as in breaking and entering to commit a felony."

"I'm convinced he'd do anything for the almighty dollar. Can I see the note Coco gave you last night?"

"Sure, it's right here." Diego unlocked his desk drawer

and handed it to her.

Simone lay the notes side by side on the desk. Diego read today's note while she compared the two of them. "Look at these. The handwriting isn't the same. The one I gave you before is messy, the lines aren't straight, and the spacing between words is erratic. Paul wrote it in the dark while watching the show upstairs so if Simon happened to be spying in the background, he couldn't see the words, just the stage. Simon must've read this final note later while Paul's was composing it, then took control and wrote a new note, and let him deliver it to the 7/11 store." Simone set her finger on one specific sentence in the latest note. "Right here. This is a sure giveaway. 'He wants you to be a part of the process and thinks its a great opportunity for you to introduce it's developments to the psychiatric industry.' Simon's too smart for his own good, but he never understood the difference between the word 'its' with and without an apostrophe. Paul would never mix them up. He was a stickler for grammar."

A sharp rap on the door startled both of them. "Room service! Jade's Juice!"

As Diego opened the door, Rafi-Simone received the delivery. "Thanks. Looks good. Smells good."

"Carrot, beet, apple, and lemon with a hint of cinnamon," Jade announced with pride. "If you don't like 'em, I'll drink 'em both. I got a question for the guest. You're the Rafi who saved the girl in the river today, aren't you? I saw it on Facebook."

"That's me. You'd've done the same."

"Probably, but you were there, and I wasn't." Jade gave her a fist bump on the shoulder. "Good on ya."

"Thanks again."

Diego closed the door and gave Simone a quizzical look. "You didn't tell me about that part."

"Rafi watched the family fall out of their canoe, but couldn't swim. I had to step in."

"Light bulbs are flicking on in my head. You're that science teacher I saw interviewed on TV after the high school shooting. I remember the bullshit reporter who seemed to insinuate Rafi was the shooter's accomplice. That pissed me off... but today... the kid's a hero." Diego replayed Jade's fist bump. "Good on ya." He flicked a finger toward the porch. "Wanna sit outside and get some fresh air with our fresh juice?"

"Yes but no. I don't want to be seen here. EDNA trucks tend to swarm around me like bees who communicate with each other and the hive. The driver who picked up Coco last night was the same guy who delivered the drug-laced meal that knocked me out last Monday night."

"Got it. Inside it is." Diego sat back down at the desk and faced her on the bed. "So you think the almighty dollar is Simon's main motive?"

"Imagine what this technology would be worth in the global market. Or to the CIA or the military, in America or Russia. The other reasons in this note Simon wrote are bogus. 'Amazing possibilities, great opportunities, he'd like me to take over the company.' All petty persuasion from his pathetic mind with a blatant bribe at the end. I don't know much about genetic manipulation, but besides perfecting his heinous process, I think he wants my DNA."

"I think you're right. Maybe even more than that. He's got a terminal disease, and the grim reaper lurking in the future can be a vicious motivator. Maybe he wants another body to live in. Yours."

"As incomprehensible as it sounds, that's what scares me the most. This morning I woke from a horrible nightmare about Simon taking control and threatening me with a fireplace poker stuck in my neck." Simone shivered as if a gust of cold air had blasted through the room. "God, I'd rather he threw me off a building than having him prowl around inside me."

Another long silent minute passed before Diego began speaking quietly, slowly piecing together the immediate future. "Tomorrow night durin' the wee hours... after your last day of this hell week... Simon is gonna do his little possession trick on you... so if you refuse to come to him on Sunday morning... he can force you to enter the domain he controls."

"Or keep me there if I go willingly."

With the trace of a smirk on his face, Diego lifted one forefinger, then pointed at himself, then at Simone, then back and forth between them. "We have to prevent that from happenin'." He leaned in closer to her. "I believe honesty and authenticity are your innate attributes, but how are your acting skills? We might have to put on a little show."

"What do you mean?"

"Even though you're an empath..." Diego gestured for her to finish the word.

"Yes..." Simone shrugged her shoulders.

"What's your official title again?"

"Empathiatrist."

"Oh, yeah. Even though you're a kind, caring empathiatrist, and I'm certainly not, we're probably alike. I'll bet you've been thinkin' of all sorts of brutally honest things you'll tell Simon when you're face to face, how angry you are with his unethical, degrading treatment of you, what a piece of shit he is, how could he do this to his own flesh and blood, etcetera, etcetera. Right?"

"I admit it. You're right."

"We... as in Diego Hood and his band of merry men and women... *we will* get you out of there. They won't know what hit 'em. But you... as in we... first need to let Simon hang himself. You need to gather evidence. To record self incrimination stated by the royal ass himself so they can arrest him and fry his sorry ass in court."

"But how're you gonna to get me out?"

"Oh, I dunno. A flame thrower, a pack of hyenas, nuclear warheads. The plan'll either be divide and conquer... or distract and confuse... or somewhere in between. I carefully selected The Fit Nest staff for their extracurricular skills. We teach, but as the saying goes, "Those who can, do. Those who can't, teach. We still do and revel in it."

Simone's frown began to curl up on the edges. "I can almost hear your calculating mind churning like when you were planning your performance for the drunken monkeys. What Queen song will you play? 'Another One Bites the Dust?'"

"Might try fireworks instead of music. With your permission, I'd like to chat with Officer Eddie and get his approval for some undercover work. Don't have give him any details other than we're stoppin' a kidnapping and diggin' up dirt on a case he's already workin' on."

"Permission granted. Eddie's a good man with a semi-open mind. He's called on me to help a few times. Considers me his human lie detector."

"Eddie was tellin' me about a slick voice recorder the size and shape of a shirt button. Comes with an identical set of fake matching buttons to replace the others. It only transmits but we'll record remotely in The Fit Nest's own version of EDNA's lab truck, the Shenanigan Van. Somehow we need to sew 'em on before you don the shirt."

"I can give you my home security code and location of keys hidden outside. I don't know who I'll be in tomorrow, but probably another patient. You really think you can pull this off? With only one day to plan?"

"Hey, I only had a few minutes to stage our show for the

monkeys. Wing it, baby. That's what we did in the service. You got a better idea?"

Simone gurgled the final sip of juice through her straw and set it on the nightstand. "I have no plan, no idea. And I'd be honored to be one of your merry women."

"You know, it's super weird to be lookin' at and hearin' Rafi when I know I'm talkin' to Simone."

"Try waking up inside an ailing old woman. Or a young kid. When I vaguely figured out what was going on and how to handle a foreign body named Amanda, it became somewhat intriguing. I'm surprised I didn't kill Coco while trying to manipulate legs perched on top of high heels. By the way, do you know if she's all right? Normally I've been able to connect with patients the day after, but I couldn't with her."

"The morning was rough, but she got better in the afternoon. I spoke with Dr. Frank. Drug and alcohol overdose."

"I was afraid of that. And surprised at how much wine she put away last night. If the alcohol doesn't kill her, the pills will. I got a couple more questions. Personal ones."

"Shoot."

"Why'd you decide to participate in this program anyway?"

"Hmm." Diego tipped his head sideways and gazed into the past. "Good question. Three easy answers. One, no one's ever appeared out of the blue and offered me that much cash for one day's work. Two, the guy was kind of a self-absorbed dick, but spewed a bunch o' psychological mumbo jumbo about how it'll help me with issues I have, or know myself better, and that resonated a little. Three, I thought 'Fuck it. Why not?' I've never be one to shy away from risky business. Besides, the program date was my birthday. It seemed like a mega-gift from the universe, and I'd kick myself later if I didn't accept the present."

"Good answer. Did you get paid?"

"Transferred into my account the next day as promised."

"How much, if you don't mind my asking?"

"Twenty grand. Not bad for a day's wage."

"Whew," Simone sighed. "This week alone is costing Simon a hundred grand, and that doesn't even include all his people. Money to burn."

"Well, I believe it's time he got burned. You know where you'll meet him?"

"No clue, but I'd guess the new EDNA building on the other side of Copper Butte near the Albright headquarters."

"I'll have Snake snoop around tonight. He's gotta choose his bird-nest view." Diego rose and paced the same circle route as Simone had. "Somehow tomorrow I'll get a copy of the building blueprints. You don't even know where you'll be tomorrow! I might not see you again till I'm followin' you to the meeting. No, too risky. Gotta get a GPS on you."

Simone sat upright on the bed, arms wrapped around her bent legs, chin on her knees, her brain playing out the possibilities. "Whoever I'm in tomorrow, I assume we'll be unconscious by eight or nine p.m., then I'll wake up in my own bed on Sunday, perhaps inhabited by Simon. Everything needs to be in place before then. I'll get up and dress like my mood these past days—beat up and black and blue. Stick your spy toys in the navy-blue blazer, the blue-striped, button-down shirt, and black jeans hanging in my closet. Black penny loafer shoes are on the floor. Two keys are concealed in a magnetic hide-a-key box stuck to the back of the green metal hose wheel mounted on the wall behind the house—one for the side office door, one for my living space. Security code is 7-9-7-5-7-3. Enter through the main front door. My bedroom's upstairs to the right. You know Ming lives in the bungalow." Simone cocked her head and smirked. "Please try to avoid her this time. By the way, I've been wondering if you got confused when I controlled you and then released you. Rafi definitely does."

"Oh, a little I guess, but nothin' like in a war zone. An explosion can deafen you and make you silly. You just re-group and go on. Plan A becomes B, C, or Z."

"That sounds like my last three days. What time is it now? Left my watch at home."

"7:35. You'd better go soon."

"Write down your email address and phone number. I need to memorize it. I have no idea whether I can contact you tomorrow or not."

Diego grabbed a business card from the drawer and slapped it on his desk. "And I need two signals from you on Sunday. Let's set 'em in stone now. One 'on your mark, get set' and one 'go for it.' We'll be poised for action, but no one knows how long your evidence sucking session will last. A minute or so before you cue us for our Oscar-winning en-try, you could just say, 'I've had enough.' But when official show time hits, I'd get crazy religious, pump my arms heav-enward, and shout, 'May God unleash his wrath onto these demons!' Hell is definitely gonna break loose."

"Hmm." Simone's eyes seemed to sparkle above a wick-ed smile as she remembered screaming "I've had enough" in Amanda's art class. "I could do that. All those words fit the anger that's been building inside me for days."

Diego pulled aside the curtain and looked out the porch door. "It's sprinkling. You wanna ride back to Rafi's?"

"Thanks but no thanks. A walk in the rain sounds good. You have an umbrella I could borrow?"

"Sure. We've got some at the reception desk."

Simone took the lead and walked out the door.

Diego called from behind. "Hey, Dr. Cowgirl. Don't for-get your hat!"

"Thanks." She pulled the brim halfway down her forehead and muttered, "I feel like a riverboat gambler in this thing."

Wordless and in their own worlds, they plodded down the stairs to the reception desk.

"Jade, will you please give our hero an umbrella?" Diego asked. "She didn't plan for rain."

"She?"

He shot Rafi-Simone a guilty look, and then stammered to Jade. "He, she, it, hero, shero... doesn't really matter around here, does it?"

"Not to me," Jade said.

He turned away, opened the umbrella and the door, then motioned Simone outside. "Rafi, I hope to meet you again. You're always welcome at The Fit House. And doctor, I have an appointment with you on Sunday."

"You're on the schedule. Thanks you so much for your help." She took his hand and shook it firmly. "I have no idea what'll happen tomorrow, but you have given me hope. However, if I wake up inside Murray Spindler, one of my most challenging patients, I might commit suicide... No, that won't work. I'd probably kill him, not me."

Diego smiled. "Plan for the worst. Pray for the best."

"Mountains and valleys."

"Yin and yang."

Simone sauntered across the street and onto the river path. The dreary rain mirrored her mood though the ozone air buoyed her spirits. And she carried a friend's umbrella to protect her from the storm. *I can't wait until this shit is over. God and Diego help me get through it.*

Two blocks before Flanagan's, Simone spotted a white panel truck parked by the curb—EDNA style, but wider with an extended rear end. She inched closer, paused behind low bushes, and surveyed the scene. Couples strolled hand in hand on the sidewalk. The driver was reading a book balanced on the steering wheel. The truck idled quietly, and she could hear music emanating from the cab.

Pulling the brim of Rafi's cowboy hat further down on her face, she backtracked on the path, crossed the street, and approached from behind the truck. Faint light shone through two windows in the rear doors. Scanning every direction, Simone crept up and peered through a thin gap between the curtains on the inside of the truck. Eyes shut and slumped on a bench, a man appeared to be sleeping. She recognized him as the same paramedic at the CAFE benefit. *Hunter again.*

Electronic devices surrounded two gurneys set side by side in the center of the truck bed. The gurney on the right was empty. On the left one, Simone's unconscious body lay plugged into life support machines like in an ICU. As Rafi's heart skipped a beat in her chest, she saw an erratic blip on the heart monitor inside the truck laboratory. She gasped in shock. Hunter suddenly opened his eyes and stared at the back window. For a split-second, both of his eyes met one of Simone's. She shoved herself away from the truck, slipped on the slick pavement, but regained her balance and sprinted back to the path as the back doors flew open and Hunter leaped out.

Rafi-Simone stooped low and ran behind the row of bushes toward Flanagan's. Hearing the slapping of feet on the street behind, she dared not look back. The light grew brighter as she neared Flanagan's. Despite the shooting incident the previous night, the saloon was packed, and a crowd of guests had lined up to enter. A security guard eyeballed or patted down every person before admitting them. She burst through the line, shoved people aside in front of the jail house next door, turned right around the corner, and sprinted up the sloping dirt road. Scraping Rafi's knees while sliding down the steep rock boundary, Simone saw

Hunter's shadow creeping along the jail house wall and dropped four-feet down into the darkness of Zara's enclosure. Her menacing growl melded into a roar ending in a surprised yip when Zara caught a whiff of her buddy. Rafi-Simone limped to her doghouse and hunkered behind it.

Hunter had begun to climb down the embankment but halted upon hearing the sounds below. He looked over his shoulder at fangs flashing in the faint light. Standing on her two rear legs, choker pulled tight around her neck, metal chain stretched to its limit, Zara snarled, barked, and bit the night air like a wild rabid wolf.

Hunter's resolve swiftly dissolved. He clambered out, surveyed the area from a safe position, and stomped away. Fifteen tense minutes later, Simone climbed the rear rock wall, crossed the walkway to the roof entrance, and ducked inside to Rafi's apartment.

Bach's mysterious organ composition, "Fantasy and Fugue in G Minor," greeted her as she unlocked the door. *Too creepy for me right now. I need silence.* She clicked off the program, took out Diego's business card, and sat at the table. Once she'd memorized his email and phone number, Simone opened Word to write Rafi a final message.

It's eight p.m. I'm sure we'll be in the Land of Nod soon. My escapade went fairly well. No drones in sight, but on the way back, I peeked into a white lab truck and saw my unconscious body laying on a gurney. Frightening enough, then one of the attendants chased me all the way to Flanagan's. Zara to the rescue! I hid behind her doghouse. Sorry, I hurt you again when I slid down the rock wall. Diego from The Fit Nest down the road lent me the umbrella. Perhaps you could return it to him. You're on your own for the rest of the night. Thanks for your support and help. I look forward to seeing you again when all this over and done!

When Simone released control, Rafi blinked back to reality and wrote her a brief reply.

Welcome back! I am very glad your venture was a success, and hope that I never have to see my own body on a gurney inside a truck. Frightening indeed! Do not worry, I will return the umbrella, apply Neosporin to my knees, and I am certain we will meet again, sooner than later.

Rafi yawned and headed into the bathroom to wash his face and brush his teeth. He slipped on his white cotton yoga pants, set down the smartphone on his mat, stooped carefully onto his skinned knees, and activated his Islamic Call to Worship. After a ten-minute session of yogic asanas, Rafi ended his day as it had begun, bowing his head to the floor three times while chanting, "Allah is the greatest. God is the greatest. Yahweh is the greatest."

Simone drifted off to sleep during the music, praying she'd awake inside anyone besides Murray Spindler.

Day 5

Saturday

DAWN HAD BROKEN but two hours would pass before sun rays hit the western side of Copper Butte, though unlikely due to a low bank of ominous clouds creeping in. An array of odors coaxed Simone from the void. A whiff of distant rain. To the left, bacon frying mixed with the stench of garbage. To the right, the honey aroma of rhododendron bushes and sweet fragrance of peony blooms. Surrounding her, the musty smell of old wood, a filthy blanket, a rotting bone. Other unfamiliar scents slipped in that her brain couldn't identify. The predominant odor was distinctly dirt—not freshly turned, black loam—but hard, packed, dusty clay-dirt.

A cacophony of strange sounds distracted Simone from the pungent air. The crackling of bacon grease in a pan. Clanks and clicks in a kitchen. Faint music and chattering from a television. The breeze whisking overhead, a harbinger of the impending storm. Crickets chirping, a tiny creature scratching the dirt, mockingbird cackles and rooster cock-a-doodles fading into echoes. The high-pitched whine of vehicles out of sight on a street.

Simone could feel she was lying on her stomach with her chin resting on the ground. *I never sleep in this position*. She lifted her lids to see a curved archway in the darkness revealing the dim grey light outside. *Am I in a tunnel?* Squinting, she raised her head for a clearer look. In her lower peripheral vision, she noticed a four-inch snout terminating in a moist black nose. Tilting her head down, she saw two tan paws stretching in front of her and a chain winding out the opening. *This has got to be a goddamn dream.* To the right, a collection of bones, to the left, three grimy yellow tennis balls. She attempted to sit up, but her movements were clumsy and limbs foreign. Her arms were nearly as long as her legs.

After tripping on the threshold as she exited through archway, Simone quickly scanned the scene. A natural enclosure with a sloping rock wall leading up to the dirt road. Copper Butte rising on the horizon. The two-story building where Flanagan's Saloon and Rafi's apartment were located. Turning her head toward the old jailhouse behind the doghouse from which she'd emerged, Simone saw her thin black tail, taut, curving upwards to the sky, and a metal-link chain stretching twenty feet from her neck to the stake in the ground. *I'm inside Zara! How low can Simon go? Now he's sentenced me to a day shackled in the rain like a criminal in medieval stocks? Or forever if his fucking experiment fails? This explains the blank entry for Saturday that Paul found on the patient list. Either someone cancelled or Simon's playing his little game by ear.*

Like a four-stroke engine, efficient locomotion on four legs required that each action coordinate with the other three. Right rear leg first, left front leg second, then left rear to right front. Simone ran awkwardly, stretching her tether to its limit. She rocked backwards and forwards, yanking the chain with her muscular upper body, trying to dislodge or loosen the stake. Her neck was raw, throbbing with pain, but the stake wouldn't budge. She lifted one paw, tried to slip off the choke chain around her neck, fell onto her side, and flailed at the choker with both paws. Panting heavily, her pink tongue hanging over her jaw onto the dirt, Simone gave up. *If I ever get back my prehensile hands and opposable thumbs, they will wring my brother's neck. Okay, Zara, I surrender to you. Show me how to walk. Teach me how to be a dog.* She took a deep breath and released control.

Zara stood up calmly with ears perked, surveyed her surroundings, and seemed to commence her morning routine. After a few laps of water from her bowl, she sniffed the breeze, and then with her nose one centimeter off the ground, inspected her entire circular boundary defined by the chain length.

Simone's fury subsided as she relaxed into observation mode. A dog lover since childhood, she'd been fascinated by their abilities and studied their anatomy extensively. She knew their sense of smell was off the human charts, but to actually experience seeing the world by smelling enthralled her. A dog's nose has sixty times more olfactory receptor cells than the human version. A person might get one page of information from a whiff, whereas a dog gathers a sixty-page report including additional data deciphered by scent molecules absorbed by their vomeronasal organ which is absent from human anatomy. Because of their rapid breathing method and air flow through the nose, dogs smell in stereo and can determine the direction of an odor.

Besides the ability to hear four times the distance of a normal human, dog ears detect high-pitched frequencies up to 65,000 Hz, three times as sensitive as the 23,000 Hz upper limit of humans. Dogs can even "see" into the past or the future. They're able to smell who has recently been in a room and hear who is coming around the corner.

When Zara completed her olfactory and auditory appraisal of the day, she sat facing the Flanagan building and gazing up at the roof.

Of course! She's waiting for Rafi! Maybe I can connect and speed up his arrival. In unison with Zara, Simone focused her consciousness on Rafi like she'd done with previous hosts. *He's dressed and finishing his bowl of granola and yogurt in his apartment. That can wait. This storm won't.* She took control of Rafi, nabbed a bone from the freezer and sent him on the route they'd taken the previous morning. When his head appeared above the parapet, she released control, and executed her plan.

While Rafi sung his familiar tune to his sweetheart, Simone took control of Zara and began pawing the ground. With painstaking though sloppy precision, she scratched a capital "I" in the dirt, then the word "AM." Trying and failing to keep her paw prints to a minimum, she wrote the name "SIMONE" and finished with an exclamation point.

In awe on the roof, Rafi watched this new behavior, and then raced across the walkway, along the sloping dirt road, and slid down into the enclosure.

Simone had often wondered about the emotions of dogs and scoffed at the idea that they only desire food and have no capacity to love people. She now experienced the joy in Zara's chest and her intense full-body wagging. *Feels pretty much like I would, minus the yelping and wagging.*

"Zara Zarina! Have you learned a new trick that is beyond belief?" Rafi kneeled beside her, petting her neck and ears. "Who are you today? I see you have a new collar with a fancy black watch."

Zara looked directly into Rafi's face as she listened to his soothing voice. *I'll bet the look of love is in her eyes, just like the song.*

After a few minutes, their frenetic play session had obliterated Simone's message on the ground and was interrupted by the landlord's arrival. Mrs. Rudd emerged from the back door of the old jailhouse and waved as she walked toward them. "Good morning, Rafi!"

"Good morning to you, Mrs. Rudd. It looks like rain is imminent."

"It sure does." Her expression shifted from amiable to pensive. "I hoped you'd visit again today. The oddest thing happened last night. A man named Hunter knocked on our door around ten p.m. and wanted to purchase Dobette... I mean, Zara. He offered us a good sum of money with the condition that we give her to you this morning. I told him I'd ask, and then he took her to his truck cuz he wanted to examine her. That lasted a half-hour." She removed a hundred dollar bill from her apron. "Strange guy. He even gave me this so you can buy dog food. What'd'ya think? Will you please take her off our hands?"

His mind skimming through yesterday's encounter, Rafi was taken aback and momentarily speechless. Zara leaned on his leg, staring up into his eyes as if she understood what Mrs. Rudd had said. "Your offer is indeed tempting but I am not sure if I am able to accept it. I know that Mr. Flanagan does not allow pets in his apartments."

"Oh, Mr. Tough Guy with a heart of gold. I'd be glad to have a few words with him." Her eyes narrowed above a mischievous grin. "If Kyle refuses to allow Zara, my husband with throw him into our jail cell."

Simone-Zara barked, tugged Rafi by the shirt sleeve, shook it back and forth, and pulled him toward the rock wall he'd slid just down.

"Zara! What are you doing? She is asking me to take you home, not that you should take me home!"

That's it! Simone released Zara, took control of Rafi, joined Mrs. Rudd again, and delivered the decision. "I gladly accept your offer. I have a friend with a home where she will be welcome for the time being." Simone placed Rafi's hand on his heart as she'd seen him do when they met. "I will be honored to introduce Zara Zarina to a new life."

"You are a good man, Rafi. You're helping us, and she deserves a better life than this." Mrs. Rudd gestured in a circle to Zara's current world as a sprinkle of rain began. "Here it comes. Let's go inside. I've got some dog food to give you. It'll be easier for you two to leave by the front door instead of scaling this wall."

"That is very kind of you. I bet Zara could do it faster than I."

"I've got an unused leash inside, but would you like the chain and stake as well?"

Rafi leaned down and gently removed the metal choke collar. "No, thank you." He shook his head slowly, deliberately. "I can promise you one thing for sure, Zara. You will never again have to endure the indignity of being chained to a stake."

Zara licked his chin, bounded back to her dog house, returned with a tennis ball, and dropped it at his feet.

"Good girl! I will bring all three of them."

After slinking along the walkway through wind and heavy rainfall, slipping in the tenant entrance of Flanagan's, and slogging up the stairs—a difficult task with one hand holding a leash and the other balancing a half-full bag of Gravy Train on his shoulder—Rafi unlocked his apartment door and introduced Zara to her new world. She carefully swept its entire floor and contents with her nose, padded in tight circles on Rafi's mat, and lay down surrounded by the invisible body of her buddy's scent.

Speaking softly, caressing her with his voice, Rafi sat squat-legged beside her and removed the black watch collar. He then rose, went into the bathroom, placed the collar underneath towels in the cabinet, closed the door and returned. He sat at his table, powered up the laptop, and slid his chair over to the mat.

"Dr. Simone," Rafi whispered, "I know you are here. When you were controlling me outside, I could hear what you were saying. I did not drop into an unconscious state like yesterday. Last night I read about genetics for an hour before falling asleep. Besides being a blueprint for the building blocks of all living things—whether it's a radish, a sea urchin, or Saddam Hussain—DNA loves to reproduce. This enhanced DNA may be evolving rapidly. For now I have hidden your black watch in the bathroom and turned on my laptop so we can communicate silently like before. Maybe I will be able to follow what you write while you write it! This is all quite exciting, scientific, and provocative."

Yeah, like a three-ring circus with me trapped in the middle circle. Immediately after Microsoft Word loaded, Rafi's fingers were keyboarding Simone's message.

Rafi, I've been able to connect the next day with other hosts but never know how long it will last. We need to talk about several things NOW. First question: what is your schedule today?

Dr. Simone, I am writing in bold italics like before. Besides taking care of Zara, my only plan is a dentist appointment for teeth cleaning at 10 a.m. Otherwise, I am at your service. Who is this friend with a home where Zara would be welcome?

His response was quick. I'm directing his hands, but he's become aware like Coco or Amanda.

Thank you for your support... again. I am that friend. You and Zara are welcome in my home. I have an ex-

tra bedroom for you, and I'm certain my two doggies will accept her. I visited the office while I was inside Diego and somehow they knew he was me. I'd like to go home this afternoon, spend the whole night, and lie on my own bed for a change. My receptionist Ming should be there, but I don't trust her, nor do I trust three dogs alone in the house! All the furniture could end up shredded.

That is fine with me. What else do I need to know?

Rafi, I was so angry when I woke up this morning, but good news has sprouted from the bad. I hate seeing dogs shackled in chains, and we have sprung Zara from prison! I rescued both my dogs from an animal shelter. When I lose my connection with you, which could be anytime, we can use these codes I learned from my first host patient on Tuesday. Amanda couldn't speak, so she used these signals with her mother. One rap or tap meant "yes." Two meant "no, thanks." Three meant "I don't know." Four raps for them meant "I'll be right there," but for me today, it might mean "I have to pee." Got it?

Got it. Next?

I'll stay here when you go to the dentist. I don't want to attract attention or hang around outside in the rain waiting for you! While you're gone, please call Diego at 541-339-8756 and tell him my host body today is a dog and that we plan to be at my home this afternoon. He, or one of his people, will be making a clandestine visit late tonight and helping me tomor-

row. He knows the security alarm code and where the key is. Please answer any of his questions and bring back any advice he has to give.

I will take care of it. Do not worry. Is there anything else?

Tomorrow morning around 11 a.m. someone will come to escort me to a meeting with the mastermind. I didn't tell you this before, but the mastermind is my twin brother Simon, who seems to have become my EVIL twin. I feel he's capable of doing ANYTHING in his power to get what he wants. He can control people like I can, maybe more effectively. Simon and his scientists developed the process. I feel certain he'll be inside me before dawn tomorrow, so in the morning, we must only speak small talk to each other. My home could very well be bugged. I think he'll be able to hear and see everything.

I will do my best. Please understand that when I touch you or pet you today, I am only thinking of Zara Zarina. I might not be able to keep my hands off her!

How funny you even have to say that! Who'd've thought anyone could be in this situation? No one, no where, no time except the present. Treat her with the TLC she deserves. I must confess I'm loving the experience of being a dog. You should try it some time!

Maybe in my next life. For now I have enough issues just trying to be me. Since this might be the last time we communicate like this, I feel the need

to share the rambling reflections in my brain.

The few facts I learned last night are quite thought-provoking, and the more scientists discover about genetics, the less we all seem to understand. 97% of DNA is classified as junk, or non-coded, and no one has determined its purpose. We know that nearly all human DNA is the same, 99.9% of it; the miniscule .01% is what makes billions of us different. That .01% of your DNA might contain a gift that your brother did not receive. Maybe there is a way you can turn his bizarre technology to your advantage.

DNA from one species can even absorb the DNA of different species. Imagining it would produce a grotesque effect, scientists planted the gene that creates a pig's eye into a fly. The fly absorbed the gene as its own and still produced a fly eye. If DNA exchange or transfer was a method used with you and me, perhaps Simon's technology is evolving faster than he realizes. Overnight I went from being inert while being controlled, to becoming aware and observing the control. You might be able to absorb Simon's DNA and make it your own.

My father used to teach me in Arabic the same message of an English idiom. "Where there's a will, there's a way." I survived my trials and have become a better man because of it. I think your will to survive shall present the way. As Captain Kirk of Star Trek always said, "To boldly go where no man has gone before." I feel confident you are capable of going far beyond where or what this little man

Simon can comprehend.

*Kind and encouraging words, Rafi. Thank you. I
don't know what time it is, but do what you need to
do. Right now I'm going to relax into this sweet dog's
life which looks like it might include a nap.*

Eight blocks away in Mama's living room at The Fit Nest,
Diego assembled his seven-member team—Sniper Snake,
Jimmy the electronics whiz kid, Smilin' Norman, Chick Fi-
let, Conan the Barbarian, weight-trainer Jade Lafitte, and
Masaru, master of martial arts—to plan the impending ca-
per he'd dubbed Mission Possible.

"I've talked with each of you about this, but let's see
where we're at so far. The next twenty hours of this distract,
confuse, and rescue mission are crucial. We might have to
destroy a few doors or windows, but I don't want any casualties or injuries. You'll have to trust me on the whos and
whys. They're complicated. Focus on the where, what, and
how. Snake, you scoped out the location last night. Please
enlighten us."

"EDNA's about a half-mile farther down the road leadin'
to Albright Pharmaceuticals which is just south of Buffalo
City. It sure ain't a fortress, more like a schizo building with
laboratories, loading docks, offices, and living quarters.
High-tech, modern design for sure—a long two-story rect-
angle with a huge bank of windows on the far end like the
cockpit of a spaceship. An outside balcony curving around
the second floor makes it look like a caterpillar with weird
eyes and big lips."

"How many spliffs did you smoke during your cosmic
tour last night?"

"One."

"How big?'"

"Mondo," Snake said with a demented grin. "Never mind. Lemme try to draw it." He sketched the area layout on a pad laying on Mama's coffee table as the team huddled around it. "The building hugs a smaller butte, and all the scientific shit is on the second floor. A roundabout at the main entrance branches off to driveways on both sides. EDNA loading bays are on the back; package drop-offs and offices face the main road. There's a security stop with a guard who checks trucks into the rear loading docks, but the rest of the driveway's clear."

"Is there some other way into the lab area?" Diego asked.

"Could be. Probably the main entrance by the round-about when you first approach the complex—chi-chi fu-fu with plants and fancy couches and two uniformed guards sittin' behind a counter that might house security monitors."

"Did you find a sweet spot where you can be our eyes tomorrow?"

"Oh, yeah." Snake seemed damn pleased with himself. "On top o' the ridge with a bird's view of control central. A cozy nest complete with mesquite bushes to hide my ass. Smells real sweet."

"Your ass... or the bushes?" Norman asked, serious like a professor. "We need clarity here."

"Definitely not his ass," Chick added. "I can smell it from here."

"Focus children!" shouted Diego, and then with an open palm gestured to Snake. "Please continue."

"The bushes smelled sweet."

Diego rolled his eyes, shook his head, and sighed.

"Sorry, boss, back to the drawing board here." Snake pointed at the sketch with his pen. "This rear control center is three stories tall. Through the windows behind the balcony, I could see the third floor is like a round stage rising out of the middle of the second floor. Guys in white coats walk up from their workstations to mastermind Simon sittin' in his wheelchair and plugged into some medical machines with a nurse and four guards around him."

Diego broke in. "Conan, any luck gettin' the building plans?"

"It's Saturday, but our secret sweetheart at the bureau promised she'd have them this afternoon."

"We need 'em. Keep on it. Snake, did you ever see Simon move?"

"He'd raise an arm or turn his head, but that's about it. I could see everything crystal clear with my binocs, and I swear one o' the guards is a guy I know... went to high school with 'im. He's even been here at The Nest a couple times. Pete Ferguson. Big dude but not a killer. I don't think any of the guards are professional mercenary-types, just local workin' stiffs. I could probably find Pete and ask a few questions."

"Good idea," Diego said, "but we can't risk it. We don't know who Simon can control."

Snake shook his head. "Weird."

"Way beyond weird," Diego agreed. "And I'm convinced Simon also caused Paul Robert's death. This mastermind thinks he and his holy quest are beyond any law. Okay, next task. We need to get hold of an EDNA delivery truck tomorrow mornin', one they won't miss to deliver Conan and me through the check point. Smilin' Norman?"

Norman eyeballed his on-and-off partner. "What'd'ya say, Chick Filet? You and me? The happy couple who calls for a pickup but picks up a driver instead?"

She returned his smirk with a thumbs-up. "How 'bout if you be the little woman this time?"

"Sure, if you let me use your kitchen knives."

"Dream on, Taserboy."

"Great," Diego said. "And tonight we need someone who is silent, invisible, and can sew. Volunteers?"

As the team perused itself, Masaru raised one forefinger.

"Of course!" Diego said with a grin. "The man who speaks softly, carries a big ninja stick, and has a satchel full o' secret skills. You and I will stake out at the kidnappee's abode. I'll snap some pics of the perps returnin' her unconscious body. Later you'll sneak inside, sew a set of buttons, one of which is a microphone, on a select shirt and implant a GPS bug in the heel of Simone's shoe. Jimmy, is the Shenanigan Van fully operational?"

"Up to snuff 'n' ready to roll, boss."

"You'll control all our communication, so make sure the earbugs work and are connected. Calibrate the GPS bug before Masaru delivers it. Get out any remote-control fireworks we have left, especially the aerial bombs, and a few pepper gas grenades. Masks for everyone and an extra for Simone. We need to look as intimidating as possible. Conan can just wear a Speedo and scare the hell out of 'em."

"Mmm. Comfy," Conan quipped. "I just bought a new one with a lovely floral pattern."

"I'm out," Norman frowned, threw up his hands and stood to leave. "Too far over the edge. Get someone else."

"Me, too," Chick echoed and started to follow him out the doorway. "No way I'm gonna be seen in public with the Barbarian in a floral Speedo."

"Hey, c'mon back," Diego pleaded. "We'll video it, post it on our Facebook page, and get a million likes."

Wearing matching smirks, Norman and Chick turned back, high-fived both of Conan's raised hands, and flopped back on the sofa.

"Okay, team, try to hang in there for two more minutes."

"You started it," Norman grunted, still smirking.

"You're right, now let's finish this. Jimmy, Officer Eddie has given us his blessing to gather dirt and prevent a kidnapping that's already been goin' on for five days. He might even ride shotgun with you in the van."

"What about your favorite minion?" Jade asked, feigning pain and suffering. "Watch the paint dry here in the store room? Rearrange your sock drawer?"

"Do not fret, minion. You have vital tasks ahead. The first one is to contact our backup staff for an eight-hour shift tomorrow. We'll all be busy as flies on Simon's shit. In the a.m. after we score the EDNA truck, Jade, Chick, and Norman will ride in a separate car, subdue the front guards, and disable the security cameras. Jade, you'll stay at the guard station and be our eyes on the main road and entrance while Chick and Norman advance. You're on your own to plan it. I'm sure you'll come up with somethin' creative."

"I can look real innocent and seductive... for a few seconds."

"You certainly can, but put some sleeves over those biceps. They could spook a gorilla." Diego folded his hands in prayer and bowed. "You know I mean that in a nice way."

"Nice way taken." Jade flexed one bicep into an impressive bulge while brushing an errant hair from her forehead. "I know you're jealous."

"That's it for now. We'll reconnoiter later on." Diego paused. "Does that mean we just connoitered? Is that even a word?"

"If it wasn't before, it is now," Jade said. "I'll find out and get back to ya."

Rafi returned from the dentist at noon and received a warm greeting from Zara already waiting and wagging at the apartment door. He kneeled down and whispered, "Teeth cleaned and Diego contacted. Shall we chat via Word?"

Simone-Zara tapped the floor twice with her paw.

"No, thanks, I guess. Does that mean your connection with me has faded?"

She tapped once, paused, then tapped four times.

"And you need to pee?" Rafi asked.

She tapped once. *I've gotta teach this trick to Dammit and Brandy. Thank god dogs can hold it longer than humans.*

"I will get your black collar. Our adversaries must not think anything is out of the ordinary."

Smart boy. He's on it.

After a rest stop by the river, Rafi put the collar back in the bathroom and joined Simone-Zara on the mat. "I spoke with Diego. He said not to worry. The plans are moving along well, and Officer Eddie has authorized the rescue. He wanted me to remind you of three things. One, make sure the specific clothing you will wear tomorrow is easily recognizable. Two and three, remember your countdown signal, 'I've had enough' and your zero hour signal... what did he say? Oh, yes, your 'hail Mary to heaven.' Does that make sense?"

She tapped once. *Wish we had a code for thank you.*

"I will grab a quick bite to eat, throw some clothes in my pack, and be ready to leave soon. And Zara, I have another juicy bone for you to chew!"

Jeez Louise, another grim trial for the vegetarian.

A half hour later, Rafi strapped on Zara's black collar, carried his bike down the stairs, and mounted it on the sidewalk. "I think there is a leash law in this city but I will not put it on you. We both know the way so stay close beside or behind me."

Rafi rode on sidewalks as much as possible, and the two-mile journey went smoothly until they were passing a strip mall on a semi-busy street. Out of the corner of Zara's eye, Simone saw a suspicious man on the opposite sidewalk, head down, ball cap pulled over his eyes and approaching an elegantly dressed, older woman leaving a jewelry store. Suddenly he sped up, snatched her purse, and dashed ahead in the direction Rafi was riding.

Simone deliberated over the dilemma and settled on a decision. *Okay, legs, let's see what they can do.* She took control of Zara and ran ahead of the bike as the man turned right at the corner.

"Zara! Simone!" Rafi yelled. "Stay close!"

Simone-Zara veered diagonally across the street, out of the man's sight lines, and picked up her pace. Twenty yards down the side road, the man ducked into an alley between the buildings.

Rafi screeched to a halt, waiting for an opening in the traffic so he could cross the street.

As Simone-Zara turned into the alley, she spotted the man leaning on a dumpster and opening the purse. She sprinted ahead, leaped into the air, and slammed him into the dumpster. The man shrieked in shock, bounced off, and fell onto his back. She pinned him down with two paws on his shoulders, teeth bared and snarling, saliva dripping down her jaw onto an aghast twenty-something face.

Rafi rode up and jumped off his bike, gawking at the scene and trying to fathom what had happened. Seeing the contents of the purse strewn on the alleyway and the look of terror in the young man's eyes, he began to understood. "Zara, do not kill him."

"Call it off... please... I was gonna return the purse and the money," the kid stammered. "Really... I just needed it today... honest... I'm not a thief."

"Do not move," Rafi commanded, holding Zara's collar and pulling her backwards. "It is a she. And right now, you are undoubtedly a thief, lying in a pile of evidence." He scrutinized the boy's face, mumbled "I know you..." and tried to place the name. "You are Becky Swanston's older brother. We met at the science fair at Hawthorne. I am Rafi, her former teacher, and I am not pleased to meet you again."

"Mr. Mansur. I remember. I'm Luke."

"Well, Luke Swanson, if you are not a thief, what are you?"

He sat up, rubbing his bruised shoulder with one hand and his neck with the other. "I'm a struggling graphic designer with a client who won't pay and a wife with diabetes who needs insulin today. I work part time at a grocery store too, but that doesn't cover the cost. I can prove it. A prescription is waiting to be picked up at the drugstore around the next corner."

"You are certainly not a very good thief." Rafi stretched out his arms, palms up. "Broad daylight. No mask. Plenty of traffic on the street."

"You gotta believe me," Luke pleaded. "She needs it now. I've never done anything like this before. Really."

The sound of an approaching siren escalated the urgency of the situation. "Okay, Luke, I believe you. I will make you a deal." Rafi spoke while picking up and replacing the purse contents. "Stay in the alley for a few minutes, maybe hide inside the dumpster, which is infinitely better than a jail cell, and I will deliver the purse to its owner." Rafi dusted off Luke's ball cap and handed it to him. "If you are gone when we return, I know where to find you and so will the police. If you are here, we shall go to the pharmacy together. Deal?"

"Deal. Thank you. I'm sorry. I was desperate."

"I understand and choose to trust you for now. I have

Scott Jones

been desperate as well. And so has Zara." Rafi smiled and patted her on the head. "She will not hurt you although I am sure those sharp fangs could. Luke, hide and survive. Zara, would you please carry the purse? You are the star who retrieved it."

Rafi's amazing. And so is Zara. I should try that trick on my patients to convince them to follow my advice. Jump onto the couch, bare my fangs, and drool on their face.

Bathed in the patrol car's rotating red lights, a small crowd had gathered in front of the jewelry store. Rafi approached the doorway, walking his bike with Zara trotting at his side. Unaccustomed to seeing a Doberman Pinscher—especially one carrying a purse by the strap—the bystanders warily stepped back, jockeying for position while recording the event on their smartphones. Once inside the store, Zara padded up to the distraught woman and dropped the purse at her feet.

"We surprised the thief around the corner," Rafi explained to the policemen. "My dog grabbed the purse, but he fled on foot. I did not get a good look at his face hidden under his cap. He ran to the east on the next street behind this one. You might be able to catch him."

After a barrage of questions and evasive answers, Rafi and Zara returned to the dumpster and knocked on the lid. Luke cracked it open and peeked out.

"I sent the police east. The pharmacy is west." Rafi rummaged in his bike pannier. "Take off your cap, put on this hoodie for now, and walk through this alley. We'll meet you there."

When they reached the drugstore, Rafi rested his bike on the parking meter, wrapped the leash handle around the metal post, and fastened it to Zara's collar. "I hate to do this, but I will return in a few moments. Leash law." He scratched her ears and smiled. "I know I need not lock my bike with Zara guarding it!"

Rafi found Luke at the pharmacy counter in the back, paid ninety-nine dollars for the insulin with a credit card, and wrote his phone number on Luke's receipt. "Deal number two. Call when you are ready to reimburse me and return my hoodie. You have one week. I might know some reliable people who could use your services, but you must first prove yourself worthy. I understand that pharmaceutical companies charge exorbitant prices and steal from the very people who have made them rich, but I hope this incident inspires you to select a different path, unlike the greedy drug lords. A noble path. The choice is yours to make, Luke Swanston."

He grabbed Rafi's extended hand and shook it with fervor. "Mr. Mansur, I can't thank you enough." Luke continued gushing as he backed away down the aisle. "But thank you for trusting me, thank you from my wife, thank you, thank you, thank you. I won't let you down!" He turned and zipped out the door.

Outside, Rafi unleashed Zara, mounted his bike, and subtly pointed to the Edna truck parked down the block. "My, oh, my," he sighed. "Life with you has been quite capricious since yesterday morning. Now perhaps we will finally be able to get you home, unless you propel us into another adventure!"

As they drew near to Simone's home, she saw the dogs in the back yard and noticed that Ming's sporty red Mazda Miata was absent from her bungalow driveway. Since many Chinese had an abundance of disposable cash, she hadn't given it another thought, but lately too many things about her seemed suspicious. *Quite a car for a young woman working as a receptionist. She's out and about so I've got to show Rafi the hide-a-key... and damn it... scratch out the security code in the dirt?*

Rafi parked his bike in the front and looked down at Zara. "Shall I ring the bell?"

Simone-Zara snorted, turned her head to the left, lead Rafi behind the juniper bushes lining the wall, and pawed the metal hose reel. He located the hide-a-key magnetic box fastened on the rear, then returned to the front door landing, and removed the set of keys. She looked up at Rafi, shaking her head from side to side. *Code first, keys second.* Bracing herself on the wall, she stood on her hind legs, touched the security key pad with her nose, then dropped onto all fours and tapped the ground seven times with one paw.

"Seven? I don't know, and I have to pee?"

Simone-Zara again shook her head and tapped twice.

"Ah, seven must be the code." Rafi entered it. "Next."

She tapped out the other five numbers as he punched them in, and the LED flashed green. Rafi located the correct key, unlocked the door, and they entered the living room.

The doggies must be outside. Dammit'll be happy to meet new friends but Brandy'll be pissed and try to defend her turf. Why didn't I alert Rafi before? I hope he gets it. He lived on the street with dogs. In her mind, Simone had played out the scene of her pampered pets confronted by a strange man and dog, a large intimidating dog, trespassing in their domain. Zara had succumbed easily to Simone's control, and during their purse snatcher encounter had even seemed to respond to subtle cues as Amanda had done. Simone didn't have to focus as intensely to lead Zara. It felt more like a partnership.

Through the sliding glass door, she could see the dogs sitting outside on the deck, alert and aware of the sounds in the house. *Act it out first.* With Zara's tail tucked between her legs, Simone crawled forward a few inches on her chest then rolled onto her back and whined.

"What is it?" Rafi asked, puzzled.

Simone-Zara stood, lifted a paw toward the door, and repeated her movements.

"I understand. A new human and a big new dog. I will open the door and step aside, yes?"

She tapped her paw once.

As Rafi approached the door, Simone could feel Zara tightening the muscles in her jaw and legs.

On the other side of the glass, Dammit wagged and stretched casually, his tongue to the side over his teeth. Straight up and tense, Brandy's tail stood stiff.

Zara tilted her head down, raised her hackles, and bared her fangs. *Okay, girl, settle down. We're in this together.*

Rafi slid open the door and stepped away.

Dammit scampered in first, gave Simone-Zara an amiable nose bump, raced over to Rafi, and stuck her head in his lap.

Both ears flattened, Simone-Zara replayed her ingratiating behavior. Brandy inched forward over the threshold like a soldier stalking an intruder in the darkness, wary, her snout sucking in air for clues. Now lying on her side, Simone-Zara yawned and licked her lips in submission.

Her tail wagging tentatively, Brandy cocked her head, one ear up and one relaxed, widened her eyes and sniffed as her panting accelerated. She stretched out into her namesake, the Downward Facing Dog yoga pose, let out a happy howl, and nuzzled the new Doberman on the neck. *The world's best doggler... well, one of two... or three!* Simone-Zara returned the nuzzle, stood slowly, and then sprinted out the doorway into the backyard.

Dammit and Brandy followed, barking and leaping behind her. The three of them raced through the yard, chasing each other around bushes and trees, wrestling, playing tug-o-war with a knotted rope, and having a grand ol' time.

This is another dream come true! Not just to feel a dog's unbridled joy, to be on all fours and experience it on their level!

After their half-hour romp, Simone-Zara, Dammit, and Brandy gave Rafi a tour of the house, starting with the kitchen cabinet that held the dog food, rawhide bones, and snack biscuits. Upstairs at the open doorway of the guest room, Brandy and Dammit waited patiently though puzzled as Simone-Zara pointed out the bed and bathroom to Rafi. *I know you rapscallions sneak in here when I'm gone, but you're being very obedient in front of our visitor.*

"My abode for the evening I assume. Yes?" Rafi asked.

She tapped once on the floor, and led him past the stairway to a larger bathroom with sauna and shower, then turned down the hallway into another bedroom and jumped onto the four-poster bed. Brandy and Dammit followed suit and stretched out, ready for a three-dog night or at least a three-hour nap, content in a room where they were welcome anytime.

"Home sweet home! I bet you have missed this. Relax. I will bring my bags up and fetch some snacks for you."

My mind is relieved, but I miss my body. Every scintilla of my being is praying this nightmare will end tomorrow.

Simone's bedroom was furnished with her ancestors' legacy. When the family emigrated from Austria to America in 1903, her great-grandmother brought the flame mahogany bed frame and armoire, empire chest of drawers, mirrored dressing table, and maroon-velvet tufted armchair. The set had been passed on to her grandmother, then to her mother. Simone's parent's had bequeathed each of their twins an equal inheritance share, and it required scant effort to convince Simon that she should receive the priceless antiques. He wanted the laboratory, test tubes, beakers, microscopes, spectrometers, vacuum concentrators, and the clinical ultracentrifuge system. Old wood was worthless except for the cash value he could extract from his sister's share.

After a peaceful, rejuvenating slumber, Simone-Zara hopped off the bed, nosed open her armoire door, and checked to see if each article of clothing and the black loafers described to Diego were where she'd remembered. *A place for everything and everything in its place... except my body.*

She padded down the stairs with her two dog shadows on either side and found Rafi reading on the sofa. She gave him a nudge on the shoulder before scratching at the front door. *This holding in Number One and Two would be hard to handle. I may be a daily slave to my dogs, but they're still slaves to me when they have to pee.*

Rafi obliged, opened the door, and waited while gazing in the opposite direction as Zara. Although the three dogs had become buds without a war over who deserves alpha status, both Dammit and Brandy had to reapply their scent over the exact spot Zara had done her duty.

Simone-Zara led the troops down the walkway to the Sensory Sanctuary for her oft routine of quiet time during the golden hours before sunset. Rafi unlocked the door, and she settled into the center of the round Persian rug's geometric pattern. Soon Brandy and Dammit's ears perked, turned toward the well-tuned whine of Ming's approaching Mazda, and scampered to the rear deck doors to meet her. Rafi sat on the therapy couch, and Simone-Zara stayed put, tense and alert. *This will be interesting to watch the reaction of Ming the Minx.*

Alarmed that Simone's dogs were not where she'd left them, Ming scanned the backyard, saw Dammit and Brandy through the sanctuary door, and headed in their direction. She unlocked the door, bent to greet the dogs, and fixed her gaze on Rafi. "Who are you?" she demanded.

Zara let out throaty growl as her hackles raised, and then lowered her ears, not in submission, in preparation for attack. *Dogs know. She doesn't like Ming.*

"I am Rafi, Miss Ming. We met a few months ago."

Her glare intensifying, Ming clamped her hands onto her hips. "What you doing here?"

"I have brought Simone home." Rafi gestured to Zara. "She has had a rough week."

"This dog not Dr. Simone," Ming scoffed. "You make joke? I call police."

Bad English and bad acting. She's just another of Simon's pawns and knows exactly what's going on. How could I miss the clues along the way? Too fucking trusting, Dr. Denial, duped by a mole right under your feeble human nose. Ming gave them access to my files. She let them into the house to retrieve my body and kept the dogs at bay. She will let them in tonight.

As Ming slipped her smartphone from her pocket, Zara leapt forward, lips curled above her sharp white fangs, her snarl morphing into a howl, and halted one yard away from Ming, poised to leap again.

Ming flattened on the wall, her free hand trying in vain to locate the door knob.

"Zara!" Rafi called as he rushed over, kneeled, and whispered into her ear. "Let us demonstrate the miracle." He stood and faced Ming. "For five days, Dr. Simone has been the guinea pig in a nefarious experiment and has somehow inhabited four of her patients, including me, until today when she woke up inside Zara Zarina here. Of course, Dr. Simone cannot speak but she can answer questions by tapping on the ground. One tap, yes. Two, no. Three, I don't know. Four, I have to pee."

As he spoke, Simone-Zara had trotted over to a shelf and rummaged through a wicker bin of toys, wooden blocks, and games she'd collected to entertain young children during their parents' sessions. She picked up a boxed deck of cards, returned to Rafi, and dropped it at his feet.

"What's this?" Rafi asked, picking up the box and opening it. "Ah, Simone has a better plan. Alphabet cards. Excellent idea!" He removed them from the box and spread them face up on the floor—fifty-two laminated cards displaying upper and lower case letters.

Simone-Zara pawed through the cards, chose a capital "I" and slid it below the rest, then completed the sentence with a lower case "am," an uppercase "S," and lower case "imone."

"Cute card trick," Ming muttered, frowning. "Proves you are dog trainer."

"Well, you could be right," Rafi agreed. "Ask her a difficult question that I could not know."

Ming thought for a moment. "What is my full Chinese name?"

The task took two minutes for Simone-Zara to spell out "Zhao YAngmiNG," substituting upper case for repeated letters. When finished, she sat back on her haunches with a smug dog smile on her lips. *So there, con artist Ming. Let's see some fake belief now.*

Ming's face was void of expression though her mind seemed to be racing as she addressed Rafi. "Maybe you speak truth. What you want me to do?"

As Rafi and Ming watched, Simone-Zara painstakingly pawed out the answer—"Rafi stAy herE"—then took letters from her first sentence for the second—"Ming day ofF. GO."

"There is your answer. She thinks this strange experiment will end tomorrow. I will tend to her, Dammit, and Brandy."

"Okay," Ming sighed. "This crazy, but Dr. Simone email

me she come back Sunday. I go to bungalow."

Simone considered the biting words she wanted to say to Ming, but didn't want to disrupt the dicey plans that lay ahead. *It'd take me forever to paw out the enmity I feel about her betrayal. Gullible Dr. Denial can play the con game too.* As Ming turned to exit, Simone-Zara's front teeth snagged her shirt sleeve and pulled her back. She grunted and pointed to the new message she was writing on the floor. "Thanks... for... FeEdiNg... DOGS."

"You are welcome," Ming shook her head and asked Rafi, "You know where dog food?"

"Yes, she showed me during a tour of the house."

As Ming left, Simone-Zara pondered the cards on the ground. *Loose ends. Need to tie 'em up. Then relax. Live each day as if it were your last.* Rafi squatted next to her while she spelled out the first message.

"Keys bacK outSidE."

"I will replace them," Rafi said.

Simone-Zara pawed away the letters to make room for message number two. "Disarm SecuRIty."

Rafi nodded.

"DamMit BrAnDy sleEp wITh You."

"Yes, I understand."

"Stay inSIde ThE roOm."

"Even if I hear noises downstairs, right?"

She tapped her paw once, and then wrote a final word. "ScrabBle."

"Scrabble?" Rafi read it out loud, his brow knitted.

Simone-Zara grabbed his sleeve with her mouth, led him to the game shelf, and nosed the Scrabble box,

"You want to play?"

She nodded, panting faster, tongue limp and tail wagging.

"All right, I hope you are a good loser. Where?"

She walked to the rug and flopped down in the center.

"I warn you. I have played hundreds of games with me and myself and never lost." Rafi grinned. "I have always finished first or second." He opened the box, unfolded the board, poured the Scrabble letters from the bag, and wrote their names on the score pad.

Simone-Zara pawed seven letters from the pile and tried to turn them face up.

"Let me help you," Rafi said, wagging his fingers in the air as if preparing to crack a safe or play the piano. "I have these handy opposable thumbs that you must be longing for. I promise I will not be taking your up-turned letters into account while I formulate my word choices. Me and myself never cheat each other."

By 7:45 p.m., they were still sitting face to face across the board, Rafi munching on a bowl of chips and Simone-Zara wolfing down a biscuit after each turn. She was ahead in the game, but Rafi formed the word "examples" which connected two red triple-letter spaces, created two other words, used all seven of his letters, and scored 197 points. Taking a commanding lead, he crossed his arms over his chest and sat back self-satisfied. "I warned you."

Simone-Zara flattened her neck on the rug and folded both paws over her eyes. To her left and right, Brandy and Dammit were still splayed out on their sides proving once again that they were capable of sleeping nineteen hours per day.

By 8:15 p.m., Diego had parked fifty yards down the block from Simone's house, his Ducati facing the direction he assumed the delivery truck would leave. Joining Masaru in his sedan, he reviewed their plans while cruising the neigh-

borhood.

"I'll signal you when the EDNA truck arrives. I suggest waitin' an hour before you enter to do your sewin'. The hide-a-key box is behind the hose reel attached to the front of the house. Here's a note with the security code, but I doubt it'll be activated. Good luck. See ya back at the ranch."

Oblivious to the covert activities outside, Simone-Zara felt herself fading into slumber, pushed her letters toward the board, and surrendered in defeat.

"Dr. Simone, this has indeed been a dream come true that I could never even have imagined. I hope Zara Zarina remembers how to play." As she plodded away to her bedroom upstairs, Rafi spoke to her limp tail, "I will complete my tasks. Do not worry. Tomorrow is another day."

Right. That's what Mom always said, but tomorrow will be a day like no other.

By 8:30 p.m., Masaru had parked his sedan one street behind the house, and now dressed head to toe in black, lay hidden on the rear roof, peering over the ridge. Across the street, Diego slunk behind bushes and tested the site lines with his infrared camera.

Inside the house, Rafi filled Dammit and Brandy's bowls with food, coaxed them upstairs into the forbidden territory of the guest room, and shut the door. They devoured their food, jumped onto the double bed, and left a narrow area on the edge of the mattress for Rafi to recline.

At 9:27 p.m., the EDNA paramedic truck arrived and two delivery men removed a gurney carrying Simone's unconscious body. As they approached the house, the front

door opened, seemingly of its own accord. From across the street, Diego flashed Masaru a thumbs-up.

At 9:53 p.m., the men rolled out the empty gurney, loaded it into the back of the truck, and departed. Diego hopped on the Ducati and followed, his camera loaded with digital evidence—infrared photos of the truck, its license plate, Simone lashed to the gurney, zoomed-in shots of the men's faces, and two clear images of Ming through the gap in the doorway as they had entered and exited.

At 10:35 p.m., with both Simone and Zara Zarina lying motionless in her bed, Masaru sat on the floor, sewing buttons and carving out a space for the GPS in her shoe.

Overlooking EDNA headquarters from the hilltop above the camouflaged bird's nest, Diego and Snake surveyed the future combat zone.

"The blueprints Conan scored confirmed that slanted window cockpit is the command center," Snake assured Diego. "I've prepared the pyrotechnics for our assault."

"I'm sure you have, in your signature style. Tomorrow we'll see what this mastermind is made of."

Day 6

Sunday

WHEN SIMONE EMERGED from the anesthetized abyss into an unconscious dream state, she found herself walking up a pitch black staircase leading to a light shining through an open doorway far above her. She felt as if she'd been trudging for hours without getting any closer to the light. As her awareness expanded, Simone realized the stairs were not stairs, instead an escalator moving downward, so every step she'd taken made no progress whatsoever. Perturbed, she picked up the pace, and soon began springing up the steps using both hands and feet like Zara would have done.

The escalator abruptly terminated on a flat platform, and Simone slid on her knees to a stop. She paused to pant, catch her breath, and survey the surroundings. Everything was gray, featureless, fifty-fifty gray, the gray area. To her left and right, Simone couldn't determine whether there were walls or merely mist. Behind her, the escalator she'd climbed disappeared into darkness; ahead another escalator moved upwards to the light in the doorway. She'd stumbled into a land beyond reason: the only way anyone could reach the platform was to buck the system by going up the down escalator or down the up escalator.

Gazing at the inviting steps moving up to the light, a surge of hope coursed through her. Simone tried to rise but her legs and arms would not respond. She struggled against an internal force paralyzing her body. Fingers twitching and muscles vibrating, she summoned every shred of energy in her being and woke up on her hands and knees in her own bed. Zara sat next to her, staring into Simone's eyes and wagging the tip of her tail tentatively as if she wanted to help.

Simone flopped onto her side and soaked in the morning sun rays streaming through the skylight, relieved yet shaking with anger. Fifty-fifty bliss and animosity. Her hand trembling, she reached over, stroked Zara's ears, and smiled. *Hey, girl. We made it. You're you again, and I think I'm almost me.* Stiff and sore from five days flat on her back, Simone dragged herself off the bed, hobbled into the bathroom, and ripped off the green hospital gown. *Gotta take a shower. My body was imprisoned for days in a van with strange men and machines. They stole my clothes. What else did they do to me?* She felt violated, disgusted, and just plain dirty. She scrubbed every inch of her skin with a loofa sponge and then repeated the procedure, trying to remove the faint medical odor still taunting her nostrils. As she toweled off, the smell of brewing coffee wafted into the bathroom. Though she'd axed coffee from her diet a decade earlier, her hosts had been devouring it all week. *Now there's a drug I need posthaste.*

Simone heard scratching in the hallway, threw on her bathrobe, and cracked open the bedroom door. Two wet noses shoved it aside, and her dog duo burst in. Dammit and Brandy danced circles around their long-lost buddy and then leaped onto the bed. Simone joined them for a snuggling, yelping, licking love fest.

Zara and Rafi watched the scene from the doorway. "It

is splendid to see you in the flesh again. Would you like a solid breakfast, or would you prefer to continue your intravenous liquid diet?"

"Think you can administer java through a tube?" Simone asked.

"Sorry, but I only found teacups in the cupboards."

"That'll do. Might even have to spike it with sugar. Doctor's orders."

While eating the fresh fruit and whole wheat toast Rafi had prepared, Simone had a rough time sticking to the small talk they'd agreed upon and swallowing the rage she felt clogging her throat. The present joy of her homecoming withered into anxiety for her immediate future. "Thanks, Rafi. That hit the spot where a pill won't reach. I'm gonna walk the doggies and take five or fifty in the sanctuary."

"Do relax, Dr. Simone. Your house sitter is on duty."

Enjoying one of the little things in life she loved calmed Simone a bit, but walking past the bungalow in back pumped her up again. *Hmm. Ming's car is gone, and I haven't seen her since yesterday. She rarely ventures out and never to church. So what's that imp up to now?* An envelope containing the answer was taped to the sanctuary door. Simone entered, squatted on the circular rug, and read Ming's letter.

Dear Dr. Simone,

Thank you for chance to work with you. I learn lot and you are nice person but it too crazy for me here. You go away without telling, patients call complaining, man come with dog and say it you. I go back to China now. My father need help anyway. May your luck be big as the eastern sea and you live for one hundred years.

Goodbye regards, Ming

No surprise here. Her dirty deeds are done. China? I doubt it. To EDNA maybe, one more pawn waiting to be moved across Simon's chessboard.

Simone stretched the neglected muscles in her back and legs, rotated her head to release the kinks in her neck, and then settled into the Lotus Pose. After relaxing each body part in sequence from toe to crown and centering her energy, Simone confirmed what she'd expected. *Simon is inside me, silent in my cells.* She could hear the familiar high-pitched whine of neural networks in her brain and the low pulse of her heart, but a subtle foreign hiss slithered through her body. *We are connected. Is it a two-way street?* Even though Simone had trained herself over the years to release toxic emotions absorbed from other people, this challenge was far beyond her experience. *Let go. Get god. Let go. Om shanti om shanti om shanti om. Please grant me the peace to meet him and the strength to defeat him.*

Two miles away, The Fit Nest buzzed with activity. A handful of stalwart members sweated through their workouts. The stand-by temps were on duty and taking care of routine business. New employee Adam, the reformed rock hurler, manned the blender at the juice bar. Franz Schubert's energetic *Unfinished Symphony in B Minor* set the *allegro moderato* mode for the staff's final preparations of Diego's "Mission Possible."

Jimmy worked inside the Shenanigan Van, a drab-gray, extended panel truck covered with dents and scratches to distract prying eyes from the high-tech gear inside and antennas on the roof. Signs on each side said "GEEKS ON THE GO, On-site Computer Service." It was the kind of vehicle people avoided, whether the van was in traffic, broken down on the roadside, or parked at any location.

A rail-thin, long-haired nerd with a waist smaller than one of Conan's thighs, Jimmy Faraday was the odd man out doing odd jobs around The Fit Nest. His indispensable skills lay in another area. He'd graduated from MIT with an Electrical Engineering and Computer Science degree at nineteen, failed in the corporate sector, and taken refuge in the weed world until finding his niche on The Fit Nest staff as the Wizard of Odd behind the electronic curtain.

As requested, Chick and Norman had delivered an EDNA truck with a driver secured in yards of his own twine. Chick looked fetching in khaki shorts, a white tee, and an L.L.Bean pocket vest to conceal her blades. Wearing a wizened, wide-brim hat, wrinkled seersucker sport jacket, and hush puppies, Norman seemed to have aged thirty years. Taser cane in hand and shuffling in circles, he continued perfecting his invalid limp.

Clad in their black SWAT fatigues, Diego and Conan stood behind the reception desk, listening intently to Officer Eddie dressed down in plainclothes. "I checked further into some unresolved issues at Albright Pharmaceuticals. In the past few months, four other employees committed suicide, off premises. None of them had records of previous mental problems nor reasonable explanations from friends or family. Sound familiar?"

"Like Paul Roberts," Conan answered.

"Exactly."

"You'll be able to hear everything in the van as we record this sibling meeting," Diego assured. "I'm bettin' Dr. Wellstone can suck a bombshell out of the bastard."

"She gets into people's brains for a living. I just hope family ties don't sway her off course."

Diego stretched a hand two feet above his head. "I think she's fed up to here with lyin' Simon."

"There was no time to get a search warrant," Eddie sighed. "And who'd've believed the circumstances anyway. So my friends, you're on your own, and I'm not really here."

"Question." Conan leaned in and drummed his calloused fingers on the desk. "If you had a reliable tip about a past and future kidnapping, could you and your boys act legally?"

"Sure, that's why I'm tagging along. What's the use of a law if you can't bend it a little?"

The front door flew open, and an apparition waltzed in, arms wide, palms up. "Hey, y'all. Is this li'l Southern belle easy on yer eyes and hard on your crotch or what?"

Conan and Eddie took a few milliseconds to comprehend that they were eyeballing Jade—now six-foot-two in three-inch heels and barely dressed in a long-sleeved cardigan sweater buttoned up to the neck and, it appeared, nothing else. The sweater accentuated her ample breasts, hugged her hips, and draped down far enough to conceal one centimeter of her lusty thighs.

Diego whistled a "whew" followed by a query. "I can see the lower ends of your legs, but do the upper ends stretch all the way to your shoulders?"

"Norman won't be needin' his Taser today," Conan said. "When the guards see you, they'll be naturally stunned."

Officer Eddie expressed his concern for the local population. "You might have to contact city hall to register those legs as lethal weapons."

"Ain't you boys the sweet ones, now? Mind if I practice a new move on you, Officer?"

"Well, I'd rather you—"

A flurry of limbs ensued. Jade twirled around as she bent low, knocked off Eddie's cap with her right heel, caught it with her left hand, dropped it into his lap, and resumed her original statuesque position.

"Okay, okay! If Diego ever fires you, I'll hire you!"

"Learned that from Masaru," she said, blowing on her red fingernails as if they were five smoking guns.

"Don't tell me you've got him wearin' high heels now," Diego teased, then looked over at Eddie. "Buddy, you can have her tomorrow."

Aged Norman yelled from the back as he gimped toward the group clutching his ivory-handled cane. "Is'at there tall drink o' water Jade's twin sister?"

Chick wedged her way through the bodies to the celebrity, stopped in Jade's shadow, and spoke to her chest. "Hey! Amazon girl! Down here! Can you spare me a couple inches of those legs? I think I'm shrinking."

"You hit 'em low. I'll hit 'em high. We can flip a coin for the middle."

As usual, Jimmy had slipped in unnoticed. "The Shenanigan Van's itchin' for bewitchin', rarin' to rock 'n' roll whenever your ready, Eddie."

"That was beautiful," Diego said, feigning a sniffle and resting his hand on Jimmy's shoulder. "Damn near poetic. You never cease to amaze me. Okay team, huddle. You too, Eddie. Get in here. Best foot forward." Seven feet joined in a circle on the floor beneath a wreath of arms over seven shoulders. "Lord, look at these motley misfit outfits! They'll think we're aliens from different planets. The clock's ticking. No time for a pep talk. Snake and Masaru are already in the bird's nest overlooking EDNA. You know what to do. Let's do it!"

As the group high-fived itself, Mama poked her head around the door frame of her living room. "Is this a prayer meeting before church, I hope?"

Seven faces turned and seven voices said, "Hi, Mama."

"It's Sunday, Diego. Try not to kill anyone. I'll fix spicey enchiladas and Grandma's guacamole for you and your disciples you return. ¡Buena suerte!"

After an extended session of chanting and meditation to set her resolve in spirit, Simone rose from the sanctuary rug and went to her bedroom. *The eleventh hour approaches.* She changed into the clothing prescribed for today's trial and sat quietly on her antique tufted armchair. At 11:05, the doorbell rang, and Simone sprung up. "I'll get it!"

Circled by three wary, growling dogs, Rafi stood waiting at the bottom of the stairway. "Good luck and god be with you."

"I'll be back soon, god and the devil willing. Thanks again for all your help." Simone opened the door as wide as the security chain allowed and stared back at the two men staring at her. "Yes?"

"Mornin' to you, Miss Wellstone." A black Lexus luxury sedan idled at the curb. The men looked like burly mechanics stuffed into stiff chauffeur suits.

"It's *Doctor* Wellstone."

"Oh... yes... doctor. We're here to bring you to the EDNA headquarters."

"It takes two of you to handle one of me?"

"Well, he's driving... and I'm... I'm his backup." He bowed his head clumsily and gestured to the Lexus. "Would you please get into the backseat?"

"No, I will not. I will follow you in my own car."

"But ma'am, our orders are to take—"

"Your orders!?" Simone snapped. "I beg your pathetic pardon. I've just returned home after being kidnapped for five days, and you think I'm getting into a strange car with two strange men? Dream on." She slammed the door in their confounded faces, winked at Rafi, and watched the men on the security screen. *Delivery lackeys. Driver's making a phone call. Obviously not management or controlled by the mastermind. So why didn't Simon just walk me into the Lexus?*

Two minutes later the bell rang again. Simone waited twenty seconds, opened the door a few inches, and peered over the chain. "What?"

"The boss says it's okay if you drive."

"Oh, how kind of him. Or her? It? Who?"

"The CEO, Mr. Heinrich."

Hmph. Sounds like a Nazi. "You two get in your shiny car and drive up beyond the carport. Then I'll go to my dull old Volvo and follow you like a good girl, okay?"

"Yes, ma'am." The man shuffled backwards away from the door. "Thank you, ma'am."

Thirty yards down the block, Jimmy and Officer Eddie sat in the Shenanigan Van watching the scene through the tinted front windshield.

"Look at that. She slammed the door in their faces!" Eddie said. "That lady's got some balls. Must've told her to get in the car. You got a pen and paper, Jimmy? I need to write down the license number."

"No need. I'm videoing the whole thing."

"What? How?"

"See the big side mirrors with the fish-eyes? I added those, and then put two Go-pro cameras in the old holders. I move 'em around with the original control buttons on the door. Installed these two little monitors in the dash so I know where to point 'em. This middle screen between us shows the GPS. The red dot's Simone, and the van's green."

"You are a genius like Diego says."

"Oh, I dunno. I got raccoon hands." Jimmy wiggled his fingers on the wheel. "Always hafta be movin' or doin' somethin'."

"Your brain has to tell them what to move."

"Ya, but sometimes it's the other way around."

"Well, when the perps start moving, give them a good head start."

"Roger that." Jimmy squinted as he looked inside his brain. "But who's Roger? Roger Wilco? Why do they always say that in the movies?"

"My grandfather served in WWII and told me years ago. When the military depended on two-way radios, they'd use a standard phonetic alphabet of words to make sure messages were clear. Able for A, Baker for B, Charlie for C, Dog, Easy, Fox, etcetera. Roger for R came to mean 'received.' Wilco means 'will comply.' These days some of the alphabet has changed to Alpha, Bravo, Charlie, and Romeo for R, but 'Roger that' still works." Eddie interrupted himself as the Lexus departed. "Show time. They're leaving. Wait'll they hit the middle of the next block."

"Roger that, Jimmy Wilco." As he checked his mirrors and began to pull out, an EDNA truck zipped by the van, turned toward the curb, and screeched to a halt in front of Simone's home.

"What's this?" Eddie held up one hand. "Hold on."

A man jumped out the passenger side and grabbed a black rubber wheel chock from under the seat. The driver slipped a small handgun into his waistband, marched up the steps, and rang the bell. As the door opened, he shoved his foot against it until the chain was taut. The other man jammed the wheel chock into the gap between the door and its frame.

Eddie could see Rafi's sullen face through the crack. The driver's body language was obviously aggressive. Even at a distance of thirty yards, he could hear dogs barking. "Are you still recording?"

"Gettin' it all," Jimmy answered, working the camera control buttons on the door.

Rafi unlatched the chain, exited, and closed the door.

The men grabbed him by the arms, led him to the rear of the truck, and deposited Rafi inside.

"I think we're witnessing a kidnapping," Jimmy said.

Eddie already had Diego online with his phone. "We got a situation here. After two men picked up Simone, two more pulled up in an EDNA truck and nabbed Rafi. He didn't look too happy."

"What? With three dogs including a Doberman Pinscher inside the house?"

"Yup. We couldn't hear what the dude said to him, but he looked damn threatening and was packin' heat."

"Fuck. Follow 'em for a while and get back to me. I do not want to lose Simone, and we need the van at EDNA. You have her location on the screen?"

"Bright and clear. I didn't tell you, but I've got an unmarked car with four casual cops standing by."

"You sly dog," Diego muttered. "Have 'em trail Rafi in case these dudes are goin' somewhere besides EDNA. Please tell 'em not to engage. I don't wanna wave any red flags that might spook Simon."

"Roger that." Eddie terminated the call and turned to Jimmy. "Follow this truck, but keep your GPS eye on Simone."

"Roger déjà vu that," Jimmy sighed. "I can see I'm gonna be sick o' sayin' that today."

Simone felt a tenuous surge of power after a few hours of commanding her own body, but she craved more information. *Simon could've driven me to EDNA in my own Volvo. Or have I only created a false perception of his control capabilities based on foolish paranoia? What's he waiting for?* She'd been a diligent girl scout in middle school and recalled the motto her leader had drilled into the troop. *"Be*

prepared. A girl scout is ready to help out wherever she is needed. Willingness to serve is not enough; you must know how to do the job well, even in an emergency." My emergency is imminent. Time to experiment to see if this connection I feel is real and how strong it is.

Approaching the road out of town to Albright Pharmaceuticals, Simone concocted a plan of action. As the stoplight changed, the Lexus turned right across the bridge, and she turned left into the center of town. *Like my dream this morning. Buck the system.*

In the Shenanigan Van, Eddie had been first to notice Simone's red blinking dot veer off the projected course. He called Diego immediately and told him of the latest twist.

"What the hell is she up to? And what the hell is happening to our best-laid plans? Conan and I are on our way out of town, same as the rest of the team."

"We're still trailing the EDNA truck about a block from where Simone turned. What do you think we should do?"

"Fuck if I know. And I'll bet you don't know if she's still following the Lexus, right?"

"We lost both vehicles when they snared Rafi."

"If the EDNA truck turns where Simone did, follow it. Have your casual cops shown up?"

"They're right behind us."

Diego slammed his fist on dash, startling their abducted EDNA driver, already a nervous wreck as he delivered a SWAT team back to his workplace. "This clandestine mission is evolving into a goddamn parade! Please keep me posted while I bang my head against the windshield." Diego hung up.

Simone watched her rearview mirror intently to see if the Lexus had turned around to follow. No sign of it, but after driving two more blocks, Simone spotted an EDNA truck far behind her. *Where are you, Simon? No emergency yet? Then how 'bout we visit the police?* She sped up, careened around the corner, and headed for City Hall. As she started to brake and swing left into the parking lot, her arms and feet would not cooperate, and instead kept the Volvo driving straight on the street. *There you are. Wherever you are, now you're right here. And I'm conscious and aware like Coco and Amanda were.*

Simone didn't try to buck the system... yet. She entered analytical observer mode for the next two blocks. *Suddenly I'm in a new autonomous Volvo. Sit back and enjoy the ride. Simon's driving the car, but how much control do I still have?* Like she'd done with Amanda that first morning, Simone tested normal subconscious movements a person might make—twitches on the face, fingers, and feet, eyelid stretches and blinks, quick and extended breaths. She slightly repositioned her hand on the wheel and tilted her head a fraction of an inch. *No response, but did he notice? Who knows? I don't want to piss him off. He might smash me into a wall.*

"Simone."

The name came from her vocal chords, tongue, and lips, but Simone did not speak it.

"Simone... can you hear me?"

She tried not to move a muscle or breathe differently than her host. *Hide inside. Let go.*

"Simon says, tell me if you can hear me!"

Hmm. He's getting upset. I'm sure he learned from his remote recordings that Coco and I spoke with each other. He's probably a jealous boy. Like Rafi said, this technology might be evolving rapidly. Maybe I have self-driving, self-en-

hancing DNA. I wonder if it works like fiber optic or phone cables that can receive and send signals? Like she'd done to connect the day after with previous hosts, Simone closed her eyes and concentrated, focusing on Simon, searching for a union. Vague images and sounds floated through her mind, distant faces, a window, something humming, but nothing that seemed familiar, meaningful, or a clear link.

The Volvo continued to drive itself back to the point Simone had turned toward city center. It crossed the bridge, let the Lexus take the lead, and the EDNA truck carrying Rafi pulled in behind. A hundred yards further, the three vehicles stopped on the shoulder.

The driver of the truck got out and walked past the Volvo, shouting at Simone as if she were an unruly dog. "Stay! Stay in the car or else!"

It's Hunter again, the paramedic, delivery boy, and resident prick. As he spoke with the two men in the Lexus, Simone realized that Simon had released control. *Thanks for the demonstration, brother dear. Exactly what I needed.*

His face set in a scowl, Hunter stalked back to the Volvo and stuck his finger in Simone's face. "If you try that little escape trick again, I will run you off the road, ruin your car, and maybe ruin you too. Got it?"

"Yes, sir, Captain Hunter, sir." Simone smirked and snapped him a salute, her middle finger raised a centimeter above the rest. She heard him whisper "crazy bitch" as he walked away.

Suddenly Hunter whirled back to the open car window. "I'm sick an' tired of babysittin' your sorry ass. Just so you know, I got your buddy Raffle in the back of that truck, and if you do not shape up, I will take him down."

A bolt of despair carved a hole in her chest, but the fury in her solar plexus forced out her words. "His name is Rafi! Don't you dare lay a hand on him!"

"Dare? I *am* the daredevil with no need for any laying of hands." He tapped the barrel of his 9mm Luger on the car door. "My buddies Smith & Wesson here'll handle him."

Jimmy caught up with Simone at the edge of Buffalo City. "We seem to be back on track," Eddie told Diego over the phone. "The Lexus is in front, Volvo's next, truck behind, and they're headed to EDNA."

"Thank you Jesus, Buddha, or Zeus! We need that van close so the team can get off these fuckin' phones and connect via mics and earbuds. Conan and I are within ear 'n' eyeshot of ground zero at the Chevron station. Jade, Chick, and Norman just pulled in. Wave as you drive by. The five of us will make our first move once I can hear Simone's voice vibratin' my ear drum."

On his stomach in the bird's nest, barely visible in his dusky camo fatigues, Snake surveyed the area through the high-powered scope on his rifle. When he spotted the van on the road adjacent to the EDNA complex, he phoned Jimmy. "Keep drivin' round the bend past the buildings. You'll see a spot to pull off in some trees on your right. The Lexus and the Volvo are in the front roundabout. They took Rafi in the rear entrance."

"Thanks for the parking tip. Call Diego and tell him I'll have us all connected in a jiff." Ten minutes later, Jimmy's voice lit up Diego's dark mood. "All mics should be hot and earbugs live."

"Okay, team. Diego here. Roll call. Say your names one at a time."

Snake waited till he heard the other seven and added a few pertinent words. "Snake here. Pretty quiet on this sleepy Sunday morning at EDNA. I finally I got eyes on the prize entering the front door with two escorts."

"Okay, listen up," Diego said. "Plans have changed. After Chick and Norman disable front security with Jade, their only task is to locate and extract Rafi. The second you three succeed, skedaddle pronto. The rest of us'll rescue Simone. Your biggest challenge is to do your duty without disruptin' the sisterly-brotherly chat before she signals the countdown to Hail Mary. I don't know how long quiet time will last. Sit tight and wait for my green light. Over an' out."

Though Simone visited Albright Pharmaceuticals two years earlier, she hardly recognized it as she'd driven by the sprawling complex. The original building seemed to have been swallowed up by a metallic cancerous growth. Vivid memories as a young girl at Albright with her father, brother, and Tall Paul still played in her heart. *Simon and I used to have a ball running around here screaming during squirt gun battles. Today our relationship reminds me of families torn asunder by the Civil War—one sibling clad in blue, the other in gray. Who's the slave holder now? Uncivil Simon.*

After parking in the roundabout, the Lexus boys led Simone toward the front entrance. Outside the double doors, a gaunt manikin dressed in a polished Armani suit and red power tie stood with arms folded tight over his chest. His leathery face cracked into a pinched grin as he held out a hand and stepped forward.

"Dr. Wellstone. Welcome to EDNA. May I call you Simone?"

"No."

"As you wish, Doctor, I am so glad to finally meet you." His hand was still semi-extended.

Simone set her gaze on his open palm, then raised it to his pallid eyes. They reminded her of the dead eyeballs on a baked flounder staring up from a dinner plate. "So far I haven't been glad to meet anyone from EDNA. Who are you, and why would you be the exception?"

Taken aback by her unabashed query, he stammered an answer. "I'm sure it's been a... a whirlwind of... of confusion for you, perhaps?"

"Yes, and I continue to be confused. Are you speaking, or is Simon flapping your jaw for you?"

He let out a nervous laugh. "Oh, I assure you that I am me, Luther Heinrich at your service, Chief Executive Officer of EDNA and Albright Pharmaceuticals."

No one says that! They say CEO. Does he think I'm a moron? Whenever she heard the name Luther, Simone didn't think of Martin Luther, the protesting Catholic, or Martin Luther King, the civil rights leader; she thought of Lex Luther, Superman's archenemy in movies from her childhood. *No one else to control right now, angry girl. Try to control yourself. Be the innocent lamb, like Diego said.* "Sorry, Mr. Heinrich. It has indeed been a stressful journey to this moment in time." *You even look like a Nazi.*

"I understand."

No, you don't. You have no fucking idea.

"Simon is waiting for you. Please follow me."

I will follow you both into hell to find Rafi.

Luther escorted her to an elevator in the back through the first-floor hallway lined with EDNA delivery offices and pressed the third-floor button.

The interior of the metal and mirror elevator created reflections of Simone and Luther stretching to infinity in four directions. She felt faint. *Too many of both of us. Get me outta here.*

"Are you okay, Dr. Wellstone?"

No, not at all. With one hand on the elevator wall and the other wiping her forehead, she mumbled her answer. "I'll be okay when this is over."

The rear elevator door slid open, and Simone stepped into a room or mezzanine or platform—she couldn't tell exactly which. The elevator was set in the middle of a long wall, the flat side of a semicircle, covered with television screens and monitors to the right and a huge Jackson Pollock painting to the left. The half-circle area in front of Simone ended in air. The outer wall was a two-story, three-panel bank of windows twenty feet beyond the edge of the floor.

This "third floor" was Simon's stand-alone throne that overlooked workstations below on the second floor, accessible via a wide single escalator dead center and stairs curving around to each side. In his high-tech wheelchair, Simon appeared to be sitting on stage, a theater in the half-round.

Whoa. It's been two years since I've seen him. He looks like a shrunken replica of his former self.

Four uniformed men stood motionless like the Queen's Guards at Buckingham Palace, two on the rear wall facing outward, and two on the stage lip watching the monitors behind him.

Beyond Simon and through the window panels that stretched up from the second-story floor, Simone could see the balcony outside and a view of the surrounding area. Eye-level with Simon, Snake scoped out the action inside from his bird's nest on the ridge.

Simon's wheelchair slowly swiveled toward her as a computer-generated voice spoke. "Hello, my dear sister. Welcome to my world. You've been a stranger these past years."

"Not as strange as you've become."

"Please come closer. My ears are failing along with my vocal chords. I see you've met Luther, a brilliant man. I doubt I'd be here today without him."

Simone didn't move an inch closer. "Well, I'd rather *not*

be here today and would prefer being without *him* right now. I came to see you alone, or should I say, you manipulated me into your domain?"

Simon politely asked Luther to leave and apologized for Simone's behavior, further aggravating his sister. "Would you feel more sociable knowing that $100,000 was transferred into your bank account this morning?"

At first she was speechless, but resentment swelling in her gut flung out a question. "Do you mind if I come back again?"

"We'd like that and hope you—"

"So I can withdraw the cash and shove it down your fucking throat!"

Inside the Shenanigan Van parked round the bend, Jimmy patched one worried officer into their network.

"Are you hearing all this, Diego?"

"Loud and clear and alarming. Is this Eddie?"

"Yeah. Whenever I've worked with her, Simone's cool as a cucumber. She's doesn't seem like herself today."

"Remember, she hasn't been herself for five days. My little lamb sounds like a lion ready to pounce. I'm afraid our quiet time won't last long."

"Sounds to me like she's already mid-pounce."

"Have Jimmy tell the troops to keep on their toes. My call to action might come any second."

Simon's body twitched as if he'd been kicked. "You seem quite upset, Dr. Wellstone."

"Does that somehow surprise you? How would you like to be ripped out of your life and stuck into a foreign body?"

"No, I'm not surprised." Simon paused. "Sad, perhaps. And angry... afraid... full of remorse. That's what happened to me four years ago. I'm still stuck, and my life continues to decline. God, my words sound even more pathetic coming through wires, circuit boards, and processors."

His reply may have tweaked a sympathetic reaction in her brain, but empathetic Simone felt each of those emotions rippling through her stomach, chest, and neck. *Are those my emotions or his? Is the enhanced DNA and our connection amplifying them?* More memories of Simon's lifelong struggle with physical infirmities flooded in. Her shoulders drooped as her crusty disposition crumbled into a delicate balance between compassion for Simon and her present task of extracting a confession from him. "I apologize for my irascible demeanor. I have been stressed, and you know I have trouble dealing with other people's traumas because I feel them as if they were mine. I'm not only upset, brother, but also amazed and intrigued by this technology, or process, or whatever you call it. I imagine you stumbled upon it while trying to stay alive."

"Apology accepted. Will you please have a seat? They brought a chair for you somewhere."

"It's just to your left," Simone said. "I'll scoot it over."

Diego's voice crackled over the earbuds. "Okay, team, our lamb has settled down, but I think Jade, Norman, and Chick should move in, careful and quiet. Let the mice play while the cat's distracted."

"Roger that," Jade responded. She drove her "Lightning Blue" Ford Escape slowly down the main entrance road, feigned a flat tire, and ten yards short of the roundabout, parked by the curb. She and Chick got out, stared at a tire, and scratched their heads. Looking as inept as possible, they jacked up the rear, failed with the tire iron, pried old Norman out of the back seat, helped him limp through the front entrance, and propped him against an inside window.

The two guards behind the four-foot counter sat up straight when two attractive women and sauntered in their direction. The short one on the right greeted Chick and Jade. "How can I help you ladies?"

Jade leaned over next to the opulent bouquet of flowers in a massive vase on the counter, read the guards' name tags, and purred, "Bradley and Stanley. Y'all related or what?"

"No, ma'am," Stanley answered, "jus' coworkers. You had some car trouble out there, didja?"

"Flat tire," Chick replied, nodding. "Tried the wrench thingy but didn't wanna risk breakin' a nail."

"Our Uncle Chester over yonder's kinda crippled an' needs a men's room real bad. Wouldn' wanna stain yer fancy floors now. 'Preciate it if'n he could use one o' yournses."

"We'll have to see some identification, ma'am."

"My name's Christy, and this here's Misty," Jade said, pinching Chick on the cheek. "Kinda like yer names." She bobbed her head back and forth sideways as she chanted, "Bradley-Stanley-Christy-Misty. It's so cool to meet real s'curity gentlemen. You guys got guns and everything!"

Stanley tried again. "We'll need to see your IDs, please."

"Misty and I both got IUDs! You wanna see 'em?"

The guards turned their heads and eyed each other. Jade could tell Stanley was willing, but Bradley was wary.

Edging around the side of the counter, Chick called to Norman at the window. "Hey, Uncle Chester. Bring your driver's license up here."

Norman hobbled ahead a couple of steps, rummaging in his jacket as if attempting to remove his wallet while eyeing the position of the security cameras on the ceiling.

Jade focused on silent Bradley. "Hey, Buckaroo, you look so big and strong. How tall're you anywho?"

"Five eleven."

"Me, too. We could trade outfits. Ya wanna?" Below the lip of the counter, Jade flashed her partners a predetermined signal.

Chick leaped into Stanley's lap, pinning his arms to his sides, and pierced the skin under his neck with a stiletto while Norman whipped out a pistol with silencer attached and popped out the four security cameras in four shots.

His hand reaching for his holster, Bradley jumped up. Jade picked up the vase as if it were a five-pound medicine ball and heaved it into his chest. He flew into his high-back rolling chair, smashed into the wall, and collapsed in a heap of flowers, greens, and shattered pottery pieces. She vaulted over the counter with tranquilizer gun in hand and fired a dart into his neck. "Time for beddy bye, Bradley." She stood on his shoulders until he faded away.

Chick hopped off Stanley as Norman stuck the Taser cane in his groin, and then busied herself slicing wires leading in or out of every electronic device she could find.

Smiling down at his quaking captive, Norman posed a hypothetical question. "Stanley, what do think would happen if a million volts zapped through your testicles? Did I say a million? Yep, that's what the specs said."

"Please don't, please," he begged. "I hate this job, but I got a family to feed."

"Planning to have more kids?"

"Maybe. Why?"

Norman flipped his coat open to reveal a black shirt with SWAT stenciled in white letters. "What does this stand for?"

"Special Weapons Assault Team."

"Smart Stanley, but that was yesterday. Today it stands

for 'Sterilized With A Taser.' Does that shock you? Would you like it to shock you?"

Stanley's eyeballs seemed to stretch the width of his face. "No, no, no. What'd'you want? What'd'you wanna know? I'll do anything!"

"Good Stanley. Two o' your boys just brought in one of ours. A young kid named Rafi—thin, dark, and swarthy." With each new question, Norman put an extra ounce of pressure on the cane. "Where is he? What room? Do you have the key?"

"Hey, team! Buy me a couple minutes." Jade shouted, dragging comatose Bradley across the floor. "I'm gonna put on his uniform and stash his ass in a closet."

"Go for it," Norman yelled. "Stanley's agreed to be on our team and lead us to Rafi."

Chick clicked on her mic. "Security secured. Snared a guard to guide us to the asset. Next update soon."

On stage in his control center, Simon droned on after his sister's calculated apology. "There's no cure for ALS. Most people live three to five years after diagnosis. I'm in year four. I've managed to retard the muscle degeneration some-what and actually strengthened my right arm." Simon raised it slowly, not a particularly impressive demonstration to others, though perhaps it bolstered his own self-respect. "I am no stranger to physical frailty, but when my power of speech and communication began to fail, I freaked out."

One of the guards with eyes on the rear monitors inter-rupted Simon's soliloquy. "Mr. Albright, sir?"

"What is it?" Simon snapped.

"The four security screens showing the front entrance have gone grey, sir."

"Never mind. Fix it later. The only guest we're expecting today is already sitting right here." Simon waved off the guard with a flick of the fingers in his lap. "Where was I?"

"You freaked out," prompted Simone.

"Oh, yes. I devoured information about ALS, 24/7. I learned about a breakthrough that allowed patients to transmit their thoughts to computers via sensors placed in the brain. I replicated it, but picturing us as kids communicating thoughts without speaking, I was certain that unique ability had something to do with our DNA. I had an idea, hired experts from around the world, and they brought it to fruition."

Okay, we're back on track... a calm habitual one. I, I, I, I. He always loved to talk about himself. A terminal narcissist from day one. "What plans do you have for this technology? You must've dreamed up so many uses!"

"It is worth billions and will revolutionize communication in many areas. If you don't mind, I'd prefer using it now and have a young scientist of mine assist us. This cumbersome method of speaking exhausts me and sounds so mechanical. When I control Taylor, he's completely unaware, essentially unconscious like you experienced with your hosts. Is that acceptable to you?"

A scientist of mine? Simon talks as if it's a machine that he owns. "Sure. I'd like to watch a connection instead of being one."

"I'll summon Taylor and won't even have to introduce you. He's me." A contorted half-smile quivered on his lips. "Watch the workstations on the lower level." Simon closed his eyes and seemed to concentrate. The scientist on the far left stood up, turned toward the platform, saluted, and sat down. The man to his right repeated the same motion, as did each of next seven scientists in their workstations. A giggle gurgled in Simon's throat. "Isn't that amazing?"

It took all of Simone's willpower to stifle her tongue

from saying *That is one of the sickest things I have ever seen. God forbid there aren't any more of you on this planet. One is more than enough.*

The final scientist in the line, Taylor marched up the curved stairs after his salute from the workstation. Blond and blue-eyed in a white lab coat, the young man pulled up a chair, and the conversation continued from Simon's last words. "You communicated with two of your hosts while they were under your control. I've never experienced that."

So I outperformed the mastermind. He must not know Rafi evolved the next day, or how I figured out how to contact Diego. "Each host was different. It took Amanda a while to become aware. Coco seemed to feel me right away, once she finally woke up. Maybe it's a female-to-female thing. I could also connect with my hosts the day after although it faded with time."

"That's impossible," Simon-Taylor said, frowning. "At the end of each day, we disabled the receptors and transmitters in the DNA-nanobots—yours and theirs."

"Impossible is the exact word I used to describe what happened to me when I found myself inside Amanda. Are you calling me a liar now?"

"No, no," he backpedaled, shaking his head, "but I am amazed. Either you have phenomenal abilities, or the technology is evolving on its own."

"Or both. Can you tell me how this brainstorm of yours actually works?"

"The specifics are beyond my comprehension, but here's a simple synopsis. DNA's main role is long-term storage of information. It's a blueprint that contains the instructions to construct other components of the cell. The only DNA we've successfully enhanced is mine and yours."

"And ours are not the same," Simone interrupted.

"99.9% the same," he countered.

"And I've learned that still leaves millions of differences in the genome which makes each of us unique. I'm sure Ming was your covert busy bee gathering my hair, fingernail clippings, and earwax for your surreptitious DNA research, now departed since her dirty deeds are done."

"She served her purpose and helped you with your practice along the way."

"Wrong," Simone retorted. "I paid her to help you."

"Do you want the answer to your previous question, or would you prefer to quibble over the past?"

"Oh, please continue," she said, biting her tongue behind a sweet smile. "My feminine curiosity is killing me."

"EDNA's organic nanobots attach to our non-coded 'junk' DNA which accounts for at least 80% of the total amount in each genome. After entering the host's cell nuclei, it dominates and seems to absorb the weaker DNA. A typical human chromosome contains 150 million base pairs that the cell replicates at the rate of 50 pairs per second. In about an hour, our DNA begins to 'take control,' so to speak."

Or evolve beyond your comprehension. "Where and when and how does this transfer of DNA or consciousness occur?"

"The delivery system is both simple and complex. We prepare the controller DNA before hand, quickly anesthetize the host in a laboratory van, roll in your body from another van, and inject the solution via IVs. For fifteen minutes, a unique process stimulates and actives the organic enhanced DNA, and like yeast expanding bread rising in a warm oven, these new blueprints decode and restructure each body. Close proximity between host and controller is essential."

Keep talking, Simon, and wrap the noose around your neck. "What's the range of this control in miles? The treatment instructions told hosts to stay within the city limits.'

"We're working on increasing the distance. Right now, fifteen miles is stretching it."

"So you carted my body around for five days in a truck? No wonder I was so damn sore this morning. How do you shut down your hosts at a specific time in the evening?"

"The black GPS watch microphone automatically activates a sedative placed in the blood stream. I see you removed yours."

"It didn't match my outfit or my mood."

He ignored her quip. "I'm very curious about your experience in the dog."

Simone spit out her next question. "The one chained outside to a stake with a storm on the horizon?"

"My people and drones were monitoring the situation. They would've intervened if necessary."

Inhuman schmuck. Has he ever uttered the words I'm sorry? "It was seamless. A union of souls."

"Huh. I found it difficult to connect with one."

"Perhaps because you don't lead from the heart, and your reptilian brain stem governs your actions."

Simon-Taylor flinched. "Harsh. I can see you're still stressed. I imagined that my dog-lover sister would cherish the experience."

Simone stifled her escalating emotions. "My stress is fading. Actually, my time in Zara the Doberman was wonderful. There's one thing I've been wondering about that I'm sure you would know because of your extensive experience."

"Oh, please ask," Simon-Taylor said, leaning forward, ready to impart wisdom and flaunt his knowledge.

"In some dicier, violent situations, I was worried about accidentally killing my host. If they died, what would happen to me?"

"Nothing at all. You would merely resume control of yourself and carry on."

"You actually experienced that?" *Oh, dear brother, please answer this one and tighten the noose.*

"In one of our trials, yes."

Simone felt gleeful and repulsed at the same time. *Hung. Dangling at the end of his own rope.* "Earlier when I interrupted you—sorry, again, I'm a bad girl, and there I go interrupting myself now—what were you going to say when I asked if I could come back? You'd like that and hope..."

"That you'd join us at EDNA in exploring this breakthrough in science. I would compensate you handsomely."

It felt bizarre looking at this clean-cut, energetic mouthpiece Taylor with Simon's torpid body sitting to the side, but nothing really surprised her after the last five days. *Always about money with you, isn't it? Raking it in or bribing your way in the world.* "It would be quite a score for me in the psychiatric community, don't you agree?"

"Oh, yes. Dr. Frank saw the potential and helped us in the beginning, but became somewhat disillusioned."

Simone almost fell off her chair and failed to disguise her shock. "You finagled Dr. Frank into this scheme?"

"He was quite willing and intrigued at first, but honestly, he needed the money. A professor's retirement income certainly couldn't cover the cost of maintaining that mansion, and the Remington fortune has dwindled over the years. You think he started CAFE with his own lack of funds? We made him an offer he couldn't refuse. It's not hard to manipulate someone's words and actions with the right inside information."

I'd call that extortion. God, I hope they're recording this. If I keep buttering him up, he'll fry himself even further. "I do like the dual name EDNA. 'Express Delivery. Now. Anywhere.' That's so clever! You must've thought of that, yes?"

"Too much time on my hands... or my mind. It's a perfect facade for delivery of goods right under the noses of the authorities."

Simone cupped her hands under her chin and leaned in. "Like what?"

"Oh..." Taylor paused a moment while Simon thought. "We'll get to that if you agree to come on board. How would you like a short tour of our facility?"

"That would be splendid," Simone said, gazing through the massive windows. "This view is magnificent." *And these are the windows in my mind while focusing on Simon when I was in the Volvo.*

After extolling the layout and gadgetry of this third-floor domain—the monitors supplying global television newscasts, stock tickers, and internal security images, the ten clocks lining the top of the rear wall which displayed the time at each worldwide Albright location, his bedroom behind the wall which appeared more like a intensive care unit with an array of medical devises and live-in nurse—Taylor rolled the wheelchair onto the escalator, pressed the start button, and motioned for Simone to follow. With a guard at their heels, they strolled around the walkway encircling his raised throne bordered with workstations and laboratories manned by EDNA's other scientists. For the next fifteen minutes, Simone mainly listened while her brother stroked his ego and reveled in his achievements. Except for an occasional pandering question, her only comment was "Still playing Simon says I see, on a grandiose scale."

Simon-Taylor only smiled, soaking in the backhanded compliment.

At the Chevron station, Diego handed their nervous EDNA driver a soda and pack of candy through the window. "You look tense, dude. Relax. We're almost done, and you can head home."

As Diego stepped into the rear of the truck, he activated his mic to notify the troops of their imminent departure. "The players inside are takin' a little tour, and I got a feelin' our lamb is fixin' to turn lion. Conan and I are movin' into strike position. Jimmy, stream the feed from Simone into everyone's ears. Everyone, you know the two cues and know what do. No more signals from me. Make me proud as a punch-drunk peacock. Over." He sat on a stool and poked his nose through the sliding window on the rear of the cab. "What's your name, dude?"

"Joe."

"Good name, my uncle's name is Jose. I'm Diego and your caretaker here is Conan, crunchy on the outside and soft in the middle like those M&Ms I gave you. I want ya to know that you're on the right side of the law, and the police are watchin' every move we make. We're rescuin' a couple friends that your big boss has snatched. We just need you to sneak us past the security check nice 'n' normal, then back up this baby to the dock by the breezeway. I suggest you split this popsicle stand cuz we're delivering hell to their doorstep."

"Okay, whatever you say."

"Joe, do they check the back of the trucks comin' in?"

"No. They only need to see me."

"Good. They only need to *not* see us." The truck cruised through the security stop, and Joe backed into the dock as instructed. "Okay, Joe-kay. You're on your own. Don't alert any of your coworkers on your way out, or we'll have to kill you." Diego patted him on the shoulder. "Just kiddin'."

Joe started to open the door and stopped. "But what about the wire around my toe?"

"What wire?" Diego asked.

"The other guy told me he wrapped a razor-sharp rusty wire around my little toe and could yank it through a hole in my shoe. He said if I move too fast or try to jump out of the truck, it'll tear off my toe."

Conan smirked. "I was joking. No wire, only the power of suggestion."

"Thank god. It hasn't been a pleasure meeting you, and I never want to see you again." Joe jumped out of the truck and made a beeline for his car in the far lot.

"That was a very creative tale you told our driver," Diego said to Conan.

"I liked the rusty part."

"You're a sick puppy, you know."

"Thank you so much," Conan agreed. "You say the nicest things."

"You ready?"

"Always."

"Hardly anyone's around today, but we're gonna do our scary SWAT walk like in the movies. I'll lead, and you keep pointin' your gun at every nook and cranny as if you expect an ax murderer to jump out of the shadows, okay?"

"Fun," Conan said.

They threw open the rear doors, stole around the corner, and snuck up on the sole guard perusing a newspaper at his station next to the elevator and stairwell door. Concealed under helmets, gas masks, and black balaclavas, they were unrecognizable.

"Hey, you!" Diego shouted. "Got a 911 call about an active shooter in your area! Have you seen or heard anything?"

The guard snapped to his feet. "No, nothing."

"Open the stairwell door so we can search the building."

"I can't do that! My boss'd kill me."

Both Conan and Diego's revolvers now pointed directly

at his head. "Really? Okay, I confess. We're the active shooters and can take care of that for him. Would you like to be the first casualty?"

"No, no!" He held up his hands in front of his face. "What the hell's going on?"

"You look familiar. What's your name?" Diego leaned over and checked his badge. "Pete Ferguson. I bet you're Snake's buddy from high school. We're from The Fit Nest. Your boss kidnapped two friends of ours and probably murdered another. Snake and my team have the place surrounded, and the police are patrollin' the perimeter. You have two choices, Pete. Open the door immediately and leave the premises, or we'll wrap you in duct tape like a mummy and throw you in a closet. Decide now!"

"I'm gone." Pete threw up his hands, then reached for his keys and unlocked the door. "I feel like I've been guarding goons here anyway."

Diego dashed up the stairs while Conan remained behind to assure that Pete vanished.

Tour completed and back in their seated positions on the stage, Simone launched into a strident interrogation. "There's one question that's really been bothering me. Why didn't you just ask me if I'd participate in your experiment? I might've said yes. Instead, you had me kidnapped."

"I wouldn't call it kidnapping."

"What would you call it then?"

Simon-Taylor shot her an insipid smile. "I'd have to blame our father. Remember how he taught us to swim? He threw us in the river and said, 'Sink or swim!' We learned quickly."

"If not kidnapping, would you call it breaking and entering?"

"We didn't break anything."

"How about stealing my patient's records? Disseminating confidential information? That's not only against the medical code of ethics; it's against the law, and I could face charges."

"Oh, come now," he scoffed. "We didn't share it with anyone else."

God, his warped mind has a song and dance for everything. "Do you have any ethics at all, Simon?"

"One. The work ethic."

"No matter what it takes, eh? Where's Rafi? Your bulldog Hunter, the fiend who drugged me last Monday night, had him imprisoned in his truck today and threatened to kill him."

"Well, Luther's bulldog is a hot head and gets a bit too aggressive. I'll have a word with Hunter. We just need to review the boy's treatment again, and you could continue to counsel Rafi here at EDNA. Can I count on you to at least consider becoming part of my team?"

Simone felt her composure poised to splinter into sharp words that would cut to the quick. She sprung up from her seat and stepped a yard away from ventriloquist Simon and his animated puppet. "Not a chance. You can count me *out.*"

"But Simone, look at what you've accomplished in a few short days! You freed Amanda from her boogeyman, hooked up two pairs of lovers, saved a drowning girl, transformed Rafi into a hero, foiled a purse snatcher. Just think of what you could do working here with me!"

You are my boogeyman, and I need to free myself. "I have another pressing question for you."

"Please ask," he pleaded. "Anything."

"I only tried to be unobtrusive and help my hosts with their lives. Would you say this control technology of yours is like hypnosis where a person won't do something which goes against their personal code of morals and ethics?"

Simon-Taylor assumed a maniacal expression of self-satisfaction. "I'd say it's far beyond hypnosis. The person becomes a helpless pawn on my board. They'll do anything that I command."

"That clearly explains the supposed suicides within your sick organization, most specifically Paul Roberts. He told me you could control him, and that he disagreed with this scheme of yours."

"He disagreed with many Albright decisions. He became distraught and deranged. His suicide was no surprise."

Stanley, the security guard coerced into switching teams, had led Norman and Chick down a basement stairway to a row of locked doors lining the hallway. They'd located Rafi in a room also housing six cages containing a spider monkey, Border Collie, German Shepherd, Poodle, Labrador Retriever, and a dead cat. With three well-placed shots from his silenced pistol, Norman had broken the chain securing Rafi to the wall.

"All these dogs are wearing owner tags," Chick said, "and I've seen lost dog posters for the poodle. We're not leavin' these prisoners behind. I had a pet monkey in Jamaica and always wanted another one." While she freed the animals, Norman and Stanley exited the room with Rafi.

A gruff voice bellowed from forty feet down the hall. "What the fuck are you doing with my hostage? An' who the fuck is your sidekick?"

"Oh god," Stanley moaned. "It's Hunter. He brought the boy in."

Hunter drew the Smith & Wesson from his waistband and skulked forward. "Keep your hands where I can see 'em and step away from the kid."

Stanley and Rafi raised both hands above their heads. Shaking like a frail old man about to faint, Norman lifted one hand and leaned on his cane, waiting until Hunter came within Taser range of fifteen feet. Chick had heard the voices and peered around the slightly ajar door.

Ten yards behind Hunter, a figure sprinted toward him. Feeling the vibration on the floor, he turned his head to glimpse a blue-uniformed blur vault above his sight line. Jade's outstretched bare feet slammed into his shoulders, hurling him facedown on the floor with such force that he slid four yards forward on the slick tiles.

Norman looked down at Hunter's numb body and demanded, "C'mon, you wimp. Get up and fight like a man."

Chick burst out with the monkey on her shoulders and four dogs behind her. "We don't have time! Fight like Norman. Tase the sucker!"

"Good call." Norman shot two metal probe darts into Hunter's lower back. "Get outta here. I'll meet you at the car. I'm gonna give him a full thirty-second pulse."

As the dogs and their three new buddies raced to the front entrance, Chick sidled up to Jade. "Hey, Amazon girl, where the heck did you learn that trick?"

"Track team in college. Pole vault, high jump, and long jump. That was a vault into a high-long jump, never before performed in public nor imagined at home."

Jade, Chick and her monkey, Rafi, and four dogs piled into the Ford Escape as Stanley hoofed it into the woods.

Chick flicked on her mic. "Asset retrieved from the assholes. Three o' your birds are flyin' home to The Nest with five more liberated hostages."

"Thank you so much for getting me out of there," Rafi said. "I am one grateful asset. How is Dr. Simone?"

"Still in the thick of it," Jade answered, "but the fireworks and official rescue have yet to begin. Wish I could be there to watch Diego, Conan, and Masaru in action."

Twenty seconds later, Norman opened the rear door to a full house—Poodle sat in Jade's lap, the monkey still perched on Chick's shoulders next to her, the Labrador, German Shepherd, and Rafi filled the back seat.

"Do I have to call a taxi?" Norman asked.

"Scrunch in the back with Angie," Chick yelled. "You're not crippled, remember?"

"Who's Angie?"

"The collie. Name and address is on her tag. She lives near here, and we're gonna take her home, right Jade?"

"If you say so." The moment Norman was ensconced in the rear, Jade screeched off the rear jack still attached and roared down the driveway.

"Nice uniform, Amazon," Chick said. "I got a butch security guard protecting me in the front seat."

"Thought it might come in handy. Are you sure you need another monkey on your back?" Jade teased. "You've already got Norman."

"Yeah, well, he's kinda cuddly too, and has always got my back."

Simone shouted the first words to signal the countdown. "I've had enough! You used the word 'remorse' earlier. Ha! I doubt you have a remorseful molecule in your entire decaying body. You haven't apologized to me once for your loathsome behavior." The finger she'd lifted to emphasize *once* now waved an inch from Taylor's face. "You controlled me in the car this morning. I could feel it and let you do it. Your own flesh and blood sister is merely flesh and blood and DNA to you." Simone paced back and forth in front of Simon-Taylor as she fumed. "Will you strap me onto an operating table, carve open my chest, and extract organs like you did with dogs at Albright? You think we can run this company together? Like fucking Siamese twins battling over one body? Bullshit! I'd throw us both off a roof like you did with Paul! This dream of yours is a goddamn macabre nightmare, and I'll have nothing to do with it. I'm outta here!" She whirled around and stomped away from him.

For three long seconds, Simon-Taylor watched in silence, and then spoke in a calm, malefic voice. "Well, my defiant sibling, we haven't quite had enough of you yet."

As the mastermind's control shifted to his sister, Taylor blinked his eyes and gazed vacantly at Simone. She felt her body tighten, and her legs became sluggish like in the dream she'd had before waking that morning. *This is the final trial I foresaw.* Curling her fingers into fists, she closed her eyes and summoned the determination of Amanda, the daring of Wild Diego, the pugnacity of Coco, the drive to survive of Rafi, the ferocity of Doberman Zara, and every gene in her being. Simone sensed Simon's control weakening and a parallel connection opening. *Go against the grain and buck the system.* She turned around slowly, faced her foe, and growled, "Welcome to *my* world, brother."

Simon's computer-generated voice crackled from the speakers. "This is im... pos... sib..."

No more words came from his inert body as the connection reversed, and Simone took complete control of her brother. The only movement on stage was a smile slipping onto her lips and puzzled looks from the two front guards.

Focusing on her host, Simone raised her brother's hand to his throat, clenched the fingers around his windpipe, and began to squeeze. *Got a sugar-coated placebo to cure Alien Hand Syndrome, bro?* Gurgling, Simon struggled to breathe as his body bucked in the wheelchair.

Four bewildered guards moved closer to Simon, and Luther rushed through Simon's bedroom doorway and onto the platform.

Relishing this reversal of roles, Simone held him tight until Simon's eyes seemed ready to fall backwards into their sockets. Luther turned and stomped toward her as she finally released control.

Red-faced and livid, Simon squawked through speakers that failed to convey the choler in his gut. "Damn you! I've underestimated your abilities!"

"We'll have to handle this the old-fashioned way," Luther bellowed in a strident raw voice that didn't match his carefully coiffed exterior. "Guards! Take her downstairs to the holding room! Now!"

Watching the four men stalk in her direction, Simone rose to the challenge. "Old-fashioned suits me just fine." With an internal prayer for Diego's troops and a fleeting fear—*I'm gonna look like an idiot if they don't hear me*—she raised her gaze and palms above her head, and screamed her plea to the heavens. "May God unleash his wrath onto these demons!"

On the word "unleash," Jimmy had punched the remote button in the van to launch the fireworks concealed near the building.

Boom! A low-altitude aerial bomb exploded, vibrating the roof and the spines of every sentient being below it. The two rear guards rushed toward Simon as sniper Snake squeezed off a shot. The bullet pieced the window and zinged into the far left clock on the rear wall, flinging glass shards tinkling onto the floor. Gas masks covering their faces, Diego and Conan burst through the second-story doors behind Simon's circular stage. Outside, Ninja Masaru raced down the ridge, snatched a concealed rope he'd hung from the balcony, and climbed upward with bare hands, his legs dangling in thin air.

Boom! Boom! Two more aerial bombs exploded as Snake continued to pick off each clock, one by one like stalled sitting ducks in a row floating in the water trough at a carnival gun arcade. Wide-eyed CEO Luther flattened his body against the wall under another shower of clock fragments. Simone kneed one guard in the groin and struggled to free herself from the other, who, though distracted by the chaos, still clutched her elbow. Back stage on the second floor, Conan and Diego split off right and left, tossing pepper gas grenades at intervals along the walkway.

Boom! Boom! Boom! Three more bombs rent the sky. Arms covering their heads, ashen-faced scientists coughing from the rising pepper gas cowered beneath their work tables. Taylor tried to hide behind his chair. Conan and Diego halted on either side of Simon's stage, anticipating the next explosion.

Protected on one side of the balcony, Masaru detonated C4 plastic explosive strips he'd fastened to the sliding double doors the night before. Moments after the glass shattered, he plunged through the smoke and flames like a black bat out of hell and seemed to fly up the escalator without using his feet. Leaping into the air toward the guard restraining Simone, he pivoted mid-air, caught him by the neck with his legs, and flipped him onto his back. As Conan and Diego advanced up the stairs, Masaru sprung to his feet, scrambled behind Simon's wheelchair, drew his sword from its sheath, and with one hand pulling back Simon's head by the hair and the other gripping the blade under the mastermind's neck, he let out a piercing war cry. "Ei, Ei, Ouuu! Stop where you stand, or Simon says no more!"

Every soul who wasn't already wheezing on the floor froze. Diego wrenched away the guard still clutching Simone's leg and pinned him to the ground with a boot on his neck, then slipped a gas mask over Simone's head and locked onto her eyes. "Rafi's safe and secured."

Apart from the hum of the escalator and people hacking from pepper gas, there was no sound in the room. His sword still under Simon's neck, Masaru moved to the side as Conan grabbed the wheelchair handles. Together they rolled it forward onto the escalator and glided down to the second floor with the mastermind. Stepping cautiously down the stairs, Diego and Simone joined them on the circular walkway. Simone took the handles and, with her three-point guards, pushed the wheelchair past the incapacitated scientists and around to the rear of Simon's circular stage.

"You up for some fast walkin', Dr. Wellstone?" Diego whispered.

"I could run a marathon right now."

"Here's hopin' your car's still in front. You mind givin' us a lift?"

"My pleasure." Simone turned and looked down at her brother, silently fuming in his wheelchair. "What does the almighty Simon have to say now?"

Simon stared at his lap and didn't meet her eyes.

"Cat got your tongue... or your whole body? The silent treatment, eh? So unlike you. See ya 'round, bro. Maybe we'll visit you in prison."

Masaru opened the double doors leading to the ground floor, let the team pass, slipped off his belt, and wrapped it around the handles in the stairwell. Diego and Conan shoved the guard desk in the breezeway against the lower doors before speeding down the delivery truck drive and weaving through a smattering of employees gawking at the smoke rising from the control center. Three men in black, two with SWAT in white letters front and back, and one Ninja warrior herding a woman suddenly seemed to be business as usual. Sighs of relief filled Simone's Volvo as she veered onto the main highway.

"Excellent work, team," Diego said, turning to Masaru in the back seat. "And you, Mr. Ninja. How'd you manage a cloud of pepper gas without a mask?"

"Discipline. Mind over matter—gas, liquid, or solid."

"I tell you what, your entrance was a grand surprise. I respect those who follow the plan, and those who are smart enough to seize an opportunity to deviate from it. When exactly did you decide to secure Simon instead of Simone?"

"While sprinting through the smoking doorway. Capture the emperor, and the empire will fall."

"Is that an old Ninja proverb?" Conan asked.

Masaru smirked and confessed. "No, I just made it up now. To be honest, I thought of an old Woody Allen movie about genetic engineering where the only thing remaining of the leader was his nose, and Woody captured it. Reminded me of Simon."

"*Sleeper*, that flick rocked," Diego said with a chuckle. "I loved the bit where Woody points a gun at the nose and says, 'Don't move, or he gets it right between the eyes.'"

After a hearty laugh, everyone seemed to wander through their own heads, perhaps replaying the roles they'd just performed on Simon's stage.

Simone broke the silence. "Thanks for everything, guys. "You all are stellar friends and kick-ass commandos. "

"It was fun," Conan said, smiling.

"Justice will not be served until those who are unaffected are as outraged as those who are," Masaru quoted, frowning.

"Ninja proverb?" Diego asked.

"Benjamin Franklin."

"I didn't know ol' Ben was Japanese," Conan joked.

"Now that you're safe and sound," Diego patted Simone on the shoulder. "I want you get a good night's sleep. Office

Eddie's postin' a stakeout with two men at your house, and Conan's agreed to crash on your couch. If Simon tries his control shit again, I want the barbarian angel to be watchin' over you."

"Thanks for your concern, but I don't think that's gonna happen again." Simone pointed proudly to her temple. "Miss Mind here turned the genetic tables on Mister Mind. Rafi will be there, I'm changing the security code, and we have a twelve-legged natural security system, four of them carrying a lovable attack dog."

"Well, to be honest like Masaru here, I wanted to make sure *I* get a good night's sleep. I'm sick o' worryin' about you, girl!" A series of honks behind the Volvo snared everyone's attention, and Diego turned his head. "It's the rest of the team. They split before us. What're they doin' behind us?"

"I'm starved," Simone whined. "Ask 'em if they're up for a victory dinner at Wong's Cafe? It's right near The Fit Nest, and I'm buyin'."

Diego phoned Chick. "You warriors hungry for a celebration at Wong's? Our happy hostage is hosting the event."

"Please extend our thanks, but our team's on a Human eSociety mission. We returned one stolen dog, two more to go, and one'll have to hang at The Nest till we locate its owner. Then we're droppin' off Rafi to see if Simone's darlings have destroyed the house. Besides, I got a monkey on my back that's comin' home with me."

Jimmy and Officer Eddie joined Simone, Conan, and Masaru for lively accounts of the day's action around a lazy Susan laden with Japanese sushi, noodles, and saki. Simone finally arrived home at five p.m. Two plainclothes policemen trailing her Volvo parked down the block.

Simone reset the security code and closed all the window blinds before flopping onto the living room rug with the dogs and Rafi. "I am so sorry to drag you into my melo-drama. Thank god Diego and his team got us out of there."

"Apology accepted though unnecessary. If neither of us had been kidnapped, the team would not have known about the stolen animals and rescued them. No rain, no showers, no rainbows, no flowers."

"Is that Rumi again?"

"No, just Rafi."

"Well, if there were more Rafis in the world, it'd be a better place. I've got some energy to burn off before my body'll let me sleep. I want a rematch."

"With whom?" Rafi asked. "Simon?"

"Scrabble."

"Oh, my. You are indeed a courageous woman! Because you foiled the mastermind, you think you can beat the Scrabble Master?"

"It's possible." She hopped up and headed to the kitchen with Rafi close behind. "I have opposable thumbs again, can rearrange my letters in a tray instead of my head, and won't fall into a stupor halfway through the game. We'll play here at a proper table." She rummaged in the cupboards and set a box on the counter. "You make the microwave popcorn and set up the board while I take a quick shower. I smell like an explosion!"

They both played masterfully, but Simone eked ahead at the end—303 to 301. "It's one to one. Two out of three wins. Final play-off tomorrow. You have to go to work?"

"No. Monday is an Irish holiday. I only have one plan."

"What's that?"

"Preparing a place in my apartment for the champion-ship trophy."

"Dream on, comrade," Simone said, rising from the ta-ble. "That's what I'm gonna do for the next ten hours."

Though peaceful and settled in her safe house, Simone

lay sleepless in bed, reliving the day, searching for any shred of Simon's control inside, worrying about his next move. *My unscrupulous brother didn't build his wealth and power by giving up. What scurrilous scenario will he concoct next?*

~

Once the pepper gas cleared, Luther Heinrich had rolled the wheelchair and its morose passenger into his hermetically sealed bedroom. Only Simon's eyes moved during the short trek. Luther quietly slouched on a nearby couch for five minutes but Simon didn't speak, only breathed and stared, so Luther tiptoed out the doorway. Two hours later, he was summoned back to the bedroom and resumed his position on the couch.

"Initiate Plan B." The crackling speakers seemed to amplify the spite in Simon's command.

Shocked, Luther's sat up straight with his hands on his knees. "Are you sure about this? I thought Plan B was still in a developmental stage."

"We have certainly learned some vital information along the way today, but the local repercussions from this fiasco will be irreparable. I am ready. The time has come. Simon says... initiate Plan B immediately."

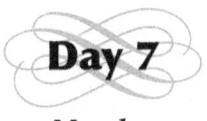

Day 7

Monday

A WAVE OF NAUSEA AWOKE SIMONE. Driblets of sweat coated her forehead and temples. Afraid she might retch, Simone rolled on her side toward the edge of the bed. The digital clock on the nightstand glowed 3:45 am. *Must be an earthquake... nearby... no... this is different.* One hand clutched her chest as a sharp pain seemed to slice her heart in half. *It's like a volcano inside me. I'm burning up! Simon?* Expecting some internal control, she rotated her feet to the bedside and stood. *No resistance, only wobbly legs.* Bracing herself on the bed post, then the armoire and wall, Simone hobbled into the bathroom and splashed water on her feverish face. As she leaned on the washstand, the dizziness began to subside. *So much for my ten hours of sleep.*

Still queasy and bewildered, Simone had no desire to lie down. She dressed and roused the dogs from their oblivious slumber. "Dammit Brandy, up an' at 'em. This room's haunted." She led them to the backyard and went into her office behind the carport. *I haven't opened my email account for days. Or my appointment calendar.* First Simone viewed her bank account online. Her previous balance of three thousand dollars now said one hundred and three thousand. *Ick. Dirty money.* After several minutes of intense thought, she wrote two checks, then skimmed through

Ming's patient communication and messages from friends wondering where the hell she'd gone without telling them.

Two patients scheduled this morning, eight and nine-thirty, both talkers, thank god. I should be able to manage listening. She called the dogs into the sanctuary and considered a morning meditation, but instead curled up under a flannel blanket on her therapy couch.

At 8:01 a.m. dogs barking snapped her from sleep. Dr. Simone Wellstone's first patient stood outside the door, rapping impatiently and peering through the glass. Middle manager Molly Wartburg went into overtime lamenting about her dead-end job at the mining company and complaining about the coworkers in cubicles surrounding her cubicle.

Lawyer Graham Beaton arrived early, fumed about traffic, his pathetic golf game, a peptic ulcer, and wouldn't cease blathering until she escorted him to his Mini Cooper and closed the car door. Ten minutes into each of their sessions, compassionate Simone had passionately wanted to expel them with six words of advice. "Get out and get a life!" Although irritating, the two patient ordeals stimulated an appreciation for the full to overflowing life she'd been forced to lead during the past week.

Walking to the house, Simone noticed the patrol car parked at the curb and found Officer Eddie chatting with Rafi in the living room. She'd never seen him decked out in a freshly pressed blue uniform. "Hey, Eddie. What's up?"

"I have news I wanted to deliver myself." He seemed more somber than usual. "You might want to be sitting down."

Simone pulled up a foot stool and obliged. "Sounds like bad news."

Eddie sighed, paused, and gathered his thoughts. "Early this morning, an explosion at EDNA rocked the neighborhood. Luckily the building was mostly uninhabited. A nurse and one guard are in critical condition at the hospital, and... your brother is in the morgue... rather... his charred remains are in the morgue."

Simone looked away and felt a familiar split in her heart. "Early this morning at 3:45 a.m., right?"

"So you heard about it?"

"No, I felt it, but didn't understand what it was. I've been up since then. Tell me more."

"We don't know much, but some outlets seem to be spinning the news." He took out his smartphone and read, "EDNA employees have stated that the facility was attacked by a band of terrorists on Sunday afternoon. Reliable sources suspect the gang may have been responsible for the explosion which caused the death of Simon Albright."

"Hmm."

"I'm very sorry for your loss, Simone. Is there anything I can do?"

"Thanks, and no thanks. He was dealt some unfortunate cards in this life and made unfortunate decisions to compensate for them. I already let go of Simon once. Before yesterday, I hadn't seen him since I visited Albright two years ago... He was comatose and flat on his back. Any sadness I felt for him evaporated when I saw a dissected dog strapped to a table in his laboratory."

After a few moments, Eddie broke the silence. "There's one thing you could do for us. We're waiting for Simon's dental records to verify the match, but could use an identification from a family member, and you seem to be the only one available. It's not a pretty sight."

"When?" she asked.

"Soon if you can. And I plan to head over to Paul Roberts' funeral at 2 p.m. if you'd like to join me."

"That's today? Cripes, I am out of touch. Sure, but I need

some time. Can you pick me up at noon-thirty?"

"Fine by me." He stood to leave. "Thanks for your help."

Simone followed Eddie to the door, bid him adieu, returned to her stool, and faced Rafi. "How are you today?"

"Okay though pensive, and I too am very sorry for your loss. There is almost too much to process from these last three days."

"I hear you, and I'm hoping life'll settle down for a while. I have an option for both of us and have made a decision that will offer you even more options."

"I am all ears."

Simone suddenly glanced toward the window as if someone had called her name. "I feel like a waffle."

"You do not look like a waffle."

Chuckling, she turned back to Rafi. "You are a funny man, but it's your deadpan delivery that kills me."

"I am not sure if that is good or bad."

"Very good. Bangin'. Icing on the cake. Has your nimble brain ever considered the origin of the word breakfast?"

"No..." Rafi replied, "but it must mean to... stop fasting, start eating again."

"Right. And I need to break the fast fast. Let's batten down the hatches and hit IHOP."

"I am not sure how to batten, nor do I know where your hatches are, but I do like IHOP!"

The stakeout cops followed the Volvo, and Simone flashed them a thumbs-up when she and Rafi entered the restaurant. Once they'd ordered, she presented her options and decision.

"I know you like facts. Here are four. One, you might not be allowed to keep Zara at your apartment. Two, even if Kyle let's her stay, it's cramped... sorry... small for a man and his Doberman. Besides, you're outside working all day. Three, I've got an vacated bungalow with a living room, a real kitchen, a big bedroom, and a bathroom twice the size of yours. And four, I'm not hiring a replacement for the missing Ming. You are welcome to move in, Zara will have a backyard and two buddies, and I could use a little help with the yard... and maybe some client accounting. You're good with figures, and I'm only good at figuring out people."

"Well, everything you said makes sense and—"

"And... I don't need an answer right now. Lemme tell you about my decision. Yesterday my brother transferred a large sum of money into my bank account as compensation for my kidnapping and a bribe to work with him at EDNA. Ha! As if! I didn't ask for it, don't need it, and don't want it. I'm giving it all away to those involved in his latest caper..." She reached into her pocket, withdrew a check, and handed it to Rafi. "Starting with ten thousand dollars for Zara and ten thousand for you." Simone smiled. "I'm sure she'll let you handle her investment portfolio."

Rafi's eyes widened as his head wobbled. "I am over-whelmed."

"So am I, and I could use a little less whelming. Your help and support has been invaluable. Sorry, but you have no choice in this decision, only another list of options to consider."

"Are you positively sure of this?"

"What do you think?"

"I think Dr. Simone seems very certain, and Rafi would be honored to occupy her bungalow and accept her most gracious offer."

"Excellent. I feel better already. Besides enlisting your assistance, above and beyond the call of duty or responsi-bility, I borrowed your body and scraped it up. If someone lent me their car and I dented it, I'd take it to the garage to be fixed and painted, and return it in better shape that when I got it."

Rafi's lips pursed into a smirk. "I do not think a garage would have a tube of Neosporin to apply on my superficial skin wounds."

Simone burst out laughing. "You're too much, you know, just too damn much."

Two Belgian waffles laden with strawberries, walnuts, and whipped cream soon devolved into crumbs floating in pools of syrup. Satiated and high on sugar, Simone paid the bill and climbed into the Volvo with Rafi. "You can check out your new digs while I'm at a morgue and a funeral—a lovely way to start the week. Maybe we can pick up a few of your one hundred things when I return. You've been living out of a backpack for two days."

"Infinitely better than my childhood in Iraq with neither a backpack nor anything to carry in it."

Dressed in a black dress and floppy black hat, Simone rode with Officer Eddie to the morgue. All of her mental preparations to view her brother disintegrated as she stared down at his blackened body on the autopsy table after the pathologist pulled back the sheet. *Good lord. This is no way for anyone to go.* "I guess that's..." she choked on her words, "that's Simon. I... I hope it was quick."

The pathologist was aloof and apathetic, a live stiff working daily with dead ones. "Do you recall any major injuries he may have received, Dr. Wellstone?"

"Simon was mainly a frail indoor person, but took up skiing and tried to conquer a mountain. The mountain won. Fractured his right tibula and fibula just below the knee."

Using a forceps and magnifying glass, he scrutinized what once were his legs. "A clean break is apparent here, next to this abnormal area on his thigh. It appears that a long piece of flesh has been carved away. I've never seen anything quite like it."

"Flying metal from the explosion maybe?" Eddie asked.

"I doubt it, though somehow this seems recent, and vaguely resembles skin graft harvesting for a burn victim, but much thicker." After a few more questions, the pathologist rendered his opinion. "We'll still check the dental records, but Dr. Wellstone's positive identification and the injury seem to be conclusive evidence."

Back in the patrol car, Simone sighed, "Well... that was disturbing. It looks like the hell he created for others paid him a visit. Maybe you can call off your official shadows, and I can get back my life."

"Does it comfort you at all that he's gone?"

"Somewhat, but it reminds me of what my mother said about weeds, worries, and cockroaches. The only way to get rid of them is to die and leave them behind."

"Is that you or Simon talking?" Eddie asked.

She whipped around her head and shot him an angry scowl. "I assure you this is me speaking."

"Easy, Simone. I wasn't insinuating you aren't you, only wondering if you were referring to you being free from Simon, or Simon being free from the law. I would've had a warrant for his arrest today. How ever they try to spin this incident, I've got a video of Rafi's kidnapping, a recording of the conversation between you two, witnesses who've experienced this bizarre technology, and incriminating yet inconclusive testimonies from EDNA and Albright employees. Whether the courts would decide it's science fact or fiction, I don't know."

"Sorry. I just have a gnawing feeling in my gut that this isn't over."

"Me too. Since you brought it up, how would I, or anyone else, really know if Simon or Simone were speaking?"

The question had no demonstrable answer, and they sat in silence during the short drive to the Presbyterian church. Opening the patrol car door for Simone, Eddie said, "We only see each other at the precinct, hospital, or in the field for some convoluted case. Now at the morgue and a funeral. Sometime we should be everyday humans and take in a movie or go bowling."

Did he just ask me out on a dateless date? He's a good man, kinda handsome, and actually seems to believe in what I'm capable of doing. "Maybe. I could use a little normal. I'll see you later. I'm gonna hang in the back like a black fly on the wall during the ceremony."

Sun rays filtered through the ornate stained-glass windows and split into a myriad of colors. First Presbyterian Church had a small congregation, but today a multitude of denominations packed the interior and straggled out the open doorways. Tall Paul, a pillar in the community had lived in Buffalo City since birth. His friends were shocked by his premature death and suspicious of the rumor that this gentle man had taken his own life.

Semi-concealed by a column behind the rows of pews, Simone pulled the hat brim over her face and perused the attendees, but saw no one she cared to meet. *Not a soul from EDNA seems to be here, not even CEO Luther, the little Nazi. Three of the scientists I saw there yesterday have been with Albright for years and worked with Paul. Where are they?*

She felt a tap on her shoulder and turned to face Dr. Frank, who launched into an apology. "Simone, I had no idea that EDNA's technology would—"

"Stop!" she whispered, raising her hand as if reprimanding a bothersome child. "It's nice to see you Dr. Frank, but today we are honoring Paul Roberts. Another day we shall meet to dishonor Simon while consuming a Flaming Blue

Jesus... or ten."

"Sorry, I understand."

"Where's Coco? How is she?"

"Home and still recovering."

"To relieve some of her suicidal stress, please tell her I'm establishing a $10,000 trust fund for Connor and his education. I fell in love with that little boy."

"So kind of you, Simone," he said, shaking his head.

"I'm hoping she continues her sessions with me. To be truly kind to Coco, we need to find a way to get her off the drugs or off the alcohol. The combination could kill her, and then neither of you will have much time left to share. Call me in a few days when I'm done recovering."

Dr. Frank faded into the crowd. Simone focused on the funeral service and the decades of memories with Paul. She thought of many warm words to say if she stood at the pulpit, but his other friends spoke them for her.

When the ceremony ended and people milled around the church yard, Simone spotted Diego, leaning on a tree alone, looking ruggedly dapper in his black Nehru shirt, black jeans, and black leather boots. She snuck behind him and hissed, "May God unleash his wrath onto these demons!"

"Run away! Run away!" Diego shouted a tad too loudly. Several people turned, profiled him in the imbecile category, and stepped away. "Look, it worked," he said to Simone while pointing at the escapees.

"Have you spoken with Eddie?"

"Yeah, seems like Simon said his last words."

"And you lead a band of terrorists. Or is it a gang?"

"Well, we did create a smidgen of necessary terror. I prefer Band of Terrorists. Could be the name of a rock group. We're more like Greenpeace or the Humanitarian League, 'a society of thinkers and workers, irrespective of class or creed, who have united for the sole purpose of humanizing, as far as possible, the conditions of modern life.' Henry Salt of the Earth, early-1900-something."

"Never heard of it or him."

"I added the 'of the earth' part. Just Henry Salt, British dude. You'd like him. Gandhi liked him. The greedy Powers That Were didn't like him. He raised a lot of hell in his time. One o' the first champions of animal rights, too. I even memorized his poem called 'A Lover of Animals.' Wanna hear it?"

"Of course."

Diego assumed an archaic pose, not unlike the Presbyterian preacher during his eulogy.

"Oh, yes! You love them well, I know!

But whisper me—when most?

'In fields, at summer-time.' Not so:

At supper-time—in roast."

"Diego, my friend," Simone said through a smile, "you always brighten my day."

"These days, most need brightening. How're you doin'? I'm sorry for your loss, but you're prob'ly not."

"You're the only one I could confess that to." She attempted to get serious but didn't quite succeed. "I have a gift for you in an attempt to show my appreciation for everything you and your BOT have done for me."

"BOT? As in Ro—?"

"Band of terrorists."

"Ah. I like it." Diego's hand seemed incapable of ceasing to fidget with the silver medallion on his black bolo tie. "We could go on tour. Diego and the BOT. Sorry, but I'm wound tight today. Too much coffee already."

"You must promise not to reveal the source of this gift."

"For you I'll cross my heart and hope to live." He took her hand, bowed in submission, and vowed, "I promise," then jerked up and demanded, "Now where's my present? Homemade brownies? A Ferrari? A large amount of cash and prizes?"

"You got it."

"Hmm. Must be a brownie," he said, shading his eyes and surveying the parking lot. "Not a Ferrari in sight."

"Are you sure you've only had coffee today? How many cups?"

"Lost count. Been up since before dawn when Eddie called. Too much to fester over."

"I'm sure you heard Simon tell me yesterday that he'd transferred $100,000 into my bank account. Well, he did, and I don't want it. I've given $20,000 to Rafi and Zara. I'm starting an educational trust fund for Coco's grand-son and sweet Amanda, whom I hope you meet some day. That leaves $50,000 for you, the BOT, and your Creative Arts For Everyone organization. You had expenses. You left your life to take care of mine. You kept my spirits up and gave me hope. You saved me, Diego Fierro." She handed him the check as the tears dripped down her cheeks. "Save it or spend it as you see fit." Simone looked up into his face, a mustached mirror image with tears dripping down his cheeks.

It took Diego a moment before he could answer. "Thank you, dear Simone. This will help many other people besides me. You are a heart with legs." He wrapped his long arms around her and spoke softly into her ear. "My tears are from gratitude... and from my memories of Nathan. This is what he used to do. I miss him, but am thankful to have found another kindred soul."

After a long hug, during which more people moved away from them, Simone said, "Officer Eddie brought me, but I'd like to leave this morose gathering. Paul's in my soul, not here. Are you feeling spontaneous?"

"That's my middle name."

"I've almost completed my humanitarian mission for the day, and The Fit Nest is part of my plan. It's four o'clock, and I'd like to show up at Amanda's apartment after she gets home from school. She's a gem and a fine thirteen-year-old fitness specimen. I want to buy a membership for her."

"I think you just did. Let's go and meet Amanda."

"Did you ride the Ducati? I didn't bring a helmet."

"Drove a car today."

"How noncharacteristically plebeian of you."

Diego let the sentence play once more in his mind. "That might be the longest word I've ever heard in conversation, and I have no idea what plebeian means."

"What common folks do, and you're definitely uncommon, bordering on abnormal and unorthodox."

"Then I consider it a compliment." Diego gestured with his head. "C'mon."

"I'll meet you in the parking lot. Gotta tell Eddie. He and his men are still my bodyguards. Think he'll trust me with you?"

Diego just smiled, letting her question hang in the air. "You want me to tell you what kind of car, or are you just gonna guess?"

"I assumed it would stand out, whatever it is."

"Not it. She... is the only 1966 Chantilly-beige Mustang within a few thousand miles."

During the ride, Simone recounted her experience inside Amanda on Day One—the bullying at school, her athletic expertise in gym class, the volleyball tournament, and her determination to slay the Boogeyman. "Besides being a sweetheart, she's a born powerhouse. When you're ready to retire, she could lead the BOT."

Pulling up in front of Amanda's duplex, Diego offered a suggestion. "Since you've had no contact with this kid lately, and she has no clue you were inside her, why don't you go in alone first and break the ice? Better than draggin' some strange oaf in behind you. Call me when you want me."

"So you're a strange oaf now, are you?"

"One of my best disguises. I'll wait here and spin some tunes." He pointed to the dashboard. "This baby'll take me back before I was born. A factory-installed, 8-track player and a stack of vintage tapes in the back—Led Zeppelin, Beach Boys, Pink Floyd." He tapped the analog clock. "This old thing here only works when the car's moving. Can't tell me the time, but I know how long I've been drivin'. Don't hurry. The clock has stopped in my world."

Simone knocked on the front door of the duplex apartment. Soon Amanda cracked it open and peered out. "Can I help you?"

"Hi, Amanda. Remember me? Dr. Simone Wellstone? You and your mom came to see me once."

"Oh, yes. I remember. You were friendly, and I wasn't."

"Well, you weren't talking then, but you seemed nice to me. Can I come in and chat for a few minutes? Is Whitney home?"

"Sure, she's taking a shower. I'll let her know you're here." Dressed in a tank top and Valleyview Hornet purple sweatpants, Amanda led Simone to the davenport and tore up the stairs two steps at a time.

Gazing around the room, Simone pictured last Tuesday's grisly scene. *Two bullet holes in the wall. Caked blood on the chair. Jack Daniel's stains on the carpet. Boy, we did a number on Darryl and this room.*

Amanda tore back downstairs and sat beside Simone. "She's almost done."

"How's school goin'?"

"Better now."

"I'm glad to hear that. Any bullies botherin' you and Toby?"

Amanda didn't answer right away. "How do you know Toby?" She cocked her head and paused again. "It was you, wasn't it?"

"Me? What do you mean?"

"You were inside me... in my head, in my body. It's weird, but I can feel it." Amanda turned and faced Simone. "You were my angel last Tuesday, weren't you?"

"You amaze me again like you did then. Yes, it was me. And I woke up in four more bodies since then."

"I knew it!" Amanda jumped off the davenport and threw her hands down as if flinging something onto the floor. "You gotta tell my mom. She's happy I'm talking, but thinks I am cray. Tetched in de head. I don't dare tell anyone else."

"Well, it's hard to accept. I did it all week, and I can hardly believe it."

"Rad an' a half. This is like the movie *Venom* where the monster's inside the hero."

"I thought I was an angel."

"You were! You were! The *Venom* monster's like an ugly angel but you're pretty. They fought off the real monster and worked together like we did."

"If you don't mind, I'd like you to meet a friend of mine who's waiting in the car. I was inside him on Wednesday. You'll like him."

"Cool beans."

"C'mon. You gotta see his wheels."

Accompanied by The Stones belting out "Time is on my side, yes it is," Diego threw open the door and stepped out when they reached the car. "Amanda Parnum! Diego Fierro." He raised one palm in front of his shoulder. "Gimme five."

Amanda delivered five, leaned to one side, and looked beyond Diego. "Whoa. Is this a Stang or what?"

"Yep, 1966 Coupe."

"It is snatched."

"No, I bought it."

"Dude, snatched means awesome, not swiped. You know, like savage, Gucci, sic."

"Right, I knew that." Diego gave Simone a wink. "Got it from a friend named Miguel Tangen, and he named her Mustangen."

"Cute," Amanda said.

"Simone tells me you are the next Wonder Woman." Diego pointed to her duplex. "Lemme see you scale that drainpipe again."

"It's not that hard."

"For you maybe. She also said you know how to handle an ice pick and a toilet cover. I like people who know how to improvise."

Simone put her arm over Amanda's shoulder. "Miss Perceptive here knew I was the one inside her before I even told her."

"Well, you're smarter than me, kid. I didn't even know Simone was in me *when* she was in me!"

"For real?" Amanda asked. "What did you think was happening?"

"I'd just zone out and wake up again. Clueless. But then, she didn't have to help me battle any bullies. She only hung around watchin' me do my thing."

"Are you two like a couple or something? Baes in black?"

"A couple of buds who came from a funeral," Simone said. "This week I found out I had a Boogeyman like you. We think he murdered our friend."

"Dr. Wellstone!" Whitney called as she walked across

the lawn. "How nice to see you again."

"You gotta tell her," Amanda whispered.

"Don't worry," Simone assured her. "I promise." She turned toward Whitney. "This is Diego, owner of The Fit Nest martial arts studio."

"Pleasure to meet you, Miss Parnum."

"Same here," Whiney agreed.

"Cool," Amanda whispered again. "My gym teacher Isabella works out there."

"I know her." Diego returned the whisper and again raised his palm. "She rocks."

Amanda gave him another five.

"Whitney, this is kind of a spur-of-the-moment visit, but I'd like to chat with you a bit. Diego wants to give Amanda a complimentary membership. And if you have time, we could take you over to The Nest and have a look-see. It's not far, just down by the river."

"If we're riding' in this rod, you can take us anywhere."

Diego nudged Amanda into the passenger seat. "I only got ancient tunes, kid. Ever hear of the Stones, Zepplin, or Pink Floyd?"

She raised five and sang her reply. "We don't need no education. We don't need no thought control."

"Three's a charm," he said, slapping her hand, "even when it's five."

During their drive, Simone gave Whitney a rundown of the week events and her financial plans for her daughter's future. Amanda listened intently in stereo—one ear on the tunes, one on the backseat conversation. When the Mustang arrived at The Fit Nest, Whitney and Simone both emerged wiping tears.

Mother hugged daughter on the curb. "I'm so sorry I doubted you, A. I wanted to believe you, but it all sounded so psycho!"

"It's okay, Mom. I'm just glad you know now."

Diego led them into The Nest and introduced Jade at the reception desk. "Say hello to our new member, Amanda Putnam. She's a fit little fighter."

As she leaned down toward Amanda, Jade's warm welcome morphed into an exclamation. "Little? You are already cut! Look at those arms, girl!"

"Mine? Look at yours. I want yours."

Jade tapped Amanda on the triceps. "You've been pumpin' somethin'. I bet you're a push-up addict... and not the girly kind."

"Yeah, and my gym teacher Isabella works me out."

"She is straight fire. I need to take some lessons from that one."

"Hey, Jade," Simone said. "Thanks for everything. I'm Simone, the helpless hostage."

"You're welcome, but I've been hearin' from Diego you're not so helpless."

"We spoke when I was in Diego and met when I was in Rafi."

"It's way better seein' your sweet face than Diego's mug. We had a blast savin' Rafi and the critters. Your wacky week reminds me of what my dad used to say about himself. "I may be schizophrenic, but I'll always have each other."

"Your daddy's DNA explains your split personality, Amazon," Diego quipped. "You mind takin' Amanda and Whitney on a tour of our fine facilities?"

"Be glad to."

A half-hour later, Simone sat with Amanda in the backseat of "The Stang," bonding like two Velcro strips. "I had to rid the world of a nasty boogeyman this week, and your determination inspired me."

"Who was it?"

"The one who created your treatment. You signed up

for it. I was drugged, kidnapped, and stuck in other bodies without signing on the dotted line. Imagine how I felt that first morning when I looked in the mirror and saw your face! Freaked me out for a while and then kept freakin' me out some more."

"So... who was it?" Amanda prodded again.

"My twin brother. Sometimes the fam is hiding your worst enemy. I wanted to use your toilet cover on him."

Amanda laughed. "You shoulda called me. We'd of taken care of him together."

"I got a question for you."

"Ask."

"When exactly did you figure out someone or something was inside you? The first time I remember is when you started speaking in the principal's office. Freaked me out again."

"Keepin' it 100," Amanda said, "probably after we busted up the bullies at the locker. You or I said somethin', and Toby said, 'You talked!' Did you say 'I did?' or did I?"

"I dunno."

"Me either. Before then I thought I was like daydreamin' or really just fell asleep. By the time you gave the class hell... sorry, bad word... especially when you screamed 'I've had enough!' I was like wide-awake and watchin' and thinkin', 'Give 'em hell for me too!" Amanda snugged up her shoulders and put on her meek face. "Sorry again."

"Doesn't bother me. Do we have to tell Mom?"

"No, no. Only she gets to say that... and some other bad words."

"Ah... the fam and its funny rules. So you like talkin' again?"

"Yeah, but like, it was kinda cool not to. The things people say when there's nothin' to say but like they just gotta hear themselves talk."

"You got one o' those high fives for me?"

Amanda obliged.

"You are wise beyond your years, girl," Simone purred. "I gotta tell you one more thing. On Saturday, when I had soooo many plans for my meeting the next day with the Boogeyman and weird stuff to try and do, I woke up inside a Doberman Pinscher."

"Noooo! Really?"

"Really. Freaked out again, chained to a stake in the ground, but it all turned out fine. She's a treasure, and we bonded right from the beginning."

Amanda was on a roll, letting it all hang out with her new sister. "You know, like, they should use this treatment or whatever it is at school. Lotsa kids need a lesson about how to treat others. What's that saying? 'Walk a mile in another man's shoes'? Or in another man's dog?" She paused and sighed, "I wish we had a dog. I love dogs."

"You and I have to do some hangin' together. You gotta visit my place again. Now I've got three of 'em. Zara Zarina the Doberman, Brandy the Irish Setter, and Dammit the Golden Retriever."

"You have a dog named Dammit!? Oops. Sorry."

"It's a great name. C'mon over, and you can yell Dammit all day long."

Diego parked at the curb, and everyone piled out. Amanda and Simone were still at it.

"Maybe we'll hit The Fit Nest together this weekend. I've been doin' too much layin' around and not enough liftin'."

Amanda turned to Whitney. "Is that okay, Mom? I got nothin' goin' on."

"Sure, sweetheart."

Amanda turned back to Simone. "Can we go visit your dogs, too?"

"Better ask Mom."

"Mom?"

"Of course, sweetheart. just don't bring one home."

After a round of hugs on the apartment steps, Simone had the last words. "I want you all to try and imagine this. The day I was inside Amanda, she... well, *we* go to a volleyball tournament after school. I'm still tryin' to figure out what the hell... sorry... heck is happening. Suddenly I... we are leaping around the court, divin' onto the floor makin' impossible saves, and spikin' the shit... sorry... crap out of the ball, and slammin' it down our opponent's throats. Talk about havin' the best seat in house. I was sittin' right inside the star player!" She bent down closer to Amanda. "See ya, sister. Five for the road?"

Amanda delivered a hard five and a soft smile.

As they drove away, Diego said, "You got a way with people, Dr. Simone Wellstone, Empathiatrist and Everyday Human Being."

"Yeah? So do you. It was a good day. Thanks for sharing it with me."

"Any time, any day, anywhere."

When Diego dropped off Simone at home, she noticed the patrol car still parked down the street and her spirits sunk. *Damn, I thought Eddie called off his stakeout. What's going on?*

She drove the Volvo to Flanagan's with Rafi to retrieve his belongings. Three dogs had to sniff every item as they carried them into his new abode. Easily hauling half of Rafi's possession in one box, Simone said, "If I tried this 100 Things Challenge, a third of my list would be chew toys, tennis balls, and rawhide bones. Do you have to lose one item to add Zara Zarina?"

"Oh, no. Zara is on a level high above things and deserves her own list. So far it contains three tennis balls, two bowls, and one leash."

Simone set up the Scrabble board in her kitchen while Rafi made popcorn. Near the end of their neck-and-neck championship game, the iPhone buzzed and Officer Eddie's name appeared on the screen.

"Hi, Eddie. What's up?"

"You okay?"

"Just fine. I see your boys are still on duty."

"I thought it best to keep them standing by. I don't want to alarm you, but this shit storm is definitely not under control."

"Eddie, do you mind if I put you on the speaker so Rafi can listen in?"

"Please do. He should hear this too."

She set the phone on the table. "Okay. Tell it like it is."

"I've had six officers working this case since dawn. EDNA trucks are delivering and employees are in the building, but EDNA's other entity is MIA. It looks like a turtle run over by a Harley—the shell's cracked but it's legs are still twitching. No one's on the second floor, and no one answers any calls, nada, zip. We only have a few names of Simon's technical staff. Their homes are vacant, no families, no info from neighbors, nada, zip again. Since we've got a video of Hunter kidnapping Rafi, I put out an APB, but he's still at large. My men spotted him near the EDNA compound, chased him into the hills, and had a damn canyon shoot out like an old wild-west movie. They lost him. This town used to be a peaceful haven. A busy day for us might be a traffic accident, a drunk pissin' in the park, or one officer helpin' someone break into their home after they accidentally locked it and couldn't find the key they haven't used in years. Now we got school shootings, demonstrations, racial tension, explosions, kidnappings, and unsubstantiated suicides or murders."

Simone didn't try to interrupt his rant, only punctuated

an occasional sentence with a yeah or uh-huh.

"When I was a kid, my dad would take his single-shot rifle into the woods for one week a year and bag a deer. No one was hunting crowds of humans with an AR-15 capable of firing ten rounds per second! During the last seven days in America the Beautiful, fifteen shoppers were killed at Walmart, twenty kids wounded at a football stadium, and a thirteen year old mowed down his brother, two sisters, and parents. What is happening to our world? I'm thinkin' of movin' to a quiet island in the Pacific Ocean."

"I hear you, Eddie. Sorry to be a thorn in your side."

"No, no, you're not. You're a rose growin' in the bramble patch. Anyway, just keep your eyes and ears tuned up full throttle, and your house locked down tight. If you get any of your inner messages about this, please let me know ASAP. It's gonna take some time to subpoena records and interview employees... if we can even find them."

"Good luck with that. I'm having all the locks changed tomorrow. Thanks so much for thinking of us." Simone ended the call and sighed, "You got any soothing advice from Rumi or Rafi?"

"Two from Rumi come to mind. 'Move, but don't move the way fear makes you move.' That sounds comforting to me, but he also wrote, "Run from what's comfortable. Forget safety. Live where you fear to live. Destroy your reputation. Be notorious. I have tried prudent planning long enough. From now on I'll be mad.' I am not sure which of these quotes is applicable for an empathic psychiatrist."

"Thanks. I'll chew on those words while you make one word on the Scrabble board. I'm down to my last six letters." Simone didn't care about winning, only finishing the game. She played compassionately as an empath would, to assure her partner prevailed.

Rafi laid down his final letter, smiled proudly, and asked,

"When will I receive my championship trophy?"

"You already have it. The Emperor's New Trophy is sitting on a gilded pedestal in your mind. No need to lose one item to receive it."

"That, Dr. Simone, is a perfect trophy."

"I've been up an' at it since 3:45 a.m., and I am bushed. Sleep tight and don't let the assassin bugs bite." As she turned to go upstairs, Simone had a notion inspired by Eddie's call. *Hmm. Maybe I should have security bars installed.* She walked from room to room, counting the windows, then stepped outside, paused, looked right, then left, and hurried to her Sensory Sanctuary. She stood in the center of the Persian rug and gazed through the five, floor-to-ceiling picture windows into her serene world. Her chest heaved and her stomach tied itself into a knot. *Bar the sanctuary and be barred from my own backyard? That's certainly not what I had in mind when I built it. My dream is crumbling.*

Feeling nauseous, as if an earthquake in her body was imminent, she locked the sanctuary, locked the front door, scurried upstairs and locked her bedroom door, splashed water on her hot face, threw on pajamas, and slid under the covers. One small wall light burned in a corner near the floor. *Maybe it is time to move on. Where? Run from what's comfortable? I used to have other dreams, but this one's the reality I chose.* A quote from Rev. Jesse Jackson that she'd shared with patients came to mind. "If my mind can conceive it, and my heart can believe it, I know I can achieve it." *I continually tell people to visualize their desires. Perhaps I need to take my own advice. Or just be patient.*

She took a deep breath and conjured up her childhood dream of being a geologist, scampering among the canyons, discovering the enigmas hidden in rocks and beneath the earth's crust. She visualized the ranch in Wyoming she'd dreamed of owning in her teens—cows in the corral, riding and camping in the mountains, hanging out with horses instead of humans. She imagined boarding a Boeing 777, flying alone to the opposite side of the world, to trek in Nepal, to bike in New Zealand, to raft down the Mekong River through Laos, Thailand, Cambodia, and Vietnam, to walk along the Great Wall of China. Her final fleeting thought was of Ming. *When she talked about China, it seemed... so exotic... so mysterious... so foreign and forboding. Maybe it's time to take that trip I've dreamed of for years...*

Day 13

Saturday

During the past five days, Simone had new locks installed in the house, office, and sanctuary, nixed the barred windows idea, and searched the Internet for airfares to Asia. Rafi settled into the bungalow and continued to help the Irish brothers complete the B&B. A small FOR SALE sign had been posted on the front window of Flanagan's Saloon and Eatery. Coco showed up for her weekly session with Simone, and on her own initiative, had flushed her pills down the toilet. Diego monitored the news for any manufactured evidence regarding his band of terrorists. The guard and nurse injured in the morning explosion at Edna did not survive.

Officer Eddie and his men continued to run into dead-ends during their investigation. They'd entered the home of Dr. Marlin Blake, one of EDNA scientists and found his dead body facedown on the cement basement floor, apparently from an accidental fall. Hunter's bloated, broken, and bruised corpse, wedged between two boulders at the bottom of a gorge, was spotted by hikers. At first it appeared to be a wilderness mishap, but during the autopsy the pathologist discovered an unidentifiable virus in the bloodstream which may have caused his death. Hunter's body now lay in an air-tight container waiting for shipment to a medical research facility in Seattle.

On Saturday at noon, Simone had picked up Amanda, worked out with her at The Fit Nest, chowed down a pizza at Papa John's, and then brought her home to meet the dogs. Sitting under the gazebo watching Amanda frolic with them in the backyard, Simone happened to glance at her silent iPhone laying on the bench. The screen showed 5:00 p.m., the scheduled commencement of her brother's memorial service. At first she'd considered attending to fulfill a presumed familial obligation, but later decided against it.

At the same moment in Kunming, China—7,000 miles away and fifteen hours ahead on the world clock—nine members of EDNA's science staff and three Chinese doctors sat at a conference table and waited for the meeting to begin at Zhao Unlimited, a leviathan entity whose tentacles stretched into a myriad of industries including communications, electronics, biological medicine, and state-of-the-art spyware. The fifty-first floor of their austere yet luxurious corporate offices overlooked the Kunming High-tech Industrial Development Zone. The outer walls of the board room contained floor-to-ceiling windows; the inner wall was constructed of teak panels and shelves lined with priceless jade carvings and porcelain vases dating back to the Qianlong Period and the Ming Dynasty. In a small chamber behind an ornate two-way mirror, three Zhao Unlimited executives and two senior security guards observed the proceedings.

The entrance doors slid open silently. Simone's former receptionist Ming—also the granddaughter of Zhao Unlimited's aging founder—strolled into the meeting followed by Luther Heinrich and his two-member Albright Pharmaceuticals management team. Ming remained standing at the head of the long sandalwood table while the team sat.

After welcoming the group in Mandarin, she switched effortlessly to flawless American English. "I don't speak Chinese, but am assuming my counterpart and host Ming gave you a warm welcome. I'd like to do the same. Simon says, welcome to Albright's new world! I hope you are settled into and pleased with your accommodations. This gathering will be brief. I wanted you to see the results of your diligent work. As some of you know, Miss Ming consented to be my host, and as I speak, my ashes are being memorialized in my hometown. Because of recent advancements in our EDNA technology, I am no longer bound to a diseased, decaying body!" Simon-Ming paused for applause, though none came. "Despite the unforeseen setbacks in Buffalo City, I consider Plan A a phenomenal success, and Plan B has gone smoothly. We now have the support and financial backing of Zhao Unlimited in a country whose laws regarding medical advancements and experimental research are more flexible, as are those covering subjects used in human trials. Our new laboratory has capabilities far beyond our previous facilities, and their staff is at our disposal. These three Chinese doctors will now conduct a tour and lead you to your new workstations. Are there any questions before we adjourn?"

Dr. Miriam Dent raised her hand. "What happened to Dr. Blake? Has his flight been delayed?"

"Unfortunately, he declined to accept our generous offer to join us, but his absence will be inconsequential. I wish you all the best of luck in your work. Like our benefactor's name, our destiny has become EDNA Unlimited. The time is ripe to initiate Plan C. Simon says... go forth and continue, collaborate, and create!"

Day 93

Monday

WHILE EDNA UNLIMITED IN CHINA surged ahead, Buffalo City devolved into the past. During the recent three months, defunct EDNA had ceased operations, and the building sat vacant as did the Albright Pharmeceuticals complex after crews had loaded its contents into an Allied Van Lines fleet of semi-trailers. The Flanagan brothers moved to Nova Scotia to begin anew. Beyond the capabilities or resources of a local police force, the Simon-Hunter-EDNA investigation had been turned over to the FBI. Officer Eddie took Simone on a few outings until he proclaimed his desire for more. She wanted less.

Select inhabitants of Buffalo City were prospering. Diego and Laurel's initial attraction matured into a best friend relationship when they both realized that the holes in their hearts could only be filled by Nathan, not each other. The Fit Nest flourished, adding advanced martial arts and self-defence courses. Amanda became an avid attendee and saw her body develop under the tutelage of Jade and Conan. Coco curbed her alcohol intake and helped Dr. Frank manage CAFE, now thriving after Diego's substantial donation. Rafi started his own custom cabinet business and remained ensconced in the bungalow with Zara Zarina.

The enhanced DNA technology continued to evolve inside Simone while sporadic connections with her five hosts reappeared. At random moments, an image from Rafi's vision would flash through her mind. With concerted focus, Simone could tap into the lives of her former hosts, and some could tap into hers. Zara Zarina seemed united with her every day. Once again Simone had a nuclear family. Her curiosity tempted her to explore this phenomenon further, but one dream took precedence. With Rafi as her live-in, trustworthy caretaker ready to watch over her home and dogs, Simone had begun preparing for a year-long sabbatical spanning the globe.

At 8:00 a.m. in Kunming, the conference room at Zhao Unlimited was filled with seventeen beings—three Chinese scientists, eight male and female operatives from a range of ethnic groups, three Zhao corporate executives, an African Cheetah lounging on the floor, a Yorkshire Terrier in one man's lap, and a Citron Crested Cockatoo perched on an armrest. Stocky security guards wearing shiny grey business suits, stiff blue neckties, and headsets stood like metal sentinels in each corner. Luther Heinrich and his management team were not in attendance. Ming's grandfather and her elder brother watched the proceedings from the viewing cubicle behind the two-way mirror. The automatic doors slid open with a faint whoosh, and Ming marched in wearing a form-fitting, red-and-gold, silk, qipao dress that appeared to elevate her five-foot-four stature. She took her position standing at the table head and waited until the room became still.

Those people accustomed to hearing her speak in America would have been surprised by her British accent absorbed during her decade of study at the International

School of London, and while achieving three degrees in Biomolecular Engineering, Nanoscience, and Wireless Communication at the University of Hong Kong.

"Welcome to Zhao Unlimited! For those of you I have yet to meet, I am Zhao Yangming, though you may refer to me by my English nickname, Ming. I'm sure you are wondering why I've summoned you here at such short notice. This auspicious day marks the commencement of a new phase in our global mission. Let me start with a summary of our stellar achievements to date before continuing with a briefing on what I shall be expecting from every one of you going forward.

"First, an update on personnel. I'm pleased to inform you that my assimilation of Simon Albright's consciousness is now complete. The era of 'Simon says' is today consigned to the Dustbin of History."

Hushed conversations and the rustle of papers scratched at the silence as a Zhao executive politely raised his hand.

"Yes, Jiang Xiānshēng," Ming asked.

"I am confused. What happened to him? Did he die?"

"Simon Albright is no more. I assume death slipped in slowly and painlessly as the ALS ravaged his cells, and the stronger DNA in my body absorbed his essence. From now on, his scientists will do as Ming says since Zhao Unlimited has purchased Albright Pharmaceuticals in its entirety, including the EDNA technology. Simon's eight surviving staff are now confined in a remote mountain facility 150 kilometers to the north. Regrettably, young Dr. Taylor took his own life while the balance of his mind was disturbed.

"Whilst in the USA, I succeeded in harvesting specimens of DNA from a wealth of first class if unwitting human donors—strands of hair, skin samples, and bodily fluids from Dr. Simone Wellstone, sperm from a host with a perfect physique and boundless energy, and a strip of flesh from Simon's left thigh. Thanks to these rich sources of raw materials and a great leap forward in our technological capability, we are now able to enhance your DNA to give you the superpowers previously possessed only by Simon and his sister. Furthermore, by coupling our satellite network and nano-engineering expertise with the EDNA technology, the previous controller-to-host range of fifteen miles has been extended to provide uninterrupted worldwide coverage."

Ming paused while her audience exchanged raised eyebrows and approving whispers.

"I imagine you are wondering what all of this means for you. On the basis of positions you occupy in global conglomerates and your success in infiltrating governmental organizations, I have selected you from our cadre of operatives to form an elite task force to be deployed in the field.

"Regarding the enhanced animal operatives among us today, as New Year's celebrations approach, they will be gifted to a range of prominent individuals. Cheetah will be presented to a Saudi prince, Cockatoo to the South Korean ambassador, and Yorkshire Terrier to an aide of the British Prime Minister. In the guise of innocuous pets, they will be ideally placed to garner sensitive information, and their handlers can control their actions from afar.

"In the immortal words of Sir Francis Bacon, *ipsa scientia potestas est*—'knowledge itself is power.' Your mission is to gather vital information and transmit it back to Zhao Unlimited Headquarters, where advanced AI systems will transform it into knowledge we can use to extend our global influence."

Ming's gaze wandered to the right for a moment as she gave a slight nod of her head to grandfather and brother behind the two-way mirror, then turned back to the table, sterner than before.

"To anyone who may be questioning his or her loyalty to our enterprise, I would advise you to remain mindful of the fate that befell the members of Simon's scientific staff. Whilst some call their current location a prison, I prefer to call it as re-education facility. Should you have any difficulty remembering that the acronym MSA stands for our Multilevel Surveillance Arrangement, feel free to use this simple memory aid: Ming Sees All."

At this point she stared wordlessly at each delegate, one by one, fixing them with the cold gaze of her serpentine obsidian eyes.

"Unlike Simon Albright, I do not designate my plans with letters, though they are precisely ordered. In Simple Simon's childish style, I could phrase my command today in this manner. Ming says... go forth and mingle." The sardonic smile playing on her lips did not diminish the severity of her previous words. "Are there any further questions?"

Apart from a yawn from the Cheetah and a bob from the Cockatoo, the room sat still.

"Then let us adjourn and be on our way. I wish you good luck and demand the best of your abilities. During your journeys, I strongly advise you to keep in mind the words of my inspirational, fellow Asian warrior, Genghis Khan. 'Remember, you have no companions but your shadow.'

Ming let time slither forward for three silent seconds before issuing her final caveat. "From this day forward... I... will be your inseparable shadow."

She then spun around on one heel, and as if foreseeing the exact moment of her exit, the conference room door slid open for a moment before closing behind her with a subtle hiss.